HERS FOR THE EVENING

Jasmine Haynes

HEAT
New York

THE BERKLEY PUBLISHING GROUP
Published by the Penguin Group
Penguin Group (USA) Inc.
375 Hudson Street, New York, New York 10014, USA
Penguin Group (Canada), 90 Eglinton Avenue East, Suite 700, Toronto, Ontario M4P 2Y3, Canada
(a division of Pearson Penguin Canada Inc.)
Penguin Books Ltd., 80 Strand, London WC2R 0RL, England
Penguin Group Ireland, 25 St. Stephen's Green, Dublin 2, Ireland (a division of Penguin Books Ltd.)
Penguin Group (Australia), 250 Camberwell Road, Camberwell, Victoria 3124, Australia
(a division of Pearson Australia Group Pty. Ltd.)
Penguin Books India Pvt. Ltd., 11 Community Centre, Panchsheel Park, New Delhi—110 017, India
Penguin Group (NZ), 67 Apollo Drive, Rosedale, North Shore 0632, New Zealand
(a division of Pearson New Zealand Ltd.)
Penguin Books (South Africa) (Pty.) Ltd., 24 Sturdee Avenue, Rosebank, Johannesburg 2196,
South Africa

Penguin Books Ltd., Registered Offices: 80 Strand, London WC2R 0RL, England

This book is an original publication of The Berkley Publishing Group.

This is a work of fiction. Names, characters, places, and incidents either are the product of the author's imagination or are used fictitiously, and any resemblance to actual persons, living or dead, business establishments, events, or locales is entirely coincidental. The publisher does not have any control over and does not assume any responsibility for author or third-party websites or their content.

PRINTING HISTORY
Heat trade paperback edition / May 2010

Library of Congress Cataloging-in-Publication Data

Haynes, Jasmine.
  Hers for the evening / Jasmine Haynes.—Heat trade paperback ed.
      p. cm.
  ISBN 978-0-425-23417-4
I. Love stories, American.   2. Erotic stories, American.   I. Title.
PS3608.A936H47   2010
813'.6—dc22

                                                    2009053450

PRINTED IN THE UNITED STATES OF AMERICA

10   9   8   7   6   5   4   3   2   1

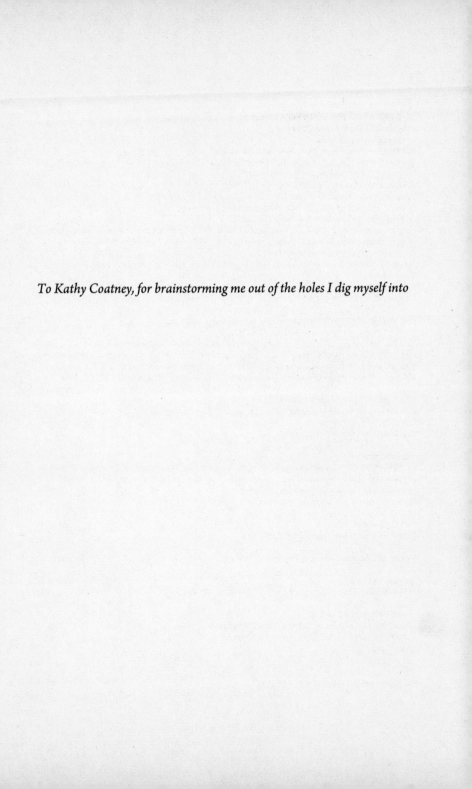

To Kathy Coatney, for brainstorming me out of the holes I dig myself into

ACKNOWLEDGMENTS

Thanks to Jenn Cummings, Terri Schaefer, and Rita Hogan for always being there. To my agent, Lucienne Diver, and my editor, Wendy McCurdy.

CONTENTS

THREE'S A CROWD

1

GOD, SHE NEEDED SEX.

Seth had been busy with a new product release, and making love had been low on the totem pole for more than a month. She'd been telling herself nothing was wrong, that he wasn't bored with her. He'd just been so busy. If Seth were game, Courtney would have dragged him into the woods right now, or even to their SUV in the parking lot. She wouldn't give a damn if anyone at the company barbecue noticed them slipping off.

It had been years since they'd done something wild and crazy like that. Working, raising the girls, building college funds and nest eggs had kept them both busy. Chelsea would be a sophomore in the fall term and Shannon a senior, graduating from college in another year.

Though both the girls had now been off at college almost a year, she and Seth had yet to get wild and crazy.

Courtney O'Brien put her arm through her husband's and smiled. Anyone else at the July Fourth picnic would believe her to be listening politely to CEO Walter Trousdale, Seth's boss. Instead, she was thinking deliciously dirty thoughts.

"O'Brien, your lovely wife is being neglected with all this business talk of ours." Walter had a big voice and a big laugh that complemented the size of his belly. He played Santa at the Christmas party without requiring any padding, and the children adored him. "She looks like she needs another margarita."

Oh, she needed something all right, and another margarita might help get her plans on the way.

The day was a scorcher, which was usual for July in the San Francisco Bay Area, but the company had rented a redwood grove in a nearby county park, and beneath the trees a nice breeze blew gently over her. The tangy scent of barbecue sauce and grilling meat tantalized her taste buds. Wine, beer, and margaritas flowed. A raucous shout bellowed from the horseshoe pit. Arts and crafts had been organized for the kids. She'd met most of the people, their spouses and children. Seth had been with NTF, Northern Thin Films, for ten years, the last two as vice president of research and development. At forty-eight, three years older than she was, with only a dash of gray in his full head of sandy hair, Seth was as handsome and trim as the day she'd married him twenty-three years ago.

Courtney fluttered her eyelashes at him. "Yes, honey, I'm parched." She waggled her plastic cup. Most of the ice had melted. She hoped he noticed the sexy pout on her lips, fair warning of what was on her mind.

Seth lowered his sunglasses so she could see his hazel eyes and gave her a look. Oh yeah, he knew. "Your wish is my command, darling." He slid his hand down her arm, laced his fingers with hers, and squeezed. He was six feet to her five foot five, and the height difference when she was wearing her flats always made her tingly.

"How sweet," Walter's wife, Irene, remarked, with a hint of jealousy. Her lips pinched, something she did often if the lines crimping her mouth were any indication. Courtney felt sorry for Walter. He was such a jovial guy, he deserved a fat and happy Mrs. Claus.

Courtney jiggled her remaining ice cubes in farewell as Seth dragged her off.

He put his mouth against her hair and blew in her ear. "Do not get naughty in front of my boss or I will make you pay big-time later."

Shivery from the minty warmth of his breath, she tipped down her sunglasses in imitation of his earlier look. "Promises, promises. Besides, I didn't do anything naughty."

His mouth flirted with a smile. "You were thinking dirty, I could tell."

"You're right," she leaned in to whisper. "Do me, baby."

This time he laughed outright, then pulled her close. "Slut."

She loved the sexy banter, the naughty name-calling. They hadn't indulged in ages, and she'd missed it. They were quiet, no one could hear, and that made it all the more titillating. Her motor was certainly running.

The drink table was do-it-yourself. Seth plopped in more ice cubes, poured the margarita, then grabbed a soda for himself since he was driving.

"Hi, Seth." The sultry feminine voice came from right behind Courtney.

In the midst of popping the can top, Seth glanced up. "Hey, Amanda."

There was something in his tone that had Courtney turning. A hint of annoyance perhaps?

In her late thirties, Amanda was petite, pretty, and dark-haired, with Catherine Zeta-Jones curves, and an enormous chest no one could ignore. She stuck out her hand. "You must be Courtney."

"Why, yes, I am."

"Seth's always talking about you." She smiled. Courtney didn't believe her friendliness for a second.

"Amanda is Walter's new admin," Seth supplied.

Amanda shrugged. "Not exactly new. I've been with the company six months. Seth has been so good at helping me understand all the nuances." She beamed at him.

Courtney glanced at the woman's hand. Wedding ring and an enormous diamond. "He's such a helpful man." She ran her fingers down her husband's arm, beaming in a cheeky imitation of Amanda. "What would we women do without him?"

Seth closed his fingers around Courtney's. "Looks like the food's ready, honey. We'd better get in line. Nice talking to you, Amanda." He pulled Courtney away.

"The food is *not* ready," Courtney murmured when they were out of earshot. "And that woman is hot for you."

Seth propped himself against the end of an empty picnic table. When the barbecue was set out, they'd darn near be first in line since everyone else was under the shade trees avoiding the sun. Or watching the kids.

"She's a pest," he said.

Courtney moved in front him, leaving enough room to hold her drink against her chest. "A very pretty pest." She wiggled her eyebrows.

"I hadn't noticed."

She took off his sunglasses, folded them, and patted them into the pocket of his polo shirt. "Liar. How could you miss those breasts?"

He squinted his hazel eyes against the sun. "All right, she's pretty. She's also married and a pain in the ass."

"Men don't mind screwing a pain in the ass as long as she's pretty. I don't see her husband in tow today, do you?" She leaned in close to lick the lobe of his ear. "Bet she was hoping you'd be here all on your lonesome."

From time to time, they'd added fantasy play to their sex life.

They might see a sharp man at the movies, and Seth would tease her. Or a sexy woman at the mall, and Courtney would ask him all the nasty things he thought the lady might be capable of doing.

Seth had a very naughty imagination. So did Courtney. They'd had some very hot sex over it.

Of course, she'd never told anyone the things they'd fantasized about. Her friends would think she was crazy, inviting infidelity. She didn't feel that way. To her, it was merely fantasy.

"What's the sexiest thing she's ever worn?" Amanda looked sexy in a pair of low-waisted shorts Courtney wouldn't have the courage to wear. She was self-conscious about her baby belly. She'd loved what pregnancy did for her breasts, but she'd never been able to lose those last few pounds after Chelsea was born.

Seth turned his head, glancing past her in the direction Amanda had headed. To the horseshoe pits. Then he plucked his sunglasses back out of his pocket, propped them on his nose, and settled his hand on her hip. "Tight sweater. Headlights."

"No bra?" With those breasts? Ohmigod.

"I didn't look long enough to figure it out."

She snorted. "Right. Afraid of sexual harassment?"

He laughed. "I got the distinct impression she wanted men to look."

"Slut," she whispered.

Squeezing her hip, he splayed a thumb along the join of her leg, then slipped away in case anyone was watching. "Not as good a slut as you, baby."

Courtney raised an eyebrow. "I bet she swallows."

He guffawed before he could stop himself, and Courtney noticed several eyes turn their way. The crowd was starting to drift closer as the scent of meat and sauce perfumed the air.

"Because you love to swallow, you think every woman does."

Some of her friends thought it was gross. Courtney never revealed that Seth's come was ambrosia. She'd never been one to talk about her sex life, but she had a prurient curiosity when it came to some of the things her friends revealed. Like Devon Parker. Divorced, she swore men were too much trouble, and she hired gigolos to take care of her needs; male courtesans, she called them. Courtney found the idea titillating, and she loved Devon's stories.

"Bet Amanda likes it doggy," she went on teasing Seth. He loved doggy. Courtney had a fondness for it, too. She got very loud while expressing her fondness.

That position had always been saved for the times the girls had sleepovers at a friend's house.

"I believe she's doing Drummond," Seth said.

"You're kidding." Drummond was vice president of sales. Not bad looking, but kind of slimy, like a used car dealer passing clunkers off on unsuspecting buyers. He wasn't in attendance today, thank you very much. He liked to cop a feel if he could. Not a breast or a butt cheek, but a shoulder or a forearm, a caress. It wasn't over the top, just . . . creepy. "You're trying to sidetrack me." She moved in on him, put her arms around his shoulders. "How would you do her? Doggy? Ride 'em cowgirl?"

"Blindfolded, tied up, and gagged. She talks too much."

She giggled and realized the margaritas were starting to get to her in the hot sun. Thank goodness they were starting to take the meat off the barbecues and setting out the salads and other fixings. "You're protesting too much."

He smirked. "It would be much more fun to watch you do Lee."

"Ooh. Where is he?"

"Don't turn around, but he's eyeing your ass right now."

Lee worked in Accounting. He was young, maybe thirty-five, with blond surfer good looks. She snuggled closer to Seth, spreading her legs slightly over his to encompass him. "What would you want me to do to him?"

"Get down on your knees, wrap your luscious lips around his cock, and deep throat him."

A thrill zinged straight through her.

"I'd rather watch Amanda"—Courtney elongated the name and dropped her voice to a seductive pitch—"take your massive tool in her mouth while I'm kissing you." She gasped. "Ooh, what about the two of us sucking you? She holds your cock for me, I hold it for her, two tongues. What do you think, honey?"

Seth almost groaned. Right when he started taking Courtney for granted, she'd pull a sexy stunt like this, getting him rock hard in the middle of a company picnic. He'd always loved her dirty mind, her playful attitude toward sex, but he wasn't as young as he used to be, and work was starting to beat the tar out of him. He'd never wanted to be CEO; he liked getting his hands dirty in the trenches. Courting the board and investors all the time wasn't for him. He loved R&D, creating products, improving existing lines, developing exciting ideas, but when a new release got off-track, as had happened now, the job sucked him dry. And not in a good way. He'd been neglecting Courtney. She needed attention, but he didn't have that much to give these days. When Courtney was in this kind of mood, he wasn't sure he could keep up with her.

"You," he emphasized, "are going to have to get two plates, because I can't stand in line with this." He glanced down. Her gaze followed.

"Ooh," she whispered, taking in his bulging shorts.

People were heading to the buffet line. He eased away from her, slid down onto the picnic table's seat, and leaned forward to bracket his Coke with his hands. "A chicken breast, salad, and corn bread, please."

"Yes, sir." She saluted, then eyed him. "A breast man today. Amanda will love that." She was off with a saucy wink and a sweet little wiggle to her ass.

At the buffet, Lee fell in behind her, saying something that made her laugh. A twinge of jealousy tweaked Seth's gut. Her fantasy games excited him, but he didn't take them as a reality, and would never share her with another man. He wasn't built that way. Not that he figured she wanted to make them real. Courtney simply got off better with a hot fantasy going between them. Seth remembered when she had to watch every Hugh Jackman movie ever made, then made him talk like Wolverine and do her doggy. Amanda had nothing on his wife. At forty-five, Courtney's gorgeous shoulder-length auburn hair didn't show even a hint of gray. With her fair skin, full lush breasts, and soft curves, he got hard thinking about doing her right now. Maybe on the picnic table in front of a crowd . . .

"Aren't you hungry, Seth?" Amanda slid onto the seat beside him, taking Courtney's spot.

Christ. Courtney was right. The woman was after him. She always had some little question, something she had to lean over and show him on the computer. She was sexy, he'd give her that, but he'd never cheated, and he never would. His marriage was worth so much more than a fuck, even a good one. Despite all her games, he was sure Courtney didn't want to give him to another woman.

"Courtney's getting me a plate." He leaned closer to the table. His cock was still hard as a diamond drill, and he didn't want Amanda entertaining any ideas that it had something to do with her. Courtney had gotten him going with the image of two tongues on his cock, not Amanda's per se. Besides, the woman was needy, not looking so much for a fling as a knight in shining armor to rescue her from her ogre of a husband. Oh yeah, she'd managed to reveal that tidbit almost her first day. For the most part, he was able to avoid her, but sometimes Walter sent her on an errand.

"It looks like she's getting Lee a plate instead." Amanda waved her fingers over her shoulder.

Every time Courtney moved ahead in line, Lee sidled up behind her. She angled herself, her elbow sticking out as she scooped salad onto the two plates she handled deftly.

Amanda fluttered her eyelashes. "Your wife's kind of a flirt, isn't she?"

2

"EXCUSE ME?" SETH COCKED HIS HEAD, KNITTING HIS BROWS TO-gether.

"I mean that in a totally nice way." Amanda gave him one of her wide-eyed looks. "She's fun."

Yeah, right. The woman was making trouble where there wasn't any. "Let's get something clear," he said. "I love my wife. I trust my wife." Courtney would never cheat, either.

A couple, the guy worked in Quality, sat on the opposite end of the table. They both smiled. Seth smiled back, then purposely let the smile die as he switched his gaze to Amanda. "Get my drift?"

Amanda nodded with a phony I'm-so-sorry rise of her brows. "Sure, Seth. I didn't mean anything by it."

Courtney's laugh carried on the breeze, Lee from Accounting still on her heels. "Here you go, sweetie." She set a plate in front of him, then sat on the very edge of the bench, pushing him slightly to make room. "Amanda, where's your food? Lee could have carried another plate." She shooed Lee with a wave of her hand. "Go get Amanda something. The poor girl looks like she's ravenous."

Damn if Lee didn't hand Amanda his plate. "I'll get another one," he said, then jogged off to the now-immense line.

Courtney leaned forward so she could talk to Amanda. "Hon, why don't you sit over there? I can't see you around Seth." She pointed to the spot across from her.

He had to hand it to his wife. The other woman had no choice but to move around to the other side. Seth could breathe again. Her perfume overwhelming, Amanda reminded him of a clinging vine. Or a Venus Flytrap. Courtney had a more luscious scent, like wisteria on a moonlit night.

She put a hand on his thigh and started heading north to the bottom of his shorts. His cock jumped.

"Are you enjoying your job working for Walter?" Courtney smiled ever so politely as she pushed her fingers between his legs and through his shorts, caressed his balls with her pinkie.

Thank goodness there weren't any kids at the table. She made him ache. His face heated. When was the last time he'd come? Weeks. He was full, hard, throbbing. He wanted to unzip and shove her hand inside.

"Walter's great," Amanda was saying. "But without Seth—"

"He's ever so helpful." Courtney smiled at him. "He's exactly the same way at home. Always going that extra mile exactly where it counts." She brushed the backs of her fingers along his zipper. He felt that stroke to the tip of his cock and back down again.

Oh man, she had to pay for this.

"So, honey," Courtney said, "that's a big, fat, magnificent"—Seth held his breath, she wouldn't—"ring on Amanda's finger, don't you think?" Courtney pointed to Amanda's engagement ring with her fork. "Gorgeous. Diamonds are soooo hard." She gave his cock a squeeze and withdrew.

Oh yeah, when he got her home, she was gonna pay.

* * *

"I'LL HOLD YOUR COCK AND GUIDE YOU INSIDE HER," COURTNEY whispered in Seth's ear.

Holy Christ, Courtney was going to make him come right here and now in front of everyone at the picnic table. She had teased him the entire meal and through dessert, brought him close to the point of total insanity. Every time Lee occupied Amanda's attention, Courtney whispered in Seth's ear about all the dirty things she wanted to watch him do with Amanda.

Amanda didn't interest him in the least. But his wife? He wanted her *now*. He wanted that naughty mind of hers devising new pleasures to blow his mind.

"Are you all right, sweetie?"

He realized he'd groaned out loud. "My head's aching." Hah! Let her do something with the double entendre in that.

She put a palm to his forehead. "Oh, you're hot."

He sure as hell was.

"It could be sunstroke," Amanda offered, all sympathy.

Little did she know, *stroke* was the operative word. His cock, his wife's hand.

"Maybe I should get you home and into bed." Her words solicitous, a naughty smile itched to get out.

Amanda's brow furrowed with concern. "You'll miss the fireworks."

Oh no, he wouldn't. Seth was damn sure of that.

Courtney gathered their plates, cups, and soda cans. "Come on, sweetie. If you get to bed now, you might feel better by the time the fireworks start, and we can watch them from the summit."

They lived in the Santa Cruz Mountains off Summit Road, and with a short drive, they could watch the fireworks down in Scotts Valley. However, since the girls were off doing their own thing, he had every intention of setting off the fireworks in his own bed.

Now all he had to do was figure out how to stand up without everyone getting an eyeful of his erection. Thank God his shorts were loose. Christ, he had to laugh. He hadn't been this hard and worked up in ages. It felt fucking good after the stress of the last few months.

They did the polite good-byes to as few people as possible, and yes, he managed to control his body.

"Want me to drive, honey?" Courtney asked so very solicitously as they reached the SUV.

"I'm perfectly capable of driving." He'd get them home faster than she would. "And you're drunk."

"I am not drunk." She snorted. "Not even tipsy. I downed a whole bottle of water with the barbecue."

Damn. She could be totally wild when she was tipsy.

The drive seemed to take forever. With every turn along the winding road back home, Courtney swayed close to him. Bracing herself on the console, she leaned over to stroke his cock.

"Oh my," she murmured, smiling with delight.

He was hard. Again. In the blink of an eye.

"You really did like the idea of me and Amanda sucking your cock together." She idly caressed the front of his shorts.

Seth wasn't quite sure what she wanted. Denial? That she was the only one? Would *always* be the only one? Or a hot, dirty threesome fantasy. "Two mouths," he said, testing, "would be double the pleasure."

"Or more," she whispered. "Like adding one plus one and getting three. Or four." She unzipped him.

"What are you doing?"

"Just drive."

He luxuriated in the touch of her fingertips as she drew him out, then blew a warm breath on his cock. His whole body was on fire. The blood pulsed in his veins and raced to his dick.

"When was the last time you jerked off?" she asked his cock.

He gave a strangled laugh. "When have I had a free minute to even contemplate jerking off?"

She'd never minded that sometimes he jerked off in the shower when she was too tired. The last couple of years, with the vice presidency, the increased number of new products, the pressure, the only orgasms he'd managed were with Courtney, and it was sometimes weeks in between. Maybe if he came more often, he wouldn't get so stressed out.

She licked off a bead of pre-come.

He groaned and took the turn a tad too wide. "Baby." It was all he could manage as she slid her tongue down his shaft, then back up, finally engulfing him between her lips.

She sucked hard on the crown, her teeth massaging him below the ridge. He thought his head would pop off. The velvety recesses of her mouth caressed him as she took him deep, slowly, so she didn't gag. He was big, but she'd had years of practice.

"Christ, you do that so fucking perfectly." He felt her smile around his cock.

She needed to hear stuff like that. It was also the truth. He'd done his share of catting around before they started dating, but no one had ever sucked him the way Courtney did. She'd gotten better over the years.

Tunneling into his shorts, she cupped his balls, squeezed gently. He fucking ached. It was so damn good. He held the wheel white-knuckled and concentrated on the road, another hairpin turn he took more slowly than he normally would. A car passed them from the other direction, and he held her head down a moment.

His legs started to tremble with the need to come. "Christ, you'd better stop."

"Uh-huh," she mumbled, her mouth full, her head bobbing.

"Baby, I'm gonna come if you don't stop." He wanted to make

love to her tonight. She'd been patient with his moods, but she needed some physical affirmation. He'd seen her looking at him sometimes, probably wondering if he'd lost interest. He needed to show her he hadn't.

Courtney didn't stop. She Hoovered him, sucking hard, and he thought he'd die.

The explosion started in his balls and worked its way out, to the tip of his cock, his gut, his chest, then the hot spurt of come up his shaft. He barely stayed on the road.

She sucked, swallowed, licked, and soothed until his body stopped quaking. Then she zipped him, straightened her hair, smoothed her lipstick—how the hell she could do that without smearing her lipstick he'd never know—and smiled at him.

"You look like the cat that ate the cream."

Her laughter tinkled through the SUV. "How very apt."

He gave her a stern look. "I want to get us home and do you properly. In a bed. With you coming a lot."

"The nice thing about you, sweetie, is that it only takes an hour for you to recharge." She licked her lips. "We have all evening."

Hell yeah. Plus Monday was a holiday, and the girls would be on their way back to school.

THE END OF JULY. ANOTHER MONTH HAD GONE BY WITH NO LOVE-making. In three weeks, the girls would be home from summer school. They'd stay home until the fall term started at the end of September.

There was a tiny rumbling in Courtney's tummy. What was wrong? Was it merely stress?

Tuesday after the Fourth of July holiday, Seth had gone back to work only to find an issue that sent the product release into the dumper. She'd thought hot sex would be the cure-all, releasing all the pressure. He wasn't . . . interested. She wanted the fireworks of July Fourth every day.

The fireworks had started with talking about Amanda. Not that she thought he'd have an affair. Seth wasn't that kind of man. He had too much integrity. Still, she abhorred the idea of perfunctory sex, something he *had* to do to keep his wife happy.

Maybe they needed more role-play in their lives. It would be hot if she dressed up like a strumpet and told him she had a date with another man but she wouldn't go if he didn't want her to. She'd blow off her date to let Seth do her instead. Wow, that would be fun. Or she could tell him Amanda was coming over to bring him some papers to sign. She'd make him hard and ask him how he'd feel if Amanda walked in to find Courtney sucking his cock. Oh, that was hot. There were innumerable things she could try. The only limit was her imagination.

She brewed her usual cup of tea at three in the afternoon. Her mother had always had teatime, including a cookie. Though she'd passed away ten years ago, Courtney continued the ritual, bringing her mom close for a few minutes every day. Of course, there was also the sinful treat of ten minutes in front of a weekday afternoon talk show. Curling her legs beneath her on the leather sofa, a pillow tucked against her midriff, she punched the remote to turn on the big-screen flat panel.

"Today we have sex consultant Tandy with us." The male talk show host was one of Courtney's favorites because he was so ridiculously outrageous. A bit effeminate, too. "Tell us, Tandy, isn't what you do a polite name for prostitution?"

A petite redhead with implants two sizes too big for her frame, the woman bristled. "Certainly not. I help people overcome their sexual issues."

"By having sex with them. And they pay you. That sounds like prostitution." With a smarmy smile on his lips, he winked at his audience.

"I show couples how to pleasure each other. Teach them to experience new things."

"But you have sex with them."

"I have to demonstrate."

"And so you have sex with them," the host reiterated. Courtney loved his tenacity with the wacky people he brought on the show. It was so amusing, her guilty pleasure.

Tandy pursed her lips and tried to explain. "Sometimes that's the only way to provide a proper visual."

The host didn't even laugh. "Do you have sex with the women as well as the men?"

"If a woman is unable to achieve orgasm with her partner, I am obligated to show them both how to go about it."

"So you have sex with the men *and* the women."

"Well . . . yes."

"And then they pay you."

Tandy blinked. Then nodded.

Even though she was alone, Courtney laughed out loud. He really was hilarious. By repeating the same thing over and over, he flustered the woman and got her to say exactly what he wanted to hear.

"What do you say, folks? Tandy is basically having hot, sexy threesomes with couples and getting paid for it." He spread his hands in the air. "Sounds like prostitution to me." His audience clapped their agreement.

People were amazing. And crazy. It took all kinds. Her one shortbread cookie finished, Courtney flipped off the TV. Sinful treat over.

A load of sun-dried clothing had to be folded, some dusting to be done, then dinner. She used to have a cleaning service once a week, but when the girls got their driver's licenses and she no longer shuttled them everywhere, she'd found herself with so much time on her hands that cleaning filled it. It relaxed her, as did cooking. Tonight, with the midsummer heat, she'd planned cold chicken curry with a tomato and broccoli salad.

She was almost to the family room entry when she turned to stare at the blank TV screen. Thinking.

3

A SEX CONSULTANT? A PROSTITUTE? THREESOMES?

She thought of Devon and her "courtesans." Essentially, the guys were male prostitutes. Devon claimed her sex life had never been better. She'd never go back to dating. She was too busy to meet men in a conventional manner.

What if . . .

No, she couldn't. Reality was never as good as fantasy. You built it up, and the real thing couldn't compare. Besides, Seth would probably freak if she suggested it.

In the kitchen, she pulled the tomatoes and broccoli from the fridge, then stopped halfway to the butcher-block island.

Two men, Seth and . . . a younger guy. Double the pleasure? No. No way. The guy would see her stretch marks and the bulge in her tummy that had never gone away after the girls were born.

She began chopping the tomatoes.

What about a woman closer to her age? Not some TV model, but a woman with imperfections who was very good at . . .

Seth loved the idea of another woman sucking his cock with her. He always got rock hard when she whispered that in his ear. She got a naughty thrill out of it, too. To actually do it? Would that be the spice to get their sex life back on track, the way it used to be? He'd gone hard as a steel rod when she said she wanted to guide his cock into another woman.

Could she watch Seth fuck someone else?

She stopped her chopping as a shiver ran through her. A good shiver. Straight down to her clitoris. Making her wet. Her nipples tightened, peaked against her lace bra. She was nuts. There must be something wrong with her. Women didn't imagine their men with someone else. They certainly didn't get turned on by it.

Yet she did. It was oddly exciting. Seth pleasuring someone else, her eyes drifting closed in ecstasy as Courtney's did when Seth put his hands on her. The sounds, moans, groans, sighs, cries. It would be like watching herself. What it would do for Seth. What it could do for *them*.

It would take Courtney to new heights.

Or she'd be jealous as hell.

She tossed the broccoli in the steamer, and cut up the chicken for the curry, setting out the apples and raisins.

She needed a therapist just for considering it. And *not* a sex therapist.

It couldn't hurt to ask how much something like that would cost, though. As long as she could choose the woman and give instructions on exactly what she wanted. Asking about a few particulars wasn't a commitment.

Picking up the portable phone, Courtney stared at it for several seconds, then punched in a speed-dial number.

When her friend picked up, she said, "Hey, Devon, it's Courtney. Long time no see. Let's do lunch tomorrow."

DEVON PARKER WORE HER BLONDE HAIR PULLED BACK SEVERELY and a tailored blue power suit that matched her eyes. Living in a ruthlessly gym-toned body and porcelain skin that never went without the highest SPF sunscreen, she'd been blessed with aristocratic features and perfect bone structure. She was also smart and the CEO of medium-sized manufacturing firm in Silicon Valley that she had brought through the economic downturn with only two unprofitable quarters. A couple of years younger than Seth, she'd worked with him at his first job out of college, and she and Courtney had become fast friends despite the fact that their lives were so vastly different.

"You look great." Devon had already ordered them both a champagne cocktail. "When are the girls coming home?"

Devon wasn't a mom, had never wanted to be one, but she always asked about Shannon and Chelsea, and she'd gone to both their high school graduations.

"Three weeks. Chelsea wants to see if she can get a short data entry stint at one of the banks for extra pin money." Courtney and Seth paid for tuition, books, and the small apartment they shared, but the girls earned their own money for all the other necessities. They needed to learn financial responsibility, and Courtney didn't believe in handing them everything.

It was almost two, the Friday lunch crowd thinning out and, thankfully, the noise level dropping. Courtney ordered the spinach salad with tiger prawns. "Dressing on the side, please," she told the perky waitress.

After ordering chicken Caesar, Devon tipped her flute against Courtney's. "I'm so glad you called. It's been ages."

For several minutes, they chitchatted about the girls, life, Seth's job, Devon's company. Lunch arrived. Okay, how to bring up what she wanted without Devon thinking she'd lost her mind?

"Are you still seeing your courtesans?" Wow. That was smooth and subtle. Courtney groaned aloud.

"Of course."

She didn't talk much about her own sex life with Devon, doubly so because Devon had known Seth before she met Courtney, plus she'd worked with him. It felt sort of like discussing marital problems with your mother-in-law. "Any interesting stories?" Jeez. That was another dumb lead-in.

Devon tipped her head like a lioness catching a scent. "What's going on?"

"Nothing." Courtney stared at her tiger shrimp.

"I like you, Court." Devon drummed her fingernails on the table. "But I'm not helping you cheat on Seth."

Courtney gasped, then glanced around to make sure no one overheard. The booth next to theirs was empty, and on the other side, two businessmen were engrossed in a NASDAQ debate. Still, she lowered her voice. "I'm not going to do that. Not at all."

"Well, you've never asked me so forthrightly before." True. Devon usually volunteered the latest titillating story. "You're acting strangely. Just spit it out."

"Here it is. I want"—she glanced around once more—"Seth, me . . . and another woman."

"Good God." Devon laughed. Now *that* drew attention. Devon didn't hold back.

Courtney waited until the attention drifted away again. "I want you to help me find the right person."

"Why on earth would you want to do that?" Devon gulped her champagne as if she needed fortification.

"I don't know why. It feels"—she leaned closer—"exciting. Besides, Seth has been working so hard, he needs a break, something to take his mind off work."

"Take him to Calistoga for a mud bath and his-and-her massages. Just not . . . *that*."

Courtney chewed on a leaf of spinach. "Have you ever had . . . more than one lover at a time?"

"No, but let me remind you I'm not married either." Devon had divorced five years ago.

Courtney started to doubt herself. Most of her friends would think her insane. She just didn't think Devon would be one of them. "Let's forget it."

"No. You brought it up, so we're going to talk about it. What does Seth say about this?"

"I haven't told him yet. I wanted to see if you'd help me find the right woman first. Through your agency, Courtesans."

Devon had explained it all to her before. She likened Courtesans to a matchmaking website, but everything was done by referral from happy clients. The agency paired a client with a courtesan. Courtesans didn't get paid, they were given gifts, which could be cash, jewelry, vacations, whatever the client and the courtesan agreed upon. They didn't get paid for having sex; they received gifts. Of course, if any of the so-called gifts were sold for cash, no one seemed to care. Gosh, that sounded a bit like the sex consultant on the talk show. There was no set amount, but when a patron proved excessively cheap, well, they stopped being matched. Oh, and the client paid a fee to the agency for the introduction.

Devon shot out a sharp breath. "I still don't get why you want to do it."

Why? Courtney leaned in, both hands on the table. "It turns me on. That's all I can say. I don't care why. When Seth and I fantasize together about another woman, I get excited, and we *need* some excitement. I don't want to hit menopause and get all saggy and only *wish* I'd done it." All right, it totally defied logic.

Devon touched the back of Courtney's hand. "I'm sorry. I didn't mean to hit a sore spot."

Courtney realized Devon *had* pushed a button. Maybe it was the girls growing up and starting their own lives. She was forty-five and feeling old, a little afraid Seth had lost interest in her. Sex made her feel young again and proved she was still desirable. "I will tell Seth when I've got it all planned. I won't spring it on him. If he says no, then we won't do it."

"All right." Devon picked up her fork again. "Tell me what you're looking for, and I'll talk to Isabel about the arrangements."

"Isabel?"

"She runs Courtesans. I'll ask her to personally set up the match. If you want, you can meet the woman she chooses."

Courtney's pulse beat fast through her veins. She'd come up with a whole fantasy as she was falling asleep last night. It was all she could do not to crawl over to Seth's side of the bed and have her wicked way with him, but he'd come home late with a tension headache, and all he'd wanted was dinner and an extra-strength aspirin. This job was killing him.

"Here's what I've been playing with. I want to do an overnight trip, on a weekend, to the wine country. Down south to Paso Robles and Templeton instead of up in Napa."

Devon picked up her champagne, considered the last fizz of bubbles. "A weekend will require a larger gift."

"I was considering using the Italy fund." She'd been saving for a Europe trip, but she no longer believed Seth would even consider taking three weeks off. A weekend was easier to manage. This seemed so much more important to do. Funny, though the idea had only come to her yesterday, she felt consumed by it. She needed it.

"Do you want a bisexual thing?"

"Bisexual?"

Devon rolled her eyes. "With you and the courtesan."

"No!" She screwed up her face. "Not me." She traced a finger-nail on the white tablecloth. "I do want things like . . ." Oh God, she couldn't say this to Devon.

"Come on, girlfriend. If you want my help, you're gonna have to tell me everything."

"She and I"—she glanced around to make sure everyone was engrossed in their own conversation, not hers—"oral on Seth. To-gether."

A smile grew on Devon's lips. Men always thought she had the sexiest smile, but she never used it at work. There, she was all business. "You are a very dirty woman. I didn't think you had it in you."

Courtney's stomach clenched. "You think I'm bad."

Devon shook her head slowly. "I'm freaked out that you'd want to screw up your marriage this way. However, if you really believe it's the right thing, I'm honored that you'd reveal all this to me and ask for my help."

"So you'll do it?"

"On two conditions. First, you tell Seth before you book the deal with Isabel."

"I will."

"Second, I want to pay for the courtesan."

Courtney gasped. "No."

"Yes. I love you and Seth. You've got the best marriage I've ever seen in my life. I'm actually jealous. If you both really want to do this, then I want it to be my gift."

That was sweet and generous, but . . . "That's too much, Devon."

"Take it or leave it."

Courtney thought about it a long minute. "This is what you truly want to do?"

"Yes. If it's what *you* really want to do."

"Thank you." She sensed Devon's certainty. "I accept."

Seth would kill her when she told him. Now she had to figure out *how* to tell him.

4

IT HAD BEEN ANOTHER HELLACIOUS WEEK AND AN EVEN WORSE day. Seth hadn't made it home for dinner, instead grabbing a bite from the deli across the street and eating it in the quality control lab. The steel wool tests weren't working, dammit. The problem was driving him nuts, and the issues were reaching crisis stage, customers calling. His only defense was that he'd told Walter the July-end release date wasn't doable, but the pressure was on.

He walked in the door at nine, and the house was dark. Except for a candle on the step down into the dining room. Setting his briefcase by the front door, he followed the candle's flame. There was another by the sliding glass door leading out to the deck. Built on the side of the hill, the house was a split-level style with a granny room underneath and an upper and lower deck. A third candle flickered on the outside stairs leading to the lower deck. And the hot tub.

Christ. He read the signals. Courtney was feeling frisky. She'd have the wine out, a sexy melody playing, the jets frothing, scented candles, imagining a romantic evening. And he wouldn't even be able to get it up.

He was pathetic. His wife shouldn't have to beg for sex, but he was so fucking tired. They'd end up having a fight and go to bed without speaking. Especially when he told her he'd need to head back into work on Saturday morning.

Well, hell, best to get it over with.

Opening the sliding glass door, sure enough, he heard the music over the bubble of the water jets. Living in the mountains, it cooled off at night a lot more than in the valley. From the head of the stairs, he could see the steam rising off the water and the play of candlelight across the trees. Hidden by redwood, dogwood, liquid amber, Pacific madrones, and birch, the deck was secluded. She'd be naked in the water. Waiting for him. He willed his cock to twitch but all he wanted to do was crawl into bed and sleep for a day and a night.

He took the stairs like a soldier to the battlefield.

"Hi, honey." Courtney gave him a sexy, sultry smile that made his heart speed up. "I've got a glass of your favorite merlot already poured. Get in the tub."

He bent to kiss her, her breasts bare as she rose out of the water to meet his lips. "Sorry I missed dinner." He began stripping out of his jeans. Working in the lab all day, he didn't dress in suit and tie.

"That just means we'll have lots of leftovers tomorrow, and I won't have to cook," she said brightly.

Naked, he slid to the seat beside her and she handed him the wineglass. He closed his eyes as the jets beat against his back. "Christ, this feels good. Thanks, sweetie."

"I understand how hard you've been working."

He patted her knee in appreciation and sipped the tart merlot, feeling the tension start to ease out of his body. He stretched his neck trying to get the kinks out.

"Tell me where it hurts," she whispered.

"Everywhere, but my neck and shoulders are the worst."

"Let me give you a rub."

Shit. That was a prelude. He didn't see any way to avoid it, so he slid one arm along the tub and gave her his back.

Courtney had marvelous fingers. "That's perfect, baby, thank you." The rub was great, but he prayed her hands wouldn't start wandering.

"I was thinking we needed a getaway together before the girls come home."

He cracked one eye open. "I can't manage the time off right now—"

She nipped his earlobe, then licked it. "I don't want you to take time off. We'll do one night. Down to the central coast for some wine tasting."

There was so much damn weekend work to get the product back on track.

"Not this weekend," she said, interpreting his silence. "Mid-month. Before the girls come home after summer finals."

Seth considered his obligations to his job versus his obligations to his wife. She put up with a lot crap—lost evenings, lost weekends. He had people working for him, good managers, who could set procedures, and the problems could be miraculously over by then. Courtney wasn't being unreasonable, and he owed her a piece of himself.

"All right, let's do it. We can leave early on Saturday morning."

She giggled and clapped her hands. "Goody-goody."

Seth was inordinately pleased with what the small offering did for her. "I love you, baby."

"I love you, too." She settled back to rubbing his shoulders and neck, working on a knot with her thumb. "Okay, so here's the other part of what I want to do."

She paused long enough for him to realize he needed to make a sound. "Uh-huh."

"I want to order a . . ." She put pressure on the knot, holding it.

For a moment, the pressure point was excruciating, then the pain vanished. The massage, her fingers, hot water, jets, a good merlot, they had their effect on him. His tension drained away. "Order what?"

"A friend to bring along."

Order a friend? He tipped his head back to look at her. She concentrated on his muscles.

"What friend? And why?" A weird sensation built in his gut, and all the tension came flooding back.

"Well, not really a friend. More like a courtesan."

"What the hell is a courtesan?" Then he remembered Devon and the naughty stories Courtney loved to tell him after the two of them had a lunch or dinner out. "You want to bring one of Devon's men?" The thought was a punch to his solar plexus.

"No," she said gently, as if she were trying to calm the wild beast rising in him. "They have female courtesans."

Grabbing her hand from his shoulder, he shifted to face her. "What the fuck, Courtney? Just say what this is all about."

"Have a drink first." She handed him his wine.

He eyed her over the rim. "Okay. Explain."

She drew in a deep breath, her breasts rising, her nipples flirting with the surface of the bubbling water. "I want a threesome like we've talked about."

He couldn't be hearing this right. His wife was suggesting . . . what exactly? "This threesome would consist of doing . . . ?" He raised his shoulders in query.

"Like we talked about." She concentrated on her wineglass. "She and I do some . . ." She sipped her chardonnay. "Sucking."

It should have turned him on. It always did when they fantasized. Reality was a whole different thing. "And?"

"You can do her for me. While I kiss you. And you can do me while she watches."

His goddamn head was going to explode. "And the next time you want to fuck another man while I watch?"

"No." She managed to meet his eyes. "I'd only feel comfortable if we did this with a woman."

He didn't believe her. "I haven't been paying enough attention—"

She put her hand over his mouth. "It's not that."

"Then what the fuck?" Maybe he was being irrationally pissed. Most men would jump at the chance if their wife said they could fuck another woman. There had to be a catch, though.

"We've talked about it so much. We should try it. If we don't like it, we never do it again." She trailed a hand down his throat to his chest, then lightly pinched his nipple. Damn. Over the years, his wife had learned all the tricks to get him going, now she used them against him. "Just once, Seth."

"Why?" In his roiling gut, he surmised it had to be because she eventually wanted to ask for another man. He'd never be ready to watch her fuck someone else. So how could she be willing to watch him?

"I can't explain why. Devon asked the same thing, and I don't have a good answer. I suppose I should, but . . ." She huffed out an exasperated breath directed at herself. "It's this thing I can't get out of my head."

"Fuck. What the hell did Devon think of all this?"

"She thought I was crazy."

He scraped a hand down his face, wiping away the sweat from the water's heat. "I can't believe you told her about this."

"She was the only person I could ask to help me find someone."

"Thank God you didn't ask *her* to do it."

"Ooh."

His eyes snapped open. "Don't even think it."

She smiled softly. "I wouldn't. Sex can screw up a good friendship." Lifting his hand, Courtney kissed the back, his knuckles. "Devon wants to give this to us as a gift."

He laughed out loud. There wasn't an ounce of humor in it. "You've gotta be kidding me."

"No. She said that was the deal, she'd help me, but only if we let her give it to us."

"I can't fucking believe this." They were both crazy, Courtney and Devon.

"This could be the most exciting thing we've ever done."

Jesus. She really wanted to give him to another woman. She'd even enlisted Devon's help in the mad scheme. Hell. "You won't be jealous?"

She took a few unbearable seconds to answer. "I don't think so. I know you love me."

He wasn't so sure *she* loved *him*. If she did, how could she give him away? Women weren't built that way. They weren't like men, who easily thought with the smaller head between their legs. Sex was sex. Women, though, their emotions didn't allow sharing.

"I want to suck your cock with her."

Christ. Upstairs, he hadn't believed he could get a single twitch out of his cock, but with her words and the candlelight sparkling in her eyes, the blood suddenly pulsed through his dick.

He could tell the second she recognized she had him right where she wanted. Her eyes widened. She licked her lower lip. "I can make this so good for you, Seth."

"You do not have to give me to another woman to make me happy." Maybe this was all about her own insecurity.

She leaned close to slide her hand down his cock. He was hard. "I know," she whispered. "But it makes me wet imagining it."

Some of the best orgasms he ever gave her were accompanied by this fantasy.

"We never have to see her again," she went on in that low seductive voice, stroking him gently. "When we fantasize about it later, we'll be remembering the real thing."

"You'll eventually hold this against me."

"Never. I'll always admit I asked for it." She cupped his balls, squeezed.

Like every other man right on down the line from Adam, he started thinking with his dick. "If you're sure this is what you really want."

"Oh I'm sure."

"Then we'll do it." He pulled her up out of the water. "Now lean on the side of the tub and put your pretty little ass in the air because I'm going to fuck you doggy style right now."

"Ooh."

He loved the sounds she made. He loved the clench of her pussy as he drove inside her.

And he prayed he hadn't agreed to the worst mistake of his life.

Therefore, the next morning, as soon as he arrived at work, Seth shut himself in his office and picked up the phone. Dialing, he waited through three rings before she answered. "Devon. We need to fucking talk."

5

OH MY GOD, WHAT HAVE I DONE?

Waiting at the roadside café off Highway 101 where Robyn was supposed to meet them, Courtney suddenly got that you-are-insane-and-should-be-immediately-institutionalized sick feeling in the pit of her stomach.

Robyn. She was their courtesan. Two weeks ago, right after Seth gave her the green light, she'd met with Isabel, described what they were looking for, specifically what *Courtney* was looking for. Isabel had offered up Robyn, a beautiful ebony-skinned woman a couple of years older than Courtney. She could have been an African princess in a former life; her features were flawless. She was by no means thin, with full breasts and curves, but her smile in the photo was what sold Courtney. A real smile, not some sultry, seductive woman-on-the-prowl smile. When Isabel asked if she'd like a face-to-face meet, Courtney declined. She wanted to be on the same footing as Seth, with no personal contact. The last stipulation she made was that if he changed his mind—or if Courtney herself did for that matter—they could call a halt at any time during the weekend.

Courtney had planned everything, the hotel they'd stay at out in Cambria, the wineries they'd visit, and one very special surprise that she'd spent hours and hours scouring the Internet to find. She hadn't told Seth what it was, though she did tell him she was dipping into the Italy fund to do it. He'd simply shaken his head with a tell-me-again-why-I-married-her look on his face.

So, the middle of August arrived, and *the* Saturday came with it. What she hadn't planned on was how nervous she'd be meeting the woman who would . . . fuck her husband.

She'd even obsessed about her clothing. For today she'd chosen a strapless sundress and sandals. After changing her mind umpteen million times until Seth had told her they were going to be late.

"Don't worry," Seth said, "she's going to show."

That's what worried her! Seated in a booth by the café's window, she added more creamer to her already overly creamy coffee. "I'm nervous meeting someone new."

"Since when did meeting new people make you nervous?"

Courtney rolled her eyes dramatically. "She isn't just any old *new* person."

The waitress walked by, slipping the tab for their coffees on the table, a subtle reminder that there were people in line for their booth. Seth rolled his hip and fished his wallet from his shorts. "We can call it off."

"No," she said, though he probably wouldn't mind if she said yes.

Somehow, she'd thought things would change over the last two weeks. That they'd have all sorts of sexy banter about the upcoming event, he'd rush her into bed the moment he got home from work every night or at least want to fantasize. Except for the night she'd told him her plans and he'd agreed, he hadn't touched her beyond the perfunctory kisses before he left for work, when he got home, and as they lay down to sleep.

In fact, she'd barely seen him. He said he was working hard so he wouldn't have to go into the office on *their* weekend. She'd wondered if Amanda was staying late, too. Ooh, bad thought. It wasn't true. That was her disappointment and nerves whispering negative thoughts in her ear.

"Come on, let's wait outside." Seth took the bill to the front register as Courtney pushed through the small crowd queuing by the entrance.

"Oh wow, do you see that?" A pregnant young woman pointed through the glass front door as a black limousine pulled into the gravel lot.

Courtney stepped out into the morning sun. It was only nine, but she had to shade her eyes with her hand.

The driver rounded the back of the limo, opened the passenger door, holding his hand out for the lady. With a regal bearing, she was taller than Courtney had imagined. Wearing a flowing burnt orange pantsuit, she put on a pair of sunglasses beneath the brim of her elegant hat. The end of the scarf she'd tied around it blew in the breeze, a trail of fall colors: orange, gold, brown, and dark green.

"Well, that's certainly an entrance," Seth muttered.

She smelled him beside her, a combination of her citrus soap and shampoo. He used whatever she had in the shower, and she loved rubbing her nose over his chest hair drenched in her own scents.

The driver pulled a small overnight bag from the trunk. The woman exchanged words with him, smiled, then palmed his hand a moment. Not a shake, probably a tip.

"She's beautiful," Courtney murmured. More so in person than in the picture. African princess height—a good three inches over Courtney's five foot five—and voluptuous curves.

"You're prettier." Seth slipped his hand through hers, lacing fingers. "We should introduce ourselves."

She glanced down at their clasped hands, touched by his sentiment, then let him pull her across the parking lot. "How do you know that's her?"

Seth leveled his hazel eyes on hers in a nonverbal "duh." What other woman would arrive in a limousine dressed like that? The tableau didn't scream courtesan; it purred high-class. Courtney felt too casual in her sundress.

By the side of the limousine, Seth stuck out his hand. "Hi, I'm Seth. This is my wife, Courtney."

Robyn shook firmly, as if they were meeting for . . . some business function. "So nice to meet you both. I'm Robyn."

Her hand was smooth and cool as she pressed her palm to Courtney's. Removing her sunglasses, she smiled. That ordinary-person smile Courtney had liked. "Perhaps we could have my driver put my bag in your car."

"Certainly." Seth pointed out their silver SUV and pulled his keys from his pocket. The driver trailed him.

"I'm so looking forward to our weekend." Robyn spoke in cultured tones, not British, but not an American twang, either. More like the educated, aristocratic lilt of Grace Kelly.

"So am I." Courtney had no clue what else to say, but she liked that Robyn didn't check out Seth's butt in his shorts or go all gooey-eyed over his physique.

Robyn leaned in. "I have some very nice surprises for you in my bag."

"Oh." Courtney suddenly felt tongue-tied as they slowly followed the men to the car.

"You're nervous, aren't you?" Robyn tucked her arm through Courtney's and laughed as if they were old friends. "Everyone is. Simply remember we're going to have fun, no pressure. Whatever happens"—she shrugged—"happens." She punctuated it with a smile to put Courtney at ease.

Courtney chided herself. She was forty-five years old, a mother of two, married for more than twenty years, college-educated with a degree in teaching, subbing for several years when they needed the money. She wasn't a brainless twit, and she had more self-confidence than this. "I love your outfit. I would never have the flair to wear something like that."

"You look lovely in that little dress." Robyn lowered her voice. "My outfit merely hides all those imperfections I see when I look in the mirror."

"I don't see any imperfections." Courtney meant it with all sincerity and a smidge of apprehension.

"See! The outfit works." Robyn laughed again. The driver turned to look as he settled her bag in the SUV next to the one Courtney had packed for herself and Seth. Seth glanced at Courtney.

"We're going to get along fine." Robyn squeezed her arm. "Tell me the fun things you've planned for us."

The sex things? Courtney decided to avoid the issue for now. This was a date. You didn't talk about sex right out of the gate. You talked about . . .everything else. "I've got a list of wineries. We can't get to them all, but I especially wanted to visit the one where they make Wild Horse Chardonnay. I love that stuff."

"Sounds marvelous."

Courtney once again found her excitement in the outing and enthused about her plans. "For lunch, there's a darling mom-and-pop café outside of Paso Robles, before you get out on the highway to Cambria." Cambria was on the coast right outside the famous castle built in the thirties.

"Everything sounds wonderful. You're very organized."

Seth hung back by the passenger's side, letting the women do the talking. Behind them, the limousine pulled out of the parking lot, and Courtney realized it was time to get this show on the road. So to speak.

"Take the front seat," Robyn said, her eyes a mesmerizing dark chocolate, "and I'll sit behind Seth so you and I can talk more easily."

"That sounds fine." She'd had visions of sitting in the back so Seth and Robyn could get to know each other, but this way, she'd get to see Seth's reactions to everything that was said. He'd also be able to see Robyn in the rearview mirror.

Seth chivalrously handled all the doors, and Courtney turned in her seat as he pulled onto the road and headed for the freeway. The trip down to Paso Robles would take about two hours. They'd be there by eleven, time enough to hit a couple of wineries before lunch.

Once up to speed, Seth adjusted the mirror, his gaze on it longer than necessary, up, down, from Robyn's face to breasts to legs. He glanced at Courtney. It was one of those wordless exchanges between married people. Her heart started to beat faster. He found Robyn attractive.

When he saw a woman on the street, it never bothered her that Seth looked. In fact, he'd started looking only after she'd begun pointing out attractive ladies. It was a game they played. Alternately, he made sure she didn't miss a hot guy. Of course, she'd had to train him on what she liked. Making love, he'd honed in how she'd gotten wet fantasizing about this one or that one. She'd do the same to him.

This was different. Up close and personal. Real versus fantasy. Thrilling yet terrifying.

Courtney hooked one leg beneath her, turning in her seat. "So tell me how you started doing this."

Seth snorted softly. Nothing like taking the bull by the horns.

"If you don't mind me asking," she added.

"Of course not." Robyn shifted, the seat belt going taut between her breasts for a moment until she settled again. "It was a fantasy of mine. Sex for hire. I met a woman who said she'd help me fulfill it by finding the right man."

"Was that Isabel?"

Robyn smiled. "Yes. I was only going to do it once."

Seth adjusted the mirror again, listening.

"I sense a 'but' in there," Courtney said.

"It gave me the biggest high, better than any drug could ever do. I wanted more of it."

Courtney had to admit there was a certain thrill to the idea. "So you started doing it full-time?"

"No, I was still working as a financial advisor at a private investment institution. I liked the job."

Devon had told her that courtesans often had other careers, that they were educated. They weren't people Isabel picked up off a street corner. "Where did you go to school?"

"Brown University. However, I wanted to move out to the West Coast."

An Ivy Leaguer. No wonder she sounded cultured. "Who wouldn't want to live out here, especially the Bay Area?" Courtney enthused. "I'm born and bred myself." At Stanford Hospital in Palo Alto. Seth was from Chicago. They'd met in college. "Don't you worry that someone you work with might find out?"

"Isabel does very careful screening and discretion is paramount." Robyn tipped her head. "You needn't fear that anyone will find out about this weekend." She zipped her lip.

"I don't." Courtney hadn't thought about it. It wasn't like she was cheating on Seth. Her parents were gone. Good Lord if the girls found out though.

"As for me," Robyn went on, glancing out the side window, "I was a casualty of the economic downturn." She turned back with a smile. "Now I am a full-time courtesan." She laughed, a pretty sound. "We have our own system for paying income taxes. Isabel has figured out everything." Her eyes sparkled with whatever ingenuity Isabel had devised to make sure the government didn't get stiffed. So to speak. "The stress is a lot less," Robyn went on. "You can't imagine what it was like trying to explain a forty percent loss in someone's portfolio. Or the guilt. Then the difficulty in convincing them when the time is right to get back in . . ." She put a hand to her chest. "In the current economic climate, pleasuring men and women sexually is a lot more fun than managing their investments."

Women? Courtney glanced at Seth. His eyes were on the road, hands comfortably guiding the wheel, cruise control set at a sedate seventy miles per hour. Despite his relaxed pose, there was a distinctive bulge in his shorts.

Oh God. Courtney couldn't help a little blip of her heart. He didn't expect *that*, did he? "So you pleasure women, too?"

Robyn's lips trembled, then she chuckled. "You'd be surprised at the number of men who like to see their wives find the ultimate pleasure from a woman's caress and a woman's lips."

Oh my Lord. Seth shot her a shit-eating grin. There was no other term for it.

"Well, that wasn't exactly what Seth and I were looking for." She emphasized by pinching his arm lightly.

"I'm glad." Robyn leaned forward to pat Courtney's hand. "I do prefer men."

6

SETH DIDN'T KNOW WHETHER TO LAUGH OR STOP THE CAR AND
run away screaming. His cock had taken on a life of its own picturing the . . . topic of conversation, as it were. Robyn was gorgeous, intelligent, and soft-spoken. She concentrated on Courtney,
not him. The discussion wasn't foreplay; it was designed to put
Courtney at ease. Somehow, instead of making it all about him
and his needs, Robyn turned it into Courtney's party. That was
exactly what he wanted. He'd barely had a free minute in the last
two weeks, which had irked Courtney to no end. He'd sworn to
himself this weekend would be all about her, about what she
needed. It wasn't just him fucking some other woman. This was
about him and Courtney. Robyn was a mechanism to bring them
closer together.

As long as it didn't blow up in his face.

"So tell me your favorite position, Seth." Robyn added a little
hmm.

Holy hell. He'd been ruminating too much and missed that
somehow the two women had finally decided to include him.

"Don't say missionary," Robyn warned, laughter lacing the
stern tone.

"I *like* missionary," Courtney said, a pout on her lips.

"Fibber," he scolded. "You like being on top." He tipped his head to catch Robyn in the mirror. "She loves to be in control."

"I do not. It's merely that when I'm on top, I can—" Courtney stopped. Laughed. Then covered her mouth.

"Come on, Courtney," Robyn chided, "tell us what you like doing when you're on top."

"I can't say it aloud." She pretended to be the prude, which she was definitely not. Then again, this was a situation unlike any she'd ever encountered.

Seth smirked. "I'll tell you what she likes to do."

Courtney shot over the console and put her hand over his lips. "You keep that to yourself."

In the backseat, Robyn laughed at their antics. "I bet you love to masturbate. Rub your clit. Frig yourself."

The words said aloud in that soft, genteel voice strummed his cock. He pulled Courtney's hand away and shoved her palm down on his cock. Christ, he was hard. He could do Courtney in the backseat on the side of the highway, he was that turned on. He scented her as if she were a bitch in heat, the sweet, musky aroma of arousal he was so damn familiar with. He could taste her pussy on his tongue. Courtney had the sweetest pussy. He loved going down on her.

The fact that they had an audience gave him a high he'd never experienced.

"Have you ever done a more exotic position? How about all fours, reverse cowgirl, standing up, or South Slav?"

"What's South Slav?" Courtney concentrated on Robyn, yet all the while rubbing Seth's cock with the bump and sway of the car along the freeway, a subtle pressure that drove him nuts.

"South Slav is when your man lays you on your back in bed, pulls you to the edge. He lifts your legs up straight and crosses your ankles before sliding his cock slowly, deeply inside you. As he moves, he kisses your feet. It's very erotic." Robyn waited expectantly, brows raised.

A throb started in his cock, spreading out.

Courtney harrumphed. "I'm not that limber."

"Hah." He adjusted the mirror slightly so Robyn would realize he spoke to her. "She walks four miles a day over the hills around our house. She's limber enough for anything."

Courtney wrinkled her nose. "Maybe I'll need a demonstration."

Robyn stared pointedly at him in the mirror. "We can certainly make sure you get all the demonstration you need."

Seth's blood hammered though his veins. Courtney leaned over and breathed in his ear, warm, wet. "Yeah, sweetie," she whispered, then licked his earlobe, "we're going to need a long, deep demonstration."

He shuddered deep in his bones picturing the night to come. He wanted to say he didn't need this, wanted to believe he was above it. Yet surrounded by the scent of so much aroused femininity, he was in danger of doing anything his wife asked.

"Courtney, are you by any chance stroking Seth's cock?"

Courtney laughed and nodded.

"Is Seth getting hard?"

She squeezed him, then reached between his legs to cup his balls, and answered Robyn with, "Uh-huh."

"Mmm." Combined with Courtney's touch, Robyn's sound of approval vibrated through his cockhead.

Oh man, he was in trouble. Big trouble.

"May I see how large he is?"

"Seth?" Courtney murmured, asking permission.

He'd had same-room sex with another couple in college, before he'd started dating Courtney. It had been new, exciting. This was ... different. Better. Hotter. More erotic. His breath seemed harsh in his throat. His heart beat in time with the pulse of his cock. It was all he could do to manage the SUV. Because of Courtney. He thought he knew her inside and out, yet this was a facet of her he'd never even contemplated. The naughty smile gracing her lips. The lascivious sparkle in her eyes. The playfulness in her touch. It was so far beyond the fantasizing they'd done. Was it possible that she wasn't jealous?

He put his hand over hers, turned long enough to capture her gaze. "It's your cock this weekend, baby, do what you want with it."

The rasp of his zipper drowned out the road noise.

Robyn leaned forward, her fingers brushing his shoulder as she peered over the seat. Her scent of almonds and vanilla drifted over him, a nice smell, yet he preferred Courtney's citrus lotions.

She moved to the other seat, behind Courtney. "The view is so much better over here."

In his peripheral vision, he got an impression of their heads together, their eyes devouring him.

Courtney reached inside his shorts. Her fingers were cool from the air-conditioning while her gaze was totally hot.

She chuckled. "Oh, you dirty man, you're not wearing underwear."

Seth gave her his best shit-eating grin. "Two can play at this game, baby." He'd gone commando, not with this in mind, but because it put him in a nastier frame of mind.

Gliding deeper into his shorts, down his shaft, making his forehead break out in a sweat, she reached for his balls.

And gasped, turning to Robyn. "He shaved," she whispered with awe.

Satisfaction ran rampant through him. She thought she had everything mapped out, in her control. He'd decided to throw his wife a few curve balls. Pun intended.

"Show me the prize." Robyn seduced them both with a whisper.

A car passed them in the fast lane. Thank God the SUV rode higher or they'd be seen. The idea shot through his cock, turning him unbearably hard and aching.

"He likes that," Courtney said, as if he were a toy they were playing with. She pulled his cock from his shorts, the crown plum-colored with need.

"Oh my," Robyn murmured with reverence.

He was a guy like any other, and the admiration in her tone kicked him a notch higher. Pre-come beaded on his tip.

Courtney captured it on her finger and raised her hand to her mouth. Her brown eyes darkened to the color of whiskey, her lips slick and beckoning with his come. The car hit the road dots, bumping over them until he corrected.

Je-sus. She liked to suck, loved to swallow, but the carnal heat in her eyes was beyond anything they'd shared. For the first damn time, Seth started to see how good this could be for them. A whole new phase of their sex life.

"Suck him, Courtney. Enough to make him crazy but not to let him come."

The seductive pitch of Robyn's voice mesmerized him. One quick glance at her, the scorching blaze in her gaze, and he was in danger of losing total control of the vehicle.

Courtney took him in her mouth. "Christ," hissed through his teeth. She'd never done it like that before, hard, sucking him deep, until her throat flexed and rippled around him. He could come right this minute, shoot off in her mouth. Instead, she was gone again, and his mind whirled in some altered state.

"That's enough for now," Robyn whispered. "We have all day to tease him."

"You're right," Courtney agreed. "He'll be pleading for mercy before we're done with him." She zipped him up and patted the aching bulge in his shorts.

The weekend had only just begun. The two of them would be the death of him. What a way to go.

COURTNEY COULD NOT BELIEVE WHAT SHE'D DONE IN THE FRONT seat of the family SUV. Holy Christmas, it was hot.

Punch-drunk on all the flirting and naughty talk, they'd made it down to Templeton before she knew it. She was dying to get Seth alone and hear what he was thinking. Then again, she was the tiniest bit afraid to learn. Coward that she was, she simply went along with the wine tasting.

"I like chardonnays and sweet dessert wines better than reds," Courtney said as they leaned on the long wooden bar.

"I'm a red girl myself," Robyn said, perusing the list of wines available for tasting.

The second winery on her list, it was smaller than the first, with only one tasting bar and no gift shop. Thankfully, it was less crowded, too. The crush at the last place made it difficult to get a taste of everything. The floors were lacquered concrete, but the wood of the bar appeared to be real oak. Three bartenders served the five groups of tasters.

Robyn pointed to a merlot at the bottom of the wine list. The bartender poured without taking his eyes off her. Robyn's elegant mannerisms had been a hit at both wineries. In fact, while the four other groups had to share the two bartenders, this guy was devoting himself to their threesome. Young, certainly under the age of thirty, he was pretty-boy handsome, dark haired, and smitten with Robyn's smile.

Lifting the glass, Robyn sniffed the bouquet, swirled the wine, then sipped. Holding it in her mouth a long moment, she swallowed. "A little bitter for me."

Their bartender pulled another bottle from the wine cabinet behind him. "Let me recommend this one instead, ma'am."

Robyn repeated the procedure with the second merlot. Sniff, swirl, sip, then she closed her eyes and gave a soft moan of pure pleasure, as if she were close to orgasm. That sound, which she made every time a particularly delicious jot of wine overcame her taste buds, was what really made her the big hit. Their bartenders couldn't get enough of her, couldn't pour the best fast enough to make sure her palate was tantalized. She had every man practically on his knees, even the other tasters.

Yeah, Seth liked it, too, watching every move Robyn made. Yet there was a distance to his gaze, as if he were assessing and analyzing a new product, taking its measure, examining its performance.

Standing next to Courtney, he flipped over the wine list. "Try this one, baby," he said close to her ear. His breath, sweet with a fruity merlot, sent tingles to her breasts.

A Riesling, one of her favorites. The young bartender tore his gaze from Robyn long enough to pour Courtney a generous sample. She sniffed the aroma. It smelled good. She swirled it. It coated the glass. She tasted it.

Oh my, it was good. A sigh of pleasure escaped.

Seth set his hand on her hip. "Let me taste."

Courtney handed him the glass. Instead, he took her chin between his fingers and kissed the wine from her lips. A long, lingering sweep of his tongue. When he pulled back, a wildfire burned in his gaze. "Oh yeah," he murmured, "*really* good."

Now Courtney was the center of attention. Every man in that small cellar wanted his wife to taste the same wine.

That kiss was hot. No married-couple kiss, it screamed lovers who'd just climbed out of bed. And were going straight home to climb back into it.

Standing on Seth's other side, Robyn slid her wineglass along the counter to him. "Taste mine."

His eyes flitted from Courtney to the bartender to Robyn, then he cupped the back of Robyn's neck and tasted the wine from her lips. More a peck than the kiss he'd given Courtney, it was no less hot, due mainly to the look in their bartender's eyes. Courtney suddenly felt lightheaded. The kid totally got what was going on. Tonight all three would share the same bed.

Seth had kissed Robyn to give their audience the thrill of specu-lation. She read it in the long steady gaze he gave her, the slight curve of his lips, hinting at a smile only she would recognize. He wanted the show. He wanted the reaction, to hear the shocked, excited voices whispering across the cellar. He wanted the kid, young enough to be Seth's son, to understand exactly what it meant to be older, seasoned, experienced. He wanted Courtney's heart to race, too.

Her heart did pick up speed. The excitement, but also the tini-est hint of anxiety. How much had he *liked* Robyn's kiss? Better than hers? She threw the thought from her mind. She didn't want to spoil a thing.

Their bartender held up the two bottles. "Which do you prefer, sir, Riesling or the merlot?"

Seth's smile was cocky, arrogant. Showy. "They're best when tasted together."

The young man's eyebrows rose to his hairline. Courtney was sure she'd heard the proverbial pin drop in the sudden silence be-fore a cacophony of whispers, voices, giggles, and laughter echoed through the room.

Oh, he was bad, so bad. Courtney wanted more of it.

7

SETH FLIPPED COURTNEY'S HAIR OVER HER SHOULDER, RUBBED HIS finger behind her ear, then cupped her nape. "Shall we buy a bottle of each, ladies?"

"I'm not done sampling this young man's wares." Courtney fluttered her eyelashes, and Seth rewarded her with a firm squeeze on the sensitive crook of her neck. The game, she found it utterly exhilarating.

"How about the Sangiovese for me?" Robyn twirled her glass by the stem.

Courtney dropped her voice to Robyn's seductive pitch. "I'd like the champagne with the hint of toasted almond."

Like a magician, the bartender had both hands moving at once, uncorking, pouring. "Coming right up, ladies."

Seth kissed Courtney's earlobe and whispered, "I'll tell you what's already up, baby."

"Yours or the boy's?" Courtney murmured as the bartender headed to the end of the counter for Robyn's choice.

Seth laughed. "Both. Better watch out for jailbait, though."

She pulled him close by the front of his shirt. "I like older men."

Her champagne suddenly appeared on the counter along with Robyn's red. "Enjoy to your heart's content, ladies."

The young man was dying to be their fourth. Courtney hadn't had this much sexy, flirty fun in . . . God, forever. It wasn't Seth's fault. It wasn't hers. They'd fallen into the twenty-year rut, the raising-children mind-set, the saving-for-retirement black hole. Time was for doing everything else that needed to be done, and their love life had taken a backseat. Robyn and this weekend were the cure.

They left with the Riesling and the merlot Robyn's young man had uncorked especially for her. He threw in a corkscrew for later, but the poor bartender never got his invite. Three's perfect, four is a crowd. As least this time.

Oh my God. She couldn't really be contemplating a foursome. She wasn't even sure if she'd like the threesome.

"You take the front seat," Courtney told Robyn as they reached the car. It was time for Seth and Robyn to do some talking. Like a go-between, Courtney had done most of the talking for Seth so far.

As Robyn had, she sat behind Seth so he could see her in the rearview mirror. He glanced at her. "Another winery, or lunch first, ladies?"

Robyn braced a hand on the back of her seat. "If you take Highway 46 toward Cambria, there's a wonderful winery with an excellent bistro. I know you had a restaurant in mind, Courtney, but I'd love this place to be my treat for the two of you. I'm sure you'll both enjoy it."

The courtesan wasn't supposed to pay for anything. When Devon hired a man, she picked up the tab for the whole event.

Devon, however, liked being in control of her men.

So why did Robyn want to treat them? *Whatever. Just take it.* Robyn's offer turned this into a date instead of sex-for-hire. Which was a good thing. Perhaps that's what Robyn intended, to enhance the illusion. "It sounds wonderful. I'd much rather try a place you already know. Right, Seth?"

His expression in the mirror was unreadable. Without the audience they'd had at the winery, he'd retreated. "Courtney loves trying new things."

Did that have more meaning than she guessed?

Robyn's voice filled with enthusiasm. "You'll love it. Promise."

"Anyone want water?" Courtney reached behind the seats, then handed the bottles around, loosening Seth's for him since he was driving. The wine had made her slightly tipsy, but she didn't want to get drunk and miss one single moment.

Seth headed out to the coast road. The day had turned hot. The air-conditioning blasted through the interior.

As Courtney had done, Robyn pulled a knee up and turned in the seat to make conversation easier. "Your husband's the complete gentleman."

Courtney laughed. "He was very naughty in there, and he needs to be punished."

Robyn gave a low, sultry chuckle. "He enjoyed inciting our bartender." She gave special emphasis to the word *inciting*.

Perching on the edge of her seat, Courtney leaned around the front seat to grab Seth's shoulder. "That's exactly what you were doing, wasn't it? Trying to make him crazy."

Seth gave barely more than a curve to his lips. "With two such gorgeous women surrounding me, I couldn't help playing a bit."

"Isn't he sweet," Robyn said. She removed her hat and threw it on the backseat next to Courtney.

"He's bad, not sweet."

"Which makes you a very lucky woman."

Courtney ruffled his hair. "Yes, I am lucky."

"Seth"—Robyn put her hand on his arm, her crimson nails dark against his skin—"you're an even luckier man to have a woman like Courtney."

He adjusted the mirror, exchanging a look with Courtney. "You have no idea how lucky I am."

Courtney glanced at his lap. His cock tented his shorts. She wanted to ask for more, yet she was afraid. How would she feel the moment he entered Robyn? The kiss he'd given their courtesan in the winery had been a mere demonstration for the audience. Now they were alone, and nothing would be for show.

Looking at Robyn briefly, her gaze was once again drawn to Seth's hard-on. Who was it for? Or was it the situation?

"Courtney, may I have your permission to feel how hard Seth is?"

Her stomach fluttered. She wanted it; she didn't want it. Perhaps that's why Robyn asked, because Courtney couldn't start it. It was hard enough to say the one word, but she did, in barely more than a whisper. "Yes."

Seth met her eyes in the mirror, the hazel shot through with something darker, something stormy.

"Seth," Robyn said softly, without the trace of seduction that seemed her trademark, "do I have your permission, too?" By asking instead of doing, she was giving them both an out if they wanted it.

"Yes." In the mirror, his gaze on Courtney was unwavering.

A heat wave rolled through Courtney's body. Her breath came fast, yet wasn't enough to fill her lungs.

Robyn leaned across the console, and Courtney caught her scent—sweet, expensive, a hint of vanilla. Courtney favored scented body lotions instead. She'd never asked if Seth wanted something more exotic.

"My, my, my," Robyn whispered, waving a hand over his shorts like a magic wand. She laid her palm over him, her hand and fingers not quite managing to cover his full length. "He's bigger than a mouthful, I'll say that much."

Courtney laughed, a nervous edge to it. Another woman was touching her husband's cock through his clothing. The sight was mind-boggling. A little terrifying. "Keep your eyes on the road, sweetie. We don't want an accident."

He didn't say a word, but shifted his legs, widening the distance between his knees, the car on cruise control.

Robyn changed direction and set her fingers down in his groin, caressing his balls. Courtney heard him suck in a breath.

"Does Robyn's hand on me make you hot, baby?"

Both of them looked at her, Robyn, up close and personal, Seth in the mirror. Courtney was horribly, terribly wet between her legs. A tad jealous, yet thrilled at the same time, the conflicting emotions adding to her excitement. She wanted her hand down between his legs, too. She wanted to feel what Robyn felt, the throb of blood through his cock, the tightening of his testicles. "Yes," she managed.

"She's squeezing me, rubbing her finger just below my nuts." Seth squirmed.

Courtney wanted to put her hand on her own pussy. Rub herself. Test her wetness. The sight set her ears roaring, her blood pressure rising.

Another woman was touching her husband.

And he liked it. Did he like it too much?

"How does Seth feel when he's inside you?" Robyn's voice was gentle, as light and seductive as the image of her hand on Seth.

Courtney's breath felt trapped in her chest, same as it did in the moment Seth entered her, the expectation, the need. "I'm so full, and he touches this spot—"

"Your G-spot."

"It's the most incredible feeling." Died and gone to heaven.

"Does he like fast or slow?"

"Both. Sometimes, I like it slow, right over that spot." Courtney found herself mesmerized by the slight, rhythmic caress of Robyn's hand over the bulge of Seth's shorts.

"Do you cry out when he makes you come, Courtney?"

"She screams," Seth said, his voice harsh. "The sounds she makes are so damn hot."

"You like it when I make all that noise?" When the girls weren't home, she let herself go.

He grabbed her gaze in the mirror. "I fucking love it."

Wow. He loved it. She was always a bit embarrassed.

"How does Courtney's pussy feel, Seth?"

"Warm. Soft. Her contractions when she climaxes milk the come from me."

"Thoughts of fucking you have made him so hard, Courtney."

A spot of pre-come marred his shorts. "That's you stroking him," she whispered.

"No," Robyn answered in a reverent voice. "It was when he started talking about the love sounds you make, the luscious feel of your pussy around him."

Courtney bit her lip. She could have climbed in his lap and ridden him right this minute. She was so wet, he would slide into her like room-warmed butter.

Robyn was seducing them both. Courtney wanted more. "I love the taste of his come."

"Tell me," Robyn urged.

"Salty. But sweet, too. Like he's been eating pineapples and oranges. I love the aftertaste of it. I love the way he pulses in my mouth when I'm sucking him."

Seth groaned, pushed back in his seat, stretched his legs, his hands clamped on the wheel.

Robyn's hand was on his cock, but it was Courtney's words that drove him higher. She felt that deep in her belly.

"How does Courtney taste?"

"Fucking sweet. She gets so goddamn wet, her juice covers my face."

Seth didn't swear often—they'd always been afraid of teaching little girls big words—but the dirty talk on his lips made her nipples ache beneath her sundress. Her juice, the juice he loved, drenched her panties.

"I'd love to watch him lick you, Courtney. I'd love to see the look on your face as you climax with his tongue inside you."

Seth choked off a sound. "Ladies, if you don't want to end up in a ditch, we need to stop right now."

Robyn leaned in, pecked his ear. "I'm sorry. I got carried away." She smiled at Courtney. "There's so much to save for later, we don't want to waste it all now."

Cotton wool filled her head. Her skin burned, her pussy pulsed. She wanted Seth more than the first night she'd had him, more than she'd needed him on their wedding night, more than the first time they made love after Shannon was born.

She wasn't sure she could wait for later. She might not make it out of the hotel once they checked in. She might not even make it through the surprise she had for Seth and Robyn.

HOLY HELL. HIS HEAD WAS GOING TO EXPLODE, AND HIS COCK WAS a throbbing ache in his shorts. His hard-on raged even as he tried to concentrate on . . . polymer densities and R factors. Work issues, usually guaranteed to make him limp as a wet noodle, wouldn't take root in his suddenly Neanderthal brain.

He sat through lunch in a fog and sipped through wine tasting in a daze. He'd dreamed of setting Courtney on the bistro table, flipping up her skirt, and dining on her instead of the croissant sandwich he'd ordered. He imagined dragging her behind a barrel of chardonnay and pounding into her until her breathy, throaty moans rose in a crescendo of orgasm.

When Courtney first brought up this plan, he'd thought of it as her giving him away, tossing him at another woman as if he were nothing more than a piece of meat. He hadn't counted on this visceral need sweeping through him. It wasn't Robyn's touch on his cock. Or her voice. It was the way she'd dragged Courtney into the front seat with her words, his wife's eyes locked on Robyn's dark, elegant hand in his lap. It was Courtney's glazed look as she described the feel of his cock inside her and the force of his need as he scented her arousal.

This was so fucking much more than he'd imagined.

After lunch and three more wineries, where the ladies did the imbibing and he did the watching, the remainder of the drive out to the coast had been light and conversational. Courtney sat in front with him, programming the motel's address into the GPS. Almost dinnertime, he pulled the car into the parking lot, the white-washed cottages fronted by small patios edged with planters of bright flowers. Across the street, the ocean crashed along the shore and walkers on the wooden pathway held their hats against the wind rushing off the sea.

In the backseat, Robyn gathered her hat and purse. "I hope you don't mind if I arrange for my own room."

Beside him, Courtney stilled. Her brow furrowed. After almost a quarter of a century together, he could read her mind. Something was wrong, Robyn didn't want to play, he'd have a huge fight with Courtney, the whole weekend would turn to shit.

Courtney could catastrophize with the best of them.

She drew in a deep breath, let it out slowly. "That will be fine." She twisted her wrist to glance at her watch. "I have a surprise planned and we need to leave in about an hour. Since we ate lunch so late, I thought we could have dinner when we get back." She raised a brow at Robyn. "Will that be okay?"

"Wonderful. I love surprises." Robyn leaned between the seats and took Courtney's chin in her fingers.

It was extraordinarily sexual, though Seth could never have pinpointed why in a million years. Yet the courtesan's hand on his wife's face excited him beyond measure, more than her palm on his cock.

"Now, Courtney, I don't want any play going on while you and Seth are alone."

"You don't?" Wide-eyed and breathless, Courtney stared.

"No. I want to watch. Whatever you two do tonight, I want to be there to see it all."

"Oh."

Oh was damn fucking right. He wanted the audience.

"Promise?" Robyn had the most amazing voice, seductive, sexy, hypnotic. Courtney was mesmerized. Her answer was a dazed nod.

8

SETH GOT TWO COTTAGES NEXT TO EACH OTHER AT THE BACK OF the complex, blocked from the ocean wind, secluded, private.

Setting Robyn's bag inside her door, he squeezed her hand. "Thank you."

"You're welcome."

He hadn't conceived of things going as well as they were. It was Robyn's doing.

Courtney had already carried their bags in, and Seth retrieved the cooler.

"Do not open the box or the cooler upon pain of death," she warned as he set the cooler by the front door next to a covered printer-paper box.

Seth was pretty damn sure the paper had long since been cleaned out. "No peeking, I promise."

The bed was huge, and a gas fireplace glowed in the corner. The coast was at least ten degrees cooler than it had been inland, and once the fog rolled in, the fire would be pleasant. She'd obviously picked the motel for romance.

"Do you like it?" She was almost hesitant.

"Yeah."

The carpet was thick, the comforter soft as goose down, and

the bed covered with huge throw pillows. They could toss them on the rug in front of the fire and toast the night to come with the wine he'd purchased.

Courtney opened her bag on the suitcase rack and unpacked, setting her cosmetics case in the bathroom, hanging a light jacket in the closet, laying things in the drawers beneath the TV cabinet. She was avoiding him.

"She said we couldn't play, not that we couldn't talk about it."

"Oh, I'm just putting stuff away." Her voice was unnaturally high.

Seth took her arm, stopped her midstride between the case and the drawers. "What's wrong?"

Staring at the steel blue carpet, she swallowed. "I didn't think we'd be alone."

"You and me?"

She nodded. "I'm embarrassed."

He laughed, short, sharp. "What the hell for?"

"You told her I screamed."

"You do." He tipped her chin up with one finger, but her eyes only made it as far as his nose. "It's fucking hot," he whispered.

"You never say *fuck*."

"I never say it in front of the girls, but I should be saying it more in the bedroom." They used to talk and laugh all the time during sex. These days it had become mostly a silent affair until Courtney screamed in orgasm. He hadn't noticed when they stopped having fun during sex. The July Fourth barbecue, when she'd sucked him in the car, was the first time in a long time that sex felt more than rote. He began to understand some of what she'd been missing all these months, why she'd planned this naughty excursion. To gain his attention.

"Do you like her?" For the first time, she met his gaze, her eyes a soft, worried brown.

"She's nice."

"Do you think she's sexy?"

"Very. You're sexier."

She scanned his face. "Did you like her stroking your cock?"

"I liked you watching. I liked having her ask all those dirty things. I like the way she talks and makes it all about us."

Courtney nodded slowly. "She's very good at what she does."

He trailed a light finger along her jaw. "Then let's enjoy what she's offering."

"I am enjoying it." She sighed. "I'm just nervous, too. About my surprise."

He wrapped his hand around her neck, drew her close to his chest. "Your surprise is going to be perfect."

Yet he wondered. How far could he let this thing go?

IT WAS THE ODDEST SENSATION. COURTNEY HAD ACTUALLY FELT uncomfortable alone in the room with her husband. They'd crossed a line. Or rather, *she'd* pushed them over it. He'd kissed another woman in a sexual sense, even if it was little more than a peck. That same woman had stroked his cock through his shorts. Courtney had been unutterably turned on by it.

Which made her certifiable.

She could be damaging her marriage. This could be an event they would never get over. Like that movie *Indecent Proposal* where Demi slept with the rich guy for one million dollars. Her marriage fell apart. Sometimes life could be exactly like a movie.

Or . . . this could be the hottest experience they ever had.

That was the problem. Her emotions were stymied. She couldn't decide. She didn't know what she wanted, or what was best. All she could think of was his voice when he said being inside her was fucking hot. He hadn't used that tone in years.

She'd do anything to hear it again.

So here they were, on the road to her surprise, her heart fluttering in her chest, Robyn sitting in the back again. Courtney still wore her sundress with a cardigan over it, but Robyn had changed into a black caftan printed with bright pink flowering fuchsias.

"Turn at the next signpost." Courtney pointed ahead as Seth drove. Maybe she should have changed, too. Robyn was stunning in her flowing black and fuchsia outfit, her skin a lovely chocolate brown.

"The castle?" Seth spun the wheel and headed through the gates. "We're taking a tour?"

Courtney couldn't decide whether his tone implied derision or wonder. "Not a tour. Something special. Private."

Seth quirked an eyebrow. From the backseat, Robyn made a sound of approval. "Very interesting," she added. "This will be a first for me." Her voice dipped. "I love firsts."

The castle had been built by some newspaper mogul back in the thirties. It was ostentatious, a modern marvel, a museum. There were daily tours. While it was a popular attraction, the restoration efforts were funded not by the price of the tours but by benefit functions and special events. When she'd seen the special offer on a website, she couldn't believe it. It was expensive, but she couldn't help herself, she had to have it for her surprise. Once she got it in her mind, nothing else would do. It would totally blow Seth's mind, and hopefully be a one and only for Robyn.

They parked in the lot, entering the fancy new arched building as most people were leaving, the last public tours over for the day. At the ticket window, she presented her e-mailed instructions and in less than ten minutes they were on a small shuttle bus heading up the winding road to the massive castle on the hill.

Their docent, a short woman with round cheeks and a florid

complexion, recited the rules. "You will have two hours. Please be back at the bottom of the stairs where we drop you off. As advertised, you will be the only people on the hill. Your access is limited to the area described in your confirmation. There is no running water on the hill and no restrooms." They'd used the facilities before they left the visitors' center. "Anything that we've left out for your use, you may leave where you find it. Otherwise, please take everything with you when you exit the hill."

Seth and Robyn shared a look. They had no clue. Courtney was glad the docent carefully didn't blow the surprise. This was going to be fun. Her strange nervousness in the cottage had all but vanished.

The van rounded a curve, revealing a magnificent view of the castle, its golden spires sparkling in the sun. They had almost two hours before sunset. Courtney snapped a couple of photos on the digital camera. "Documentation," she said when Robyn glanced at her as if she were a tourist.

Well, goodness, she was! This was once in a lifetime and ungodly expensive. The Italy account would now fund a tapestry restoration, and this weekend would be with her forever, like tandem skydiving or zip-lining through the jungle.

The docent gave them the virtual tour. "You can see some of the bison on the slope there. We also have zebra, Barbary sheep, and sambar deer remaining on the ranch from the days when this was Mr. Caine's animal preserve. Over there, you'll see the polar bear cages. The arbor"—she pointed to the right—"was a two-mile-long horse trail beneath the lilacs."

The scrubby hillside gave way to flowering bushes and fruit trees, their branches drooping beneath the weight of luscious oranges and lemons. Finally the shuttle pulled up at a set of concrete steps leading to a marble frieze of Roman gods.

"Everything you requested is at the top of the stairs." The lady gave Courtney a severe smile. "Remember, two hours. The van will be waiting here."

Courtney felt like Cinderella whose carriage would turn into a pumpkin in only two hours.

Seth held her hand as she exited the van. "You've outdone yourself this time, baby."

"You ain't seen nothing yet." She grinned as he courteously extended his hand for Robyn.

The evening was quite warm. Down by the ocean, the breeze had cooled everything off, yet up here on the hill, the sun was brilliant and the air surprisingly still.

The van pulled away. They were alone in paradise.

Seth grabbed her hand, stared at the frieze in marvel. "How did you manage this?"

"Secret." She didn't want him asking how much it cost. Then she took Robyn's hand. "Let me show you our surprise."

Robyn's hand was cool while Seth's engulfed her with heat. Her sandals slapped on the concrete stairs, and they stepped onto the marble decking beside the magnificent blue pool.

"The famed Bacchus pool." Robyn's voice dripped with awe.

Marble statues surrounded the olympiad pool: dolphins, cupids, gods, goddesses. A small temple had been erected on one side, hodgepodged together from various ancient ruins with differing column styles from Ionic to Doric. Three cushioned rattan chairs sat by the pool, the sun beaming on them, each laid out with a plush bath-sized towel. Champagne chilled in a silver bucket, and three champagne flutes stood at the ready.

She held out a hand, encompassing the pool and the cozy setting. "Champagne and an evening swim."

"I didn't bring a suit," Seth said, his eyes sparkling.

"Neither did I," Courtney answered. "We'll have to swim in the buff." She laughed. "The water isn't heated."

He shuddered. "Uh-oh, shrinkage."

She pressed up against him, putting her hand to the front of his shorts. "You don't have to worry about that, sweetie."

Robyn wandered to the edge, slipped off her sandal and dipped her toe in. "Cool, but not too bad. At least it was hot up here today." She unzipped her cotton caftan, and let it drop to the marble.

She was gloriously bare beneath, as if she'd known something like this would be expected, though Courtney had given no hints, not even to Isabel. Long, toned legs, hour-glass figure, and large, firm breasts, Robyn wasn't thin, she was lushly proportioned, sexy, and feminine.

She stole Seth's breath. At least that's how Courtney interpreted the stunned look on his face. Robyn turned, diving in a graceful arc into the pool.

She surfaced, shrieking. "Oh my God, it's cold, but lovely." She splashed water at them—"Get in, you guys"—then paddled away on her back, her breasts bouncing proudly, nipples dark, large, and taut.

Courtney touched Seth's arm, and he came out of his trance. "Do you want me to open the champagne, baby?" he asked.

She wanted to glance down to his cock, but was afraid she'd find him bursting his seams. Over Robyn. Which was what he was supposed to do, but . . .

"Yes," she said before she could finish the thought. "I need champagne." A ripe, juicy strawberry lodged at the bottom of each glass.

He popped and poured, handed her a glass, then raised his, tapped her flute gently. "To a wonderful surprise." The sun behind him, his eyes were dark. Courtney grabbed the camera to snap a photo of him. He was so perfect.

They sipped in unison. "Do you really like it?" she whispered, suddenly unsure of herself, of the money she'd spent, of the things she planned for the rest of the night.

"You're fucking perfect." He sealed the words with a kiss. "Now take off your clothes."

A thrill shot through her at the hunger sparking in his eyes. She wriggled her shoulders and let the cardigan fall to the chaise lounge. Turning, she pulled her hair to the side and said, "Unzip me, please."

Robyn splashed in the water, watching them.

Seth dropped a kiss on her shoulder, then the top of her spine as he slid down the tab. Gliding his fingers beneath the spaghetti straps, he slipped them off her shoulders. Robyn turned onto her belly and kicked to the side of the pool, hanging on the edge. Courtney's dress fluttered to the marble. She stepped out of it, then slid her feet from her sandals. Seth trailed a finger down her back to the crease of her butt. More than anything, she wanted to tip her head and see if he was looking at Robyn. Whose breasts did he like better? Courtney's were full, but breast-feeding had taken its toll. Robyn's belly was smooth. Faint stretch marks lingered on Courtney's tummy even after all these years.

Seth leaned down, bit the soft tendons between her shoulder and neck, and Courtney thrilled to the fact that he concentrated solely on her. Reaching around to cup her breasts, he pinched a nipple. She shivered, closed her eyes, and pushed back against his rock-hard erection. Then he pushed her forward and into the water.

She came up shrieking, the same as Robyn had. "Oh my God." The cold water choked off her breath for a moment, then she met Robyn's eye. They both came out with "shrinkage" at exactly the same moment, then dissolved into peals of laughter.

"I'm not getting in there if I'm going to have shrinkage," Seth said emphatically.

"Strip," Courtney ordered.

"Take it off, Mr. O'Brien," Robyn demanded.

They both paddled to the pool's marble edge, folded their arms, and stared expectantly.

Truthfully, Courtney couldn't describe the feeling. The Bacchus pool that thousands of tourists dreamed of swimming in—they had it to themselves. Skinny-dipping. Champagne and strawberries. She shivered with pure delight.

"Come on, don't be a weenie," Courtney challenged.

"I'm not a weenie," Seth declared.

He wanted to put on a show for them. Courtney read it in his stance, the curve of his lips, and the bulge of his shorts.

She had her husband right on the edge.

9

"TAKE IT OFF, TAKE IT OFF," ROBYN CHANTED. COURTNEY JOINED IN.

Grabbing his shirt by the neck, Seth yanked it over his head. Muscled chest dusted with hair, dusky nipples, flat abdomen, he was a man in his prime. She'd take him any day over some wimp in his thirties.

"Show us the rest, hot stuff," Robyn catcalled.

Flipping off his deck shoes, Seth unbuttoned, unzipped, and shoved his shorts off his hips to kick them aside.

Complete and utter silence reigned on the hill. Courtney saw her husband through Robyn's eyes, a magnificent male animal, predatory in the aggressive jut of his cock. Long, thick, pulsing. Her mouth watered.

"Shrinkage is certainly not a problem," Robyn mused, taking in her fill.

Courtney should have been jealous at another woman getting the complete eyeful. Yet she was proud. Seth was hers. And he was fucking gorgeous.

With a mighty roar, he took off at a run, jumped, pulled his knees to his chest, and hit the water in a tremendous cannonball. The girls shrieked and laughed, wiping the spray from their faces.

He broke the surface, then backstroked across the pool, his cock standing proud.

"He's quite a sight." Robyn's gaze followed his progress.

"He's quite a man," Courtney agreed.

"This was a wonderful idea."

"I wanted something over the top."

Robyn arched a brow. "We haven't even gotten to the really fun part yet." She dove beneath the water, pushed off from the wall, and glided into the middle, coming up next to Seth as he made his way back across. With a big smile, Robyn dunked him under. He came up sputtering, grabbed her around the waist, and flung her into deep water. They laughed, playing like children.

A pang nudged up under Courtney's rib cage. She'd let herself be left out for the moment. Ducking beneath the surface, she braced her feet on the wall and shot into the middle where she could see their legs working in the water. Tugging on Seth's hairy calf, she pulled him down with her. Bubbles burbled out of his mouth. Wrapping an arm beneath her breasts, he swam up to the light shining into the water, lifted her, tossed her.

"Oh my hair, you've made it a mess," she shrieked, pushing it out of her face, water streaming down.

Robyn jumped up to dunk Courtney with a two-handed shove on her head. When she cleared the water again, Seth was dunking Robyn. A moment later, he hauled Courtney against him and took her down, sealing his lips to hers in a searing kiss. Her legs tangled with his, his cock hard against her belly. Oh no, shrinkage definitely was not a problem. With the exertion and the heat of his kiss, the water didn't even feel cold anymore. Her nipples beaded, and that wasn't the cold either. He broke the surface once more, wrapping her legs around his waist and swimming with her to the steps.

They were both breathing hard, their skin icy, their hearts racing. Robyn's cold fingers slid down her spine. "Kiss him for me, Courtney."

Courtney pushed Seth back against the steps, spread her body over his, their torsos bare above the water, and kissed him. Lips, tongues, open-mouthed, seeking, taking.

Seth's blood roared through his ears and his cock pulsed. They'd gone from laughing and playing to throbbing heat in sixty seconds flat. He wanted to bury his cock in her.

He wanted Robyn to watch. "Take a picture," he ordered, pointing to the camera Courtney had left by the champagne, then gave himself up to the taste of his wife's lips.

He was aware, moments later, as Robyn nuzzled up against them on the pool steps, the camera on and lying within reach. Wet, naked female bodies surrounded him. He was nuts with the feel of all that skin. Courtney devoured him like never before. Threading his fingers through her hair, he anchored his mouth on hers and slipped his other hand down between their bodies, pinching her nipple, stroking her abdomen, tunneling between her legs. She opened over him, and he slipped into her moist channel.

Down between Courtney's legs, he felt the stroke of Robyn's fingers across the back of his hand and thought he'd shatter into a million pieces. He tore his mouth away for a breath of air.

"Are you sure this is private?"

Courtney nodded, her gaze shell-shocked.

"Then suck me, baby," he muttered. "Christ, I need your mouth on me."

She slithered down his body, sucked his nipple, bit him lightly. Spots danced before his eyes. Robyn's body heat, so close to theirs, set the water boiling.

He shifted to the top step, his cock breaking the surface, and Courtney went down between his legs. Curling her fist around him, she took his shaft deep into her mouth. He closed his eyes, groaning, and when he opened them again, Robyn's gaze consumed him. Her nostrils flared, her eyes coal dark and hot. "More pictures, Seth?" she asked.

He could do nothing more than nod. Oh yeah, he wanted documentation, too.

The sex was raw, heated, elemental. Courtney sucked hard on the tip, the way he loved, driving him higher. He had to beat back the orgasm that rose like a tidal wave. Not yet. Too soon.

Robyn reached out to pinch his nipple. Hard. Pleasure-pain flashed down to his balls. He screwed his eyes shut. Christ. Too much. Not enough. God.

"Courtney, stop." Robyn's voice, soft yet steel-edged.

His eyes flashed open. Courtney stilled with his crown between her lips, the sight so gorgeous, so powerful. Yet he could breathe again, and the climax receded a hairsbreadth.

"We don't want him to come so soon," Robyn said gently, as if Courtney were a child.

His wife blinked, came back to herself. She'd been as carried away as he. Robyn was right, though, too much, too soon, too fast.

"Lick him lightly along his shaft." Robyn's voice caressed him as Courtney followed her instructions, gliding her tongue down to the base of his cock.

"Now his balls," Robyn cooed.

He'd shaved smooth this morning, but Courtney had never been a nut girl. Until now.

She licked around, under, over, then sucked one ball into her mouth. Holy mother. He was instantly an inch longer, a stone harder.

"Now motorboat him."

Courtney popped him free. "Motorboat?"

Robyn nodded. "Yeah. Like this." She dipped down into the water and blew bubbles out her mouth.

Courtney laughed, then repeated the action against his balls. It was unique, different, hot.

"Like it?" Robyn asked.

"Fucking fantastic," he said, fast losing himself in the sensations.

"Now take him slowly into your mouth, Courtney, as deep as you can go."

Seth held out his hand. "The camera."

He gazed at her on the view screen. Christ. Gorgeous. Courtney slid her lips over his crown, down, down, down. He documented the intensely erotic sight.

"Relax your throat," Robyn coaxed.

His shaft disappeared into her mouth, and finally nudged the back of her throat. "Look up at me, baby." Her eyes were like melted chocolate in the camera's lens.

"Let him in all the way." Robyn laid her hand on the back of Courtney's head with a gentle pressure. "A little bit more."

Impossibly, she took him. It was sheer heaven. His hips moved on their own, lightly pumping. Courtney pressed her fingers into his ass, urging his cock deeper.

"Holy shit. Fuck." The words fell from his lips, his eyes closed, and he flexed.

She was gone, cool air on his hard cock. He opened his eyes to meet her gaze.

"I want Robyn to do this with me."

How many times had he heard that? Her fantasy. Christ, he wouldn't be a red-blooded American male if he hadn't gotten right into the fantasy, too.

The chill of the water seeped into his bones. He set the camera aside on the edge of the pool, away from the water. What would she do or say later if he agreed to this?

"Please," she whispered.

Robyn soothed a hand down his arm as if she understood the thoughts knocking like billiard balls inside his head. "It'll be together, not just me."

The water swished around his legs as Courtney moved to his side and Robyn settled down next to him.

His wife held his cock, dipping her head to run her tongue from base to tip. Robyn angled her head the opposite direction, and tongued him from crown to balls.

Two mouths, two tongues, two feminine bodies pressed against him. Shit, fuck, he was going to hell. He closed his eyes so he couldn't see who was doing what and the sensations intensified. He slid deep down a throat. A hand teased his balls. Slurping, sucking, Jesus, even the sounds drove him wild.

"Watch," Courtney demanded.

He was their tool. He did what she wanted. Eyes open, he drank in the sight as Robyn held his cock in her fist and guided Courtney down on him, her lips engulfing him, taking him deep, deeper, deepest. They switched, Courtney holding, Robyn's mouth sliding down. His wife's eyes glowed, swallowing the sight whole as if she relished the finest of her sweet wines. Finally, both mouths at once, as if they were kissing each other as well as his cock. The heat, the excitement, two heads bobbing over him, worshiping his cock.

He snapped a picture, wanting Courtney to see it for herself later. Then everything became pure sensation.

"Jesus, I'm gonna come." The cry was almost torn from his throat. He was on the hairy edge, Courtney sucked, Robyn palmed his nuts, touched that sensitive spot by his ass. He pulsed, rocked, pumped, then at the last moment, he yanked on Courtney's arms. "I need to come on your breasts."

She rose, and he spent himself on her chest, covered her

beautiful thick nipples with his come. Before she could rub it in, he fisted his fingers in Robyn's hair and said, "Lick it off."

Courtney's eyes went wide. Robyn looked from one to the other. He gave the back of her head a push. Courtney had her fantasy, and he had his.

She acquiesced with the briefest of nods and leaned against him. Robyn sipped his come from the upper swell of her breast. Their bodies covered his legs, his still-throbbing cock. Robyn sucked a droplet from Courtney's nipple, and his wife moaned.

The sight was so fucking hot, his cock surged again.

Robyn trailed from one peak to the other, licking, sucking. Courtney arched into the sweet sweep of another woman's mouth across her body. Her nipples were turgid buds, a deep, luscious aroused red. Her fingers bit into his thigh where she held on. Until Robyn had cleaned away every trace of his come.

Courtney opened her eyes, met his gaze; her lips parted, her breath quickened. She was the most beautiful creature he'd ever seen.

"I want some champagne," she whispered.

She was going to need it. Because this show she'd asked for had now become his.

COURTNEY COULDN'T BELIEVE SHE'D DONE THAT. OR RATHER THAT she'd let it be done to her. Did it make them even, that Robyn had sucked Seth's cock and licked Courtney's breasts, laving her nipples, sending a thrill shooting straight down to her pussy?

Oh Lord.

She'd let another woman lick her breasts. She wasn't sure how she felt about it. Odd, to say the least.

Seth had loved it. The heated look in his eye allowed her to give herself up to sensation.

Poolside, they'd enjoyed champagne and strawberries and the last of the sun as if nothing had happened on the pool steps. The shuttle took them back to the car, and half an hour later they were back at the cottages.

"I brought some things with me for dinner," she said as they piled out of the SUV. A feast they could fuck over, that's how she'd thought of it, filling the cooler and her big cardboard box with goodies.

As Seth unlocked their cottage door, she stopped Robyn with a hand on her arm. "Come in. Eat with us."

"Of course." Robyn still backed toward her own cabin. "I'll be right over."

Courtney was afraid to let Robyn go. If she was alone with Seth, if she thought about what they'd already done and what they were going to do . . . she wasn't sure she could go through with it all.

She didn't want to sound like a weenie by begging, either. "Okay, see you in a few." She waggled her fingers and headed to her own open door.

She'd put her clothes on, and it was going to be damn hard to take them off again. In the heat of the moment, you could do all sorts of things, but give yourself a minute to think, and bam, you lost your courage. It was all the stopping and starting. When she'd planned the weekend, she'd thought of the wine tasting, the meals, the Bacchus pool as flirty fun, foreplay, all leading up to the big moment. Yet now it was a matter of regrouping her courage after each naughty encounter.

There were even pictures of her debauchery, too.

She'd barely closed the door when Seth grabbed her around the waist and tossed her on the bed, coming down on top. He took her mouth before she could get a word out.

Oh God, what a kiss. No staid married kiss, nor a passionate first love kiss, it was a rediscovery of things lost, a lush melding of lips and tongues, then backing off as he whispered, "You naughty slut," and took her again. His tongue invaded, driving deep, sucking her under with the sweetness of fruit and champagne. Again he backed off, nipping her earlobe before he murmured, "You're too fucking hot," and came back for more. He didn't give her a moment to think or doubt, not even to breathe, his hands on her breasts, fingers pinching her nipples, knee between her legs, cock hard against her belly, and his voice: "Fuck the hell out of me, baby."

This was exactly what she'd wanted, for the weekend to bring them to a whole new level of their sexuality and need for each other.

Seth's heat and desire overwhelmed her, and Courtney missed the knock on the door. Until he slid off her, leaving her with her legs splayed and her dress high on her thighs.

Robyn laughed as she entered. "Are you two starting without me?"

The special moment Courtney had shared with Seth died.

10

PULLING HER DRESS DOWN TO COVER HER BUTT AS SHE CLIMBED off the bed, Courtney tried to sound normal, as if nothing had happened and nothing had been lost. "Seth was accosting me, or I would already have dinner out."

He snorted. "Shall I open both the red and the white we got this afternoon, ladies?" He'd set Courtney's Riesling to chill in the ice bucket.

"I'd love a glass of merlot." Robyn tossed a bag on the bed, then joined Courtney on her knees, helping to unpack the cooler and the cardboard box filled with all the goodies. "Ooh, you've got lots of fun stuff."

"Cheese and fruit and veggies and crackers."

"I love this kind of smorgasbord." Robyn popped a grape in her mouth. "Here, Seth." He leaned down to hand her the merlot, and she popped a grape in his mouth, too.

Courtney's heart stilled. Somehow the tiny act shocked her. It was so . . . intimate. More than Robyn sucking Seth's cock with her. More than the peck he'd given for show at the winery.

Yet Robyn seemed to think nothing of it. "Shall we eat by the fire? The pool chilled me a bit." She squeezed Courtney's knee. "Despite all the hot action going on."

Courtney found her voice. "Oh yes, the fire. The fire, that's what I had in mind." She waved a hand at Seth, as if she were as unaffected as Robyn. "Can you flip the switch, honey?" It was a gas fireplace. "And throw down some of those pillows off the bed?"

In the end it was a cozy meal on a big platter by the cheery fire, all three of them leaning on pillows, Seth in the middle.

Courtney dipped a carrot stick in the dip, then laid a dollop of brie on a cracker and handed it to Seth.

"Thanks, baby."

"Now tell me how you managed to rent the Bacchus pool, Courtney." Robyn prepared two crackers, one brie, one Cambozola cheese.

"I saw a package on eBay for a night's stay in one of the servant's rooms in a castle tower. It included a private tour and breakfast on the patio. I followed the links to a website where they had all these cool packages you could buy." She glanced at Seth. "I couldn't afford the overnight stay, but I thought two hours in the pool would be fun."

Robyn held out the Cambozola cracker, feeding it to Seth. He ate from her fingers without a thought.

Courtney experienced that same bump in her heart rate. It was the strangest thing. Why did feeding Seth bother her more than watching his cock slide between Robyn's lips? The thought was totally ass backward. Courtney's only defense was to dip a strip of red pepper in the ranch dressing and feed that to him.

As if they were fighting over him.

Robyn was so pretty and elegant, intelligent and soft-spoken. Seth had moaned as she sucked him. He licked his lips after she fed him a cheese-laden cracker.

He'd tasted another woman. How could he go back to the same old tired wife after this?

"Courtney, do you need a refill?" He held up the bottle. She'd finished her Riesling without noticing and held out her glass.

"This is delicious cheese," Robyn said.

Courtney prayed she wouldn't feed Seth another bite of it. "Cambozola. It's Seth's favorite."

Robyn touched his hand with the tip of her index finger. "He's got very good taste."

Courtney felt that touch as if Robyn had suddenly wrapped her hand around Seth's cock and started stroking him. *I can't do this.* Yet she didn't know why. What had changed between the hot, naughty pool play and this moment?

Robyn smiled, raising a knee, her skin brushing Seth's leg, the caftan falling away to reveal the inside of a firm thigh. "I'll have to remember that name."

What name? Courtney had no idea what she was talking about. Oh. The cheese. She was losing it. "It's very good with sweet fruit. Try it on an apple." Courtney slathered a slice with cheese.

When Seth reached out to pass it over, she pulled away, making sure Robyn took it from her fingers, not his.

She was jealous. She couldn't deny it. She didn't want Seth feeding Robyn or vice versa. She didn't want to see them kiss. Not after that deliciously hungry kiss Seth had given her on the bed.

How was she supposed to say she'd changed her mind? She'd planned the weekend, talked Seth into it, hired a courtesan, paid a freaking fortune for two hours in the Bacchus pool. And now she wanted to back out when they were about to get right down to it?

"Delicious." Robyn's gaze was on Seth.

Courtney thought she'd scream.

"Take off your clothes, Courtney." Robyn popped a cherry tomato in her mouth.

"Huh?" A flush rose to Courtney's face. She wasn't ready for this to start.

"Take off your clothes. I want to see Seth drink wine from your belly button and eat a grape out of your pussy."

Oh. She shivered.

Seth laughed out loud. "I like you, Robyn. You say what you want."

"You two whet my appetite earlier. I feel like upping the stakes." Robyn petted Seth's arm. "You can come more than once in a night, can't you?"

"I could come right now." He stared straight at Courtney as he said it.

Robyn clapped her hands. "Good. Because we have so much more to do tonight." She leaned past Seth, dropping her voice to a whisper just for Courtney. "I want to see him take you."

The evening was getting away from her. Courtney was losing control. Yet Seth looked at her with the reflection of the fire in his eyes. The memory of his kiss, the way he'd grabbed and taken, tossed her on the bed, it played on her needs. The two of them together were seducing her. Since Seth had yet to say he wanted to do Robyn, Courtney let herself be seduced.

Rising, she unzipped her dress, the material caressing her hips and legs as it slid to the carpet.

Robyn threw it across the room after Courtney stepped from the pool of fabric.

"Aren't you getting naked with me?" It was fine being naked but only when you didn't have to do it alone.

"No. This is all about you now." Robyn lowered her lashes. "I want to help Seth pleasure you."

Courtney felt that deer-in-the-headlights sensation. What did that mean? She was a jumble of emotions. Was Robyn going to . . .

"Only what you want, baby." Seth played with her ankle. "Let us take care of you."

She latched on to the one important thing. He wasn't asking to fuck Robyn; he wanted to pleasure his wife. Right now, that's all Courtney cared about, the sexiness of a threesome without the fear that Seth would find the other woman's body preferable to hers.

He patted a pillow. "Lay down."

The fire leapt in his gaze. Her knees weakened. Robyn pushed the platter aside, and Courtney lay back against the pile of pillows between them.

Seth kissed her gently, ran a hand down her abdomen to the very edge of her pubic curls, and stopped. Her belly trembled.

Robyn retrieved the bag she'd tossed on the bed. "I'm going to put a bit of this on your nipples." She drizzled liquid from a bottle, then smoothed the gel around each nipple.

Heat rose. Courtney swallowed. Her nipples puckered to the light touch of Robyn's fingers.

"It's a heat gel," Robyn explained. "Does it feel good?"

"Yes."

"Lick her nipples, Seth." Robyn cupped Courtney's breast, plumping the flesh for his mouth.

He sucked her deep, and Courtney moaned, her body rising all on its own, heat flashing down to her core. "Oh my God."

"Feels good, doesn't it?"

Her nipples tingled, Seth's moist mouth heating the gel until her breasts burned. "Yes. God. That's intense."

Robyn dribbled cold white wine on her other nipple. "Suck it off."

Seth ministered to that breast, the hot and cold an electric combination.

Robyn set a grape in her belly button, added a couple of drops of wine and demanded of Seth, "Eat it."

He licked the wine and sucked the grape from her body. His nose tickled. Courtney laughed. Her anxiety was receding. If she didn't think of the moment she had to trade places with Robyn, she'd be fine.

"You need to strip down, Seth." Robyn waved a hand at him. "I want to see both of you naked and tangled together."

It was Courtney's move to tell Robyn to throw off her caftan and join them, but she couldn't. Just as she hadn't wanted to see them feeding each other, she didn't want to see Seth's hand reaching for her breast or his mouth on her nipple. Maybe she could get back into that idea later, but not now.

Her husband rose to his full magnificence, tossed off his shirt, and stepped out of his shorts. His cock jutted proudly. Her breath simply stopped in her throat. He was so perfect.

"Touch him," Robyn whispered. "He's gorgeous."

Courtney reached up to stroke his hard length. "He always amazes me with how hard he gets," she said, almost to herself.

Robyn closed her fingers over Courtney's, squeezing until Seth hissed in air, then she pulled Courtney's hand away. "Not too much. First I want him to make you come."

Courtney turned, met Robyn's chocolate brown gaze. "I've never come in front of anyone else."

"That's why it's going to be so hot and exciting for all of us." Robyn pulled Seth to his knees between Courtney's legs. "Blow on her."

He nestled at the juncture of her thighs, put his hand to her pussy, and opened her folds. His warm breath caressing her sent a jolt of heat to her clit.

"She needs the warming gel," Seth said.

Seth held her open as Robyn drizzled the gel on her clitoris. It trickled down, leaving a wave of heat in its wake. They worked on her in tandem. It was suddenly, inexplicably, the most erotic thing she'd ever experienced. Even more than sucking Seth's cock as Robyn held his base.

"Rub it in," Robyn directed.

Seth did as he was bid, stroking her clit with his finger, dipping down to gather more of the gel. He circled, tantalized, teased. Courtney writhed.

"Is that good, baby?"

"Oh yeah." She was seeing spots before her eyes.

"Now for something succulent right out of her pussy." Robyn studied the platter, made a selection, holding out a slice of apple.

"You can't put that in me."

"Oh yes, we can." Robyn's hand disappeared between her legs, slipping the bit of apple into her channel without actually touching Courtney.

"Eat her and suck it out." Robyn's eyes gleamed with circles of topaz around the irises.

Seth bent to the feast. His mouth on her clit, he licked, sucked, the gel tingling, heating, making her mad. Robyn caressed her thigh, squeezing lightly, soothing. Dipping down to tug the apple from her, he ate it, covered with her juice, his lips glistening as he gazed along her body. Courtney went mindless. He played her with fingers, lips, mouth, teeth. Her eyes closed as she writhed on the pillows, Robyn's touch could have been on her, too, and she wouldn't have noticed or cared. Her climax tore through her like wildfire. Seth held her down as she bucked. Finally, she subsided amid the pillows, covered her face with her arm, and gave a laugh laced with a hiccup.

Robyn pulled her arm away. "Don't be embarrassed. That was beautiful. Wasn't it, Seth?"

He held her with a deep gaze. "It was fucking gorgeous."

"We have more in store for you, too." Robyn patted her flank. "Lift." She shoved a thick pillow beneath Courtney's butt, then removed the one beneath her head. "Lie back. Seth's going to fuck you, and I promise it'll be out of this world."

11

EVERYTHING WAS PERFECTLY ON PLAN. COURTNEY WATCHED HIM with wide, dazed eyes after that magnificent orgasm. She was wet, her body open and beckoning him.

"Tell him how much you want him to fuck you, Courtney." Robyn's voice was like a tune you couldn't get out of your head, urging them on, forcing them higher. It was exactly what Seth had wanted, needed. Robyn played her role flawlessly.

"I need it," Courtney whispered.

It wasn't enough for him. He knelt between her legs, pulled her thighs around his hips. "Tell me how much you need it."

"Please, Seth." In the flickering light of the fire, her eyes were almost black. Her auburn hair fanned across the carpet, her fingers clenching, unclenching. "I want you inside me. I love how you feel deep inside me." Reaching down, she took his cock in her hand. "You fill me up to my heart."

That's what he needed to hear. He dredged the tip of his cock in her sweet juice. "Only me," he murmured.

"Only you."

It was like a vow, the courtesan their witness.

"Say it," he urged. "Tell me what you need me to do."

"Make love to me."

"More."

"Fuck me."

He closed his eyes, drank in the dirty word on her lips. "Fuck yes."

They'd made love their entire married life, and it had been great. But fucking was primal. It was that feeling you had when you saw the woman of your dreams and your heart drummed out *I want, I want*, when you imagined pinning her to an alley wall and fucking until you were senseless. It was cutting out early on that last afternoon meeting because you had to get home and have her, because all day you'd imagined driving deep inside her. That feeling had gone MIA from their marriage. Trying to get it back was what all the fantasizing and teasing had been about.

"Mmm." Robyn made a sweet sound. "I'm going to pour the lube on you." She looked at Courtney. "I swear you're going to adore the sensations when Seth's cock is balls deep inside you."

She drizzled it on him, the liquid heating his skin, a few drops dribbling down to Courtney's pussy. Setting the bottle aside, Robyn slathered the lube all over his cock and testicles, preparing him as if it were a ritual. Her touch was fucking hot as he knelt poised between his wife's legs.

Courtney watched. She didn't say a word. She blinked, once, twice, then raised her eyes to his. They were like warm liquid chocolate. Christ. He so wanted Robyn to touch his wife's sweet little clit. Yet he recognized that was way too much.

"Take her, Seth." A hand on his dick, a palm on his rump, Robyn guided him, the crown of his cock breaching Courtney.

Courtney closed her eyes, sucked in a breath. "Oh God."

"The gel's extraordinary"—Robyn licked her lips—"isn't it?"

A brief nod seemed all Courtney could manage.

"I love the sight of a big, thick, bare cock taking a sweet pussy like your wife's." Robyn leaned over them, taking in every hot inch as he filled Courtney. "That's what's so sexy about monogamous relationships. No condoms."

The woman he talked to, Isabel, had prepped Robyn perfectly. She'd said everything he requested, did everything he'd asked. He wanted Courtney to take it all in. They didn't need another woman, they didn't need another man. Although he had to admit, Robyn as their voyeur was goddamn hot, having her direct their play intensely sensual, her voice urging them on an aphrodisiac.

"Your pussy feels so good, baby." In fact, she had never felt this good. Courtney's plan had opened his eyes to all the new possibilities that lay before them. With the girls gone, they could do anything, fuck in the hot tub, the living room, on the kitchen counter. He could make her scream.

"Do you like it, baby?"

"You're so hot inside me." She moaned. "That's good. Ooh." She sucked in a breath, let it out with a groan, lifting her hips into him as he hit that sweet spot, the G-spot.

"Let's try South Slav, Seth." Robyn was full of all sorts of exciting ideas. "Raise your legs, Courtney," she directed, her eyes trained on Seth.

He slid his hands up Courtney's calves, placed her feet on his shoulders.

"Now cross her ankles," Robyn said.

Courtney shivered, contracting around him. He kissed her instep, soothed her with a long stroke down her shins.

She writhed, then laughed, ending in a deep sigh. "That tickles. And it feels so good. Seth, fuck me, please, fuck me like that."

He took her slow, needing her to feel every ridge and ripple of his cock along her G-spot. She writhed and moaned and Robyn caressed his ass. "How do you like it, Seth?"

"Fucking unbelievable." Courtney was so damn wet, the gel

hot on his cock. It was all too incredibly good. He pumped, flexed his thighs, loved his wife with all his strength.

"Time for another surprise." Robyn reached into her magic bag, retrieving a vibrator. She held it up for both of them to see. Simple, neat, no fancy frills. "It's perfect for what I want you to do." Picking up Courtney's hand, she wrapped her fingers around the toy. "Hold it on your clit, down far enough to caress Seth's cock at the same time."

Courtney laughed, her mirth lacing her words. "I don't have the strength to do that right now."

"Oh yes, you do, sweetheart. You can do anything with your husband." She flapped a hand at Seth. "Put her legs down. Spread her around you."

He liked the instructions. They added another element to the excitement and the intimacy. He couldn't quite say why. Doing everything Robyn told him to do was like showing his wife he was willing to bare his soul for her, anything to prove she was the most important thing in the world.

Courtney slid the vibrator down over her clit, bumping his cock, caressing the tip of it along his shaft as he pumped slowly. "Christ." He let out a long sigh.

Robyn raised a brow and smiled. "Like that, don't ya, Seth."

"Oh yeah."

"Courtney," she said, "tell me how it feels."

"Ohh." She moaned. She groaned. Real words seemed to fail her. "Oooh."

"Say it," Robyn demanded, going down on her elbow at Courtney's side. "Tell Seth how good it feels."

"It's so fucking perfect."

He loved that word on Courtney's lips, the heat in her voice, the slight waver of her excitement threaded through her words.

"Oh, Seth. Ohh, ooh, ahhhh." Her sounds shot him higher. She bucked, tossed her head, and gripped that vibrator hard.

"Faster, Seth," Robyn urged. "She wants it harder, deeper. Hold her here, use this angle." She revealed exactly what his wife wanted as only another woman would. With every surge of his cock inside Courtney, he felt how right Robyn was. Courtney loved it. He had never fucked her like this. He'd never seen her this wild. Her nipples were diamond hard, her breasts pink-tinged, her skin flushed. Color rode her cheekbones, and she squeezed her eyes shut.

"Oh God, oh God, oh God," she chanted for him. The position afforded him a luscious view of her whole body, his cock taking her, her pussy lush and pink, the hard nub of her clit as she rode the vibrator.

"Fuck her, Seth, fuck her hard."

The vibrator pushed him closer to the very edge. As he pounded into her, his cock throbbing, his balls hard, aching, he felt himself tumble over. Courtney's pussy contracted around him, milking him. He shouted, she screamed. Fuck if they didn't come together and it was so goddamn good, so amazingly fantastic, he didn't even have a comparison, just the stars shooting before his eyes and Courtney's voice talking to God.

COURTNEY'S EARS WERE STILL RINGING FROM THE FORCE OF HER climax. It wracked her from the inside. It turned her over from the outside. Her throat ached from the scream that had been torn from her. Her eyelashes felt glued together, and her body still trembled. She opened her eyes despite the effort it took.

Seth looked down at her with awe, that was the only word for it. He stroked her thighs, her butt, reached beneath her and hauled her closer. His cock still filled her up.

"It's never been like that," she whispered. "I love you."

He pulled the pillows from beneath her butt, threw them aside, then came down on top of her. She wrapped her legs around his hips and locked her ankles.

"It can always be like that if we want it to be." Braced on his elbows, Seth stroked the hair from her temples.

"Thank you, guys, that was awesome."

Courtney had almost forgotten that Robyn was there. She turned her head. The courtesan lay stretched out beside them, her head propped on her hand. "Thank you for letting me be part of such a beautiful moment." She reached out, just a finger, stroking Courtney's arm. Throughout the day and evening, she offered non-threatening touches, friendly, caring, seductive in a strange way because they were intimate yet lacked eroticism.

It hit Courtney again why they were there. So that Seth could fuck Robyn. She'd somehow forgotten. After that cataclysmic orgasm, her husband was supposed to fuck another woman. In her heart she couldn't take it. She could not watch. She could not allow this. There was something terribly wrong with her that she thought this would be the solution to her need for attention, to be wanted, to be desired.

"What's going on, Courtney?" Seth cupped her face in his hands and forced her to look at him. He lay a hairsbreadth above her. "Tell me what you're thinking."

She wanted him to be the one to back out. She wanted him to be the one to say he didn't want Robyn, that he wanted only his wife. Yet, looking in his eyes, she realized he was not going to say that to her. She had arranged this, she had talked him into it, she had paid for it with her blood, sweat, tears, the Italy fund, and a little help from Devon. Courtney was the only one who could call a stop to it.

Yet she wasn't sure how.

Devon had been so right. She should have thought more about how much she could handle. How there truly was a huge difference between fantasy and reality.

She did the only thing that came to mind—joked her way out of it. "Wow, honey, you've come twice tonight. Are you sure you're capable of getting it up again for Robyn?"

Something sparked in his eyes. His face hardened. He pulled free of her and stood. She felt exposed and vulnerable in a way she hadn't at any other point during the evening, not when she stripped off her dress, not when she sucked Seth's cock with the courtesan. She rolled to a sitting position, wrapping her arms around her knees.

Seth grabbed his shorts, yanked them on. "You're right, ladies. My pecker's done for the night." He gathered the platter and the wine bottles from the carpet. "Robyn, it's been nice, but I'm bushed."

Robyn still wore her caftan; she'd never undressed. Courtney wished she'd brought her own robe to cover up with. Instead, she rose to pull her sundress up her legs, then the straps over her shoulders, and reached behind to zip it. "We'll see you tomorrow?" she asked.

Robyn merely glanced at Seth. "Talk to you later."

He opened the door for her. Stopping a long moment as some odd and frightening nonverbal communication flashed between them, Robyn said, "Be nice," then she was gone, the door closed, the cottage silent except for the flutter of the gas fireplace.

Courtney was left alone with her husband.

12

HIS BLOOD HUMMED WITH EXCITEMENT, ADRENALINE, AND ANGER. What the fuck? Everything had been going according to plan. Until Courtney had challenged him to fuck Robyn.

Or insulted his virility. He was forty-eight, not freaking seventy-eight. He could get it up again, goddammit.

He'd given her the best freaking sex of their lives and she'd negated it with a flippant joke.

"Well, that was fun. What did you think?" she asked, her voice too high and falsely bright, as if she didn't know how to gauge his mood. After twenty-three freaking years of marriage.

He found himself stomping into the bathroom like a child. "Yeah. It was great."

She followed him to the door. "Are you mad, Seth?"

He took a deep breath, steadying himself. He was too old to play the I'm-not-speaking-to-you-right-now game. "Yep, I'm pissed."

"I'm sorry. I was nervous. That's why I said that about you getting it up again."

"That was a minor technicality."

"No, no. I shouldn't have said that in front of Robyn. I'll call her back and apologize. We can start again." She glanced at her watch. "It's only ten."

He closed his eyes. Why the hell had he gone in the bathroom anyway? To brush his teeth, get ready for bed. Instead he started pacing. She moved out of the way before he ran her over. Slamming a hand against the switch, he shut down the gas fire, then he threw the pillows back on the bed.

"We don't have to clean up now, Seth."

He turned on her. "I'm not going to fuck some other woman just because you want me to."

"I didn't say you had to fuck her." She'd taken two steps toward him, now she took one back. "But I thought you liked her. You seemed to love it when she was sucking your cock. Didn't you love it?"

"You know goddamn well it was hot having two women suck my cock."

"Good, then—"

"This isn't tit for tat. I'll be goddamned if we're going to start fucking other people. Or going out on dates. This is not a fucking open marriage."

Her eyes widened, a flicker of nervousness flitting through her gaze. "I never said it was."

"And I'm not watching you do another guy." He slashed his hand in the air. "So you can get that thought right out of your head." He paced, his stride eating up the length of the cottage so fast he had to turn and start back the other way.

"That wasn't what I was thinking—"

"Don't lie to me. You're pissed because I've been working too much. You want more excitement."

"That's not—"

"Well, I'll give you fucking excitement." He was on her before she could turn and run. Grabbing her beneath the armpits, he tossed her onto the bed amid the mountain of pillows. Before she could move, he was on top of her, pushing up the naughty little sundress she'd tempted him with all day. He found her pussy, delving deep, two fingers to the knuckles. "Christ, you're wet."

She gasped at the intrusion, and her eyes turned the color of melted dark chocolate. "Seth, please—"

"No fucking *please*. You want sex, you've got it, baby. All you can handle." He pumped inside her, riding the ridge of her G-spot, his thumb on the nub of her clit at the same time until she writhed on the bed.

The sweet scent of her sex clouded his head. He needed to taste her, show her no one could do this the way he could. "I'll make you come until you pass out." Christ, her pussy was hot and spicy like mulled wine, fragrant and sexy. She shoved her fingers through his hair and rode his mouth, arching, twisting, grinding.

"Seth, oh my God." She moaned, and those were the sounds he wanted to hear.

He lifted his head long enough to order, "Say my name."

"Seth, Seth, Seth." She chanted and didn't stop, her pussy clenching around his fingers, milking them as if they were his cock filling her.

"Tell me it's never going to be this fucking good with anyone else."

"Never, Seth, never."

He licked her again, sucked the nub of her clit hard, worrying it with his tongue, just as she'd sucked the head of his cock in the Bacchus pool tonight.

"Scream, baby. Scream loud for me."

She panted, moaned, ooh, aahed, then he felt it, that special contraction, the beginning, then she thrust up against his mouth, clamped her legs around his ears, her body undulating. She cried out his name. Only his name.

He rode her climax until she pulled back from him, crawled mindlessly across the bed to get away from the intensity. He followed, yanking at his shorts, freeing his cock, rolling her beneath him, sliding deep into her contracting pussy, so wet, so fluid. He barely had to move, letting her aftershocks do all the work.

"Repeat after me," he whispered next to her ear. "You are mine, and I am yours."

"You're mine, and I am yours."

"I don't want to fuck anyone else."

"I never want to fuck anyone else." She rocked against him. "Fuck me now, please," she begged.

He gave her what she wanted. "You're the best there ever was."

She hugged him fiercely. "You've always been the best there ever was." A sob threaded through her voice. "You always will be."

He held her chin in his hand, pushing deep inside her. "Look at me, Courtney."

She met his gaze, hers bewildered, heated, almost dazed.

"I never wanted to fuck Robyn." He punctuated with a deep thrust. "It was always my intention to have her watch me fuck you." When she didn't answer, he circled her throat. "I told her that's what I wanted. Only you."

Her pussy rippled around him, ratcheting his tension higher, his orgasm suddenly rushing up at him.

"I love you," he managed. "Say it."

"Oh God, Seth, I love you. I love you."

With one last thrust, he drove them over the edge together.

* * *

"I PLANNED IT ALL WITH HER," SETH SAID, SNUGGLING COURTNEY close beneath the comforter. He'd pulled off her dress and tossed off his shorts. "The vibrator, the new positions, everything."

"When?" The one word was the most she could manage.

"After you talked to Devon. I told Isabel that was the only reason I had for doing this, that I called all the shots. I never intended to fuck Robyn. Or anyone else you chose."

It was exactly what she'd wanted to hear. And hadn't had the courage to ask for once she'd started the game. Her husband had far more courage than she did. "I was wrong," she murmured, playing with the matt of hair around his nipples. "I wanted to get the fire back. I wanted something to excite you and bring you back to me. When we got right down to it, though, I didn't want to watch." She rolled her head on his shoulder to look at him. "That's why I said that."

He stroked tendrils of hair from her face. "How did it make you feel watching her suck my cock, holding it for her?"

"This is going to sound strange. Like why is there a difference between watching you fuck her, versus helping her suck your cock, but there is." She blinked, taking a second for one quick inner glance. "Maybe that's why. It was me helping, but it was still *me*. Fucking her, it would have been the two of you."

"So you'd be excluded."

"Yeah."

He kissed her forehead. "What we did this weekend was so damn hot, baby. You were fucking gorgeous sucking my cock in the pool." He reached for the camera on the bedside table. Courtney hadn't even noticed he'd put it there.

He turned it on, flipped through. "Here, look at this," he whispered in a reverent tone.

Snuggling close, she gazed at the shot. Her, eyes on the camera lens, Seth's cock in her mouth. He was right. She was absolutely fucking gorgeous. She'd never felt more so in her life.

"I want more of that," he said. "More of you looking so damn hot and sexy and erotic." He set the camera aside and turned out the light. Pulling her tight into the circle of his arms, he tipped her face up to his. "It still has to be about us, not anyone else."

"What do you mean?" She tried to read his expression in the moonlight through the cottage's window.

"I mean that I loved being kinky. I loved having her watch us, telling us what to do. We should explore more of that."

"You mean like same-room sex?" Oh yeah, she'd learned all the terminology while exploring the Internet.

"Yeah. Dirty pictures, sex parties, clubs, watching people, performing for others. Like we did with Robyn. Maybe even an audience. Kinky shit." She could swear his eyes sparkled as his listed his naughty litany.

"I'm shocked." Yet she heated clear down to her toes.

He tweaked her nose. "You opened my eyes, baby."

"Do you really want all that?" A thrill ran through her.

"I want to explore it." He gathered her close, trapping her face against the warm, salty skin of his throat. "But I'm not letting another man touch you." His voice rumbled against her cheek. "I'm not getting inside another woman. This will always be about us. Agreed?"

"Agreed." Her heart beat faster, his words like ownership, possession.

"I will never let work come between us again."

"Oh Seth, I've been such a bitch. I'm sorry."

"You haven't. I neglected your needs. Never again. I love you, baby, I always will. Kick me in the ass when I seem like I'm taking you for granted."

"And I love you." She pushed up onto one elbow. "Kick me in the butt if I ever start whining again."

She settled back into his arms. Perhaps they'd needed this to figure out what their limits were, what they could do together and what they couldn't, to remind them that marriage needed tending, it needed nurturing, and that love should never be taken for granted.

THE STAND-IN

1

HUNTER NASH WAS INTELLIGENT, ARTICULATE, TRUSTWORTHY, ethical, and loyal.

She made him sound like a Boy Scout. Devon Parker certainly wasn't thinking of her second-in-command as any Boy Scout. That was her whole problem. She had the hots for her tall, sexy-as-sin, black-haired, blue-eyed CFO. Watching him in action was akin to foreplay for her. Today, she was content to sit back and let him duke it out with the auditors. As CEO, Devon was here only as a show of GDN's—Grant Digital Network's—solidarity.

"I don't appreciate the implication that someone on my team is being less than forthcoming." Diplomatic, Hunter also had a will of iron. When he believed he was right, he didn't bend under pressure. Having hand-picked each and every member, he trusted his accounting team implicitly. He would not let the outside auditors impugn their integrity—or his.

Thus the need to drive up to San Francisco to meet face-to-face with the new partner. The company had a September 30 fiscal end, and this was the new guy's first year-end audit with them. Myron Denwal, a thin man with pale skin, a forehead marred by deep worry lines, and type-A dark circles under his eyes, spread his hands on the table. "All we're saying, Hunter, is that Jenna has created an overhead file so complicated it may easily mask any miscalculations that could potentially overstate your inventory values."

"Have her sit down with your lead and walk him through it." Hunter sat back in his chair at the conference table. "Though I'm surprised he'd need the assistance."

A slam. The spreadsheet wasn't rocket science. With a marketing background, even Devon understood the file. Hunter had been having run-ins with Larry, their lead auditor. The kid was taking the fast-track to manager level on the backs of his clients by trying to prove negligence and fraud. When compared with Hunter's domain, both negligence and fraud were oxymorons. And the kid, he was just a plain moron. Devon had complete faith in Hunter. If he said Jenna had nothing to hide, then she did indeed have nothing to hide. Devon also liked the girl. She'd been their cost accounting manager for more than a year.

The corner of Myron's eye started to twitch. "At this point, I believe we need a third-party intervention between them." He rubbed at his lid as if that would make the nervous tic recede.

"I would be happy to explain the file, Myron." Hunter gave him a genial smile, but beneath it Devon sensed the leashed tiger.

Myron clasped his hands in a tight grip, his joints cracking. "I meant third-party intervention from outside Accounting."

It was tantamount to saying Hunter couldn't be trusted, either. It appeared as if the new audit team was out for blood, creating an adversarial working relationship that would do none of them any good. After the last few years of accounting scandals, the general atmosphere between public accounting and private industry had taken a nosedive. Where once you went to your auditors for advice, you now kept everything as close to the vest as possible. In her opinion, a few bad apples had screwed the entire profession and made life with your auditors a pain in the ass. It didn't necessarily mean the reporting was any better or more honest. Except in Hunter's purview.

Hunter had the makings of a great CEO. She was well aware he would move on from GDN, sooner rather than later. Selfishly, though, she wanted to keep him forever. What would the company do without him? What would *she* do?

Devon leaned both elbows on the table and steepled her fingers. "I have the utmost confidence in both Hunter and his team, Myron. As you will learn once you've been through an audit with us." Though she was fast beginning to consider they needed to find another audit firm. That, however, wasn't the issue at hand. "I am familiar with the file." Jenna had given a detailed presentation to management when she'd constructed the overhead rates. "I will sit down with Larry and explain the basics to him." This was, in fact, the solution she and Hunter had devised before the meeting began. He was to be the heavy, she was the conciliator. Sort of a good-cop/bad-cop routine.

Myron opened his mouth, closed it. Like a fish.

"Or do you wish to call my integrity into question also?" She pinned him with a look.

Between her steady gaze and Hunter's hard stare, sweat gathered in the creases of Myron's forehead. "I assure you this has nothing to do with mistrust."

"I suggest you accept my offer then. Or do we need to discuss this further with a more senior partner?"

He blinked, sucked in air. "No. Your offer is satisfactory."

She smiled. "Perhaps you would like to be in attendance when I conduct the session with Larry."

"No, no, Devon"—underscored with vigorous head shaking—"I'm satisfied."

"Good." She rose, meeting adjourned. Auditors weren't generally a stupid bunch. In fact, she had great admiration. They had a bad reputation to overcome after the series of shakedowns, and the majority, in her opinion, were pretty damn good at what they did. It was Myron and Larry who were inept. The kid saw himself as some sort of investor avenger, ferreting out accounting evildoing and making a name for himself as hard-core and no-nonsense. Myron should have reined him in. What a team the company had been saddled with. Pulling out midstream, though, would not be good.

Damn. She was really bad off, because that last thought made her contemplate sex again. With Hunter. Though she could *want* all she wanted, but she could never have. *That* wouldn't fly with the audit team. Collusion would be their first assumption.

Five minutes later, the meeting over, Hunter took her elbow, guiding her onto the empty elevator car. So polite. His touch sent a hot shiver through her.

"That went well," he said.

She turned to him, liking the fact that she could still look up to him despite her three-inch heels. In the main, Devon didn't like having to look up at men. Hunter was different. Always had been.

"He's an asshole," she answered. She'd known Hunter more than ten years. They'd worked together at Simcoe Systems, moved on to other jobs, but she'd always had great respect for him. When she took over as CEO at GDN four years ago, he was her first choice as CFO.

They'd both been married back then at Simcoe. Now they were both divorced. She was also his boss.

Hunter unbuttoned his suit jacket. "We're stuck with him, unfortunately."

"And we're stuck with that little pissant Larry."

He laughed. "Your language is definitely colorful today."

With Hunter, words popped out of her mouth, she was that

comfortable with him and their working relationship. "I say it like it is."

"You always have."

In the garage, he led her to his car, beeped the remote, opened the door, and handed her into the passenger seat. In the coolness of the interior, his aftershave, something sexy and smooth, still lingered from the earlier drive up to San Francisco. His touch still heated her skin, reaching all the way to her belly.

Now *that* was bad. And getting worse.

He climbed in, shut the driver's door, and the masculine scent intensified, tantalizing her senses. She closed her eyes to breathe him in, letting him fill her as he backed out and headed down the ramp for the exit.

"You want to stop for lunch?" he asked after paying the exorbitant parking fee. That was San Francisco for you.

"No," she said, eyes still closed. The attraction had been slow-growing, infiltrating so subtly she hadn't recognized it for what it was until it was too late to eradicate. Now she could only make sure she didn't put herself into nonwork situations with him. "I've got a meeting with Garrison."

Hunter snorted. "Our illustrious S&M veep has his head up his ass."

Devon couldn't help the answering smile. The moniker was their private joke. Garrison was her Sales and Marketing vice president. Hunter had coined the S&M phrase. He had a bawdy sense of humor he kept in check while in a work environment. They were friends. He didn't worry she'd misconstrue. The mere allusion to sex did not constitute sexual harassment. However, that was her personal opinion. As a matter of company policy, she had to display zero tolerance. Garrison had stepped over the line with one of his subordinates.

Hunter's lips curled in a semi-smile. "It's humorous in a rubber-necker sort of way."

"What the hell was the man thinking?" she mused, head back against the seat. Garrison's antics had put her in a very difficult position.

"What the hell was his *wife* thinking? That's what I want to know."

Devon blew out a sharp breath. "God only knows."

Garrison had committed the sin of having an affair with his administrative aide. He'd compounded the stupidity by e-mailing her from his home computer. Which his wife discovered. She'd started calling his peers in the company, all the other VPs, including Hunter, to ask if they knew anything about Garrison's affair. Everyone was too dumbfounded to reflect properly before they answered. Only Hunter kept his cool and told her she should discuss it with her husband. She didn't. She called his boss. Which would be Devon.

"I'm not saying what Garrison did wasn't bad. You never screw your subordinates." It was a proverb Devon had been repeating to herself. "Or anyone else in the company for that matter." Especially at the senior level. It looked bad. "She went further and laid out her personal business for all the world to see."

Despite being a midday Friday in San Francisco, Hunter made it to the freeway with a minimum delay. "Unfortunately, she's tied my hands," Devon said as he merged into traffic. "If she hadn't made it so public, we could have gone for some sort of disciplinary action. As it is, I have no choice but to ask for his resignation."

Per company policy, she wasn't even required to give him severance. His resignation was better than getting canned for misconduct. Garrison had two kids in college. People talk, word gets out. It would be difficult for him to find another job at his age. Devon had come up with the strategy in tandem with Human Resources, but she wasn't happy with it. There were no winners. Not the company, not Garrison, not his wife, not his kids. Garrison's admin quit before she was fired. Devon sighed.

Hunter reached over to pat her knee. "He made his own bed, Devon. It's not your fault."

"I understand that," she answered, concentrating on the conversation rather than how much she enjoyed his comforting touch. In a very noncomforting way. "But firing people has never been one of my favorite things." Despite having the reputation for being unemotional and a hard-ass.

"Yeah, I realize that." He squeezed her knee this time. He didn't mean anything by it. He couldn't guess the shivers the touch sent through her body. He couldn't know how the heat of his hand skewed her concentration. "Have a good soak in the tub tonight, and you'll feel a lot better."

She'd once told him of her not-so-guilty pleasure. Steaming water, bubbles, chocolate, champagne cocktail, and a really good book. Problem was these days when she was having a good soak, a sexy novel wasn't enough. Fantasies of Hunter kept wandering through the pages of her mind. Funny how everything came back to Hunter. Garrison and his peccadillo with his AA, the mention of a hot bath, her mind had a way of twisting every thought back to Hunter. She needed relief. But what? Not one of her male courtesans. More and more often, she found herself closing her eyes to imagine it was Hunter doing all those things to her. There had to be a way to tame this need. Maybe a new man. A substitute to take the edge off.

Because no matter what, Devon was not going to go the way of Garrison by compromising her relationship with Hunter for a little hot nookie.

2

THE IDEA CAME TO DEVON IN THE MIDDLE OF THE NIGHT WHEN SHE was masturbating to fantasies of Hunter Nash. She called Isabel first thing Saturday morning.

"I need a stand-in," Devon said a few hours later as she stroked a delicate black-and-red feathered Mardi Gras mask.

Isabel had agreed to meet her if but only if Devon was willing to accompany her on an impromptu shopping trip. Isabel was attending a Halloween ball the following weekend.

"A stand-in for the real thing never works."

Devon laughed. "You sound like the voice of experience."

Isabel winked. She was off-hours from Courtesans. At least Devon thought so, but who really knew with Isabel. She was almost always available for a call. The few times Devon had been forced to leave her a message, she'd called back within half an hour. Isabel lived and breathed Courtesans, providing the ultimate pleasure for her clients. Thus she was always elegantly attired, even if it was pairing a silk blouse with designer jeans. Today was an ultrafeminine, soft gray pinstriped suit with a formfitting tailored jacket, the skirt long, hugging her rear and flaring at the bottom, her hair piled high in the usual elegant topknot.

"So tell me why you've used a stand-in," Devon wanted to know.

"They're all stand-ins for someone we knew a long time ago, aren't they?" Isabel's mouth was a gentle smile, her eyes unfocused for a moment. "It's a long story."

Devon had been utilizing Courtesans for almost five years, since her divorce when she realized that relationships in general, and men specifically, could be a pain in the ass. Truth to tell, the only decent relationships she'd ever had with men were working relationships. Her friendship with Isabel had blossomed over time, and while Devon considered herself an open book, Isabel had always been more reticent about personal details. Devon didn't take it as an affront to their friendship.

Isabel held a white latex nurse's uniform against her. "What about this?"

It was short and tight and sexy as hell, at least from a man's point of view, but, "Not you. You need to be . . ." Devon tipped her head one way, then the other, letting her gaze slide over Isabel's lithe form from head to toe. "Cleopatra."

Isabel laughed, a pretty, musical sound. "I don't feel like getting bitten by my asp."

Devon quirked an eyebrow. "How about Marie Antoinette?"

"I fancy holding on to my head."

"Catherine the Great?"

"Isn't there something about her dying while having sex with a stallion?"

"Stallions are good," Devon mused.

"Not an Italian stallion, a real stallion, a horse."

Devon couldn't help the laughter. "Okay, not your style. So what do you want to be?"

"Sleeping Beauty's stepmother."

Devon laughed until it hurt. "You're more like everybody's sexual fairy godmother."

"I haven't a clue what to choose," Isabel moaned. "Let's talk about your stand-in instead. What do you want?"

They wandered through the store, picking up costumes, casting them back onto the rack. "I want a stand-in for Hunter." Over coffee, drinks, lunch, dinner, Devon had slowly revealed her growing obsession with her CFO. "I'm surprised you hadn't already guessed."

Isabel winked. "I had an inkling." She held up a pleated schoolgirl outfit, discarded it when Devon guffawed.

Devon pulled a photo from her bag. "I want someone with his general stats, his approximate age, forty, forty-one. He's six two, about one-ninety-five, black hair, blue eyes." She handed over the picture that had been taken at a company Christmas party.

Isabel perused the photo for a few very long seconds, raised just her eyes to glance at Devon, then puffed out a breath. Finally, as if it were an afterthought, she made an appreciative sound. "Not bad looking," she understated, then gave Devon a direct look. "Why don't you just do him?"

"It's against company policy."

"Darling. You can do it discreetly without hurting anyone."

"It could jeopardize his career."

Isabel snorted. "What about yours?"

Devon thought of yesterday's meeting with Garrison, the condemned-man look on his face, the watery eyes when she told him to submit his resignation. The interview had been exceptionally painful. "My career, too."

"If it's consensual, it can be considered personal business. You're an adult and wouldn't let it affect how you make your decisions."

"It's the appearance of impropriety." Devon held out an Elvira dress.

Isabel shook her head. "Too common." She drew in a deep breath. "He could be good for you. He's divorced, you're divorced."

Despite their marital statuses, she still couldn't justify a relationship with him. If the auditors—Myron and flunky Larry—were ever to stumble across something like that, they could start talking collusion, cooking the books, cookie jar accounting, et cetera, all of it fraud. No, she couldn't risk that, for Hunter's sake and for the sake of the company. "It's not possible."

"I understand, I get it." Isabel flipped through another rack of endlessly common costumes. "So, how do you want this to go down with the stand-in?"

"I'd like it to take place in my office."

Isabel gave an incredulous laugh that didn't have an ounce of mirth. "You're worried about company policy and jeopardizing your career, yet you intend to do this in the office?"

Devon had thought about that issue all morning. "If it's not at work, it's not going to seem like the real thing. Most of my fantasies about him take place in my office." She had to have it this way or it wouldn't alleviate the pressure.

"Naughty girl," Isabel chided.

"It sounds crazy, but I'll figure out when the cleaning crew is done, the auditors have cleared out for the weekend, and the place is completely empty. Late on a Saturday night." She'd make sure nothing would go wrong.

Isabel shook her head sadly, as if she thought Devon were delusional. "You know what they say about the best-laid plans."

"I'll check card key access for the last few weekends, and choose a time when the building is consistently empty."

"It's your neck."

"No, it's my fantasy." She was aware it was near insanity, that it was risky, which made the idea even hotter. Yes, it seemed at odds with her desire for discretion and following company policy. Yet she was willing to take the chance to get what she needed. If she didn't play it out the way she'd built her fantasies, she was afraid the obsession would go on. She had to purge Hunter from her system. Lying in bed last night, going over and over every detail, it seemed the only way.

If by some off chance she was caught, it would only be her at risk, not Hunter, not GDN. She was a lot more willing to risk herself to get what she needed than to jeopardize anyone else.

"All right." Isabel stared at the picture. "I have a man in mind, his name is—"

Devon held up a finger, shushing her. "Don't tell me his name. When he walks in, he is to *be* Hunter Nash. That's what I'll call him, that's how he'll refer to himself. He's a CFO. He's divorced. He has two children, a boy and a girl in their early teens. Everything he says has to fit with Hunter Nash."

Isabel scoffed again, then quickly softened it with a smile. "You're a freak."

Devon laughed. "Yeah."

"I'll work on it. I can probably get the correct stats, but I'm not going to find his twin."

"I realize that, but as with everything else you've done for me, you'll do the best."

Huffing out a breath, Isabel pointed at the abundant racks. "There's not a damn thing here."

"You're not an off-the-rack kind of woman."

Isabel bit her lip, still staring at the jumble of costumes. "I'm usually not. I guess I don't care to impress. I was looking for quick and easy."

"Quick and easy in costumes? Or men?"

"Both."

"Do you need to talk, girlfriend?" Devon was there if Isabel needed it.

"He's not worth talking about."

Then why go out with him? Devon thought it, but didn't ask. There was way more to this story and Devon suspected a whole lot of understating, but Isabel was a mystery until she wanted to reveal herself.

"Now help me find that perfect costume."

Devon hoped in return Isabel would find her the perfect match.

BY WEDNESDAY, DEVON HAD IT ALL PLANNED OUT. SHE'D CHECKED card key access. The cleaning people came in on Sunday, not Saturday. On weekends, especially during audit time, people were in and out. Hunter tended to do Saturday mornings. No one had carded out or set the alarm any later than five thirty on a Saturday. If she could arrange it for *this* Saturday, it was Halloween with lots of parties or taking the kids out for trick or treating.

Now she needed to hear from Isabel. It was four o'clock on Wednesday and she'd been carrying her private cell phone all day, practically to the ladies' room, she was so anxious. Wrong word. *Excited.* She wanted this, needed it. She didn't take most personal calls at work and she didn't use her work phone for personal use, either, but she'd been feeling jumpy for days wanting to put her strategy into action.

It was planned, she was ready. All she needed was the right man.

When the cell rang only five minutes later, she almost jumped. The displayed number: Isabel's. Her desk facing the door, Devon glanced up to see where Robert, her admin, was. Outside her office at his desk, nearby to call through the open doorway if necessary, not close enough to eavesdrop.

"Devon Parker here," she answered formally, as if it were a business call.

"You gave a tough order, darling, especially since you wanted to shoot for this Saturday."

Devon swiveled her chair slightly. She didn't want her voice carrying straight out the doorway. "Never too tough for you, Wonder Woman."

Isabel gave that lovely tinkling laugh that always had men turning her way. "I should not have let you talk me into that costume."

"It's perfect. And you'll find me someone equally as good."

"Under the circumstances, I did pretty darn well, considering the enormity of the task. Funnily enough, the best choice is the man I originally thought of, but I didn't want to shortchange you so I did some further scanning through the files."

"I had no doubt you'd be thorough." Devon shivered with anticipation.

"He's an out-of-towner. Is that okay?"

"If he's the right one for the task, I'm fine with that. Where from?"

"Seattle." Courtesans' headquarters was located in San Francisco, but Isabel maintained satellite offices in most major U.S. cities and hubs abroad, such as London, Paris, Amsterdam, and Frankfurt.

"The flight cost shouldn't be too astronomical then." As the client, it was Devon's responsibility to pay for incidentals such as travel. To get what she wanted, the extra cost was worth it. "Book the best price possible, if you could."

"I already have my T.A. working on it." Isabel employed a full-time travel agent who got her clients the competitive fares and rates.

"He'll need a car, too. I don't want to pick him up. This needs to feel exactly as if—" She cut herself off, glancing past her door. No one paying attention. Though she should have closed it before she even answered. She'd almost said too much, catching her runaway mouth just in time.

"I'd thought of that. In order to have him pull off being your Hunter Nash, he'll need access to the building."

"I can't give him . . ." She paused, weighing the best way to say it. "I'll be at the entry. Once I return to the designated place, he can follow in five minutes." That didn't sound untoward if anyone overheard.

"I'm going to need a write-up of all the details you want him to be aware of so he can fit them into his conversation."

"I can do that. I'll send you an e-mail tonight." Devon didn't intend to give away Hunter's personal details, but she did want verisimilitude, enough to make the encounter seem real.

"What time do you want him to arrive on Saturday?"

"Nine p.m." She crossed her legs, brushing off lint that had gathered on her skirt. "I'll also send you details on how I want the scenario to play out."

"I've never known a woman"—the smile in Isabel's voice made it clearly across the airspace—"who plans out her fantasies to the nth degree the way you do."

"It's how I work and how I play," Devon answered with a like smile. "But some improvisation from him is fine."

"Your organization skills amaze me. I need to take lessons."

"Hah," Devon scoffed. "That's the pot calling the kettle black." Isabel was just as exacting.

"If you come up with anything else you want, add it to the e-mail."

"Will do. And thanks." Seriousness invaded her voice. "I really need this."

"Yeah, and you're going to pay a pretty penny for it, so you should get everything your little heart desires."

Devon wasn't extravagant. She had a decent car, a decent home in a decent neighborhood, a decent wardrobe, and when she ate out, she patronized decent restaurants. Nothing over the top, and thus, she had a very decent investment portfolio that she'd managed to keep above water despite the erratic markets. Her one extravagance was her sexual playtime. She didn't indulge often, but when she did, she was determined to get exactly what she wanted and was willing to pay for it. "Call me if anything gets in the way."

"Will do," Isabel echoed her.

Disconnecting, she snapped the phone closed, turned once again to her desk and the folder on—

She almost shrieked. Good Lord, Hunter stood in her doorway.

3

"I-I DIDN'T HEAR YOU," DEVON STAMMERED. HOW LONG HAD HUN-ter been there? What the hell had she said? Her heart raced like a stampede of stallions in her chest.

He looked at her, his head cocked slightly with animal-like concentration. "Sorry, didn't mean to disturb you."

"D-Did you want something?" She shot the words off too quickly, close to rudely, and dammit, she even stuttered again. She needed to get control of herself here. "Duh. Of course you did or you wouldn't be here. More bad news from the auditors?"

Her blood still thrummed with adrenaline. Looking at him, breathing him in as he sauntered farther into her office, was like mainlining an aphrodisiac. Her body pulsed with need.

"I wanted to let you know Larry has signed off on Jenna's overhead spreadsheet." He stopped in front of her desk, but didn't sit.

She tipped her head back to look up at him. "Great."

"Your explanation did the trick."

Larry was a bit of a dope, his questions first-year accounting, a class she'd had to take as part of her business degree oh so many moons ago. The kid thought a big mouth made up for a lack of IQ. She had the feeling Jenna's overhead calculations were only the first of many problems he was going to harp on before this audit was over. "Glad to help."

Hunter's perusal unnerved her, his gaze falling to her personal cell, then rising to her face. Silence usually didn't bother her. She was always the one who could wait it out. Not so this time. "Anything else?"

"Yeah. The investors' conference next month in Sedona. Are you attending?"

"I haven't made my decision yet." She'd been too busy planning her obsessive fantasy. Bad, very bad. She'd never allowed the personal to interfere with work before, not even during her messy divorce. "What are your thoughts on it?" she asked, giving herself time to regain her wits.

Last year, this particular conference had been in New York and the cost for two executives was prohibitive, so Hunter had represented the company. The Sedona resort chosen for this year was quite reasonable, comparatively speaking, and the airfare into Flagstaff much cheaper even with a rental car. A couple of weekends before Thanksgiving, it wouldn't interfere with the holidays, either. She usually spent the day with her parents in Monterey, and Hunter wouldn't want anything getting in the way of seeing his kids.

Hunter crossed his arms. "If we're really going to consider doing that public offering late next year to finance the new enterprise system and capital equipment upgrades that Manufacturing says are critical, then you should put in an appearance."

Glad-handing prospective investors was part of her job. Market conditions hadn't been favorable for the last few quarters, but the outlook for next year was picking up. "All right. I'll have Robert make the arrangements."

"Makes sense to have him make mine as well and take advantage of the fee discount for multiple registrations."

Her teeth wanted to chatter. Hunter, business trip, Sedona, her. It didn't mix well. Too much time in a confined space with him, but she couldn't say they needed to take separate flights and rent two cars. Really, her obsession was getting in the way of the job. Thank God she was taking drastic measures this weekend. "Sounds great. Can you forward him the details?"

"Sure." Hunter didn't turn, still towering over her desk.

"Anything else?" She moved her phone, picked up a pen, set it down, then grabbed the folder she'd originally been searching for when he entered.

He eyed her. "You okay?"

"Of course." Not. She picked up her pen again, clicked it once, twice.

"You seem . . . fidgety. I've never seen you fidget."

"Don't be silly." Je-sus. Would the man ever leave? She barely managed not to drum her fingers on the desk.

"It was all fine with Garrison?"

"Yes, fine. That was last week." She made a face.

Finally, he backed away, holding up his hands. "I'll let you get back to work." He turned, said something to Robert on the way out, probably about the conference.

He'd picked up on her signals. She'd communicated completely nonverbally that something was off. It was the shock of seeing him there. She told herself he couldn't have gotten anything out of what she said. She'd been careful.

Saturday night couldn't come fast enough. She was too jittery and jumpy with nerves. This courtesan session would be therapy. It might take more than one appointment to achieve the cure.

SOMETHING WAS UP. HE DIDN'T KNOW WHAT.

It's how I work and how I play.

Devon could have been talking about anything, any "scenario" that needed "improvisation," Hunter mused as he returned to his office down the hall. Something about Garrison? Maybe he was going to sue for wrongful termination—not that the idiot had a leg to stand on—and she was devising strategies with HR. Maybe she'd taken up acting classes as a hobby. He hadn't intended to listen, but the way she smiled, the lilt of her voice, her unguarded expression in profile . . . Yeah, the moment stunned him. She seemed so damn . . . new and different. And captivating.

Then her words caught him. She could have been referring to any number of things, work, personal, private.

Innocuous enough, yet his gut said it was sex. The color rising to her cheeks when she saw him, the soft flush of her skin, a quickened breath, and the nervous shift of her eyes, around the room, touching on him, bouncing off, dropping to his belt buckle, then past him to the door.

God help him, he'd gotten hard looking at her. She'd stammered and fidgeted, acting so unlike the Devon Parker he had worked with for over ten years. She was usually in charge and comfortable in any situation. Forthright yet diplomatic. He'd never seen anything publicly ruffle her aplomb. Sure, Garrison threw her, and he'd witnessed other situations get under her skin. Hunter was one of the few who detected those subtle nuances. Their friendship was close enough for her to trust discussing those things with him.

She'd never acted like that, the way she had in her office. She couldn't wait to get rid of him.

It was sex. It had to be. She was talking dirty at her desk, and he'd caught her.

Hunter entered his office, closing the door, then rounding his desk to flop down in his chair. Elbows on the armrests, he laced his fingers. It was warm for the end of October, and the sun beat through his window, shining on his computer screen, not that he was looking at it anyway. His office didn't have the feminine trappings of Devon's, no prints on the walls or ornamentation, but it had plenty of room for a conference table where he held his strategy meetings, a large whiteboard that printed out whatever was written on it, and a couple of chairs in front of his desk for anyone wanting to park their butt and talk. Someone usually did, especially during audit. On the whole, he was an open-door kind of executive, but right now, he didn't want anyone interrupting his thoughts. About Devon.

Christ, she'd gotten him hot. And bothered. She was an intelligent woman and extremely pleasant to look at, but off limits. First, they were both married. When they came together again, she was his CEO. He didn't do work relationships. Six months after the divorce, he'd dated a woman from the office. Dating was a whole new ball game versus flirting in the halls. It ended badly, and going to work every day became a nightmare, his personal business all over the break room. Devon was a different kind of woman. With her, nothing would make it to the water cooler. She was still off limits. They were friends. He'd never wanted to jeopardize that.

Until five minutes ago in her office, when he'd experienced a need-to-know that bordered on insanity. For a moment, he wanted to reach across her desk, pull her up by the lapels of her tailored suit jacket, his face right in hers, and force her to tell him how she played.

Because if she played anything like she worked, holy hell. Bringing that level of concentration, dedication, and focus to sex, with all the gusto she applied to the job, he could only imagine. For Devon, everything was about her career. He figured that was the reason for her divorce. After her job, she didn't have anything left over to give a man. It was never something he held against her.

He admired her for it. In a lot of ways, she thought like a man—unemotional in a work setting. He'd never fancied her a sexual creature. She was unattainable, controlled, look but don't touch, a virtual ice queen.

His eyes had been opened. He wasn't going to be able to shut them again. He wouldn't be able to stop seeing that sensual smile on her lips or hearing the sexy note in her voice.

Oh, man, was he ever in trouble now.

TWO DAYS LATER, HE HADN'T REVISED THAT OPINION. FRIDAY. IT had been a freaking long week with the auditors. And he'd noticed Devon in every meeting. Hunter had always paid attention to what she said, now he noticed *her*. Her scent, expensive, subtly sweet, and evocative. Her legs, long, toned calves with defined muscles. He was a leg man, and he found himself wishing her skirts were shorter, affording him a glimpse of thigh. He had eyes in his head and a nose with which to breathe, so he'd seen all these things before. Now he drank in the details like fine wine on his tongue.

Christ, he needed to get his head out of his shorts. Or out from underneath her skirt, metaphorically speaking.

Shoving a folder into his briefcase, he realized he'd have to come in for a couple of hours tomorrow morning. With the office relatively empty on a Saturday, he could get a lot of work done without interruption.

His personal cell phone vibrated on the desk. He kept it with him for the kids to use in an emergency, though they usually didn't bother him at work. His message icon blinked. Odd. He'd been in his office for the last fifteen minutes, and the phone hadn't rung. Someone must have dialed directly through to his voice mail.

He punched in his password, and listened. She didn't give her name, but he recognized the voice. She surprised him; he hadn't had dealings with her in quite some time. The message? Holy Christ. He listened to it twice. It was an offer he didn't intend to refuse.

THE ALARMS WERE SET AND THE LIGHTS OUT WHEN DEVON ARRIVED at the GDN corporate building. The company had two Bay Area campuses, corporate headquarters in Mountain View, with the executive staff, Accounting, IT, Human Resources, and Sales and Marketing, and their manufacturing facility in Milpitas, with Engineering, R&D, Production Control, Quality, Shipping and Receiving. Production worked three shifts, but Corporate was empty and dark at eight-forty-five on a Saturday night.

She breathed a sigh of relief. Her office lay off the reception lobby at the end of the main hallway. She would see him pull into the lot and had instructed that he park his car behind the building so it wasn't visible from the street. Still, her heart pitter-pattered. She wasn't used to hijinks, yet the element of risk added a thrill.

Her pumps were spiked, red suede, the heels sinking into the plush carpeting. She'd chosen a red power suit, one she usually reserved for board meetings. The fitted red jacket was molded to her breasts and waistline, then flared at the hips. Made of the same material, the skirt stretched tight over her rear end, falling below the knee, its forties-style pencil lines forcing a sway to her hips as she moved. She wore her hair up in her usual knot, her only outward concession to the naughty activities of the night being a few tendrils of blonde cascading to her shoulders.

Hunter had seen the suit before. Imagining the look in his eyes if he knew the lingerie that lay beneath made her feel sexy as hell, and she added a little wiggle to her walk.

Sauntering through the outer office, past Robert's desk, she unlocked her door. A large corner office, an oak conference table and four seats lay to the right, a loveseat and two armchairs with a small coffee table took up residence to the left. Her polished desk and computer credenza fit right down the middle beneath the window. The office served as workspace yet was hospitable enough for entertaining customers. The prints on the wall were her personal possessions. She favored nature art, birds in flight, a woodsy path, a mountain lion's eyes blinking in the underbrush. She spent more time here than she did at home, and the prints soothed her.

The antique carriage clock on her desk ticktocked closer to nine. She checked her lipstick in a compact mirror, then removed several condoms from her purse before laying the bag in her bottom desk drawer. The condoms she carried to the side table by the sofa, setting them unobtrusively behind the lamp.

Ticktock.

Back at her desk, she gazed out at the parking lot dotted with islands of hawthorn bushes no longer in bloom. She'd driven around the building to make sure the back was as empty as the front.

The beam of headlights flashed across the road as a car turned into the cul-de-sac. Her blood began to pulse wildly. There were four other businesses along the street, but the vehicle passed by those entrances, heading straight ahead to GDN's lot.

She swallowed, her throat parched. A date with a courtesan had never affected her this way before.

The headlights flashed up, then down as the car bumped over the driveway.

She held her breath, knowing she was silhouetted in the window, her office lights behind her.

Following the outside border of the parking lot, the vehicle disappeared from view around the building. Devon glanced at the carriage clock. Nine p.m. exactly. Leaning over the desk, she flipped on the reading lamp. Her stomach fluttered as she closed the blinds behind her credenza, shutting out the night. Retrieving two bottles of water from her mini-fridge, she left them on the coffee table, then closed the window blinds behind the sofa as well. At the door, she switched out the overhead lights, leaving the room aglow with only a soft illumination. The setting was as perfect as she could make it.

She backed out, turned, headed down the hall.

Showtime.

4

DEVON'S HEELS DETONATED LIKE SMALL EXPLOSIONS ON THE FAUX
marble tile of the lobby. She'd never realized how loud that was.
With the reception lights on, her features in the window's reflection were starkly superimposed over the form of a man waiting
outside. Damn, she should have left the lights off.

At least he was tall like Hunter.

Reaching for the door's metal handle, she realized her hands
were shaking. Devon curled her fist, willing away the tremors.
Nervousness was stupid. She shoved on the door.

Rather than a gasp, she took one sharp intake of breath. Her
insides melted, her knees weakened, her nipples peaked against
her jacket's lining.

Damn. The man was Hunter's doppelganger.

More than six feet of gorgeous male, thick black hair, midnight
blue eyes, a hint of dark beard on his square jaw, a deep navy suit
that made his white dress shirt gleam brighter in the overhead lights.

"Wait two minutes, then take the hallway on the right," she
instructed. "It's the last office. The door will be open." She pointed
to the bank of light switches by the front entrance. "Turn off the
lights here and the ones in the hall." She pivoted on her heel, leaving him to catch the door before it slammed.

She'd sent Isabel an e-mail describing the courtesan's role, possible things he could say, all with the intention of pretending that Hunter had walked into her office for a brief chat about some work-related topic.

From there, it was up to the stand-in to seduce her.

She hurried down the hall, nearly catching a heel in the transition from tile to thick carpet. By the time she reached her office, she was panting. This was crazy, but she had to have it. She'd lost her mind. Hopefully the stand-in would help her get it back. Her heart raced like the first time a man had put his hand on her thigh. She wanted Hunter's hand on her. Up her skirt. Inside her panties.

Sitting down behind her desk, she opened a meaningless folder. Her skin flushed hot. Between her legs, she throbbed.

He stopped at the door to the outer office, outlined by the hallway light. He flipped it off, leaving only Robert's desk light on to illuminate the outer office. The beating of the carriage clock filled the silence, matching the rhythm of her heart. He moved like a mountain lion on the prowl, stopping once again at her door, both hands on the jamb. Her heart drowned out the ticktock of the carriage clock.

Hunter. She could almost smell him.

"Hey, Devon, got a minute?" he said. His voice, only a fraction off Hunter's deep resonance, strummed her body. She liked the sound of her name on his lips.

"Sure, Hunter. What do you need?"

He paused long enough for her to understand he'd need a lot more than a minute. He sauntered into her office, staying beyond the pool of desk light, then held out a hand. "Closed-door meeting. You mind?" he asked.

Her throat was parched, her skin jumpy. "Must be serious."

"Oh yeah." His voice dipped a sexy note. Just as Hunter's did when he made one of his bawdy comments. He closed the door, leaned slightly against it, and she was almost sure she heard the snick of the lock. As she'd instructed. He was perfect.

She held out a hand, indicating one of the conference table chairs. "Have a seat."

He pulled it to the desk, parted the lapels of his jacket, and sat, his hands idly in his pockets. In the soft lighting, he was enough like Hunter to make her panties slick. Yes, there were differences if she looked closely, his nose longer, more flared, lips thinner, eyes a little closer together, but in the soft light, she could pretend away those differences. Isabel had done a damn good job in her choice.

"What's up?"

His mouth quirked, and he adjusted slightly in his chair. "Something big."

She almost laughed. Except that he was a tad too blatant. Hunter wasn't. "The auditors up in arms about something again?"

He nodded slowly, took his hands out of his pockets, laying them along the armrests. Big, masculine hands. Like Hunter's. She'd imagined those hands on her so many times.

"Larry's got issues with the . . ." He paused as if he couldn't remember what Larry was supposed to have issues with. When he smiled, she knew he was playing with her. "The reserves," he said at last.

The smile got to her. Hunter had been wearing that sexy grin in the photo she'd given Isabel. The smile was so good, the courtesan might very well have practiced in the mirror.

"What kind of issues?" she prompted.

He rose, rounded the desk, the air currents carrying his scent to her. Damn if it wasn't Hunter's scent, sexy and male. "Boot up your computer, and I'll show you."

She was actually breathless as she swiveled in her chair to tap the start button on her laptop. He boxed her in against the credenza, tall, all male, powerful.

He leaned close and whispered, "I'll cover my eyes while you type in your password." His minty breath bathed her ear.

She glanced at him. His eyes were indeed closed, his face in shadow, reminiscent of Hunter. But not. She looked away quickly, chiding herself. She would not spoil this by harping on the subtle differences.

Watching him once again, noticing his long lashes, she tapped out the keystrokes. "Okay, we're in."

"Get into the Internet," he said.

Directing her mouse, she clicked on the appropriate icon. She utilized only a small ergonomic secretarial chair, which was easier on her back than a desk model, and he moved behind her, bracketing her with his arms. His big body surrounded her and set her temperature soaring.

He logged in to a Google account called StallionHunter. She laughed, knowing Isabel had put him up to it after their talk about Catherine the Great's stallion. The e-mail he opened came with a photo attachment.

"This is what I want to show you, Devon," he murmured, as he bent low against her, his chin right down at the crook of her neck. He clicked on the attachment entitled, "What I want to do to you."

The graphic photo bloomed across the screen. She sucked in a breath, pushed back, her head against his shoulder.

A man, a woman, no faces, just bodies. Beautiful, trim, muscular bodies entwined. It could have been her. It could have been Hunter. He'd crawled down between her legs, his dark head nestled there, his mouth against her pussy.

The stand-in seduced her with words and explicit pictures. "I could never tell you, Devon, I had to show you." He pointed, leaning close to whisper in her ear. "This is what I imagine every evening as I drive home, every night as I lay in bed with my cock in my hand."

She could almost feel his tongue on her clit. Hunter's tongue. He *was* Hunter in this moment.

"We work together," she whispered. "We shouldn't do this."

"I'm gonna go fucking crazy if we don't." He beguiled her with the need threading through his voice. "It consumes me. It's what I imagine, feel, smell, and taste every time I close my eyes." He blew warm breath on her nape. "When I come, you're all I see."

Oh God. *She* was the one going fucking crazy.

"Just once, Devon." He nipped her earlobe. "We'll never talk about it again." He swiveled her in the chair so they faced each other, the computer in her periphery. "One taste, Devon." He laid a finger on the screen right over the image of his head between her legs. "One orgasm," he murmured.

"Hunter—"

He cut her off with a finger against her lips. "Christ, it makes me hot the way you say my name. I've wanted you fucking forever." His eyes blazed a deep ocean blue the exact color of Hunter's when he took on Myron. Probably contact lenses, but who the hell cared. He said the right things. That hadn't been in her e-mail to Isabel, yet he anticipated what she needed to hear.

"Say you want me, too," he begged. "I need to hear that you want me as badly as I need you."

He was so damn good. Worth every penny she'd pay for the performance. No woman could withstand him, especially not when he was her fantasy.

She let him take her over. "Yes, Hunter, I want you." It felt so good to finally say it aloud.

"Tell me what you want me to do to you." He held her chin in his big hand, so close his face was slightly blurred, turning him completely into Hunter. "I need to hear the words."

"Kiss me, you fool."

He laughed. Not quite Hunter's laugh. She had to stop those thoughts. He *was* Hunter. *Go with the fantasy, Devon.*

He cupped both cheeks in his palms. "I thought you'd never fucking ask."

Hunter didn't curse. She loved that he did it now.

His lips were smooth, warm, his mouth tasting of sweet mouthwash. She opened to him, gave him her tongue. Oh Lord, the man could kiss, not a wet slobber, but a melding, a foray, backing off to angle his kiss the other way. Tasting, savoring, getting his fill of her, as if he'd dreamed of this moment for months.

The way she'd dreamed of it. Devon sank her fingers into his forearms and held on. The ride was exquisite. With her eyes closed, he was all Hunter. He kissed her breathless, mindless, whispering sweet nothings to her every time he lifted his lips. Sweet nothings, dirty nothings, hot and sexy nothings. She was drowning in his taste, steeped in his scent, mesmerized by his voice.

"Come here." Hands at her rib cage, he lifted her from the chair, setting her on her feet. "I want to feel all of you against all of me." He crushed her to him, his tongue sweeping into her mouth. She wrapped her arms around his neck and hung on. He was big, muscled, and hard against her belly. All that cock wanting her.

"Hunter, I need . . ." She stopped, drew in a breath.

"What do you need, baby? I'll give it to you."

"Take off your jacket." She'd fantasized slipping the knot of his tie, undoing his shirt, slipping her fingers inside. Would he be hairy or smooth? She'd never seen Hunter without a shirt.

"Whatever you want, baby." He undid the button, and she shoved the jacket off his shoulders and down his arms. He tossed it into the darker recesses of the office. "What now?"

He didn't overwhelm, letting her set the pace. "Your tie," she said. Reaching up to pull the knot, she loosened the tie and tossed it on the desk. "Now your shirt."

He hadn't worn an undershirt, and she found bare flesh as she popped each button. He shivered when her fingers touched warm skin. Devon met his blue eyes. "Are you acting?"

Damn. Of course he was. It was all an illusion.

He grabbed her hand, squeezed. "Say my name, Devon."

"Hunter," she whispered.

He sighed with satisfaction, then pulled her hand down to the front of his slacks. "Does this feel like acting, Devon?" He rubbed his cock with her palm. Good Lord, he was large. "That's all for you. I've known you for ten years, and I've lusted after you from day one, but we were both married then." He massaged his cock with her hand, pulsing, throbbing under the pressure. "When you made this job offer, I truly thought about turning it down so I could have you in my bed. During the four years since I've worked for you, there's not a day gone by that I haven't wondered how your pussy tastes, how your mouth will feel wrapped around my cock, how tight you are, how damn fucking good it'll be buried balls deep inside you."

She moaned, closed her eyes. "Oh God, yes, Hunter."

"Finish undoing my shirt and lick my nipples, pinch them." He gritted his teeth. "Because I like it."

Her hands trembled, she shook inside, and when his shirt hung open, she wanted to lick and suck all that smooth flesh. Hairless except for a few strands right around the nipples. She took one flat rosy nub in her mouth and sucked hard. Her fingers dallied with the other, rolling the peak between her thumb and forefinger. She pinched, hard. Hunter hissed in a breath and groaned. Yes, Hunter. He said all the right things, and to her, he *was* Hunter.

"I told myself it was only the last few months that I've wanted you." She raised her eyes as he cupped her cheek.

"It's been longer than that, hasn't it?"

"Since forever," she whispered, feeling the dawning of truth. "Even when I was married." Even when her husband had been making love to her, she realized that Hunter had somehow crept in. It was probably why his face came to her first when she needed a new CFO.

He unzipped her blazer, but held the lapels closed. "You've imagined me undressing you." It wasn't a question.

"Yes." The word was a mere breath. Oh yes, the times she'd imagined him, slowly, seductively, or quick and dirty, popping buttons, tearing fabric.

Pulling the blazer apart, he revealed the camisole she wore, underwire to cup and mold her breasts, but sheer to reveal the deep color of her areoles. The lingerie fit tightly over her belly and hips, ending in ribbons with garter snaps, but he wouldn't figure it out until he raised her skirt. She'd wanted to appear businesslike on the outside but sexy as all get-out on the inside, like white chocolate filled with raspberry liqueur.

"Christ, your breasts are beautiful." His voice dripped with awe and reverence. Slowly, so slowly, he raised one hand and stroked the bud of a nipple with his index finger. She immediately peaked.

He lifted his gaze. "What else have you fantasized?"

Her pussy was wet and throbbing. "You, Hunter, going down on me on the couch." She pointed. "That one."

He swallowed, his Adam's apple bobbing, and she was reminded of the day Hunter caught her on the phone with Isabel.

"Your fantasies make me nuts." He backed up, pulling her with him, then turned, lacing his fingers with hers and leading her to the sofa.

"Clothes on," he murmured as he pushed the coffee table out of the way with his foot. Holding her gaze, he accordioned her skirt in his fingers, and tugged it slowly, inexorably upward. "Every time we're in a board meeting," he said, "I dream about bending you over the conference table and fucking you from behind."

Heat sizzled through her.

The skirt was tight; he pulled harder. "When we're having cocktails with customers to discuss contracts, I envision putting my hand up your skirt and fingering you."

It was dirty and oh-so-sexy. Her pussy turned creamy.

He yanked the skirt to her waist and palmed her butt. "You're not wearing panties." He pulled back to survey her. Black stockings fastened with the camisole's garters. "You're so smooth," he whispered.

"Do you like it?" She shaved herself bare, loving the feel of her naked pussy as she walked or drove or sat or moved.

"I fucking love it." He slipped one finger along her pussy lips. "You're wet already."

"Touch me, Hunter. I've waited so long for this."

He parted her, nudged her clit, circled. Her body jerked.

"Christ, I need to taste you." He damn near shoved her down on the couch, then spread her legs, as if he couldn't get to her pussy fast enough. His intensity thrilled her, sending a new rush of moisture through her.

She'd thought her obsession had been about wanting Hunter. Deep inside, though, it had always been about him wanting her just as badly. Mutual desires.

Bending his dark head to her moist center, Hunter blew on her. She moaned. "More, please, more."

He drew her clit into his mouth. Throwing her head back against the sofa and closing her eyes, she threaded her fingers through his hair. Tightening her thighs, she clutched him to her, riding his tongue. "Yes, oh God, yes," she cried out.

He sucked and circled, dipped down to slide his tongue in her pussy, then back to suck her clit. A finger, then two entered her, finding her G-spot and sending her shooting off a cliff in what felt like two seconds flat. She chanted his name, "Yes, Hunter, please, Hunter." So damn perfect.

The stand-in was the best idea she'd ever had.

5

HUNTER PARKED HIS CAR IN THE LOT NEXT DOOR. AS HE PULLED IN, he noted Devon's car parked at the back of the GDN building, another vehicle next to it.

He glanced at his watch. Dead on nine-thirty. He closed his door quietly, not that he figured anyone inside GDN would hear him, then stepped over the small hedgerow separating the two parking areas. The blinds of Devon's office were closed. There might have been a light on, but he couldn't be sure.

When he used his card key, the alarm didn't beep. Someone had already disarmed it. The lobby was dark, only the outside lights falling through the window illuminated the tile floor. He cocked his head, thought he heard a sound but couldn't be sure. Standing at the mouth of the executive hallway, the view was straight into Devon's admin's office. A desk lamp burned. That was all.

The sound again. A woman's voice? A moan?

The voice mail played in his mind. *There's something you need to see.*

He moved silently past two doorways, HR VP and Garrison's old office. His heart beat in his ears.

Devon's office. Nine-thirty tonight. Don't come early or the play might not have started.

He didn't know exactly what the message meant. He had no clue what to expect. Devon had mentioned improvisation and the message referred to a play. He was, however, convinced of the prurient nature of that conversation. There was no way he'd have missed showing up tonight.

At the entry to the outer office, he knew for sure that was a woman's voice, but through Devon's door, the words were indistinguishable. He stopped once again right before it, realizing the door had not been pulled completely shut.

A woman moaned. There was no mistaking the heady sound. His cock felt it, rose to it.

He put a finger to the door. Swallowed. To open it constituted an invasion of her privacy.

He wouldn't, if not for the voice on that voice mail. The madam of Courtesans. He'd utilized their services a couple of times, on a lark, introduced through an old college chum of his. The encounters hadn't given him the connection he enjoyed during sex.

Isabel would not have left that message lightly. Had Devon put her up to it? Somehow he thought not. Devon Parker was straightforward. She would have left the damn message herself.

A feminine groan drifted through the slightly ajar door. He swore it was her. Devon. Privacy be damned. She was in the fucking office with the door unlocked. She couldn't be expecting complete privacy. And he wasn't walking away.

He pushed. The door, barely latched, snicked open. The lighting was minimal. Now he felt her pleasure sounds deep in his gut.

She moaned. "Yes, yes, please."

He pushed the door wider.

Devon Parker reclined on the couch, her desk lamp softly illuminating the tableau. Her suit jacket fell open to reveal a lacy black camisole. Her skirt bunched beneath her hips, she held her legs spread wide. A man's dark head bobbed between her thighs. She fisted her fingers in his hair and rocked against his mouth.

Hunter froze, his breath trapped in his throat, so damn hard, he ached. She was gorgeous. She was a wet dream. She was hot as Hades. Her body rocked against her lover, wordlessly begging for more. Her eyes closed, she made hot little throaty noises that sent his blood pressure soaring.

What the hell was he supposed to do? What did she want from him? Join? Watch? Salivate? Maybe she wanted him to see what he could have had all these years if he'd had the balls to ask.

She writhed. Fuck, he wanted to be that mouth on her, that tongue tasting her.

"Yes, Hunter, please, Hunter, God, Hunter."

Blood roared in his ears. She was calling his name. She was asking for *him*.

"Yes, Hunter, do it like that, exactly like that." She tossed her head back and forth on the couch. "Oh Hunter, you don't know how many times I've dreamed about this, wanted you like this."

Somehow, perhaps by miracle, everything fell into place. Devon had hired a courtesan to play him, Hunter. Part of the game was for him to watch. The madam of Courtesans—or Devon herself— had set him up to be there.

And watch he did. Her orgasm blossomed, her body shaking with it, and she cried long and low, ending with his name, "Hunter," soft yet recognizable.

He wanted to see the flush on her body, feel the quake in her limbs, but he could only watch. It was so damn fucking beautiful.

Before she'd even come down, the courtesan rose, hauled her across the couch and laid her flat. "Do you want me to fuck you, Devon?" The light hit the side of his face, and damn if he didn't look a bit like Hunter himself, dark hair, same build.

"Please, Hunter, yes, yes, please do it, Hunter."

She said his name as if she were trying to convince herself it was really him.

The man reached into his pocket, came out with a condom packet. Unzipping his slacks, he pulled out his cock, then gave the foil a practiced tear with his teeth. Rolling on the condom expertly, he pulled Devon's leg to his shoulder.

"Tell me who's fucking you, Devon."

"You are, Hunter."

The courtesan rewarded her with a deep thrust. Her cry melted into a moan.

It was the hottest fucking thing Hunter had ever witnessed. Almost like watching himself in a mirror. He wished to heaven he could see Devon's face.

"Do I feel good?" his substitute asked, body pumping against her, inside her.

"Hunter, yes, there's never been anyone like you. Never."

The guy looked up, shot Hunter with his gaze. "You crave this, don't you, Devon. You're going to beg for more. Every day, every night." He knew Hunter stood beyond the door, and he wanted him to hear every word. "You'll never want me to stop, will you, Devon."

"I'll never want you to stop, Hunter." Tears leaked through her voice. "I'm going to want this forever."

She screamed his name as she came.

Hunter was a goner.

MONDAY MORNING, TO QUOTE A CLICHÉ, DEVON WAS WALKING ON air. It was amazing to give herself over to the fantasy. She didn't have to be in control, she wasn't the boss, she didn't have to impress or dictate or run the show. She didn't even have to hide her feelings. She simply allowed the stand-in to direct everything, while she let it all go.

She'd never had sex like that. She'd always had an agenda. With her husband, it had been to placate him because he claimed she was a workaholic, putting him second. With a courtesan, it was to make sure she got her money's worth, every last orgasm she deserved and wanted.

With the stand-in, all she had to do was close her eyes and indulge her fantasies, let him be Hunter. It had been a taste of freedom she might very well have to indulge in again.

Devon entered the conference room for the weekly executive staff meeting she held first thing Monday mornings so the VPs from the Milpitas manufacturing facility could stop on their drive in. Wearing high heels that were an inch taller than her usual, she was the second to arrive. "Morning, Stinson." VP of R&D and Engineering.

Stinson mumbled a greeting. Maybe it was the introversion of an engineering mind—though she'd met her shares of extroverted engineers—but Stinson never spoke clearly. The tall, lanky, slightly unkempt professor type, he possessed a brilliant mind, but had a harder time with the social skills. No one was perfect, and he'd gotten them out of many a hole with a slightly jumbled inarticulate dissertation that was nevertheless pure genius.

Merrimac from Manufacturing and Gigi from HR arrived next. Gigi was their only female VP. Her head count was small but her bailiwick huge. Devon had pulled HR out of Accounting and Admin last year. Wells sauntered in, taking a seat next to Gigi. Director of IT, Wells reported to Hunter, but due to the update she wanted on the search for the new integrated computer enterprise system, Devon had invited him.

Hunter came last. At that first sight of him, a flush rode through her body, heated her skin. He'd warned her he might be late due to a conference call, but he'd managed to keep the tardiness down to a minute.

"Let's start with the audit update, Hunter." She loved saying his name, remembered how it rolled off her tongue as she pleaded for the first orgasm, then another.

She didn't care about the meeting agenda or the audit or the computer system or the search for a new S&M VP. She let his voice caress her, intensifying the silky slide of her lingerie beneath her staid business suit. Stockings, garter belt, thong panty, lace bra. It wasn't her usual work fare, but this morning, the urge had been irresistible. Her breath quickened. Her pulse beat at her throat. She was warm and wet remembering Hunter's touch. That was the beauty of Saturday night: For all intents and purposes, the man who'd made love to her *had* been Hunter Nash. She loved the sexy sensations stealing through her. She felt like a woman instead of an automaton.

"Thank you, Hunter." She smiled at him. She'd heard every word of his report, absorbing the timbre of his voice.

He tipped his head, giving her a look. She usually asked a lot of questions. That was her style. Today, she didn't care to hear more. Any problems, he'd handle them. He was capable. They all were. That's why she chose them.

"Gigi, how's it going on the executive search?"

Gigi rattled off the steps she'd taken, yet Hunter still perused Devon's face, her body language. Did he sense something different in her? She pushed back slightly from the table, crossed her legs, rocking her foot. His eyes dropped briefly to her high heel. She imagined he could see all the way up her skirt to the lace top of her stockings. And that he'd remember the stockings she'd worn for him on Saturday.

Again, the perfection of the night allowed her to put the real

Hunter there with her. Electricity arced between them. Delicious. She could walk around in bliss all day imagining that she was boffing her CFO on the side. The ruse had actually worked for her.

Hunter cleared his throat.

Devon realized Gigi had finished her accounting. The meeting went on as she deliciously, blissfully relived every moment of Saturday night.

Back in her office an hour later, she sat at her desk, her attention focused on the couch. Door closed, she held her private cell phone. She hadn't called Isabel yesterday, wanting to savor the moment without explanation or comment, deciding what she liked best about it, how it could be improved.

"Hey, you," Isabel answered, obviously reading the caller ID first.

"You were genius," Devon congratulated her.

Isabel purred. Devon could almost see her buffing her fingernails on her sleeve. "I assume you were pleased."

"The resemblance was uncanny."

"You'd be surprised what the right hairstyle, clothes, and lighting can do. How about the performance? Worth it?" Isabel liked her clients to be happy and her friends delirious.

"It was worth a helluva lot more." She didn't, however, mention the price she'd paid. Isabel never liked specifics about remuneration going out into the airwaves. No one ever said aloud that they *paid* for sex.

"Were you able to fool yourself?"

"Yes." She thought a moment about how much she wanted to reveal. "I never thought I'd like giving a man the control."

"Don't tell me you let down your legendary reserve?"

"Smart-ass."

Isabel's laugh was delightful. "Seriously, sometimes you can be rigid."

Her? Well . . . yes. "They need to be apprised of exactly what I like and do everything the way I want. That's not too much to ask." So she was asking for the world: She was also paying for it.

Isabel laughed. "But you liked letting *Hunter*"—Isabel stressed the name—"decide what you needed."

"He surprised me." Devon didn't usually like surprises. This time, she'd loved it. "I'd enjoy seeing him again."

"Gee"—Isabel snorted—"I'll beg him to do it as a favor."

The facetious tone meant the stand-in had reported positively. Of course, Devon paid him handsomely, but even with a courtesan, money wasn't the only factor. Some people, it didn't matter how much they paid if they didn't show the proper respect and appreciation. "I have to go to Sedona on a business trip in a couple of weeks. I'd like to see him there."

It was freaky, true, but she wanted to play the next date as if she and Hunter were being naughty at a work function. She'd seen it happen, John and Jane from So-and-So company getting tipsy and flirty in the bar, then sneaking up to one or the other's room. They thought they were fooling everyone, but you could practically scent the attraction on the air. She'd never done it, but always found it extremely titillating. In fact, she'd once mentioned such a fantasy to Isabel, she and Hunter in a hotel restaurant, his hand suddenly finding its way up her skirt. It wasn't possible to pull it off exactly that way since the real Hunter would be at the same conference and she couldn't afford to be seen in public with a man who looked so much like him. She'd have to devise another way of playing the scene to maximize the naughty feeling she craved.

Damn, had she simply traded one obsession for another?

"I'll set it up." Isabel paused overlong. Something else was coming. "Is this really working for you?"

"Absolutely." One obsession for another? It didn't matter. This morning she'd looked at Hunter without the desperation. She could replay the whole thing as if it were him, get the kick, and not end up with that overwhelming, frustrating need burning in her belly. She might have daydreamed in the meeting, but it had been . . . different. Which sounded like rationalization, but honestly, she felt more normal than she had in ages.

Her desk phone beeped and Robert's voice came through. "Do you have a minute for Hunter?"

The intercom was loud enough for Isabel to hear. "Ooh, he wants to see you," she cooed as if they were teenagers.

"Stop that," Devon chided, then punched the TALK button. "Tell him to come on in, Robert."

"It's an invitation he won't be able to refuse," Isabel murmured. "I'll get back to you. Toodles."

Devon had to laugh. Toodles? Who said *toodles*, except maybe Paris Hilton? Isabel always popped out with something completely unexpected, and Devon liked her more every time.

She set the phone down and undid the top two buttons of her blouse.

6

SHE MYSTIFIED HIM. HUNTER HAD WALKED INTO THE CONFERENCE room Monday morning, and Devon had given him that smile. Not *a* smile, but a sexy, satisfied cat-that-ate-the-cream smile, her skin flushed pink. As if he'd been the one making her scream on Saturday night. As if they shared a secret. It made him nuts. He couldn't figure out what was going on in her mind, but she looked at him as if the taste of his come still lingered on her tongue.

Holy hell, he'd looked through that door and gotten an eyeful. He was a goddamn peeper. It wasn't enough that the man fucked her; no, he'd pulled out, stripped off the condom and fed her his cock, crooning to her—and maybe to his cock—the entire time. She'd eaten him alive.

A cold shower when he'd arrived home hadn't done a damn thing. Instead, he'd taken his own cock in his hand and worked himself to the image of her taking another man deep down her throat.

Devon Parker sucked cock like a goddess. The guy had jerked and groaned for one hell of a long time, telling her how hot her mouth was, how well she sucked. Playing the scene out behind closed lids in the shower, he imagined her lips on his dick, her hand massaging his balls, squeezing, caressing. The hot, sexy little sounds she made were for *him*.

He damn well better not shut her office door when he went in there or he'd have her flat on her desk with her legs spread. She had him that worked up.

"Go on in." Robert pointed a thumb over his shoulder.

"Thanks," he said, passing the man's desk. In days of old (last week), he'd simply have knocked on her door and walked in without preamble. Robert would have stopped him if it was something he shouldn't interrupt.

The worst thing was, he'd manufactured an excuse to see her. It slid idiotically off his tongue as he stepped into her domain. "Can I show you something on the screen?" He pointed to her computer on the credenza behind her.

She gasped, her breasts rising, and he suddenly realized she had two more buttons undone than in the meeting.

"What do you want to show me?" There was a slight catch to her voice.

"It's nothing disturbing," he said, because her eyes indeed widened as if he'd disturbed her.

"No, sorry." She shook herself, held up a hand. "It reminded me of something else."

He rounded her desk, stood behind her as she hit the screen saver. Her scent played havoc, subtly sweet and laced with . . . the musk of arousal? What the hell had she been doing in here with the door closed? Staring at the couch, remembering, and getting hot all over again?

Oh yeah, he'd gone fucking nuts.

"Pull up the cash forecast," he instructed. The file was in a shared folder accessible by password only to him, Devon, his general accounting manager, and her subordinate who prepared the spreadsheet.

When the file came up, he pointed to a number, then took the cursor from Devon's hand and highlighted the accompanying comment. "We're going to have to deal with this." A sizable past due receivable, he'd already made the appropriate calls. Normally, he'd let his accounts receivable clerk handle it, but the amount was so large, he'd gotten involved. He didn't need Devon in on it. He'd needed an excuse to get close.

"Do you want me to give Bowman a call?" she asked.

"Let's wait and see if we need to escalate." They wouldn't have to. "I wanted to make you aware of it."

She glanced up at him. "I saw it this morning, but I figured you'd handle it with your usual style." She smiled. It wasn't the cat-that-ate-the-cream smile, but it got him going anyway. "Thanks for making sure, though." She turned once again and shut down the file. From his angle above her, he could see straight down her blouse to her cleavage. His heart trip-hammered. She had full, milk-white breasts. A hint of nipple showed above the lace of her bra. He wanted to touch.

Holy hell, he'd lost his mind. She'd never studied him the way she'd done today. She'd never unbuttoned her blouse that far. Did she know he'd been watching Saturday night? Had she planned it? Was this some look-but-don't-touch game she was playing?

"Anything else, Hunter?" She swiveled in her chair, her knee brushing his leg.

He forced himself to back up. Saturday night had changed something fundamental. She was as sexual and hedonistic as anyone else. She probably always had been, but now he *knew* it.

Despite himself, Hunter smiled. "Nothing right now," he said. She was playing a game, and he was dying to play it with her. She had her rules, he didn't care. That's why it was going to be so fucking fantastic, because he had no idea what the game was or how to play out the hand.

"I'll see you later." He headed for the door, turning at the last moment to catch that sexy, tantalizing smile again.

Oh yeah, things were different. *She* was different. He wanted her lips around his cock in the worst—or best—way possible.

When he reached his office, he pulled out his cell phone, punched in a number, and a woman answered. He was going to set about adding his own rules to the game right now.

MID-NOVEMBER ARRIVED, AND ROBERT HAD BOOKED DEVON A SUITE at the resort where the investors' conference was being held. Basically the conference was a schmoozefest of people who had money and people who wanted money. You talked about how great your company was, what a sound investment you would be, and convinced the shakers and movers to open their wallets. She often entertained in the room after the day's activities were over, which was why she needed a suite rather than a single room. You didn't invite people into your bedroom, and you never invited one person to your suite alone, of course, especially a man. That was asking for trouble.

The suite was, however, hers after all the schmoozing was said and done. Devon intended to use it to its full extent after Friday, the last day of the conference, after the last dinner and the last cocktail. She'd arranged for an extra night she would pay for herself. Devon was a stickler. No one could accuse her of charging anything personal on the company expense account.

It would have been so much easier if Hunter hadn't decided to take another day, too. "You don't have to stay Saturday because I am," she told him. "I'll hire a car to take me to the airport on Sunday morning." She planned to return with the courtesan since she was paying for his rental car.

"I've a mind to do a few rounds of golf."

"It'll be too cold for golf." The daytime temperatures for November in Sedona were mid-fifties to low sixties.

"I'll be fine as long as it doesn't snow."

"Men," she said softly. She was hoping for snow flurries to get rid of him. If he saw the courtesan . . . she didn't want to imagine what he'd assume.

"Women," Hunter said with a chuckle. "Relax and enjoy." He was behind the wheel of the rental car, having chosen the scenic route from Flagstaff rather than the highway. Though a much shorter distance, it took longer but Hunter claimed the vistas through Oak Creek Canyon and Slide Rock State Park were worth it.

"Oh my God," she breathed as he came out of a turn to a magnificent view of a red rock butte jutting into the sky.

"Was I right?"

"God, yes." She wasn't a nature girl, but one couldn't help but be in awe of the majesty.

He pulled down his shades and glanced at her.

"What?"

Pushing the glasses back up the bridge of his nose, he set his attention to the road as it meandered into another turn. "I like the way you say, 'God, yes.'"

Over the last couple of weeks, he'd tossed out several strange comments. They almost sounded like double entendres. Devon was afraid she'd been revealing too much with her body language, her attire, her glances.

Was he starting to suspect she had a thing for him? Good Lord, that wasn't why he was staying over, was it, hoping to get lucky with her? No, no, and hell no, the man was off limits. She had her substitute, and he would have to do.

"You want to go hiking while we're here?"

She looked at him, tried to see inside his mind. "High heels are not appropriate footwear for hiking." Though she did have her workout tennies.

She couldn't allow herself to spend that much time with Hunter. Alone time. Off-work time. It was bad enough sitting next to him on the plane, his body heat practically jumping across the armrest. She did not travel business class on such a short flight and sandwiched next to him on the plane . . . Lord, *sandwich*, she was making up her own double entendres. After the flight, the car was only marginally better. With bucket seats, at least she wasn't touching him, but his scent still tantalized her. For some reason—lust and obsession—her gaze kept falling to his trousers, wondering. She crossed her legs trying to tamp down the burgeoning sensations between her legs.

"You need to let go, Devon. There is life beyond work."

She snorted. "You sound like my ex-husband."

"I am *not* anything like your ex." A touch of growl laced his voice.

She cleared her head with a deep breath. "I'm sorry. I'm edgy. Too much sitting still." She'd never quibbled like that with Hunter. Her obsession was getting to her. She needed another night with her stand-in. She needed to stop wondering how big Hunter was, what his taste would be, how his skin would feel, if his chest would be smooth or dusted with soft hair, whether his nipples were sensitive, if he'd like them pinched . . .

How he compared.

"Apology accepted," he said.

She wanted to crawl over the hand brake between them and discover the answers to all the questions running around in her mind.

"This is silly," she muttered aloud.

"Arguing?"

She searched for something other than the truth. "No, attending the conference together. One of us could have handled everything. Two is a waste of company money. Besides, you should be at the office to oversee the audit." She could hear the desperation leaking into her voice. The last two weeks she'd been telling herself she was fine, her obsession had dropped back down to mild attraction, yet here it was flaring out of control again.

Maybe she'd have Isabel send the courtesan tonight. Which made him sound like a wrapped package that could be shoved in the cargo hold.

Hunter didn't fight her by saying it was a two-person job or that he had a capable staff handling every aspect of the audit and he was only a phone call away. "You would have missed the beauty of Sedona."

As he spoke, the towering red rocks fell away and the view expanded to the Sedona valley rimmed by distant buttes. The resort they were headed to was at the southern end. Somehow the sight worked magic on her. Or perhaps it was Hunter's calm voice and laid-back attitude.

She was here. She enjoyed his company. At the end of the three-day conference, she was going to screw the heck out of her stand-in and pretend he was Hunter. It was a win-win. Unless she got all edgy and ruined it.

7

THE WOMAN COULD WORK A ROOM LIKE NOBODY'S BUSINESS. There were workshops on economics, investment strategies, mergers, due diligence, acquisitions, market instability, et cetera, but the real business was networking. Devon was a master. She had the men eating out of her hand after the Wednesday evening cocktail reception, and the female attendees were equally impressed. She walked the walk, talked the talk.

He wanted her straight up against the elevator wall. Or on his room's balcony, with the amazing view of Bell Rock and Courthouse Butte in the background. He'd sat out there despite the chill of approaching dusk, a glass of wine in his hand as the sun set, painting the red rocks with spectacular hues. He wished Devon would let down her guard enough to watch it with him.

Thursday, he wanted to jump across the dinner table when he perceived she was too friendly with a money man from Minneapolis.

Friday, his jaw ached from all the teeth clenching he'd done. He wanted an hour alone with her, just one. She'd managed to avoid any one-on-one time, even for a second.

Saturday, he saw her through the workout room window. In a zebra leotard and black leggings, she revealed every curve. He was ready to cut out on his golf date, but she'd asked to borrow the rental car for some Sedona shopping. He'd invited her to dinner that night. She said she wanted a long soak and a good book.

With a couple of phone calls, he'd learned all about her weekend plans and what she was preparing for. Him. Only *not* him. It was the other one, the twin.

Maybe he needed to take the direct approach and ask her to have an affair with him. He would even take plain old fucking, he was that enthralled.

At eight-twenty Saturday night, he knocked on her suite.

Holy hell. She opened the door wearing the sexiest little black dress. Short and velvety soft, it flirted with her thighs. He'd never seen the top half of her knees. The bodice plunged, the material draping her breasts in artful folds. The long sleeves ended in points below her wrists. Her stockings were fishnet, the heels of her shoes fuck-me high. Her blonde hair caressed her shoulders and bare nape. He'd never seen her hair down.

She'd done this for the other one. His eyeballs suddenly ached with jealousy. He barely knew where to find his voice. "I thought I'd fill you in on how the golf game went with Metro." He hadn't been wasting time to gain the extra day with her.

She glanced at her watch, then once over her shoulder.

"You have a date, I'll be quick." Oh no, he wouldn't. He intended to be here when her date arrived. He'd bulldoze his way inside if he had to.

"All right, a quickie." She blushed as if she suddenly heard the dual meaning of the word, then opened the door wide to let him in.

The large sitting room opened onto a balcony with a fantastic view of the red rock bluffs. At least it would be in daylight. A long sofa and armchair grouping took up one corner opposite the flat-panel TV. The computer workstation was tucked away by the bedroom door. A bottle of wine chilled on the dining table. Two glasses. Beside them lay an attractive plate of specialty cheeses, crackers, and fruit.

He eyed them, eyed her. She didn't offer an explanation for why she'd claimed a desire for tub time in order to get out of dinner with him. Her nose tipped in the air.

The haughty façade turned him on. Inside she was probably screaming for him to get on with it. "They'd like to visit the plant." He'd played golf with an investment group out of Seattle. Before doing a public offering, you had to feel out the interest level. If financial institutions didn't back you or your stock price dropped significantly, you could end up getting a lot less than you'd planned on.

"Sounds good." Devon was not normally a two-word-answer person.

"I would prefer that they come after the 10K has been signed off." The report to the Securities and Exchange Commission was the final result of the year-end audit process. "I'd like to have the earnings release to give them."

"I agree totally."

Okay, that was three words. She glanced again at her watch, a twist of her wrist and a slide of her eyes, probably thinking he wouldn't notice. Hunter noticed everything about her.

Her perfume was different, more exotic. Beneath the soft velvet, the beads of her nipples revealed how thinly laced her bra was. If she wore one at all. A pulse beat at her throat.

"Do you have any questions about them?" he asked.

"Not right now. After I've had some time to mull it over, I'm sure I will."

Devon always had questions. It was time to look at his own watch. Two minutes to go until the scheduled appointment. "Good. We can talk more on the plane tomorrow." He turned, made a move to the door, stopped. "Do you want to do breakfast in the morning before we head out?"

He could almost feel her hold her breath so she wouldn't scream at him. "That would be fine. Seven-thirty?"

Damn, he shouldn't find this so amusing. He pretended to consider that a moment. "Or I suppose we can catch a bite at the airport after we turn in the rental car."

She huffed. "Whatever you decide."

He'd made his decision. He was going to have her tonight. He'd thought of nothing else for two weeks, worked it, arranged it. The courtesan, who should be walking down the hall to her door right now, would play a big part in making it happen.

The man had damn well better be the punctual type. Hunter didn't have a lot of excuses left. "Let's eat here. The food will be better."

Her nostrils flared. "Okay, fine. Seven-thirty."

"We should probably load up the rental car first," Hunter added.

Devon shot out another breath. "All right." Testiness hardened her consonants. "I'll meet you in the lobby with my bag at *seven-thirty*," she emphasized. What was up with him? Devon had never known Hunter to be so indecisive. He usually said, "this is what we'll do," and it was up to her to object if she didn't like it. That applied to a major business crisis or something as simple as where they'd take a vendor to lunch.

She wanted to scream. *Get. Out.* The other Hunter would be here at any moment. This was the dumbest idea she'd ever had, arranging for his services while on a business trip with Hunter. She felt darn near naked in the fishnet stockings, garter belt, short dress, the velvet draping her breasts, and no damn brassiere. If she leaned over even the slightest, the low-cut cowl neck would reveal everything down to her navel.

"Then we're set," he said, his expression bland. He didn't care that she had another date or had used an excuse to get out of dinner. Nor did he seem to find it a big deal if he happened to be here when the man she'd dressed up for finally arrived. Dammit, he'd seen the wine and the platter. It appeared as if he was stalling in order to check out her date.

Well, it was a *big* freaking deal to her.

Rat-a-tat-tat.

Devon froze at the knock, her limbs seizing up, as if Hunter seeing his doppelganger was the end of the world. As if he'd *know* she'd hired his lookalike to fuck her.

It was completely mortifying.

Until she remembered that resemblance was in the eye of the beholder. People rarely saw that in themselves. Maybe he wouldn't pick up on it.

"Ah, Devon, do you want me to open the door for you?" The hint of a smirk curled his lips.

She could swear he was laughing at her.

"No, I'll get it." She had to make sure the stand-in didn't call himself Hunter. Rushing past, she yanked the door open. Her heart had been pounding for the last ten minutes. This must be what it felt like for your husband to catch you with your lover ten seconds after you'd both pulled your clothes on.

"Hi." She practically dragged the courtesan inside. "This is Hunter Nash," she said quickly. The man had been instructed to refer to himself as Hunter, to build her fantasy. She had to somehow communicate it was so not cool at this moment.

He extended his hand to Hunter. "Kenneth. Nice to meet you."

The name shocked her. Kenneth. With his hair cut like Hunter's and a dark gray suit and tie against a white shirt, he looked more like Hunter than Hunter did himself in the casual golf attire she wasn't used to. The bone structure was different, sure, but Isabel was correct. Hair style, clothing, and a sexy grin went a long way.

They shook. Hunter sized him up, a quick flash of the eyes, up, down, but he gave off no clue as to whether he saw the similarity. "It's great to meet a friend of Devon's."

Was he teasing? She wanted to shoot him.

"Any friend of Devon's is a friend of mine." Kenneth—really, this was ruining the whole fantasy—closed the door, then slipped his arm around her waist. "Right, sweetie?"

She tipped her head back. What's up with *that*? They were *both* teasing her. "Sure, *honey*." She used the endearment, but sent Kenneth a glare.

He took her chin in his hand as he had that evening in her office, and gave her a kiss with enough tongue to liquefy her bones. At least it would have if the real Hunter hadn't been watching.

She pulled back. "What are you *doing*?"

"You make me crazy in that sexy dress. I had to have a kiss." His eyes glittered for her the way she'd always imagined Hunter's would when he was horny. "I'm sure Hunter doesn't begrudge me a brief kiss." He glanced up. "Right, man?"

"Not at all." Good Lord. *His* blue eyes glittered in tandem with . . . the other guy's.

Something was off in this whole scenario.

Kenneth chuckled, arm across her back hitching her closer, his hand splayed over her rib cage, gently nudging her breast. Hunter's gaze dropped, and she could have sworn his breath quickened.

The courtesan nuzzled her hair. "I have a feeling old Hunter here wouldn't mind watching at all."

She swallowed. How had she lost control of the situation?

"Watching is great." Hunter speared her with a blazingly hot look. "Participating is so much better."

Devon gasped, pulled free, and stepped back toward the door. "Now wait a minute here—"

Kenneth reeled her back in, brought his lips to her ear. "This is your fantasy," he whispered, his fingers rising inexorably to her breast. "Take it." Her nipple came to life with his brief, but hard pinch. "You may never get another chance." He retreated enough to lock eyes with her.

She couldn't say a word.

Still holding her trapped in his gaze, Kenneth pointed to the table. "Pour her a glass of wine."

"I'm not getting her drunk in order to want this," Hunter stated flatly.

A look passed between the two of them. A corresponding chill shot through Devon. "What's going on here, Hunter?"

He stared at her for . . . ever, then shot a quick glance at Kenneth. "I was in the office late on a Saturday night."

Pins and needles jabbed every extremity. "*Which* Saturday?" Of course, she already knew.

"There is only one Saturday that counts." His answer said it all.

Good Lord. He'd seen her. Her skin heated, her face burned, her vision blurred. Like the Wicked Witch, she wanted to melt into a puddle on the floor and drain away unnoticed through the grout in the entry tile.

"I've thought of nothing else but being a part of it ever since." Hunter didn't move, didn't try to touch her, yet his eyes caressed her body as if he'd used his hands. "You can't possibly imagine how much I want you."

As much as she wanted him. She wasn't alone in this obsession. As terrifying as it was to have her secret revealed, she wasn't the only one anymore. *He* felt the same things. The tension stretching across her chest had the slightest give, but for one issue. "How did you know about tonight?"

"I know about Courtesans." Not a single muscle on his face twitched. His gaze didn't flinch or flicker.

Once again her body froze, time suspended. He knew of Courtesans. It still didn't make sense. How could he have connected all those dots? She jerked a thumb at the stand-in. "*He* told you that's where he came from?"

The courtesan stood there, arm still anchoring her to him, fingers brushing her breast, and let Hunter field the questions.

"I received an anonymous voice mail to come to the office that night, and I recognized the woman's voice."

Isabel. She was the only one. "How could she do that?" Devon shook her head. It was a violation of the trust clients placed in Courtesans, in Isabel herself. She preached confidentiality. "I'm her client."

"You're her friend." Kenneth tucked her hair behind her ear.

That would be how Isabel thought. Devon was no longer a Courtesans' patron; she was Isabel's friend. Isabel had never considered Hunter off limits once they were both divorced. Business and pleasure *were* separate. Instead of supplying a fantasy, she provided what she believed Devon truly wanted: the *real* Hunter, not a stand-in.

"It's a gift she wanted to give you." Kenneth turned her chin to Hunter, forced her to look at her CFO, her employee, the man she'd lusted after for months. "Tell him you need it," he murmured.

She couldn't breathe. Hunter captured her with the blueness of his eyes. Her gaze dropped. He was big, hard, filling out his slacks. His arms were still bronzed from yard work in the summer sun. His chest beneath the fitted polo shirt was muscled, tantalizing. A lock of dark hair nudged down onto his forehead.

"It's your choice, Devon. I asked Isabel to tell me the next time you were with him." He didn't say Kenneth's name or look at him. "I'll leave now if you ask me to. I don't want you to feel coerced." He took one step, a hand out, like a man trying to reassure a frightened animal. Then he smiled, a devastatingly sexy smile that melted her and drenched her panties. "But I *need* this," he said, undermining her desire to be pissed as hell. "You have no idea how badly."

Despite another's arms around her and his hand on her breast, Hunter was the only man in the room. She'd ponder how he'd tricked her tomorrow. She'd deal with Isabel's definition of friendship later. Maybe she wouldn't give a damn later.

Because, God help her, Hunter was everything she'd dreamed of for the last year. Kenneth was right, *this* was everything she wanted.

Everything times two.

"Stay," she whispered.

8

HUNTER'S HEART DAMN NEAR JACKHAMMERED THROUGH HIS CHEST. "We need a glass of wine to celebrate."

Devon stared at him wide-eyed. Now that she'd agreed, she'd freaked herself out, but he knew her well enough. Once she said yes, she meant it.

He uncorked the bottle, a sweet dessert wine she favored. He poured, drank deeply, the sweetness caressing his throat as he swallowed, topped off again, then filled the second glass, and set the bottle back in the ice bucket.

She stood within the courtesan's hold. Without letting go, the man propelled her forward, deeper into the room, almost as if he were presenting her to Hunter, and it somehow made the moment hotter. Slipping his hand beneath the fall of hair at her nape, Hunter held the glass to her lips. "Drink."

She sipped. He didn't force her to take more than she wanted.

"Now taste me," he ordered. Blood rushed through his veins.

His hand a guide on the back of her neck, she rose slightly on her high heels, tipping her head back. Finally, after ten years, her mouth touched his.

Holy Christ. He drowned in her scent, in the sweetness of her lips. She licked him first, along the seam, entreating him to open.

He wanted nothing more than to devour her. She tasted sweet like the wine, fresh like winter air, and the hot spiciness of feminine arousal intoxicated him. He took her tongue deep, then forced a retreat and took her mouth. Her nipples hardened against his chest, and he felt the imprint of a male hand as the courtesan teased her breasts.

He'd never done a threesome, never thought he'd want to share, but watching her that night had done something to him. He wanted to see as well as do. He wanted to watch her be tasted as much as taste her himself.

Kissing her, he stole a hand between them and worked her other nipple. She moaned and writhed, rose high on her heels to wrap her arm around his neck, and consumed his mouth as if it were the spoils of war.

Together, he and the courtesan drove her closer to ecstasy, then, as if telepathy existed, they pulled back at the same moment, leaving her frenzied, bewildered, wanting, craving.

She blinked, focused, glanced from him to Kenneth and back. Her chest rose and fell. She licked her lips. "Which one first?" she whispered.

The courtesan tossed his jacket on a chair, stripped off his tie, and undid his shirt to the third button. Moving behind her, he bent his knees, holding her hips and grinding his pelvis against her ass. "You don't have to choose. We can both play at once." He raised his eyes to Hunter's as he rocked against her. "I suck your nipples, he licks your pussy." She moaned for them both. "He fucks you, you suck my cock. It's interactive. Nobody gets left out."

She laid her head back on his shoulder and pierced Hunter with her gaze. There was no coercion; she wanted this, she knew what she was doing. He reached inside her bodice and cupped one bare breast, flicked the nipple, then bent close to lightly bite the turgid bud.

"Hunter." She moaned. He'd heard her say his name exactly like that before. With the other man's mouth on her pussy, then his cock buried inside her. His name, not Kenneth's. Her pleasure enflamed him.

He rewarded her, taking her nipple deep, sucking.

"Plea—" She cut off.

He glanced up. The courtesan held her chin, devouring her mouth. She arched and squirmed between them.

"Lift her dress for me," Hunter demanded.

Kenneth tore himself away, grabbing the velvet on both sides and tugging it up over her hips. Hunter palmed her. The way she looked at him, direct, no wincing, tightened his chest. Her mouth, bare of lipstick yet plump and red from Kenneth's kisses, turned him inside out.

"Your panties are damp," he whispered.

"You make me wet." Not "you and Kenneth" or "you and the courtesan," but him. Just him.

He stroked her through the damp scrap of fabric, then raised his hand and scented her on his skin. "You smell good."

"She tastes even better," Kenneth said.

For a moment, it pissed him off the man had been there first. His boiled blood. Just as quickly, he ratcheted back to simmer. Without Kenneth, he wouldn't have this at all.

Caressing her once more, he held her gaze. "Have you ever had two men before?"

She shook her head.

"I've never shared with another man, either."

Kenneth laughed wickedly. "You two don't know what you're missing."

"We're going to make you feel so fucking good," he promised her.

Her eyes darkened, pupils dilating, and her panty crotch dampened beneath his touch. "You've never said *fuck* before," she muttered.

He barked out a laugh. "Oh, I've said the word."

"Not to me."

"You're too much of a lady for the normal use." He moved away from her heat and hooked his thumbs in either side of the thong's elastic. "But tonight, *fuck* is exactly the right word."

"Yes," her voice a mere breath.

This may be his only time with her. Tomorrow, she could force them back to their usual roles, coworkers, colleagues. He wanted a night she'd never forget, so she could never forget him this way, a sexual way.

He slid down her body, going to his knees before her. She was gorgeous, a pretty, plump, trimmed, and suckable pussy visible through the sheer black thong.

"Hold her skirt up for me."

"Yes, sir," Kenneth quipped.

"I love the garter and stockings." Hunter traced one lace top with his tongue. Her skin was fragrant with a sweet lotion, smooth and soft. He glanced up. "Do you always wear stockings and a garter belt under your business suits?"

She shook her head.

"From now on, you always will. I want to sit there knowing what's under your clothes."

She blinked. He could feel her wanting to fight the demand. Devon didn't take orders, she gave them. Yet finally, she nodded.

He rubbed his nose against her mound, breathing in her spicy, sexy scent. She wore the black thong over the garter belt for easy removal. He drew down the high-cut confection slowly, over her hips, her ass cheeks, then rolled it down in front to reveal the barely there thatch of trimmed blonde, then the plump lips of her sex.

"She's got the prettiest pussy," Kenneth said from above.

"Yes," Hunter agreed.

Devon snorted. "A pussy isn't pretty."

"You poor woman," Kenneth groaned.

"A woman's pussy is a beautiful thing. And yours," Hunter added, "is one of the prettiest I've seen." He wasn't particularly adventurous, he hadn't done a lot of screwing around, so it wasn't as if he had hundreds to compare or that he'd ever really stopped to notice before, but Devon inspired him. He kissed her pubic bone for emphasis. "Beautiful," he murmured.

"Whatever." There was a note there that belied the offhand word. She was pleased.

Sliding the thong down her legs, he lifted one foot, then the other. He held the satiny scrap to his nose, memorizing her lush scent before handing the panty to Kenneth for a repeat performance. All the while, her gaze heated.

"I want to touch you first," Hunter murmured.

"Okay." It was clear in her low, husky voice that she wasn't used to being told what would happen every step of the way.

He wasn't normally so vocal, yet it enhanced the pleasure, prolonged it. In case it never happened again, he wanted the night to last forever.

He caressed her butt cheek with one hand and slipped his index finger between her folds. She inhaled sharply as he grazed her clit.

"She likes it," Kenneth interpreted the sound. "She wants more."

"Give her more," Hunter said, concentrating on his own play. "Pinch her nipples." He looked up to find her gaze on him, eyes ablaze with desire as Kenneth rolled and plucked the tight beads. "Visualize," he told her in a low voice. Four hands to pleasure you, two mouths, two cocks." He caressed slowly, gently, sliding over the nub of her clit, wetting his finger. She swallowed. "Give her some wine," he ordered. "She's parched."

Kenneth grabbed a glass from the table, holding it to her lips for a long swallow of the sweet drink. Then Kenneth drank deeply, handing it to Hunter. The sensuality of sharing wasn't lost on him as the cool wine slid down his throat.

He immediately put his tongue between her pussy lips, touching her while his mouth was still cold.

"Oh." She gasped, ended with a moan.

Her juices were as sweet as the wine. She writhed against his mouth, and with one brief glance up, he saw the courtesan had taken control of her nipples again, working them, pinching. He'd once been told a woman's nipples had a direct line to her clit. With her parted lips and lowered lids, now it was fact.

He spread her pussy, gaining better access, and worshiped the erect bead of her clit with his lips and tongue, sucking, licking, caressing. Her body pumped and grinded, begging for more without words. Kenneth crooned to her, hot, sexy words that heightened her fervor.

She cried out. "Hunter, please, stop, I'm going to come."

"We want you to come," Kenneth said. "All night long."

She tangled her fingers in Hunter's hair and pulled. "Not yet, I'm not ready yet."

He eased away with a last lick.

Her breath came fast and hard, and her eyes shone as she stared at him. "It's too fast," she whispered, "too soon."

He felt an accord with her. He and the courtesan were still dressed, she was the one exposed with her dress tugged up to her navel. They hadn't even made it past the table, and here he was taking her standing up.

Hunter smoothed the velvet dress down over her thighs, then rose to cup her face. Capturing her lips without asking, he forced entry inside her mouth, tasting her tongue, swirling, tangling, her body pressed tightly between his and Kenneth's, a hard cock at her belly, an equally stiff erection at her spine. He pulled back, laced his fingers with hers, and guided her to the sofa.

"Bring the wine and cheese, Kenneth. Put it on the table."

The guy was a courtesan; he didn't mind being the lackey.

Standing by the coffee table, Hunter ran both hands down Devon's arms. "Undress me."

She blinked. She was not the CEO in the boardroom or the executive at the head of the table. She was a woman, and tonight she was his.

9

DEVON HAD UNDRESSED MEN BEFORE. SHE'D JUST NEVER UN-
dressed Hunter. She'd had men give her oral sex, really good oral
sex, but they weren't Hunter, the object of her obsession. Truthfully, she'd never been obsessed before. Never allowed it. Hunter
was different, she couldn't help herself. That's why she'd stopped
him from making her come. It was too fast. She needed time to
savor, time to process, time to make sure she never forgot one single moment of it. Because it could never happen again.

"Your shirt or your pants first?" she asked.

He smiled. She was fast becoming addicted to that smile.
Kenneth's wasn't the same, though she couldn't pinpoint how
or why.

"Take off whatever you want." Hunter had a way of looking
at her, too, his gaze penetrating deep. She'd felt it at work, yet it
had so much more fire tonight.

"I want your chest." Hair or no hair. Like Kenneth. Or not.

He held his arms out. "Go for it."

She tugged the polo shirt from his slacks. Kenneth flopped
down in the armchair to watch, one of the wineglasses in his hand.
The other, her lipstick prints on the rim, he'd set on the coffee
table along with the fruit platter, a handful of condoms, and a

bottle of lube. Kenneth had certainly come prepared, but then he was a courtesan, after all.

Devon slid her hand beneath Hunter's shirt, her fingers making contact with his warm skin, and forgot all about the stand-in. Sliding up his sides, she pushed the material to his armpits. *Oh. Oh my.* A dusting of dark hair arrowed up from his navel and covered his pecs. She brushed her hand over the soft mat. Not too much, not completely bare, perfect.

"Arms up." He did as she said, and Devon pushed the shirt off. Hunter finished the action, tossing the red polo at Kenneth.

He laughed, batting it aside. It wasn't Hunter's laugh, she clearly heard that now. "You guys are too damn slow," he complained. Rising, he popped the buttons down the front of his dress shirt and at the cuffs, shrugged out of it. A nice chest, but he didn't have quite the breadth of Hunter's. He unbuckled his belt, shoved his pants to his ankles, and toed them off along with his shoes.

Kenneth was unapologetically hard, letting out a sigh of relief as if the pants had been constricting his blood flow. "That's better." Lounging on the sofa, legs spread, his cock jutting high, he waved a hand at them. "I'm ready for the show." He drizzled wine on his cock, hissed in a breath, then stroked himself, a bead of pre-come oozing from his cockhead.

Her heart beat erratically. Sex permeated the air, dizzied her. She'd never watched before, never been watched.

Hunter tilted her chin toward him. "Are you sure you want him here for this?"

"Yes." She wanted two Hunters. Her hand to his belt, she pulled it free, slipped the button on his slacks, grabbed the tab of his zipper, and tugged it down. Unlike the stand-in, Hunter wore briefs, the tighty-whiteys outlining his cock.

She felt him hold his breath as she slid her hand through the open zipper to cup his sex. "You're huge," she whispered.

Hunter exhaled sharply.

From the couch, the stand-in snorted.

She glanced at Kenneth. "You're pretty darn impressive, too."

"Thank you, my dear." He reached down with one hand to squeeze his balls, and his cock grew another inch. The man turned masturbation into an art form.

But Hunter was Michelangelo's *David*.

All at once, she shoved both hands inside Hunter's slacks and pushed everything down, going to her knees to pull off his shoes and socks as well. His clothing strewn across the carpeting, he stood gloriously naked, his cock bobbing in front of her face.

"I'm not gay or anything," Kenneth said, "but that's one helluva cock you've got there."

For the longest moment, Hunter stood silent, staring at the other man. Then he laughed. "I guess I should say thank you."

"I want to see Devon suck it. Watching a woman suck another man's cock gets me fucking hot." Kenneth no longer played his Hunter role. He'd somehow mussed his hair so that it stood on end, and without the suit, it was hard to see the resemblance she'd found so marked.

"Suck me for him," Hunter urged, his fingers brushing the hair back from her face. A droplet of pre-come beckoned even as he said the words.

"I've never really liked oral sex much," she mused. Sucking Kenneth that night had been fine because she imagined it was what Hunter would have liked. She'd wanted to please him as if he were Hunter. She raised her gaze. "But I want to suck you, Hunter. I want to taste you."

She recognized the irony of being on her knees before him. In the office, she was the boss, he was the employee. Here, their roles were completely reversed.

He fisted his hand and held his cock out to her like an offering. "I'm all yours."

Who was the taker and who was the takee, the woman on her knees or the man begging? She'd never picked up the nuances before, the power in a man wanting your mouth on him.

She understood all about power.

Licking away the drop of pre-come, she closed her eyes. "God," she whispered, as if she'd tasted something sacred.

"More," Hunter murmured.

She circled her tongue around the plum of his cock, then closed her lips on him and sucked. He rewarded her with a groan and another drop of sweet juice. Taking Hunter in her mouth made sucking cock a ritual. Her pleasure was in his taste, the salt of his come, the sweet of his skin, the hardness of his flesh. And in *his* pleasure. She glided her lips down as far as she could go. He filled her mouth, yet there was room to hold his base tightly in her hand.

"My balls." Need edged his voice.

She cupped, rubbed, squeezed the sack gently as she sipped and sucked his cock. This was Hunter in her mouth, her hand, his taste on her tongue. That alone made her dizzy.

She let him fall free, ran her tongue down his shaft, then sucked one nut into her mouth.

"Fuck." He groaned, fisted his fingers in her hair.

She sucked the other nut. His legs trembled. His head seemed to fall back boneless on his neck, breath sharp and harsh through his nostrils. When she took him in her mouth again, he was harder, thicker, the veins throbbing.

Devon thrilled to the knowledge that she'd done this to him.

"Don't let him come yet."

She jerked, Kenneth's voice startling her. She'd forgotten they weren't alone.

The velvet of her cowl caressed her nipples. Hunter's come tantalized her tongue. The sound of another man's voice as he watched them made her wet.

Hunter cupped her cheek and slowly slipped from between her lips. "Suck him for me. I want to watch while you *know* I'm watching."

Her mouth watered. Hunter ordered, and she obeyed. She wanted to do anything he asked. She needed him hot, hard, and aching as she did to another what she'd given to him moments before. Her emotions about it were all jumbled, what she *should* feel versus what she actually felt. It should be awful to be shared, like a sex object instead of a woman. To be told what to do. A normal woman would be angry he'd tricked her. Yet everything about tonight excited her. Relaxing all the inhibitions, letting go of the need to control. The freedom *not* to have to make a decision. Yet feeling the power of it all, too. Such a seductive dichotomy.

There was only one word to say. "Yes."

Hunter held out a hand as if she were a queen and helped her to her feet. "A sip of wine first." He put the glass to her lips as she drank, then swallowed from the same spot. Setting it down again, he shoved the coffee table farther from the couch and led her to Kenneth as he reclined against the cushions.

Hunter pushed her to her knees, then hunkered down behind her, draping her body with his, lips at her ear as he whispered, "I want to watch every moment." His voice made her creamy. "Take him," he urged.

When she held Kenneth, she couldn't feel the difference, but it came as she slid him between her lips. He was still thick and large, but she didn't have to stretch as wide, and her mouth came closer to his base. His taste was salty-sweet; Hunter's was simply more. Hunter himself was more.

Behind her, Hunter groaned his appreciation as he raised her dress over her butt. A heated touch, a warm breath, he kissed her high on her hip before he trailed down the crease of her buttocks. Entering her pussy with his thumb, he stroked a finger over her clit.

Lord. She sucked, and her body moved of its own accord, pumping, forcing Hunter to fuck her with his hand. Kenneth moaned and arched, shoving his cock deeper down her throat.

"Christ, that's hot, baby." Hunter crooned encouragement to her. "You're so fucking wet." And more. "I love the sound of his cock in your mouth. Tell me how it feels." The last was directed at Kenneth.

"Ah shit, man, she sucks so fucking hard on the tip, it feels like she's sucking my soul out."

"Yeah," Hunter whispered.

Devon figured it was a good thing.

"Make her do that thing to my balls," Kenneth pleaded in a strangled voice.

Hunter circled her clit. "Lick his balls, baby. Suck them into your mouth. Make him crazy."

She was crazy with sensory overload, Hunter's body surrounding her, his fingers in her, on her, slipping, sliding, his scent in her nose, his taste lingering on her tongue, melding with Kenneth's.

She nibbled down the outside of his cock and licked the tender flesh of his sac.

"Harder," Kenneth begged.

She sucked him inside her mouth, swirled her tongue against his flesh. He arched and cried out.

Hunter pulled her off, holding her hips, his fingers damp with her juice as he nipped the side of her neck like a lion anchoring his lioness. "I want to fuck you like this."

She wasn't even naked yet, and she didn't care. "Yes."

"Say my name."

The courtesan had said that when it was a game. Now it was real. Her pussy clenched with need. "Please fuck me, Hunter."

"Hold on to Kenneth's thighs, but don't suck him."

She did as she was told while Hunter grabbed a condom from the coffee table and donned it, his fingers brushing her backside. Grabbing the bottle of lube, he coated his cock and drizzled the warm liquid down her butt crease, soothing it into her flesh until it heated.

"Oh." She wriggled, the sensation intense.

"Nice?" he asked, rubbing his cock against her opening.

"Yes."

"Yes, what?"

He wanted his name. She had to give it to him. "Yes, Hunter, I love it."

He eased inside her, slowly, an inch, then another. So big, so thick, filling her. She squeezed Kenneth's thighs, her nails sinking in. She didn't even realize until he groaned, arched, and wrapped his hand around his cock to stroke himself as if he liked the small pain.

Hunter began to move, and oh, my, *God*, it was good. His broad length found her G-spot like a homing device. The tip of Kenneth's cock bobbed in front of her, the crown purple with need. He stroked faster, harder, his hand twisting, engulfing, retreating. Hunter tossed him the lube, and he drowned his cockhead in it.

Devon hung on to his thighs as Hunter leaned low over her, thrusting higher, shoving her closer to Kenneth's cock.

"Christ, you're tight." Maybe because she'd never had children. "I love the feel of your pussy, Devon." He seduced her all over with words just as he had while she sucked Kenneth. "I've dreamed about this," he whispered, "I've jerked off envisioning it, I need it. Fuck, Christ, I've wanted you." He put his finger to her clit and combined with his cock on her G-spot, she lost her mind. He throbbed inside her, pulsed, stretching her walls as her body jerked.

Without his prompting, she gave him what he'd asked for earlier, his name. "Oh God, Hunter. Fuck me, Hunter, I need this, Hunter, Hunter." His name over and over as she trembled with release, a never-ending sensation that seemed closer to heaven than she'd ever gone.

10

HE FELT COMPLETE. IT WASN'T A GUY TYPE OF NOTION, YET BURIED inside Devon, his cock still pulsing with an out-of-this-world climax, it was the only rational thought Hunter had.

She lay with her face practically in Kenneth's lap, breathing hard yet otherwise unmoving. Hunter stroked away the hair covering her face, kissed her temple. "Devon?"

She mumbled unintelligibly.

He'd fucked her but he hadn't wanted her to suck Kenneth at the same time. Because he wanted that for himself, to witness Kenneth filling her, drink in her moans of pleasure, watch her body jerk and shimmy with orgasm. All while his cock was in her mouth. Perhaps the idea had been born the night he watched Kenneth take her on her office sofa. Come to think of it, there was no *perhaps* about it.

"Have you ever had a man in your pussy and a cock in your mouth at the same time?" He glanced at Kenneth. The guy wore a big smile.

She stirred. "You told me not to suck him," she said.

Kenneth tipped her chin. "What he's saying, sweetheart, is that he wants me to fuck you while you suck his cock."

She glanced back at Hunter, her eyes midnight blue and questioning.

"I want to watch how good he makes you feel. When I fuck you, I can't think, much less watch your face." He pumped slightly inside her, his cock not as hard after the climax, but still erect. It would be no time at all. "I want to see your pleasure." Like a drug high, he needed to relive the emotions of that night, the first time he actually allowed himself to see Devon. "Let him make you feel good," he urged.

"Order me to do it for you," she whispered.

In ten years, he'd never told Devon to do anything. When they were peers, they'd exchanged ideas. As her CFO, he suggested a course of action to her. She always made her own choice, her own decision.

There was the key. Devon was turned on by someone else being her decision maker. He'd never have guessed it, but hell, he'd give it to her the way she wanted it and get off on the role-play himself.

He pulled from her delectable pussy, stripped off the condom, tossing it in the trash by the desk.

She turned her head on Kenneth's lap to watch his every move. He'd come not five minutes ago, but this side of Devon set his cock raging again.

"Stand up," he told her.

She braced herself on Kenneth's thighs and pushed to her feet. Her dress, now resembling crushed velvet, slid down to cover her thighs.

He tipped his head. "Shall we have you naked or dressed to fuck him?" He stroked his chin thoughtfully. "Dressed. That'll be sluttier."

Her eyes sparkled. He marveled that this was the same Devon

Parker he'd known for so long. She looked softer, gentler. She'd always been womanly, feminine, yet for tonight, she'd lost the hard edge she was capable of. Fuck if it didn't make his head spin with desire.

"Hand him a condom."

She grabbed one from the table. Kenneth ripped open the package and rolled the latex over his erection, then bathed himself with lube.

"Now how do I want to see it?" Hunter mused aloud.

Peaking above the neckline of her dress, her nipples were tight buds, the areoles a deep, aroused shade of rose.

"Ride him backward," he ordered, "your back to his chest."

Kenneth shifted on the couch, sitting upright against the back cushions. He patted his lap for her. Devon straddled him, knees bent, legs spread over his cock. Her pussy glistened with her juices.

"Slowly," Hunter directed. "I want to watch him enter you an inch at a time." He wasn't sure he'd survive it. Holding out a hand, he simply said, "Lube," and Kenneth laid the bottle on his palm. He coated his fingers. "I'm going to put this on you." The liquid warmed his skin. It would drive her higher.

She blinked as he trailed one finger over her clit and down to her opening.

"Do you like this, Devon, my touch on you while his cock is so close to your pussy?"

"Yes."

"Yes what?"

"Yes, Hunter."

Fuck, she was hot. He might very well be the one who went crazy. He rewarded her with two fingers inside, lubing her. She squirmed, her eyelids fluttering.

"You loved fucking and sucking Kenneth in your office, didn't you?"

"Yes," she whispered, her eyes mere slits, open only enough to see him.

"You loved saying my name while he fucked you."

"Yes, Hunter."

"You're going to love fucking him now because I told you to do it."

She moaned as he slowly pumped her with his fingers. "Yes, Hunter."

He withdrew, sliding slowly across her clit. "Fuck him for me." He tipped her chin up. "And watch me the whole time."

"Hunter," she whispered, as if saying his name now was total acquiescence. Taking Kenneth's cock in hand, she rubbed him in her lubed pussy.

Hunter sat on the coffee table to watch, legs spread, arms braced behind him, cock rising.

Kenneth's hands on her hips guiding her, Devon took the head of his cock inside, squeezing slightly.

How had it come to this? she wondered, enjoying the freedom from decision making, then sucking, and finally allowing a man to make her fuck another for him. This wasn't what she'd envisioned at all. Yet it was so damn hot, she couldn't imagine doing anything but what he demanded. Hunter's eyes ate up the sight, mesmerized, his cock hard, flexing involuntarily against his belly. He told her what to do, yet she had the ultimate power over both men. Such an intense mixture of emotions. Her eyes wanted to close with the feel of hard cock inside her, yet she forced them open to savor Hunter's deep gaze.

A sigh slipped from her as she fully seated herself, Kenneth's cock deep. He flexed inside, and she groaned.

"Fuck him slowly," Hunter murmured, nostrils flared like a racehorse, his eyes dark.

She steadied herself with hands on thighs, knees tight to

Kenneth's. Her muscles worked, making the pleasure that much more intense. She was wet, never more so, the sound of it filling the room along with Hunter's harsh breath.

He stood. "Suck me."

The order made her hot, a fresh rush of cream inside her. Hunter put his hand to the back of her head and brought her mouth down to his cock, immersing himself in her.

"God, yes," he whispered.

She felt the power a submissive must experience when she has her master by the balls. She is told what to do, yet he is a slave to what she gives him by that very compliance.

She rode Kenneth and sucked Hunter, taking them both. Kenneth's fingers bit into her hips, forcing her to a faster pace as Hunter fucked her mouth. The room heated and steamed, the sounds of their sex bouncing off the walls, the moans, groans, the cries, the scent of come and her own juice, the smell of healthy sex, and Kenneth's shout, the spurt of his climax inside her, his cock throbbing.

"Fuck," Hunter gritted out. "Devon. Jesus. This." He pushed deep, jerked, cried out her name, and filled her mouth with his come.

She held his hips as she might a delicate cup she drank from, and her own orgasm struck with the first taste of him on her tongue.

She returned to herself with the insistent nudge of Kenneth's cock inside her. Tears had leaked from the corners of her eyes, her temples damp. She'd slumped to the side and found herself cradled in Hunter's arms.

Held by one man, another's cock still inside her, Devon opened her eyes, and for a long moment, it felt as if she were looking at the tangle of limbs from above. An out-of-body experience.

She had fucked and sucked her CFO. And loved it. "Hunter."

He must have heard something in her voice. "Don't say a word," he said into her hair, then pulled her fully across his lap, and Kenneth fell free. "Be with me and don't think." ·

"I was only going to say it was good, Hunter."

"Liar," he chided, because of course she was going to start overanalyzing it tomorrow when they flew back home, and Monday when they saw each other in the office, she'd already be regretting.

Kenneth rose, muffled around, his footsteps padding over the carpet, followed by the rustle of clothing, the chink of his belt buckle, the squeak of the chair as he sat to put on his shoes.

That's what courtesans did, they left at the appropriate time. His envelope had been under the fruit platter. He would take it as he left. She didn't say *thank you* or *good-bye*. The door closed, and there was only Hunter's warm body against hers and his breath sweet across her hair.

"Let's go to bed," he said.

She was afraid to get in a bed with him. What if she never wanted to get out again? "I don't think—"

He cut her off. "Don't think. This is still tonight, not tomorrow." He gathered her in his arms and carried her to the bedroom, setting her amid the bedclothes she'd neatly folded down before the evening began. Quietly, gently, he undressed her.

He didn't make love to her, he didn't fuck her. He simply held her until she slept.

Nothing in her life had ever been as perfect.

FUCK. DAWN WAS FAST APPROACHING. HE ONLY HAD A COUPLE OF hours of darkness left. *Tomorrow* would be here when the first rays of light stretched across the green grass of the golf course. Even now, he heard the sprinklers chunking rhythmically outside the window. He didn't have much time.

Hunter held her body flush against his, her skin warm and fragrant with exotic perfume and hot sex. Tonight had surpassed his wildest dreams, not just about Devon, but *ever*. With the morning light, however, she would morph back to CEO Devon Parker.

He didn't know how to hold her longer. Maybe he shouldn't even try. Maybe they were meant to have only this one fantastic night.

Except that he'd had a taste, and like drinking a magician's elixir, he'd been bewitched. He'd controlled her tonight, but tomorrow, he'd have no hold. Devon Parker, CEO, wouldn't give it to him.

Damn if he wouldn't have the last say, though. One last thing for her to remember when she was alone in her bed.

He shifted. She rolled to her back. Dipping down low over her belly, he stroked her. She squirmed, her legs falling apart. Hunter traced her delicate pussy lips. She was still wet from the night. Her body jerked slightly when he found her clit, then she sighed. Slowly, lingeringly, he dipped inside her, wetting his finger, sliding back out to circle her clit. She arched, sucked in a breath. He played her. Her skin heated, and her nipples peaked. She moaned, spread her legs, giving him total access. Last night when he brought her to bed, he'd noticed a stash of condoms on the side table. She'd left nothing to chance. Neither would he.

He hit a sweet spot, and her lips parted in a soft moan. She twisted, rolled her head on the pillow. Her eyes remained closed. She could have been asleep, dreaming a wet dream. He was hard as a piling, and it was no dream. Grabbing a condom, he left her long enough to don it. She writhed on the bed, touching herself.

He entered her. She was wet enough to take him without the lube. Christ, she was tight, like a young woman, her body supple, her skin smooth and soft as if she were ten years younger. Holding her hip, he filled her slowly. She pushed her head back into the pillow, arched into his thrust, and when she sighed this time, he imagined his name in the sound. Deeper, higher. Her body clenched around him, milked his cock, squeezed. He pulled her legs to his waist, changing the angle, heightening the penetration. She clutched his arms and let him take her.

She came hard, tightening around him, first her pussy, then her legs, then her arms, as if she were trying to take every last inch of him inside. He bit the tender skin on the side of her neck when he climaxed, and swallowed every sound, every groan, every cry that wanted out.

There were no words, she never opened her eyes. When it was over, she rolled to her side, wriggled into the pillow, and sighed as if she'd never woken up. He didn't believe it. Tomorrow, they'd both pretend the night had never happened. Monday, it would be a distant memory.

11

DEVON DIDN'T KICK HIM OUT IN THE MORNING, NOR DID SHE invite him into the shower with her. She simply smiled and said, "I'll nip in the shower, pack up, then meet you in the restaurant at seven-thirty," as if she hadn't just climbed out of the bed in which he'd made love to her. Denial. She was going to pretend last night hadn't happened.

The lock snicked a moment after she closed the bathroom door. Hunter had no choice but to leave. If he wanted to keep any freaking dignity at all.

Over breakfast in the dining room, she discussed the follow-up e-mails and letters they should compose and distribute.

In the car, she studied the scenery.

The silence grated on his nerves. "Let me explain to you about Courtesans."

She continued to peruse the view out the passenger window, pine and evergreen sprouting up as the elevation rose. "There's no need to explain. I understood last night."

At least she'd finally mentioned last night. "I used them a couple of times," he said, "but it's been a year or more since then."

She turned then, her gaze as flat as the ocean on a windless day. "I use them all the time. They're convenient and you don't wake up with them in the morning."

Fuck. That was harsh. "I know you're capable of being a bitch, Devon, when you feel someone needs to be put in their place." She'd just never done it to him before.

A beat of silence. "I apologize. That was uncalled for. We had last night, and there's no need to rehash anything. You've used Courtesans, I use them, Isabel took matters into her own hands, we had a great time, end of story."

"Isabel didn't say anything about you or Courtesans when she called me. She didn't reveal your secret."

She puffed out a sharp breath, indicating the true state of her emotions. "How was it not revealing my secret to tell you to come to the office? How was it not revealing a connection when she told you my plans for this weekend?"

"I called her and said I needed to be there when you met with him again."

She didn't flinch. "She told you. Which broke her confidentiality agreement with me."

He had no answer for that.

"I don't care about that, Hunter. I enjoyed it. The whole episode was very hot."

He wondered if she could say it any more coolly. "I agree."

"Isabel still has to provide an answer to me."

"I'm sure she will." He'd never asked Isabel her reasoning. He didn't care. He'd simply wanted in on Devon's fantasy. Now he didn't want out.

It was clear Devon wasn't giving him a choice.

She pulled her purse closer, fingers on the snap. "Will it make you feel better if I ask her right now?"

He cast her a sideways glance. She was treating him like . . . a spurned lover. Trying to placate, offer an explanation for something that ultimately wasn't going to change.

He should have stuck to peeping on her. It was easier. Christ. He laughed out loud.

"What's so funny?"

"You wouldn't get it." Hunter waved a hand. "Sure, call Isabel. I'd love to eavesdrop."

"Fine, whatever." Devon fished her phone from her purse. She had Isabel on speed dial, not for Courtesans but because Isabel was supposedly her friend. It disturbed her that her *friend* had made an executive decision of that magnitude. Yet at the same time, she wouldn't have given up last night with Hunter for all the gold in Fort Knox. She'd tasted so many new things: two men—two men like Hunter, no less—a cock in her mouth and one in her pussy, four hands caressing her. The intangibles, such as being watched, which was exciting all on its own, the seduction of having her will usurped, the thrill of knowing Hunter's taste, his scent, the shape, size, and texture of his cock, the saltiness of his skin, the softness of his chest hair beneath her fingers. So many things, the best of which was waking in the middle of the night to his hands on her, then his cock in her. She'd always sent her courtesans home before she slept. When she was married, she'd slept like the dead, and her husband never would have woken her for sex. Hunter gave her those things, the memory of which she would cherish.

She couldn't very well castigate Isabel for giving her all that. Then again, she couldn't allow her friend to believe it was fine to take liberties where Devon's career was concerned. Mixing business and pleasure was not part of her personal code. Hunter needed to hear it, too.

She hit Isabel's speed dial.

"I thought you'd be calling," Isabel answered.

If Hunter hadn't been listening, she'd have lightly gotten her point across, perhaps something like, "Naughty, naughty, Isabel," or "I've got a bone to pick with you." Hunter's presence called for something more serious.

"We discussed this and I told you my reasons for wanting to keep it on a fantasy level. You ignored me."

Isabel kept her tone equally steady. "You two are perfect for each other."

Devon snorted. "Don't tell me you've known who he was all along." Every time Devon poured her heart out regarding her obsession with Hunter, over all those long dinners. Now *that* would really piss her off.

"I didn't realize it until you showed me his picture."

Devon remembered the odd look at the Halloween store. "You should have told me right then."

"You'd have freaked and called the whole thing off."

"I like to make my own decisions, Isabel." Except that the thing she'd enjoyed most about last night was *not* having to make a decision. She glanced quickly at Hunter to see if he noticed the irony. He studied the road ahead, his fingers tight on the steering wheel.

"I thought you needed help to see what was right in front of your nose."

"Don't help me, Isabel." She heard the edge in her voice and didn't like taking her turmoil out on Isabel. Even if she was justified. "What I mean is—"

Isabel cut her off. "You're right. I overstepped the bounds of our friendship. It won't happen again."

A friendship should have no bounds. That's what friendship was all about. Damn. She never should have started this with Hunter bearing witness. There was no choice but to see it through, though, or risk permanent damage to her relationship with Isabel. "I know you care about me, and you did what you thought was best, but talk to me about it next time instead of doing it behind my back."

"I apologize sincerely, Devon." A sharp inhale of breath. "I'm so used to interpreting what my clients really want that I forget to ask my friends."

"You're forgiven. I have to go, we're getting on the plane." She used the little white lie. "I'll call you later."

She disconnected after Isabel's good-bye. "There," she said, snapping her phone closed. "Issue resolved. We don't need to analyze it ad nauseam. It's over and done, back to work tomorrow."

"Yeah." Hunter tapped his fingers on the steering wheel. "Work as usual tomorrow." He removed his sunglasses from his shirt pocket and slipped them on. The day was cool, but bright. Devon did the same.

Since the only sound was the rhythmic swoosh of the tires on the road, she once again stared out the window.

Well, that was the end of that odyssey. Kenneth wouldn't work out again. He had his own name and his own personality. And he wasn't Hunter.

Despite what Isabel thought, business and personal still didn't mix any better than oil and water.

The problem? Now Devon *knew* what she was missing.

AFTER A FULL WEEK, THEY WERE BACK TO NORMAL. THEY DIDN'T mention that night, didn't eye each other as if they remembered every second, every breath, every touch.

Yet Devon woke each morning, her pussy wet, her nipples hard, her breath fast from some erotic dream about him, his taste and the feel of him inside her. As with Kenneth, her vibrator no longer did the job.

Monday at five in the evening, seven days, thirty-six hours, and thirty-five minutes since Hunter had last touched her, Devon snapped the clasp on her briefcase. She had a few errands to run before her dinner meeting with Joseph Stewart, potential S&M veep. She winced at the title; it reminded her of Hunter and his bawdy sense of humor. Joseph had worked at Simcoe Systems with her and Hunter. She'd heard through the grapevine he was looking, and she'd always been impressed with his work ethic and his astuteness at reading people.

At the restaurant, the maître d' led her across the elegant, quiet, dimly lit dining room to a secluded booth in the back corner. Her heart stopped. Wham, bam, splat. She couldn't breathe for the life of her.

Seated next to Joseph, Hunter nursed a drink. She almost asked him what the *hell* he was doing there, stopped herself only a second away from freak-out.

"Hey, Devon." Joseph rose, stuck out his hand, shook hers hard. He'd always had a strong grip. Mid-fifties, he'd lost all the hair on the top of his head, whereas the last time she'd seen him his hairline was merely receding. Never on the thin side, he'd gained a bit more middle-aged weight.

"Hope you don't mind that I gave Hunter a shout." Joseph jerked a thumb at him. "I figured getting two opinions was better than one, and it works both ways."

"Not at all." Seated in a booth, she was forced to sidle around next to Hunter. He smelled good, all male and woodsy. She wanted to ask who really called whom, but that would be bringing Joseph's actions into question. "Two heads are better than one." Somehow it sounded like a double entendre. Hunter's lips twitched.

For the next hour, they talked about GDN, the product lines, the customer base, the sales and marketing needs, the executive staff, what the company could bring to Joseph, and what Joseph could bring to GDN. He was sharp, he adored his kids and wife, and he wasn't about to seduce his administrative aide.

During dessert and coffee, his cell rang. He glanced at the caller ID. "It's my wife." He smiled, and Devon admired that he didn't glower as many men would have. "I'll be back in a minute." Climbing out of the booth, he flipped open his phone and was already talking as he headed to the back of the restaurant and the restroom hallway for privacy.

"Did you put him up to this?" she asked once Joseph was out of earshot.

"You mean being interested in the job?" Hunter gave her a singularly innocent look she didn't buy for a minute.

"You know I mean inviting you to this meeting."

"No."

"No what?"

Hunter sighed. "He called me after you spoke to him and wanted to know the scoop. Like I would have done. Like you would have done."

"So you invited yourself."

He raised his eyes heavenward. "No. He suggested it."

"And you agreed."

An edge crept into his voice. "Of course I agreed or I wouldn't be here. A week ago you would have invited me yourself."

"A week ago we hadn't—" She cut herself off.

"Fucked?" he supplied for her ever so politely. "You wanted to pretend it never happened, and I've played by your rules. *You* won't let things get back to normal."

Damn him. He was right. He'd treated her exactly the same as he'd always treated her. She was the one who was afraid to sit next to him in a quiet, elegant, romantic restaurant, the conversations hushed, the servers in crisp white shirts and black pants, candles flickering on the white tablecloths. Devon took a deep breath. "I'm sorry. I jumped down your throat for no reason."

Something sparked in his eye. She'd made another double entendre. It seemed inevitable with Hunter. She was fixated on sex whenever she was around him. And when she wasn't.

Joseph returned but didn't take his seat. "Sorry about that. Emergency at home. I need to take off."

"I hope everything's okay," Devon said politely.

Joseph grinned. "Emergencies are subjective. Nothing life threatening." He spread his hands and his smile. "Thanksgiving coming up, family arriving. *Everything* constitutes an emergency when my wife's mother is coming." He parted his suit jacket to pull out his wallet.

Devon waved away his money. "We're courting you for the job, we'll pick up the tab."

Joseph nodded his appreciation. "I'm very interested."

"So are we. HR will be in touch to have you interview with the rest of the team."

He saluted, turned on his heel, and left Devon alone with Hunter and every single one of her desires for him.

Hunter wasn't the one who scared her. She was afraid of herself.

12

HUNTER HAD SWORN TO HIMSELF HE WOULDN'T TRICK HER AGAIN, but Joseph Stewart had called him a little after five. Devon was already gone when he went looking for her.

Their waiter topped off their coffees and took away the signed credit card slip.

Alone again, Hunter said, "Stewart's a good man."

"He'll be a good fit for the team." Devon toyed with her coffee cup.

"We need to talk."

She pursed her lips. "We *are* talking."

"About *us*," he stressed.

She glanced around. "Please keep your voice down."

She was trying his patience. The dining room wasn't full, the tables were spaced a decent distance apart, and theirs was in a dim back corner. No one could even see them well. "Move closer so you can goddamn hear me."

He was surprised when she did what he told her to do, sidling around the booth's circular seat. Her fear of being overheard was greater than her terror of him.

"There is no *us*." Her voice was quiet yet emphatic.

It was taking advantage, but he shifted even closer, his thigh scant inches from hers. "I don't like that you're jumpy every time we're in the same room."

There were several things in that statement she could have taken umbrage with. "*You* don't like it?"

This was the Devon he knew so well, but he sure as hell liked the one who obeyed his orders. "Yes, *I*"—he gave her the same emphasis—"don't like it. You don't look me in the eye. You disagree with every suggestion I make. In short, everyone in the office knows there's something up." There definitely was something up beneath the table. She'd driven him crazy during dinner, how she smelled, the way she tasted her food, laughed, talked. Even arguing with her didn't tone down his reactions.

"That is completely untrue. I've been totally normal."

He eyed her. Her breath came fast, breasts rising and falling beneath her suit jacket, her nostrils slightly flared like a highstrung filly, her mouth tense. "*Normal* like you are right now?"

She stopped long enough to take stock of her body's reactions, then sighed. "I'm nervous about it."

"Because you're in denial." He expected her to get all uppity again.

Instead, she leaned forward, elbow on the table, her cheek propped on her fist as she looked at him. "Denial about what?"

What was she looking for? A dissertation on how great it had been? A declaration that he wanted more? She needed a demonstration.

"Denial about *this*." He slid his hand along her thigh, between the buttons of her skirt. All day he'd been looking at those buttons. Calf length, the skirt buttoned down the front, but Devon had left it undone from the knee down, her legs encased in black stockings. He'd wondered: garter belt or panty hose, thong or bare?

He had to know.

"What are you doing?" She didn't stop him as he undid two more buttons, sliding higher up her thigh.

"What I've wanted to do all day long. You wore that skirt to make me nuts."

"I didn't." Her gaze was unfocused, bewildered.

He slipped another button loose. "I can smell you. You're wet, aren't you?"

"Yes." The word wasn't even a whisper, just a parting of her lips.

Their coffees were full, the check had been processed, their waiter was taking care of other patrons. Hunter pulled her thigh over his, spreading her legs, opening her to him. The long white tablecloth would cover the view of whatever he did. "You've been dying for me to touch you all week, haven't you?"

She swallowed. "It's all I've thought about."

Triumph sizzled through him. He quested higher, finding the top of her stockings. Question one answered, garter belt. His gaze locked to hers, he didn't miss the slight widening of her pupils. "It's all I've thought about, too. Let's stop denying. We're going to do it again."

She didn't answer.

Higher. He found her pussy, bare, wet. She shuddered. Question two out of the way. "I'm shocked," he said. He hadn't expected Devon to go pantiless at work.

She drew in a long breath, let it out. "I suppose subconsciously I was hoping for something like this." She spoke without a smile. The realization didn't please her.

Turning toward her, he leaned an elbow on the table, hiding the movement of his arm from view. "I would have fucked you any time you asked."

She closed her eyes, opened them. "I know."

It was written all over her. That was the problem. Hunter wasn't going to let it stop him. He would make her see how good they were together. How much better they could be.

Sliding between her folds, Hunter found her clit unerringly. Devon almost bit her lip in ecstasy. It felt as if she'd waited forever. Wrong time, wrong place, but she couldn't help herself. Hunter's fingers made her wild. She couldn't have stopped him if the waiter came over or the world threatened to end with an earthquake. She needed this, had to have it.

Devon sank her fingernails into his forearm. He stroked, rubbed, and circled her clit slowly. Heat rose to her face. Her lips parted on puffs of air. His eyes were intensely blue, hot, burning. For her.

"You're going to come for me."

She whimpered, it was so good. So wet, he slid and slipped in all her moisture, faster. The shockwaves started in her belly, shimmying out to her fingers and toes, shooting back to the very spot he touched her. The world quaked around her. She didn't cry out or faint. She trapped every moan and sound inside. The effort only increased the magnitude, six-point-five, seven-point-oh, eight, then off the Richter scale.

She came off the high to find her fingernails biting into her palm, a tear at the corner of each eye, and Hunter buttoning her skirt. She wondered what he would have done if it been a tighter fit with no buttons. Have her hike it over her hips?

Lord. What had she been thinking?

Ah, of course, she hadn't been thinking at all. That's how it was with Hunter. She straightened her hair, pushing back a tendril that had fallen loose. "I'm not usually a do-anything-anytime-anywhere kind of woman."

"If you accept that this thing is unstoppable and simply go with it, you wouldn't have these flare-ups."

She laughed, not because he was funny, but more that he was completely correct. She was out of control because she wouldn't give in. If she was discreet about it, then she wouldn't spread her legs for him in the middle of a restaurant during the dinner hour. Even if it had been one of her hottest fantasies come to life. "I am not going to get caught with my pants down like Garrison did."

"Totally different situation. He was cheating on his wife and stupid enough to let her figure it out. You and I are both single, consenting adults." He picked up her hand.

She removed herself from his grasp and shifted away. "We don't touch in public."

"I agree."

"No flirty sexual innuendos at work."

He made a rude noise. "Spoilsport."

"No more than once a week, no spending the whole night with each other, and we don't tell anyone what we're doing."

His eyes flattened, and his shit-eating grin disappeared. "So we're just fuck buddies."

"I prefer *friends with benefits*."

Jaw tensing, he stared at her. "I don't."

"Take it or leave it." She sounded like Devon Parker, bitch with brass balls, and tried to soften it. "This is to protect both our careers."

"I'm not worried about my career." His voice was stone cold.

That got her back up. "Because you're the man, and men can do whatever they want, whereas a woman has to be careful. Any hint of scandal can ruin me."

"May I hark back to the fact that Garrison, a *man*, got himself fired?"—she winced at Hunter's reminder—"I don't intend for that to happen to either of us. Besides, no one cares about consensual adult activities between single people."

Why was he being so difficult? "Fine. People don't care. We're still doing it my way." She grabbed her purse from the seat beside her. "I'm leaving. You should wait five minutes."

"For Christ's sake, as far as everyone here is concerned it was a business dinner."

"Hunter." That's all she said and began shimmying out of the booth.

He grabbed her arm, held on. "When we're in the bedroom, everything's *my* way." His eyes glittered like glass.

Devon shivered. In the bedroom, she'd do whatever he said.

GODDAMMIT. FRIENDS WITH BENEFITS WAS NOT WHAT HE WANTED. Hunter watched her go, then waited the requisite five minutes. Why the fuck was he doing what she told him to? They were adults. If they wanted to have a relationship, they could goddamn well have a relationship.

He'd learned something huge in the last month. He wanted Devon Parker in his bed all night long. He wanted to call her on the phone in the middle of the day and talk dirty. He wanted to take her to dinner, to a movie, for a walk in the park, and out with his kids to a Sunday football game. He wanted her without all the secrecy and sneaking around.

He wouldn't let her paranoia stop him.

SHE'D MADE A DEAL WITH THE DEVIL. TRUE TO HIS WORD, HUNTER didn't make a single sexual innuendo, not even a sly remark. In fact, he rarely smiled at all. But he didn't forget what she'd promised him.

Tuesday night, he called her cell at eight-thirty. Without even a hello or asking if she was busy, he said, "Saturday night. You will come to my house at seven o'clock. You will be wearing a coat, high heels, and nothing else." He disconnected before she could answer yes or no.

Her parents lived in Monterey. She was going down only for Thanksgiving Day, and would be back in town for the weekend. She didn't have to ask for his address, having attended work-related social gatherings he'd hosted at the house.

She'd be there wearing nothing but a coat and high heels.

Wednesday, she planned on letting everyone go by noon for the holiday. The crew was small anyway, as many chose to take the week off.

The auditors, however, had their full contingent. Five minutes before noon, there was Larry the Lead taking up space in her doorway. She really could not like that man.

"Larry, what can I do for you?"

He advanced into her office. "Got a question for you." Tall, lanky, his hair overlong, he reminded her of Jughead from the old Archie comics.

The thought made her smile. "Sure. Have a seat."

He mistook the smile, because he grinned back, all teeth. A bit like a shark. She'd cottoned on to the fact the beam on his face had nothing to do with pleasantries. He didn't sit. Instead, he laid an expense report on the desk and slid it toward her. "Can you tell me what this is?"

Oh yeah. That look was definitely a shark moving in for the kill. Devon rose. She wasn't taller, even with her heels, but she sure as hell wasn't going to give the kid the advantage of towering over her while she sat.

"This is my expense report. What are you doing with it? I just turned it in last week."

"We're obligated to review significant activity that takes place between year-end and the 10K release."

"This isn't significant."

He laid another expense report side by side with hers. Hunter's. "You, the CEO"—he tapped her report—"and Mr. Nash, the

CFO"—he tapped Hunter's—"at a resort in Sedona together is significant."

Shit. They knew. Despite her worst fears realized, she would *not* fold in front of this man. "It was the annual investors' conference. We attend every year. It happened to be in Sedona this year." Her tone said "big deal."

He yanked her page from the desk, stabbed a finger at the hotel line. "You didn't put Saturday night on your expense report." He tossed it back down, and she caught it before it flew off the edge. He grabbed Hunter's and stabbed again. "Here we find Saturday night charged to the company."

She let her brows knit together—"Yeah?"—and leveled him with a look that clearly said she considered him an imbecile.

He jabbed both expense reports at once. "You flew home on the Sunday flight together, Ms. Parker." He gave her a smirk. "So where did you spend the night on Saturday? In Mr. Nash's room?"

Her heart was beating so fast she thought she'd faint. Guilty, guilty, guilty flashed before her eyes like a neon sign. *Never let them see you sweat.* She was a CEO because she was capable of controlling her emotions.

"Consider carefully, Ms. Parker," he said, a slight sneer on the title. "Fraternization between executives could be an indicator of collusion."

She laughed and was sure, *absolutely* sure it didn't sound hysterical or guilty. "I do not understand your desire to find fraud." In exact opposition to his stabbing and jabbing, she gently picked up her expense report and gingerly flipped to the attached hotel bill, drawing a finger along the last line. "You'll see right here that I paid for Saturday night with my personal credit card since I took a spa day. Mr. Nash, on the other hand, spent the day with an interested investor and therefore his Saturday night stay was a company expense."

Larry the lead asshole's face muscles drooped, his shoulders slumped. "Oh."

"If you were to properly peruse all the attached documentation, you wouldn't need to take up my time with idiotic questions." She handed both expense reports back to him. "Please make sure you return these to the appropriate accounts payable clerk when you're done with them."

At least three inches shorter than when he entered, Larry took the reports, backed away, his eyes brown like a whipped puppy.

"Close the door on your way out." She did not sound pleased this time.

With the snick of the latch, she slumped into her chair.

This was what Hunter didn't understand. They might be single consenting adults, but they were under scrutiny. They'd skated on this one because Larry the lead asshole hadn't done his homework. Next time, he wouldn't make the same mistake. Though they'd done nothing illegal or unethical, they were under his puny microscope, and any "fraternization" would land them in hot water. Devon would not destroy their careers for the sake of a little nookie.

Saturday night at his house with only high heels and a coat was not an option. It could never be an option.

13

"YOU'RE JOKING, RIGHT?" HUNTER COULD ONLY LOOK AT DEVON AS if she'd lost her mind. Or rather, her mind was completely unfathomable to him. "Larry didn't find anything wrong because we didn't do anything wrong."

Devon had closed his door and now paced the length of his office. Her suit was a staid gray, severe lines, nothing feminine, and her hair was pulled back so tightly it must be giving her a headache. "It's the *appearance* of impropriety," she insisted.

"There is no *appearance*." He almost threw up his hands in exasperation. They twitched at his sides. "We went to a conference the way we've done several times in the past. We weren't extravagant, and we didn't bilk the company. There's no wrongdoing."

"We had sex," she whispered on a hiss.

"Yeah. It was fucking great. We're going to do it again." He took a step closer and lowered his voice. "And again."

"That's what I'm trying to tell you. We can't *ever* do that again. If someone finds out, it'll ruin us."

He rounded the end of his desk, yanked back his chair, but didn't sit. "I don't have time for this lunacy." He had to pick up the kids from their mom's in half an hour. He was taking them up to Santa Rosa for Thanksgiving with his parents. They'd return

Friday night, and the kids would do a mock Thanksgiving with their other set of grandparents over the weekend. He and his ex-wife traded holidays. One year he spent Christmas with them, the next year Thanksgiving. It sucked, but it was the only way to work it.

"What about Garrison?" Devon kept riding him.

"Garrison's wife called his boss and every other member of the fucking management team." He tried deep breathing, but it didn't stop the harsh note in his voice. "*That's* what sunk him."

"The issue was doing his subordinate."

"No, it was his wife's big mouth." Even Devon had said that the day she had to ask for Garrison's resignation. "You're twisting the story to support your paranoia."

"I am not paranoid." She gave him her best bullish look.

It was possible he was being a prick, wanting what he wanted without any compromise and regardless of her feelings. "Okay, you're not paranoid. Let me say it this way. I want you. I want to have sex with you. I want a relationship with you. We are two consenting adults, and no one's going to give a rat's ass. So either you want this"—he paused for impact, eyes on hers—"or you don't."

She bit her lip. Devon Parker never bit her lip indecisively. If she voiced one more doubt— "It's a bad idea."

"I've made a decision." It might appear to her that the words were spur of the moment, split second, but it was something he'd known had to come eventually. Maybe he'd been putting it off because of her, but it was the right move, the right step. "Here's my solution to our mutual problem. Joseph gave me a heads-up that Richardson over at National Dynamics is getting his ducks in a row to retire."

She looked at him as if she couldn't connect the dots.

He connected them for her. "My career path does not end at CFO. I intend to rise to CEO, chairman of the board, et cetera. It's time for me to climb another rung of the ladder." He knew the people and the products at National Dynamics. The company was a good fit for him and vice versa.

Devon blinked, then her jaw dropped. "You're going to desert me in the middle of this horrendous audit with Larry the lead asshole nipping at my heels?"

"No, Devon. I am not going to desert you." Didn't she know him better than that? Didn't she have more faith? He wanted to reach across the desk between them and shake some sense into her. "By the time any move I make gets squared away, the audit will be over, the 10K will be filed, and the proxy will be approved and off to the printers."

She shot out a breath, spread her hands. "What about the public offering?"

"It's a year away, Devon. Plenty of time for anyone else to come up to speed. Plus we've got a good accounting team, things can almost damn well run themselves."

"I can't believe you would do this over sex." She folded her arms beneath her breasts.

He gritted his teeth, his jaw tensing. "It doesn't have to be this way."

"So this is an ultimatum? Either I have sex with you the way you dictate it or you leave?"

He leaned both fists on the desk and glared at her. "Jesus Christ, Devon, that's not what I mean at all, and you fucking know it. I can't hang around forever as CFO just to bolster you."

She glared, eyes narrowed. "Oh, so now I can't do it on my own."

He took a deep breath because if he didn't calm down, he'd

say something they'd both regret. "We've got an opportunity here to have a relationship, and at the same time I can meet my career goals."

She swallowed. "Whether you leave or you stay doesn't make any difference," she verbally slapped him. "We can't have a relationship even if you've left the company. If we did, they'd go back and consider our actions together while you were still here." She wasn't going to budge an inch.

He pointed a finger at her. "Here's how I see it. You don't want to admit there's any solution at all." He pulled back, buttoned his suit jacket. "I'm going to be late picking up my kids. You cogitate on it, Devon. If you're at all interested in making this thing between us work, you will be at my house on Saturday. If you don't show"—he stretched his lips in a smile without humor—"I'll understand you're indifferent to it. Quite frankly, my opinion is you're afraid of having a relationship. You got burned in your marriage, you've played around with your courtesans ever since, and stayed as far away as possible from any commitment or obligation."

She shook her head slowly, lips parted, eyes wide. "I can't believe you're doing this."

"What I want is a decision. I have never known you to have such a problem making a simple decision."

Her lips flattened, the lines of her body militant. "You want a decision, fine. Here it is. I won't be there on Saturday. But I wish you all the best of luck in your new job." *This* was the Devon he expected. Pushed, she'd come down hard.

She stalked to the door, opened it, and left it open after she passed through. No dramatic slamming. That wasn't Devon's way.

Was it her? Was it him? Were they both uncompromising? He couldn't quite comprehend that he'd ended a ten-year relationship with a woman he admired over a sex thing that had lasted little more than a week. Sex really fucked things up.

* * *

SEX RUINED EVERYTHING. HE'D LEFT HER, JUST LIKE THAT, WITH AN ultimatum, be there or forget everything. Devon gritted her teeth. She was right, and this had nothing to do with her fear of relationships or her anger with men. She was not angry at her ex-husband. They were different, she accepted that. She was over it. She loved her courtesans. They were easy, went home when you told them to, and didn't ask you to have inconvenient sex. Everything was on her terms.

None of them made her feel the way Hunter did. That was the whole issue.

Devon stuffed her briefcase with paperwork she'd look at over the holiday weekend. She'd spend Thanksgiving with her parents, but with so much to do she'd return the same night.

Damn Hunter for mentioning her marriage. He was wrong. He was pushing too damn hard, using every trick in the book.

Then she heard herself, the number of times she'd said men were too much trouble. She'd said something very much like that to Courtney O'Brien all those weeks ago, that she preferred courtesans because men were a pain in the ass. *Was* she afraid of relationships? No. No way.

Worse, though, was Hunter's other accusation. Had she been holding him back?

The argument kept her awake much of the night, it haunted her along the highway during the hour and a half drive to her parents', and it made her uncharacteristically quiet with them once she got there. She and her dad barely shared two sentences in the TV room after her initial kiss on his cheek. Her father seemed to have lost much of his joie de vivre after he retired several years ago.

"Mom, here, let me get that for you." She walked into the

kitchen to catch her mother pulling the oversized roasting pan from the oven.

"I've been lifting the Thanksgiving turkey out of the oven for the last sixty years," her mom said. "And I'll be doing it for at least another ten."

Devon had simply taken it for granted that what her mom said was true. "That pan is heavy."

Her mother tsked, independent as always, and set the pan on the bread board. That's where Devon got her independence from. Her mom was eighty-three, and still took her daily three-mile walks, worked two days a week at the church thrift shop, delivered the Sunday altar flowers to hospital patients. The list went on and on. Yet, she'd seemed more fragile over the last few months, moving more slowly. Devon had been rushing at such a fast pace herself that she'd seen the changes without actually taking stock of them. She visited most holidays, but that didn't amount to more than five or six days a year. Monterey was only an hour and a half down the freeway from Silicon Valley, a three-hour round trip. She drove that distance three or four times a month for business meetings, yet she couldn't manage to see her parents more than six days a year. It was unfathomable. It had to change.

"I should get down here more often for a visit," she said.

Her mom poked and prodded the turkey, squeezed the legs with a piece of paper towel to see if the bird was ready. She didn't believe in meat thermometers. "Honey, we understand you're busy. You're a big CEO. You take after your dad, a workaholic." She threw the paper towel in the trash and wiped hands gnarled with arthritis on her apron. "Look what you've made of yourself. Your dad and I are very proud of you."

"My priorities need to change so that I can visit with you and Dad more often."

Her mom went up on her toes to kiss Devon's cheek. She was only four eleven now, and barely came to Devon's shoulder.

"I'm not a workaholic," Devon added.

"It's a term of endearment, sweetheart." Her mother laughed. "Don't try to deny it." She shrugged. "That's you. We accept it."

Devon stuck a fork in the potatoes boiling on the stove. "They're done. Do you want me to mash them?"

"That would be wonderful, honey."

After dumping off the potato water into a pan for her mom to use in the gravy, Devon retrieved the masher from the drawer. Maybe she needed to rethink a lot of things. She'd told Hunter she wasn't afraid of relationships, but were the auditors and Garrison's antics excuses not to have a relationship with Hunter? Her parents weren't getting any younger, but neither was she. She wouldn't be a CEO forever. When she retired, what would she have to fill the place of her career?

She mashed the potatoes as she contemplated, then she set the serving dish on the warming plate.

"Would you get your dad a glass of sherry, dear?" Her father loved his Bristol Cream.

She took the bottle down from the cupboard. Her dad was five years younger than her mother, yet he seemed ten years older. Once he'd retired, he quickly wearied of fixing things around the house and aiding in her mother's charities, and he started a downhill slide, favoring his easychair and the TV on mute. Devon was an only child. She didn't have any kids of her own, so her parents didn't have any grandchildren. Once her father lost his work—he'd been CFO for a large aluminum company—he didn't have anything left to fill the empty space. Just as Devon would have nothing, not a daughter to visit her, not a spouse, not even a lover. Hunter was right. She used her career to avoid relationships

210 · Jasmine Haynes

with men, and she'd relegated him to nothing more than a co-worker. Not even a friend. It was possible she'd screwed up the only chance she had at the best man she'd ever known.

She took a good long look at her mom and decided she wasn't going to screw that relationship, too. "I didn't bring a change of clothes, but I'll spend the night anyway. That okay with you, Mom?"

"Sure, honey." Her mother didn't even look up from the cheese sauce she was making for the cauliflower. She didn't have a clue about Devon's inner turmoil.

It wasn't so easy to fix what she'd messed up with Hunter.

14

AS THE OLD SAYING WENT, HUNTER HAD CUT OFF HIS NOSE TO spite his face. Instead of trying to reason, he'd issued an ultimatum. With Devon, it was the worst thing he could have done.

He'd had a great holiday with his folks and the kids, but the empty Saturday night loomed, made worse by the fact that he was well aware Devon would never give in by arriving at his door. He didn't give a damn about his instructions for nothing but the coat and high heels, he just wanted her to show, to at least be willing to talk. Yet the fact remained, after he left the company, he wanted Devon by his side for all the world to see. Today, despite it being a holiday weekend, he'd called Richardson at National Dynamics, told him he'd heard the news, and they'd made a Monday dinner appointment. This particular opportunity might not pan out, but there would be another. He wanted the career advancement, but the more he thought about leaving, the more he craved having Devon. Everything was open to them once he no longer worked at GDN, but it would be a cold day in hell before he'd make her see that. If she wouldn't give up her work code for her husband, why would she give it up for Hunter? Even if she consented to an affair, he'd moved beyond that. He needed more. He believed she needed more, too, if she'd only admit it.

He poured himself a glass of wine and shot a DVD into the player. Saturday night and he was home alone watching a movie. Truthfully, who was the uncompromising one?

He wasn't even engrossed in the action flick when the doorbell rang. Glancing at his watch, his heart started to pound. Seven o'clock on the dot.

When Hunter opened his front door, he half believed Devon was a figment. She wore a calf-length, cream-colored cashmere coat. Above the coat's lapels, her throat and cleavage were bare. Her heels spiked at least four inches, her ankles delicate, her calves firm, her skin smooth. And all bare.

"May I come in?" Her lips were painted a deep burgundy that suited her coloring, her lashes long, eyes outlined and brushed with a purple shadow that glittered in the porch light.

Dazzled by her, he didn't say a word, just held the door wide.

The high heels tapped on the tile entry as she entered. "Do you need me to prove I'm wearing nothing underneath?" She trailed her fingers over the coat's tie.

"No." He needed to understand what she proved by being here.

She stepped in on him, closer, her sweet, sexy scent intoxicating him. He didn't need alcohol to get him high. All he needed was her.

"There's no stand-in, Hunter," she said, her voice a low, seductive pitch. "Just you. Just me." Her breath was sweet with cinnamon.

Like a starved man cast away on an island for five years, he was dying for a taste of her. In that instant, he didn't give a rat's ass about a relationship, about his career, the corporate ladder he strove to climb, or getting reamed by Human Resources or the auditors for fucking his boss.

"In the bedroom," he ordered. He wasn't going to jump her right in the tile entryway.

"Which way?" she asked.

Devon had been to the house for cocktail parties and business functions, but she'd never gotten the grand tour past the bathroom. He had a four-bedroom house, keeping two for the kids, one for his office, and the master for himself.

"Down the hall"—he pointed—"last door on the left."

Watching her sexy fuck-me heels sink into the plush carpet, his higher brain ceased to function. He wanted her in those shoes and nothing else. Whatever her arrival meant, he'd figure out later.

HUNTER'S BEDROOM WAS MASCULINE WITH CHERRYWOOD FURnishings. The bed's duvet cover was a simple navy, no extra pillows, no extra fuss. The pictures adorning the wall were of his kids. No vases or knickknacks festooned the bureau or chest of drawers, no doilies sat beneath the bedside lamps. Devon turned at the end of the bed and faced him.

In the doorway, he braced both hands on the jamb. His pullover sweater was red, his jeans black and molded to his body with wear. A five-o'clock shadow marred his chin. He was the most handsome man she'd ever seen. It wasn't merely her body involved. He engaged her mind, tugged at her heart. She'd never experienced this immense feeling with a courtesan, the overpowering need to touch, taste, savor. Not even with Kenneth, the stand-in. Hunter was the only man who meant anything, the only one to make her body hum even when he wasn't there.

She was here to tell him that and so much more, but for now, she was his willing slave.

"Drop the coat," he demanded.

She received the same delicious thrill she'd felt in Sedona. Her skin flushed, her clitoris throbbed, and her thighs were wet with her desire. Dropping the coat to the carpet, she stood naked the way he'd instructed, naked in more ways than one. His eyes roved her body, their brilliant blue deepening to midnight.

"This isn't going to be a simple fuck, then you walk out, Devon."

The whisper of words seared her mind. "I know."

"Get on the bed," he directed. "Don't remove the shoes."

"The heels could ruin the bedspread."

His eyes blazed, his voice roughened. "I don't give a flying fuck." The word was a not a curse. It was a promise.

Her breath quickened, blood raced through her veins, and she shimmied backward across the bed.

"I was going to make you suck me off," he said. "That's not enough." He advanced to the edge of the bed. "I need to come inside you. Not in your mouth or on your face or over your breasts."

He braced a hand on the mattress and trailed a finger through her drenched pussy. She gasped, the sensations sharp, shooting up inside her.

"My cock will own you," he murmured. Backing off, he stood, tore his shirt over his head and tossed it, undid his belt. Unzipping was a vision, his cock bulging against his jeans, the unveiling a masterpiece.

"You are so beautiful." She bit her lower lip, entranced by him.

The sweeping look he gave her body was the return compliment. "Spread your legs. Touch yourself."

Leaning back, propped on one elbow, she drew a finger down the center of her pussy, grazing her clit, sliding inside herself to test the heat, the wetness. Returning to her clit, she parted her folds so he could see the plumpness of her sex. She hissed in a breath, her pleasure rising.

"Don't come," he warned. "Just play. Keep yourself on the edge, but don't you dare push yourself over."

He shucked his jeans and stood before her in his true naked glory, cock jutting. He crawled across the bed like a predator, a sleek jungle cat, then went back on his haunches between her knees, pulling her spread legs across the bulging muscles of his thighs. "The drawer," he said, "open it."

She loved every order, every demand. Loved that he made her stroke herself. The sexual glitter in his deep ocean eyes. The heat of his flesh against her. She loved every single thing about this man from his mind to his body to his heart. His gaze made her creamier.

Her clitoris throbbed beneath her slow, sweet caress. She hadn't let up; he hadn't told her to. With this newest command, she leaned over to his bedside table, opening the drawer to discover an open package of condoms and a bottle of lubricant. He didn't offer an explanation, and despite all her courtesans, a bolt of jealousy sizzled through her. In spite of her good intentions, she'd become proprietary about him.

She passed him a packet and the lube. He put on the condom, poured liquid down the crease of her pussy and over the head of his cock, and entered her. There were no preliminaries, yet she was wet and more than ready to receive him. Like the lioness being claimed by her lion. He slammed home and she almost lost consciousness.

Filling her, huge, demanding, he rocked inside her. "Let me tell you how it's going to be, Devon." He thrust balls deep, held still.

She raised her thighs to his hips and locked her feet at the base of his spine. "Tell me, Hunter."

"You are mine." Out, in with another deep lunge, nostrils flared, hot male all the way.

She blinked, her pulse beating at her temples and in her ears.

"Say it," he demanded.

"I'm yours, Hunter." They were words she could never take back. Deep in the heart of her, she didn't want to take them back.

He moved inside her, his cock stroking her G-spot, bringing it to life. She shoved her head back into the pillow and moaned.

"No more courtesans." He branded her with the heat of his body and the command in his words.

She raised her hips to meet his next delicious plunge. At the same moment, he gripped her butt and yanked her to him.

"Oh God." She tossed her head, hair flying.

"No more courtesans," he repeated, grinding against her writhing body.

"Only you, Hunter." She moaned and groaned, undignified sounds, yet she loved letting them loose for him.

He kept up a steady stream of demands as his cock drove her closer to the edge of heaven. "You will dance in my arms, eat at my table, bathe in my tub, and sleep in my bed. You will be my lover."

"Yes, Hunter." Sobs of pleasure flooded her voice and a tear leaked from her eye.

"You'll never fear telling people you belong to me." He came down hard on top of her, buried his face in her hair. "You will love me," he whispered, "because I need you to."

She wrapped her arms around him. "God, yes, Hunter. I love you." It had taken her ten years to recognize it. Afraid to face it when they were both married, afraid to ask him once they were both divorced. It was easier to deny, yet she'd had to have him close, until her obsession took over. The obsession she'd tried to tell herself was only physical and could be managed by a stand-in.

"You will cherish the love I have for you as I cherish yours for me."

The tears fell from her temples into her hair. He loved her. She cried out as his cock rode her sensitive G-spot. "Yes, Hunter." She'd give him anything he asked.

"Say it," he commanded through gritted teeth.

"I love you."

He lost all control, pounding into her, driving her higher, thrusting her over the edge, and she screamed, his name, that she loved him, needed him, would always need him.

Somewhere in the cataclysm, she was sure she heard his voice, his words, "I will always love you."

HUNTER CRADLED HER IN HIS ARMS.

"Can I take the shoes off now?" Devon asked.

He laughed. "Yes."

She kicked them off. He turned her chin, forced her to look at him. "I mean what I said, Devon. I love and accept who you are. I've been an asshole." He smiled. "Not as bad as Larry the lead asshole, but an ass nonetheless. Yet I can't accept some secret affair with you, hiding in corners. There's a way to work this out." He held her tight a moment. "I'm not giving you up for some fucking job."

She stroked his cheek. "I've been unreasonable. Valid points, but I took them too far. You'll make the best CEO, and I'm going to put myself behind my words. Whatever you need."

"I need you to agree that we have a shot." He couldn't compromise on this. "I want a relationship, a commitment. I want you to admit you're mine and I'm yours. That we're not going to hide *us* behind closed doors. I have no clue why I missed seeing how damn good we could be together." He chuckled. "Maybe I needed your stand-in to open my eyes."

She tucked her forehead against his neck and played with the hair on his chest. His cock stirred, but he needed to hear it all before they got back to the good stuff.

"You were right." Her breath brushed his skin. "I always had to be the strong one. If I wasn't, I was afraid everything I'd worked for would be torn away. I was so strong that it did get taken away and my husband left. Yet I went on the same way." She nuzzled him, licked his throat. "I've had the hots for you for months, years even. I thought sex would solve the problem, but the problem is *me*." She gave a laugh that ended in a sigh. "I'm scared of a relationship and a commitment and of getting hurt again. But you"—she trailed a hand down the center of his chest, and his heart pumped harder, faster—"I love you, Hunter Nash. I want to sleep in your bed, wake up in your arms, see you at the breakfast table."

He suddenly felt lightheaded.

"You've spoiled me, Hunter. A stand-in will never work again. You're irreplaceable."

He grabbed her chin, kissed her hard.

She pushed back. "I will say," she added, her voice a sexy drawl, "having two Hunters at once, Heaven help me."

He laughed. "You naughty woman."

"That's not replacement. It's double the fun."

"And double the pleasure," he whispered. "Your wish is my command."

"Oh no, my sweet man." She stretched sinuously against him. "You're the one who gets to command me."

SURRENDER
TO ME

1

HALEY VENTURA HAD CURVES A MAN COULD SINK HIS FINGERS INTO.
Simon Foster wanted nothing more than to worship those curves.
He'd be so damn good for her. And she for him.

Seducing her would have been so much easier if she didn't hate
him.

Strike one was falling in love with her when she was married
to his business partner and former best friend. Not telling her that
said business partner, former best friend and her husband, was
having an affair made for strike two. Strike three, bearing the
news that Artie had died of a heart attack in bed with his lover.
And the strike *out*? The fact that it was Simon's bed they'd been
using. Haley never believed Simon didn't know they were meeting
in his house.

Simon hadn't purged his emotions for her. It simply seemed
shitty to seduce the widow before her husband had been in the
ground a year. Even if Artie had been cheating on her.

Haley's year was up.

Now all Simon needed was a strategy. He didn't usually plan
out a seduction, but Haley was special. He figured he'd only get
one shot, and he didn't want any fuckups.

Maybe a Valentine's Day thing. That was only a month away.

He wasn't the roses, hearts, and romance kind of guy, though. She'd see right through him, and think he was just horny. Simon had to admit he was always horny. Turning fifty sure as hell hadn't reduced his sex drive.

He was considering horniness and Haley as he pulled his truck into Foster-Ventura's parking lot. A contracting company specializing in remodels and insurance work, the guys were in the field most of the time, so they rented only a small suite of offices out of a larger building in Saratoga. The Saturday morning was bright and unseasonably hot for January. Even in the Bay Area.

The real bright spot? Haley's SUV was parked by the front door. The sight gave his heart a kickstart. Haley, an accountant, did the books and all the receivables and payables for the business. That hadn't changed with Artie's death. Now Haley was half owner. Construction was generally slower in the winter, but the couple of weeks of good weather had seen a miniboom for them. They also did demolition work, fires, water damage, asbestos removal. Most contractors didn't have the proper asbestos licensing, which gave Foster-Ventura a leg up on the competition. As for Haley's schedule, it was year-end for them and all the accounting work that went with it. She'd always been a hard worker, something he'd admired from the moment she came to work for the partnership twelve years ago. He should have snapped her up right away, but he hadn't even thought about settling down back then. So he missed his chance. Because Artie was ready for her.

Water under the bridge. He climbed out of the truck, slammed the door, and took the three steps to the front entrance in a single bound.

The door was locked—kinda strange—and the front office was empty. He rounded Haley's desk. She'd refused to move into Artie's vacant office, preferring to stay out front. Simon figured she didn't want any more reminders than necessary. Artie's office was strictly storage space now. Colored fish swam across her computer monitor. A quick glance into the break room showed she wasn't there, either. She must have run across the street to the Starbucks. He only had a couple of things he wanted to check, so instead of booting up his own machine—in his office—he tapped Haley's keyboard. She wouldn't mind. They had a LAN and shared files.

She had a spreadsheet up, but he popped over to her open Internet window. It took long moments for his brain to catch up with his eyes. Mostly because he couldn't imagine Haley looking at . . . ads for casual sex?

No way, that wasn't her. She was a sexy lady, but sort of prudish. Simon had closed his ears to the stuff Artie said. He'd refused to discuss their sex life. As a couple, they'd been his best friends. At one time. Before Artie starting cheating. And Artie's excuse? Because Haley wasn't a firecracker in bed. Didn't want to be. It even embarrassed her.

The ad's subject line emblazoning the screen wasn't prudish at all.

You know you want to be my sex slave.

Holy hell. She was into bondage?

He couldn't help reading, mesmerized. It wasn't a coarse, crass advertisement for dirty sex. It was a story. He read as if he were seeing straight into the deepest, darkest corner of her heart and soul.

Be prepared. You will do whatever I say and love it. I call as I am walking to your door. Unlocking it, you wait for me. On your knees . . . wearing nothing but a pair of sexy high heels. I close the door, stand in front of you, and undo my jeans. Taking my cock out, you slip the head into your mouth. I run my fingers through your hair as I caress your throat with my cock. Your tongue is all over the shaft and head and it keeps me hard. Finally I pull out and order you to give me your hands. I shackle you with wrist cuffs, pull you close, and place a thin leather collar around your neck. With my finger through the ring in your collar, I lead you to your bed, sit you on it, and fasten both wrists to the headboard. You belong to me now. I kiss your lovely neck, lick your abundant breasts, and suck on your luscious nipples. You feel my hard cock between your gorgeous, sexy legs. I pinch your pretty skin, leaving a few nice red marks so you can remember me after I'm gone. Something you can look at in the mirror the next few mornings when you finish your shower. Kissing and licking my way to your hips, I move between your legs, placing my mouth over your beautiful pussy lips. You shudder with delight. I suck on the inside of your thigh. I love the taste of you. Holding your chin in my hand, you are my captive, my slave, and I remind you that it is the weekend. No one is expecting to hear from you until Monday. You are mine to do with as I wish for days.

Do you like this fantasy so far? Do you need to hear more? Do you want to meet me and be my slave?

Simon's cock pulsed as if it had a life of its own. And fuck, it wanted Haley. If she'd been standing in front of him, he'd have bent her over the desk and taken her hard and fast. Maybe he would have tied her hands first. Christ, maybe he'd have tied himself up in her long, silky, touchable chestnut hair.

Flipping to her Internet history, he checked out the other ads she'd viewed on the site. Three of them, all submissive or bondage stuff from being cuffed or tied to spanking, phrased eloquently enough that it didn't seem a man could have written them. Or they were written by men who understood how to tap into the feminine psyche. Sexy and titillating without being crude and obscene, they appealed to a woman's need for fantasy. He was about to click into her e-mail to see if she'd answered any when he caught himself. What the hell was he doing? Spying on her. Invading her privacy.

Simon had never done that. Never gossiped, never spied, never stuck his nose in someone else's business. That code had ruined his relationship with Haley. As much as he'd thought Artie was an ass for cheating, he'd never felt it was his right to tell Haley. Somehow, because of his feelings for her, to tell felt self-serving.

Yet here he was, spying on the very woman whose trust he hoped to regain. It was a momentary lapse into thinking with his dick. He was better now. Simon shut down all the windows he'd clicked on and maximized the spreadsheet file the way she'd had it.

Fuck. No little fishies swimming back and forth. She'd realize he'd seen something. It couldn't be helped. He was above changing the screen saver wait time to hide his dirty deeds. However, if they came back on before she returned, he'd call it providence. In the break room, he poured himself a cup of coffee, then headed down the short hall to his office, passing the restroom.

And stopped. He'd heard a sound. There it was again, more clearly identifiable as a . . . voice. Inside the restroom. A wave of heat rolled through his body, and the dick he'd gotten under control flared to life, hot, hard, and ready for action.

She moaned again. Oh yeah, that was a moan and that was Haley. They had a receptionist who came in three times a week, but not on Saturdays. Saskia was a sixty-five-year-old grandmother. He couldn't picture her locked inside the restroom moaning like that.

Mother of God, he could picture Haley. He couldn't *stop* picturing her. She was masturbating. She'd gotten hot looking at Internet sex ads and run to the restroom to relieve the built-up tension.

The moans came faster, sharper, louder. She cried out, and there was no mistaking her voice. She came forever. Simon thought his head would explode. Or his dick. His breath caught, his heart pounded, and his palms began to sweat.

If he stayed there much longer, he'd start jerking off in the corridor. The break room seemed the only logical place to hide out. If he went to his office, she'd guess he'd heard. His hands were shaking as he added another spoonful of creamer and stirred. The coffee was now milk-white and undrinkable, but he drank anyway to keep himself busy. No woman had ever affected him this way, and he'd had more than his share of ladies. He'd truly cared for a good number of them, too, but only Haley had ever made his heart pound like this. Maybe it was because he'd been her friend without fucking her. She was, in fact, his only female friend. Or at least she had been until Artie's frantic lover called him to say she thought he'd died in Simon's bed. Simon had called 911, but Artie was already dead from a massive coronary.

Haley never forgave Simon. As his punishment, he'd started craving her more. Now he had the hot memory of her moans and cries to add to his storehouse.

He had to make his move soon. What if she answered one of those ads?

A smile grew on his lips, like the Grinch when he decided to steal Christmas. What if she answered an ad?

And it was his?

DAMN, SHE'D NEEDED THAT. WHEN HALEY TURNED FORTY A COUPLE of months ago, her hormones started raging as if she were a teenager. All she thought was sex, sex, sex, cruising personal ads to titillate herself. Pathetically, she'd even started carrying her vibrator in her purse.

Haley washed off the instrument of her perversion, put it away, tucked her long-sleeved tee into her jeans, and buckled her belt. She hadn't been with a man since Artie'd died. He'd destroyed her faith, in men, and worse, in herself. She didn't want to put herself out there again. Ever. Lord have mercy, though, her libido had gone into hyperdrive. How long till menopause? Didn't a woman lose sexual desire then?

She'd lingered this morning, longer than her usual quickie, but it had felt so good, and she'd needed the multiple orgasms badly. Might have been better to be more quiet about it, too, but letting go made the climax that much harder. It was Saturday, she had her privacy. Throwing away the paper towel and slinging her purse over her shoulder, she opened the door. Now that she'd satisfied one urge, she needed a mocha in the worst way.

She almost screamed when Simon ran into her coming out of the break room. He was so big, he dwarfed her, tall compared to her five two, with big shoulders and a wide chest. He smelled good, like hot, sweaty sex.

"How long have you been here?" Her skin flushed from head to toe. She'd been so *loud* in the restroom.

He held up his mug. "Long enough for coffee."

She glanced around the doorjamb to the back of her monitor. She couldn't remember what she'd left up on her computer desktop. Not that Simon would bother looking at her PC, but it still left her flustered. She'd been reading and getting hotter and wetter and hornier, then she'd grabbed her purse, with only enough presence of mind to lock the front door, and practically ran to the bathroom.

She backed off to scan Simon's face. Same laugh lines and silver eyes that matched his hair. She'd always thought him handsome. They'd been friends a long time ago.

Then Artie died, and she saw how she'd been lied to.

Why the hell couldn't she let go of the bitterness?

"I'm making myself a mocha. You want one?" she offered. She might be an angry, bitter bitch but she tried to be civil. They owned the business together. Simon had never offered to buy her out, and no way could she afford to buy him out. Artie had left her with a load of debt, credit cards she'd known nothing about. She'd finally gotten a handle on her finances, consolidating, securing a second mortgage on the house to take advantage of the lower interest rate. At least she could sleep at night now. Hmm. Her lower stress level could be another reason her libido had resurfaced.

"Yeah, thanks, a mocha would be great," Simon answered, but didn't move aside. Was there something in that silver-eyed gaze?

Please don't let him have heard.

Finally he backed off, letting her pass.

She shoved her purse far back on the countertop, making sure it was latched shut. Wouldn't do for Simon to see what was inside. Pulling the coffee from the freezer, she then retrieved the milk from the fridge. Odd how she felt about Simon. Artie was the one who cheated, yet she'd felt the betrayal so much more keenly over Simon. He was her friend, he knew about Artie and that woman, yet he'd never told her.

She heated the milk and hot chocolate in the microwave, otherwise the mocha chilled too fast. Steaming wasn't enough.

"Want me to tamp the coffee?" Simon said, almost at her ear.

She gasped. "Don't sneak up on me like that."

"Sorry." A smile lurked. More often than not, Simon was laughing at something. Always good-humored, Simon never seemed to get down or depressed. He took the coffee from her hand. The muscles of his arms bulged as he compressed the espresso grind. She had to admit that with his superior strength, he could pack it harder, which allowed her to steam longer.

Why did that sound sexual?

Her clitoris throbbed. Her breath seemed shallower. Simon was so . . . male. He'd always had this physical effect on her. She might have acted on those feelings way back when, but Artie had warned her, citing a laundry list of reasons. Simon wasn't the settling kind; he thought of women as sex objects; he wanted variety. Simon was a horn dog, as much now as when they'd first met. The difference between him and Artie was that Simon never professed to be anything else. He'd always treated her with respect, too.

Artie had been the charmer—or the snake oil salesman depending on how you looked at it. He brought in the new customers with his fancy talk, but it was Simon who produced the repeat business. He was more low-key, sure, but he got the company into demolition work and on the approved vendor list for insurance companies. That's what saved the firm when the economy tanked. Though she'd only begun to comprehend all these things months after Artie's death.

She'd allowed Artie to charm her the same as he did everyone else. She'd believed him when he claimed he *was* the settling kind.

Sometimes Haley wished she could have talked to Simon about it all. The debts. The other woman. How long had Artie been cheating? Right from the beginning or . . . later? After all the fights about money, after the accusations that she was trying to control him? When?

But Simon had deceived her by omission. She'd lost both her husband and her best friend on the same day, and she could never forgive Simon for betraying her that way.

2

FOR THE TWO HOURS SIMON WAS IN THE OFFICE ON SATURDAY, HE was pleasant, kept out of her hair, busied himself in his office, got her a sandwich from across the street, and ate with her, informing her about events at a couple of the job sites, and generally acting as he always acted. No personal comments or questions. Like her, he was civil. Though she very quickly had come to realize that Simon hadn't allowed Artie to meet in his house, that Artie used his key without Simon's knowledge, she still couldn't forgive Simon for the things he'd kept from her. And Simon had never forgiven her for accusing him of lying and condoning Artie's actions. They simply didn't talk about it, and the business went on. They were polite. Like this morning. Haley decided he couldn't have heard her in the restroom or seen the personal ads on her computer. He would have had *some* reaction if he had.

She did, however, decide it was a bad idea to cruise the Internet at work. The oddest thing happened, though. A day and a half later, when she pulled up one of those naughty ads on her home computer Sunday night, an image of Simon popped into her mind. His arms as he tamped the coffee for her. His ass in khaki work pants as he left to get her sandwich. His deep laugh. His earthy, masculine scent. The heat of his body when he stood beside her.

It was her raging hormones making her notice all that stuff. Artie must be rolling over in his grave right about now for all he was missing. He'd once gone so far as to call her frigid. Honestly, it was their timing that was off. He was horniest in the mornings when she had so many things to do before going to work. Now, she wanted it morning, noon, and night.

Carrying the laptop to the couch, Haley sat cross-legged. Wearing soft flannel pajamas, she sank into the sofa cushions, a glass of white wine on the side table. She clicked on her favorite personals site, then suddenly hung back. Was she getting obsessive with this? She'd never answered an ad. She enjoyed the titillation. A healthy forty-year-old with normal urges—so there, Artie—and no partner to share them with, what was the harm in looking at some naughty ads?

She scanned down until she found a heading she liked, then clicked on the link to read the ad.

Remember how it felt to have your fanny spanked? How the sensation of warmed flesh and the sound of a nice swat goes right through you and makes you crazy. You miss a good old-fashioned spanking. And you can't tell your friends because you're ashamed of your desires. So what is a poor girl to do? Let me help you. If you would like a nice, warm, flesh-arousing spanking, it's my specialty. I will be completely clothed, you will either be naked from the waist down, or in panties with your bum exposed for me to swat. Afterward, you will be able to walk around the rest of the day with that warm sensation of a nicely spanked ass. I have spanked a good dozen girls over the years.

Are you next?

Her clit throbbed deliciously, and the erotic scent of her arousal rose to her nose. She wasn't terribly into the spanking ones, but she loved the way this man wrote. He made her feel his hand on her ass. So many of the ads were plain disgusting. She loved the ones where the writer seduced her with his words.

The next one she clicked open, the guy wanted to chain her facing a wall while he played with her. She would never call herself submissive, but there was something about those ads. Artie claimed she was controlling, but he spent money as if there was an inexhaustible supply. Even before the whole credit crisis came down, she believed in living debt-free, paying the credit cards off every month.

When she found all those bills he'd been making minimum payments on, she'd actually hated him. More than for cheating on her. This was a worse cheat. He'd threatened her very security.

For the last few years of her marriage, she'd craved a real man, not a boy who indulged himself in expensive toys all the time. Part of her wanted to let go and have a man take care of everything, be responsible for everything. She'd felt like she was the parent with Artie, always tugging on his leash. Which was probably why he started applying for credit cards without her knowledge.

Somewhere in all her trials and tribulations with Artie was the appeal of the submissive ads. While she had to obey, she was also taken care of and rewarded with more pleasure than she could imagine. All she had to do was let go of her control. In the safety of her living room, she got wet imagining it.

She'd never actually do it.

Her eye fell on one ad way down the list, its subject line provocative. It was more than twenty-four hours old, but she didn't care about that.

Surrender to me and I will give you everything you need.

She clicked, her skin already heating. She loved the ones with a story format. They hooked her as if a hot sexy voice murmured the story right in her ear.

"Face the wall," I tell you, and you do exactly as directed.

With my foot, I knock your legs farther apart, spreading you wider. "I smell the scent of your hot little pussy," I say. You moan and writhe though I haven't even touched you yet.

I slide my hands up beneath your short skirt. "Bad girl," I murmur, as I find that you aren't wearing panties. That wasn't part of my clothing instructions. "You'll need to be punished for that." I can't resist sliding down the crease of your ass, between your legs, skimming along your dirty, naughty wet pussy. "Have you been playing with yourself?"

"No," you whisper.

"No what?" I stroke your burgeoning clit, making you tremble.

"No, Master, I haven't played with myself."

"Good girl." I ease back out, taste your sweetness, scenting you on my fingers. I contain the moan rising in my throat, but my cock is hard. I want you badly, you can never know how much, but I must maintain the illusion that I am the master and you are the slave, though the reality is I am yours as much as you are mine.

"Hands behind your back," I say.

You assume the position. I fasten the nylon restraints.

"Turn around." I'm only a breath away from your face. I could kiss you, but you have not proven yourself. I know you will. You are dying to give me everything for your reward, to show me how special you are. All you have to do is anything I ask. "On your knees," I say.

You fall gracefully to your knees before me, my cock bobbing close, so close to your lips, beckoning. You swallow. I know how

badly you want my cock, my come, but first you must be punished.
I stroke myself to full hardness, a bead of pre-come oozing to the
tip. "Do you want to taste it?"

You moan. Your eyelids flutter. "Yes, please."

"Please what?"

"Please, Master."

Haley's breath felt trapped in her chest. Wildfire rushed across her skin. She fell into the rest of the ad as if it were her dream man whispering everything she wanted to hear.

Does my story appeal to you? Are you wet reading it? Imagine all
I offer. You will be mine, and there will never be anyone else for
me. I will never tire of tending to your every need. No man has
ever made you feel so special. Surrender to me, be my love slave,
follow my commands, and you will have everything you've al-
ways desired.

Haley clicked the reply link before she could mull over what she was doing.

"Yes, please, I need this," she typed, almost hit SEND, then realized how stupid that was. This was her regular e-mail with her real name. She had another address she used for shopping online, so she didn't get inundated with spam. She logged into that account.

Dammit. The high was gone. The immediacy. She wasn't even wet anymore. Her mind had kicked in and shot her down. Dumping the laptop on the sofa, she reached for a sip of wine. The wine was dry, expensive. She didn't allow herself many indulgences, but a good glass of wine once in a while was another of her sinful pleasures. She savored a bottle, taking a couple of weeks to finish it. Artie didn't have a clue about the art of savoring, and he hated it when she complained that she'd had one glass only to find the bottle damn near empty in the refrigerator door.

"Do you realize how often you think about Artie?" she said the words aloud, to make herself hear them. He'd been dead a year yet everything was still about him. She needed to move on, dammit.

She glanced at the laptop, tapped a couple of times to get back to the e-mail. With a cut-and-paste, she copied the ad's e-mail designation over to her shopping account, then typed the same words.

"Yes, please, I need this."

It was only an anonymous e-mail. The ad was over twenty-four hours old so the guy might not even answer. Maybe he'd already found his submissive. It didn't matter. She needed to get out of this hole she'd dug for herself ruminating over Artie and everything that had gone wrong. A few anonymous e-mail exchanges with a man she'd never meet was exactly what she needed. She deserved some fun in life.

Haley hit SEND.

SIMON'S HEART BEAT RIGHT OUT OF HIS CHEST. HE'D DESIGNED THE ad specifically for her after reading the four she'd been looking at. Pulling them up on his own computer, he'd studied the language, the nuances, then added things he thought would touch a nerve for her. He hadn't truly expected her to answer. Receiving about fifteen hits, he'd weeded out half as being 100 percent not her, a couple even being from men wondering if he liked to dominate males. Five of the others, it had taken one e-mail exchange to figure it out. The other three, he'd averaged four messages to determine it wasn't her.

This one, he could practically smell her need in those few short words. Hers. Only hers. He recognized the e-mail address as one he'd seen her use online.

He dashed off an answer. "Tell me why you need this."

He'd created an account she wouldn't recognize. Before she figured out who he was, he wanted to whet her appetite for what he could do for her. Of course, once he told her, which he would do before they talked on the phone or met, she'd probably never speak to him again. It was a chance he'd been willing to take. He had to get her to see beyond the face she encountered damn near every day at the office, beyond the man she thought had betrayed her. He wanted to get back to what they'd had before Artie turned into an asshole. He wanted that old camaraderie with the added bonus of hot sex. He wasn't a dom in the BDSM definition of the word, but he could give her what she craved—acceptance, love, desire, passion. All the things Artie had never learned a woman needed.

Simon saw her for the jewel she was. If he had to issue a few orders to get her to believe that, he'd do it.

His inbox lit up. So did something inside him.

"Because I'm tired of being the one in control," she wrote.

He saw hints of living with Artie in her statement. Artie had raged about how she micromanaged his life. *Haley's a fucking spoilsport. Why do you need that? Why do you always have to have the best? You've already got one of those, why do you need another?* He could hear Artie's voice mimicking her. He'd never told Artie he was full of shit. Not that Artie would have listened, but it would have shown loyalty to Haley. Because she'd been right, Artie always made her play the bad guy.

"Let me be the one in control." He couldn't fix the things he'd neglected to do over the years, but he would be her future if she'd let him in.

He had only a limited amount of time before she asked his

name or, hope against hope, wanted to meet him. Learning everything he could about her desires was paramount. He dashed off
another e-mail before she'd even answered the last.

"Tell me your deepest, darkest fantasies. The ones you've never
shared. Not even with your best girlfriend."

It could backfire. When he revealed who he was, she could
very well hate him more than she already did. The potential reward was worth the risk.

3

HER SKIN PRICKLED. HALEY RUBBED HER ARMS. SHE USED TO BE normal, standard, even somewhat vanilla sexually. After reading so many naughty ads, she found herself terribly excited by the racy, kinkier ones.

She'd never thought to reveal her newfound interests to anyone.

"I'm afraid." Once she'd sent off the e-mail, she realized it was the epitaph for her life. She wasn't a risk-taker. Another of Artie's complaints. Every decision was based on fear.

The answer was quick to arrive. "Trust me with your secrets."

Haley laughed out loud. How could she trust him? He'd put out a bondage sex ad on the Internet, and they'd exchanged a handful of e-mails. He was nothing more than a dot-com address, for heaven's sake.

Haley slumped back against the sofa cushions, the laptop heating her legs as it rested on her thighs. That was it exactly. He was an e-mail address. He wrote a bondage ad. He wouldn't consider her a freak any more than he'd think of himself that way. He was probably the one person she could tell absolutely anything to and still be completely accepted.

There was one thing she wouldn't do, even on e-mail. "Are you married?"

"Single. Never been married."

Good. She didn't want to be a part of adultery, even on e-mail. Telling him her fantasies was no risk at all. She was already warm and tingly just contemplating it. She thought about asking his name and what he looked like, but that would spoil the image she wanted to create in her mind. If she didn't ask questions, he could remain the perfect man. "Give me a few minutes to write my deepest, darkest fantasy for you."

He was waiting for her, his reply almost immediate. "I'm a patient man if it means getting what I want."

An Artie comparison immediately filled her head, and she thrust it back out. Artie didn't belong here tonight. She wanted to have fun; it had been so long since she'd had hot, sexy fun. She'd never done anything like her deepest, darkest fantasy. She'd never told anyone, either.

Haley began typing.

I lie awake at night sometimes with so many naughty thoughts running through my head. I imagine my commanding, forceful lover tying my wrists to the rails of the headboard, then my ankles to the foot of the bed, spreading my legs wide. He teases me, blowing on my pussy, trailing a scarf over my breasts, making my nipples hard. I'm so wet and ready for whatever he has planned for me. He forces me to do things I didn't think I'd like, but he's never rough, and he makes everything so electrifying. This time there's something different; he doesn't undress but remains fully clothed while I'm completely naked and exposed. It thrills me yet terrifies me, an exhilarating combination. I have no idea what to expect.

Until he opens the door to another man. My whole body stills, my breath catches in my throat. What are they going to do to me? I've never been with two men. My lover tells me he's going to watch while this other man goes down on me. He wants to see me come from another man's mouth, another man's touch. I fear that I'm not enough for him anymore. As soon as the thought flits through my mind, his lips are at my ear assuring me how exciting and hot it will be for him. I'm still afraid, but it doesn't matter what I want because I have no choice but to submit to his will.

Haley stopped in the writing of her tale, her body humming, sexy goose bumps pebbling her skin, her face overly warm. It was more than the excitement of her fantasy. It was telling *him*. Wondering if it would make him hard, if he'd want to stroke himself reading her words, knowing her thoughts. She went on.

The man removes his clothes. He's older than me, handsome, well built. Like my lover is. I'm jittery with nerves and anticipation. My lover tells me he won't blindfold me, that he wants me to see another man licking my pussy, and that he loves watching me submit to his desires. Forcing me to let go of my inhibitions makes it hotter for him. Whatever excites him does the same for me. He frees me.

The handsome older man climbs on the bed between my legs. He trails his index finger down my pussy, then parts me and licks my clit. My lover demands that I lock gazes with him, his eyes silver hot, while the other man licks and sucks me. He sits on the bed next to us. It's the sexiest, most intriguing sensation. All the while he talks, asking how I like it, how it feels. I answer between sharp breaths because it's so good. He reaches out, pinches my nipple hard, twisting slightly. That unique pleasure-pain he makes me feel shoots straight to my clitoris. I moan and grind and arch, riding the wave of building climax. His deep, sexy voice, the man's warm, wet tongue, it's more than I can handle, and I come hard, pulling at the restraints he's put on me, crying out, tears leaking

*from my eyes. I come back to myself to the touch of his fingers at
my temples, through my hair, while the other man is kissing my
inner thighs. I have a feeling they aren't done with me yet.*

Simon's cock was an aching iron shaft in his jeans at the end
of the reading. Holy hell. She was hot. Artie had his head up his
ass when he said she was a prude. He simply didn't know how to
free her inner slut. He hadn't appreciated her enough to discover
the hot, sexy, naughty woman she truly was. Fuck Artie. He'd blown
it, screwed around on her, and he was gone. Now it was Simon's
turn. He was not going to fuck up. He loved women, everything
about them: the way they smelled, how soft their skin was, the
taste of their lips and their pussies. But he'd never been in love
with a woman he was fucking. He imagined love made the experience that much more intense.

Sex with Haley would be better than any fantasy he'd had as a
horny kid.

"I need to come right this fucking second," he typed. She'd
love knowing what her words did to him. He shot off another
quickie. "Do you masturbate to this fantasy?"

He counted the seconds. There were too many of them. "Yes." She
answered only the second question, but his gut told him she liked
the first comment just as much. The thought of her lying in her bed
touching herself sent another wave of blood rushing to his dick.

He cruised over the things she'd written. He noticed that she
didn't call the man *master* or *sir* as in the traditional dom/sub relationship. She referred to him as her lover. He also noted her use of
"silver hot" referring to her lover's eyes. He'd seen that on the
first run-through, and his heart had skipped a beat or two, but he
wouldn't give it too much meaning. Not yet.

There were other things that stood out. "You would only do
this if he forced you?"

This time she was quick on the keyboard. "Only if I was tied down so I couldn't fight it. I'd have to surrender to his desires, whatever he wanted."

"That's damn sexy," he zipped off. *Surrender to me.* He'd written the words specifically for her. He'd been so right. She wanted to surrender, needed to.

"The idea of forcing you to comply makes me hard," he added in another e-mail. His trigger finger was getting too happy, sending off missives before he thought them through. Starting a chat would be easier, but the delay waiting for her next e-mail gave him an extra kick.

"All my responsibility would be taken away," she wrote.

"You'd be free."

"Yes. I would be forced to let go of all my inhibitions. Because I wouldn't be able to stop him."

She wouldn't want to stop him, that was the whole point for her. Not that he'd call her a control *freak*, but she definitely could do with allowing a bit of her control to fly out the window. She wasn't looking for the true dom/sub relationship, she simply needed justification for letting go.

"Let's do a little mindfuck here." He sent that off to gauge her reaction.

"What's a mindfuck?"

There was a bad mindfuck, screwing with someone's head, but there was also a very good one. "What you did to me with your fantasy. Seducing me with your words."

She was gone too long. Haley wasn't fastidious, but she didn't cuss a lot, either. Maybe *fuck* offended her.

Then she was back. "Mindfuck me."

Shallow breaths, an ache in his chest. She made him *feel*. He wanted this so badly his eyesight blurred a moment. "Pretend I'm your lover." He closed his eyes to savor the fantasy. "Will you do whatever I tell you?"

He could feel each individual beat of his heart against the wall of his chest. He'd had so much sex, started when he was fourteen, initiated by an older woman, and he'd enjoyed each and every encounter to the utmost since. Minus a few, but whatever. Yet his gut had never trembled with this need. He'd never been on the edge waiting for a word. Even with Haley, despite his emotions about her, he'd never allowed himself *this* feeling. First she was Artie's, then she hated him.

Now, he wanted every single heart-pounding, frantic, insane moment. It was more than the dance and tease of seduction. It was his next breath.

"If you were my lover, I would have to do whatever you told me to."

A fire shot to life in his belly. Christ, he hadn't a clue what he'd been missing. He'd only had the physical, but the mental part . . . man, it was exponential. He spun her a story of his own, emulating her style.

Here's what I would force you to do. You would have no choice. You would comply. I untie you and tell you that you must do things to this man. You nod, but I see the fear in your eyes. I lean close, my lips brushing your temple, and I tell you how pleased I will be if you obey. That you are my special one. You need to be pushed to your limits. I must know you are mine completely, willing to do whatever I ask. I untie the scarves I've bound you with.

Hell, he couldn't remember what she'd used as restraints, but the point was pulling her into *his* fantasy. He was getting into it, too, hard cock, aching balls. He would come by his own hand tonight to thoughts of her, and the climax would be explosive. While he jerked off when necessary, he'd always found it paltry compared to the real thing. With her driving his thoughts, no sex act, done alone or otherwise, was paltry.

First I would put you on your hands and knees, with him stand-ing beside the bed. I would make you suck him for me while I stroked you lightly from behind, just the brush of my fingers over your ass, gently over your sweet wet pussy, reminding you that I am there, watching you. Loving how well you suck. Because I know exactly how good it feels. You close your eyes and dream you're sucking me. His legs begin to shudder with impending cli-max, and I make you stop. We're not done. I don't want him to come.

Now I force him onto his hands and knees on the bed. I hand you a big, thick dildo. "Fuck him," I say. You tremble, your eyes wide, looking from him to me. You need this, to show your domi-nance over a man. You are my submissive, but at heart, you're a switch, needing some of that power for yourself as well. I will give that to you if you allow yourself.

Like a frightened doe, you take the dildo, test it in your hand, its weight and feel. Dual-headed, you can grip it tightly and have total control. "Do it," I command. This will be so good for you. You love it, fucking him until he spills his seed all over the bed without even touching himself.

Haley's body flushed from head to toe. His words shot emo-tions through her like lightning flashes, sizzling her nerve endings. How could he have guessed this when she didn't even realize it herself. As much as she craved letting go, she craved power. They went hand in hand. Using a dildo on a man was almost punish-ment, even if in his scenario, the guy enjoyed it enough to come. It was cruel yet a delicious thrill tingled like pins and needles along her flesh. She imagined the man was Artie. She imagined being in control. As much as Artie claimed she'd dominated him, he'd ultimately been the one in charge. Now was her chance to turn the tables on a man. The idea was Machiavellian, but it excited her like no other fantasy. Probably because she'd never dared to imagine such a thing.

Now she wanted it, but she didn't want him to get the impression she was bitter or sadistic. "That would be a good addition to the fantasy."

Two seconds, maybe three. How could he type that fast? "Liar. You want it so bad you can taste it. Put your hand in your panties and tell me how wet you are."

He made her burn. It was part of his mindfuck, and he was so damn good at it. Without even dropping the laptop, she had her fingers in her pussy the way he'd ordered her. She was creamy, her flesh hot, her clit throbbing. Laying her head back on the sofa, she stroked herself, moaned, imagined it was her faceless, nameless lover. She shot so quickly to climax that she almost let the computer topple against the coffee table, catching it as orgasm rippled and rolled through her body.

She could barely type when it ended. "Very wet. I accidentally came without your permission."

"You'll have to be punished."

"Yes, please."

"LOL," he wrote. "You are a true submissive."

She wasn't. She merely wanted someone to help her let all those inhibitions go. She wanted more of what this man did to her. If she'd known this was what answering an ad would be like, she'd have done it two months ago. Except it wouldn't have been him. "Was that the end of your story, with the dildo?"

"No."

"May I please have the rest?" She sounded oh so sweet.

"Yes, you may."

She sipped her wine, waiting, blood pulsing through her veins. She jumped when her e-mail beeped. Little shocks raced all over her body as she opened and began to read.

After I've watched my fill, I have decided that I will have you. I planned to tease you and withhold myself, but you've been so good, so hot, you deserve my reward. You love my cock, you love the way I fuck. Unzipping, I let myself free, then I haul you up off the bed to wrap your legs around my waist. The door is only steps away, and I slam you up against the wood, pulling your head down for a long, sweet kiss. You love being manhandled. I fuck you there, against the door, hard, fast, while our friend watches from the bed. You cry out my name as your climax begins. Your hot little pussy clamps around my cock, squeezes, works me, and I can't hold back. Jesus H. Christ, you're the best I've ever had, ever will have.

She felt herself floating away as if she'd had another orgasm. It was the fantasy. More, it was him. The way his mind worked, his dirty talk, his intuition into what she needed.

"You give very good mindfuck," she threw back.

There was no doubt about it. Haley was hooked.

4

DAMMIT, SIMON HAD COME INTO THE OFFICE AGAIN. ON A MONDAY morning he should have been checking in at the different job sites, but no, he had to come into the office. Saskia, their receptionist, wouldn't be in until nine, and Haley had thought she'd have the half hour to herself.

Which was why she'd sent out the e-mail first thing when she came in. She should have waited until tonight when she was at home and everything would be private, but no, she was a horny bitch and couldn't wait.

"You want some coffee?" Simon stuck his head out the break room doorway.

"No, thanks, I'm fine." She smiled, but it didn't feel much more than a stretch of her lips. She had her e-mail open on her computer, but hidden by several other windows. As soon as Simon went back to his office, she could check it for the five-hundred-thirty-first time. Then, swear to God, she'd shut it down.

She input some payables, listening to the rustle and clink in the break room. His footsteps faded away. She clicked over to her e-mail window.

Nothing. Her heart sank to her toes. She couldn't bring herself to close her inbox.

She'd weighed the pros and cons all night long. Should she ask to meet him? Should she keep it e-mail only? What were the risks? He could be a serial killer. A rapist. Except she was willing. She'd told him she wanted to be tied up and have naughty things done to her, even by another man as well. So it wouldn't be rape, but he could hurt her physically. There was also blackmail, though beyond her own embarrassment, nobody would care what she did.

Driving to work, she knew she was going to do it, but her brain was still firing off a list of doubts. By the time she'd booted up her computer and opened her e-mail, she'd decided to ask him to meet her for coffee. A public place. A nonsexual meeting. Her pulse had raced when she hit SEND, and for a long moment she felt dizzy looking at the monitor, as if the screen saver's fish were up and swimming at a maddening speed. What mattered was having done it. She'd done *something* to get out of the rut she'd been in.

That was half an hour ago. He hadn't answered. Then Simon came in and ruined everything. Of course, she was paranoid he'd pick up vibes out of the air itself.

Suddenly an e-mail appeared in her inbox. Goose bumps ran up and down her arms. The fish started to swim before her eyes despite the fact that her screen saver wasn't up.

It was him. "When and where?"

The ad had been placed in Saratoga, but that didn't mean he worked or lived there. "Do you know Hobee's at the Pruneyard?" She lived in Los Gatos. The Pruneyard in Campbell was close enough without being in the same city.

"Yes. Meet me there now."

She wanted to laugh, with both disbelief and excitement. "Not now. I'm at the office." She couldn't explain to Simon why she would leave before Saskia even arrived. "After work." She wouldn't be checking her watch, worrying about time while she was with him.

"Lunch," he sent back.

The bargaining titillated her as much as the sex talk, as if he were saying how much he wanted her. She could do lunch. Most of the time she ate something she brought from home. "Lunch is fine." She stopped, drew in a deep breath, and typed again. "I have one thing to say. Please don't lie to me. You must tell me the truth." After Artie, she couldn't abide a lie. She thought of Simon. "No lies of omission, either." It was a lot to put in an e-mail to a man she'd never met, but she wanted him to understand her rules up front. It was easier said when they weren't face-to-face where he could read all her emotions in her eyes.

His rapid reply took her off guard. She'd figured he'd at least consider his answer longer.

"I will never lie to you," he wrote. "Not even a lie of omission. You haven't asked my name."

She hadn't wanted his name. It was supposed to be anonymous. She'd never intended to meet him, either, yet here she was changing the rules on herself. "What's your name? What do you look like so I can recognize you?" She'd envisioned him handsome, tall, with a perfect body, but what if he was gross?

"My name is Simon."

The world started to spin out of control. Her body shuddered involuntarily. She glanced to the hall leading to the two offices. "You didn't say what you look like." Her fingers shook so badly she had to retype a couple of words before she hit SEND.

He shot off his replies so quickly, it was as if he already had his answers typed up. "You know exactly what I look like, Haley."

She grabbed the arms of her chair, knuckles turning white. Her emotions rushed up, choking her. He'd known all along. Which meant he'd looked at her computer on Saturday. Spied on her. He'd probably even written the ad to trick her, assuming she was a pathetic, horny, middle-aged woman who would jump at his sexy, titillating words.

Goddamn him.

She stood so fast, her chair went rolling, slamming into the wall. So angry she couldn't see straight, she whacked her hip on the edge of the desk as she rounded it, but the pain didn't stop her.

His door was open. She slammed it shut behind her. "You asshole. How many responses did you get?"

Seated in his chair, feet propped on the desk, his keyboard lay in his lap to type. "About fifteen."

"How many did you fucking answer?" The word slid off her tongue as if she used it all the time, and she didn't *fucking* care.

Her anger didn't faze him, the crinkles at his eyes pronounced as if he were laughing at her. "Only yours. I deleted the ad after you replied."

A horrible, terrible wave of relief washed through her body. That pissed her off even more. "You are a liar, you have always been a liar, and you will never change."

He brought his booted feet to the floor and gently laid the keyboard on his desk. Ever so gently, as if it took great effort not to slam it down. Then he stood.

"I have never lied to you."

"You lied about Artie."

"I failed to tell you things you didn't want to hear. Whether you want to admit it or not, that's not the same as lying. If I *had* told you, you would have hated *me*, not him, which you did anyway, so it didn't make a damn bit of difference."

"That is crap." She didn't yell, but her breath came fast and harsh in her throat.

He stalked to her from around the desk. At six feet, he towered over her. Sometimes his height made her feel petite and feminine.

Now it made her anger boil. "Let's forget about Artie. You lied with that ad. You tricked me. Got me to tell you things I never would have said if I'd known it was you."

"Exactly. You never would have told me." He leaned down, crowding her, forcing her to back toward the door. "If you didn't *want* me to know, you shouldn't have been frigging yourself in the bathroom so I could hear."

Her face went up in flames, and without even a conscious thought, she raised her hand, bringing it hard against his face. Time stopped as she stared at the red imprint.

She hadn't meant to, honest to God, she hadn't.

"Feel better?" he whispered, his eyes the color of smoke.

"No," she answered just as softly. Oddly, she felt like crying. Tears pricked her eyes. It was the anger, all the things she'd lost, the good friend he used to be, how during the worst of the fights she'd had with Artie, she'd actually wondered if she'd chosen the wrong Foster-Ventura partner. Losing Simon had been worse than Artie's cheating. She'd had no one to turn to for comfort. She'd had to handle everything on her own, find out about the credit cards and the debt all on her own. Because of the lie that was like a wall between them.

She would never feel better.

"You don't have to forgive me," he said, and she only realized she'd closed her eyes when his voice stroked her nerve endings. "All you have to do is let me give you the fantasy we talked about last night."

Her lids shot open. He was so close, his earthy scent filled her head, his body heat sizzled over her skin. "Let you tie me up?"

He moved with the grace of a jungle cat, faster than a big man should be able to, thrusting his hands beneath her armpits, hauling her up along his body, then shoving her back against the door. Without thinking, she wrapped her legs around his waist, her arms about his neck.

Like his e-mail fantasy. *Her* fantasy.

"Let me down." Her voice lacked any conviction. Because, heaven help her, he felt deliciously warm and hard against her body. She tried telling herself that it had been so long, any man would feel as good.

"Last night you wanted me." He shifted his hips, his cock at the juncture of her thighs. "I sure as hell want you."

This wasn't right. No matter what, Artie would always be between them. Simon was her friend. No, wait, she'd told him he *wasn't* her friend. "Last night I wanted a figment of my imagination."

He grabbed her chin in his big hand, forced her eyes to his. "You wanted *me*."

Why did he have to feel so perfect? Why did it have to be so damn sexy to be slammed up against a door, his body surrounding her, hard, demanding? She swallowed, her gaze falling to his lips, wanting, needing.

Except this was Simon.

"You were my husband's best friend. I would never even *think* about you in those terms." Somehow she'd morphed them from last night to the twelve years they'd known each other. To her shame, she *had* thought of him like that.

His jaw tensed. "Artie's been dead a year. You haven't had a man between your thighs in all that time." He rolled against her, punctuating his words. "I will be that man."

She should have spit in his eye. The presumption. And yet. He was so *right* between her legs. *Simon*, so right in a way she'd never let herself truly acknowledge beyond a few fleeting thoughts she'd shoved away quickly. The command in his voice was like an aphrodisiac, setting her blood on fire. Even as she writhed against him, trying to wriggle away, he pinned her to the door with his hard body, slid his palms up her arms, and shackled her wrists in one big hand.

Her body wanted to come. Falling completely still against him, it took all her will not to allow orgasm to overtake her. She couldn't breathe, couldn't talk, couldn't blink. Or she'd lose it all to him.

"I will give you want you need," he seduced, his chest expanding with a breath, caressing her breasts.

She was afraid even to shake her head lest she lose control. "Let me go," she managed.

He held her with his body, his gaze, his will. "Kiss me first."

Her eyes were drawn to his mouth. She wanted to taste him more than anything in her life.

"Force me," Haley whispered.

Simon took her chin in his fingers, his palm cupping her throat, her skin soft, fragrant, the slight musk of her arousal clouding his mind. His cheek still stung lightly with the imprint of her hand. He'd deserved it, taken his punishment. Now he wanted this. With the first taste of her lips, his knees threatened to buckle. He didn't know whether she opened her mouth voluntarily or he plundered, but she took him deep, sucked his tongue. The groan was his, the moan hers. His body moved, rocking, fucking her with clothes between them. He was up and over the edge in seconds, wanting to tear her T-shirt to get at her luscious breasts, rip her jeans apart to ease his fingers into her pussy.

He had to release her jaw when she wrapped her arms tight around his neck. Ah God, she tasted so sweet, her body clinging to his, her soft hair falling all around his face and shoulders in a cloud. He braced one hand on the door, the other beneath her ass, and rocked into her, taking her with his mouth, his whole body, everything except his cock.

Jesus, it was Haley, with twelve years of wanting launching into his kiss. He devoured her, but damn if she didn't do the same to him, her fingers fisted in his hair, holding him as if she'd never let him go. She tugged on his hair, backing off to breathe, moaned, pierced him with her deep brown eyes, then attacked his mouth once more. Being above him, she controlled the kiss, angling her head for a deep assault. A firecracker? She was a tidal wave dragging him under, tossing him, drowning him in her scent and taste.

She groaned, tore her mouth away, her head thumping against the door. "Put"—she had to breathe before the next words came out—"me down."

No, please, no.

Yet he let her body slide down his, her legs, her breasts, her skin searing him. Her feet touched the floor, and she pushed. He didn't move.

"I kissed you," she said, unblinking. "Now you have to let me go."

He wanted to shout his frustration, but he'd agreed. Simon backed off, his body on fire, his lungs working overtime, his heart shriveling.

Without taking her eyes off him, she eased open the door, slipped out, and closed it behind her.

Fuck. Fuck. Fuck.

How could she walk away from the power of what had happened between them?

Because she couldn't forget and she couldn't forgive. He touched his cheek where she'd slapped him. Putting out that ad to get past her defenses was a worse mistake than all the others he'd ever made.

This time, he'd lost her for good.

Maybe. Probably. Whatever. Simon was *not* giving up.

5

OH MY GOD. THAT KISS.

Haley locked herself in the restroom, hunkering down on the closed toilet lid. A full bathroom with a stall shower, Haley had made it a girlie place, with a wicker stand containing extra tissue, TP, soap, and cleaning supplies, a flowered curtain tacked around the top edge to hide everything. Two bright prints of Mardi Gras masks hung on the wall above the toilet. In the mirrored cabinet over the sink, she kept her makeup. A pretty plastic curtain covered the shower. Working with all men, except Saskia, making the bathroom feminine was like staking a claim, or drawing a line in the sand. *If you mess with my bathroom, I will mess with you.* She fought to maintain that bathroom's neatness with every guy that walked through their door, even Artie. They'd all knuckled under in the end, cleaning up after themselves, giving in because they finally figured out she'd *never* back down from this one thing. She hadn't thought it was that much to ask, but men, they didn't get it about not peeing on the toilet seat or wiping down the shower so it didn't grow mold or gather soap scum.

The only one who hadn't put up a fight was Simon, not because he couldn't win the battle. He was probably the only one who could win since he'd been the one to give her the most respect.

This was about the right of ownership. Simon and Artie owned the projects, made all the business decisions, got the job done. She owned that damn bathroom. And the books. She didn't mess with the jobs, Simon didn't mess with the bathroom or the books.

He'd trusted her with his accounting, trusted she'd pay the bills on time, collect the money, file the taxes. In return, he respected her desire for a clean bathroom. He never called her a neat freak, never tried to sneak money out of the petty cash, never wrote himself checks he conveniently forgot to tell her about. He respected *her.*

Mercy, there was so much more than that. The way he'd helped remodel the house, countless weekend hours, the thank-you dinners she'd made him, the fun they'd all had late into those evenings, talking, laughing, Artie telling his stories.

Maybe she'd become so mad with Simon because he was a living, breathing object at which she could direct her anger. Because Artie was dead, and she couldn't direct it at him.

Haley touched her lips. Simon's body had imprinted itself all over her. His warmth, his smell. She could still feel the hardness of his cock between her legs, relish his sweet, cinnamon taste. He was like a glass of champagne sparkling in her mouth.

Artie had never—

She slapped her hand over her mouth as if she'd spoken aloud. She'd loved Artie when she married him. She'd loved him when he died. It was just . . . different. Every argument, every time you go to sleep angry or stomp out of the house, it changes how you love somebody. Yet Artie had never kissed her that way, not in the beginning, certainly not at the end. Never with a passion that quite literally stole her breath, suspended her in time where all that existed was him, his mouth, his body.

Only Simon had ever made her feel that intensity. It scared the bejesus out of her. He was a man to stay away from if she wanted to protect herself from ever getting hurt again the way Artie had hurt her.

Haley unfolded herself from the toilet lid. She couldn't hide in the bathroom forever. She'd kissed him, touched him, wanted him. Now she was going to have to deal with it. Ignore it? Yeah, great plan.

Simon leaned against the wall opposite the restroom door, arms folded over his chest, legs crossed at the ankles, the toe of his boot propped negligently. A relaxed, easy stance, as if he didn't have a care in the world. All muscle, the man was enough to make any woman drool. His hair, the silver shot through with his original dark brown, didn't make him older. As the cliché went, it only made him better. He'd turned fifty his last birthday, setting off the smoke alarm with all the candles Saskia put on his birthday cake. Fifty years on Simon was prime.

Ignore what happened in his office? He'd flipped a switch she couldn't turn off again.

Yet she made one last-ditch effort to pretend. "It's all yours." She flapped a hand in the bathroom's direction.

Simon didn't say a word. He didn't move. He simply focused his smoky gray eyes on her. And waited.

His stare unnerved her. She swallowed. "It was a mistake."

One side of his mouth tipped. It might have been a smile. Or a grimace.

She glanced around the wall to the front office. Saskia still wasn't in. Her watch read five minutes to nine. Shock. It seemed like hours since she'd sat at her computer. That's what Simon did her to her, messed with her senses.

Finally, the rock spoke. "Once."

Her pulse skittered. "What?"

"We make your fantasy come true one time."

Heat arced from his body to hers over the small space between them. Haley started to shake on the inside. He wouldn't see, but she felt the quakes right down to her toes. "That's not a good idea." Dear Lord, she wanted it. He'd done a number on her last night. A total mindfuck, to use his word. Today, he'd turned it physical. If she hadn't become such a horny slut on her fortieth birthday, she might have been able to fight his power. But she couldn't fight herself.

"Once," he repeated, his gaze piercing, like a predator with his quarry in sight. "If you don't like it, you walk away."

If she *did* like it? Oh no, she wasn't stupid enough to ask that question. She wanted to close her eyes, but his scent would still envelop her, his heat surround her, and the images from his story would overwhelm her.

"I will give you what you want."

She'd crossed a line with him. His voice would forever hold the power to seduce her now. Had he known that when he put out the ad like a cat setting a trap for a mouse?

Oh yes, she was caught. "If I agree, who would the other one be?"

His lip twitched as if he realized he had her right on the edge of surrender. "I've got a lady friend who can find the perfect man to let you do the things you want."

She couldn't remember anymore whether they were sexual acts *she'd* wanted or merely what Simon wanted *for* her. Somehow he'd made his fantasy hers and vice versa. "*If* I say yes, tell me exactly what I'm saying yes to." She was afraid she'd give him more than she ever dreamed if she didn't make him spell it out.

His pupils widened, his nostrils flared, as if he were breathing her straight into his lungs. "You are my slave for the night. I tie you down, I find the man to pleasure you the way you deserve while I watch. We turn the tables on him and you take him with a dildo, giving you all the power. When it's done, I fuck you."

All the air was sucked out of the short hallway. She couldn't form a word.

The front door opened. Saskia loudly hummed a bombastic tune. "Yoo-hoo. Anyone here?" she singsonged, her words tinged with a Scandinavian lilt.

"Haley." With her name, Simon's voice branded her.

"I'm back here," she called out, then looked Simon full in the face. "Once. That's all."

"Agreed." He smiled, a wicked grin that lit a fire in her core. "Unless you decide you need me twice."

She was afraid she wouldn't let him go at all.

SIMON COULDN'T BUDGE FROM HIS POSITION AGAINST THE WALL. She had him by the balls with the sweet sway of her delectable ass as she walked out to greet Saskia, the lingering scent of her shampoo or lotion or whatever the hell it was that captured him, and the phantom feel of her body in his arms. He was fucking seduced. Head over heels. A goner.

If she took him once and walked away, he'd die. He'd never thought himself capable of such depth of emotion. It was both a joy and a misery. She held his heart in her hand without a single clue. Was it a lie of omission not to tell her he loved her?

The truth would not set her free. Instead, it was a club to the head, shackling her with an obligation. Just as he hadn't told her about Artie because the act would have been self-serving, revealing how he felt about her was equally self-serving. *Love me or you're responsible for breaking my heart.* Emotional blackmail. He despised it when a woman tried it on him so he sure as hell wouldn't use it on Haley.

No, his emotions were his own to deal with, good or bad. If she came to share his feelings, then he'd tell her.

In the meantime, he had one chance to show her how good they could be together. Straightening away from the wall, Simon went to his office, closing the door behind him. He dialed the phone, flopped back in the chair, and propped his boot heels on the desk.

"I do not book animal acts, Simon."

He laughed from his gut. He'd once asked Isabel to locate a Great Dane for a lovely lady of his acquaintance who'd made the request of him. He always obliged a lady if he could. Though he was pretty damn grateful when Isabel said she didn't have any Great Danes in her kennel, so to speak.

"You find me so predictable, Isabel, but this time I'm going to shock the hell out of you."

She snorted. "I doubt it."

He liked the woman. She was striking, sexy, well put together, smart, and possessed a wicked sense of humor that snuck up on a man. As madam, she spent the majority of her time booking courtesans and making sure her customer base was completely satisfied. Not many were privy to the fact that she entertained her own private and very select client list. Isabel did the choosing, not the other way round. She'd taken Simon because she liked his attitude, respectful of women, but willing to try most any damn thing she proposed. She'd been known to pair him with her clients, too, if she couldn't find a good match with one of her courtesans.

Simon had few limits, and Isabel appreciated that. Animal acts, thankfully, had never been one of her suggestions. He'd never followed through on the Great Dane, one of the few times he'd failed to accommodate a woman's request.

In contrast, what he wanted was almost vanilla. "I need a male submissive for a lady friend."

He could hear the light drum of Isabel's fingers on her desktop. "What's the level of pain involved?"

Isabel did have one or two courtesans who enjoyed a high

degree of physical and mental abuse. It was a need some people had, and she found clients who wanted to fill the role. She wasn't comfortable with violence or humiliation herself. It didn't do anything for Simon either. "No pain. He needs to be willing to let my lady take him with a dildo and give her a lot of oral pleasure. I'll say when he gets to stop."

"*Your* lady?" A curious note laced her voice.

He hadn't meant for it to slip through, but neither would he deny it. "Mine," he confirmed.

"Well, well, well, Simon, you have indeed managed to shock me. I never thought I'd see the day."

"She's special, and *this* needs to be special."

"Tell me more about her so I can make the perfect match." Isabel was all about the perfect match. It was a point of honor with her.

"She's petite and requires someone of medium height and build, preferably older, my age, bald." He stopped midstream, realizing he'd described Artie, and felt the rightness of it in his gut. He wondered if Artie had ever worshipped Haley's body the way she deserved. Simon had the feeling the answer was no. Well, he would *make* Artie worship her, even if it was an illusion. "I want him to be fifty years old, five ten, one-hundred-eighty pounds, brown eyes, and bald."

"*And* a submissive? That's a tall order, Simon. Seriously, at that age, they're somewhat more dominant."

"I know you can find one. He doesn't have to be *a* submissive. He merely needs to be willing to follow all my instructions in how I want him to pleasure her and allow her to use the dildo on him."

"I love the way you say 'merely.'" She sighed. "I'll see what I can do."

Bless her heart. Isabel always made it sound as if he was asking for the moon so that when she came through, she looked like a miracle worker. "I'd like to arrange ASAP. The sooner the better." He didn't want to give Haley enough time to change her mind.

"Ooh. Desperate to impress, are we, darling?"

He chuckled even as something ached around his heart. "You have no idea."

"Then I simply can't fail you, can I."

Isabel rarely did. Never say never, she'd had a couple of royal fuckups or she wouldn't be human, but for him, she'd always come through. Sometimes he wondered what thing in her past had driven her to the life she'd chosen. Perhaps she'd had a love affair gone bad, but that explanation seemed too trite. Yet there were times she'd gone thoughtful on him, out of the moment, as if he reminded her of someone. He'd never been quite sure whether that was a good or bad thing for her.

"Simon, if she's the one, I hope this works for you."

"She is the one."

He just wasn't sure anything would work with Haley. It might have been too late the day Artie died fucking another woman in Simon's bed.

6

FRIDAY MORNING, HALEY'S CELL PHONE VIBRATED WITH A TEXT message.

"Come into my office, baby. I need to bend you over my desk and fuck you bad."

Simon. He'd been texting naughty messages since Monday. From his truck, a job site, when he was out to lunch, late at night, and yes, even from his office. Sexting, he called it. She called it foreplay, part of the mindfuck he was so good at. She'd been in a constant state of arousal since she'd agreed to this "date." His sexy missives kept her high, so that she didn't rethink, worry, or change her mind. She never replied, she never complied, but she didn't delete the texts, either. At night, alone in bed, she'd read them all again and masturbate to the emotions he evoked.

Five minutes after he'd sexted her, he appeared by the break room door. "Need a mocha?" A sexy, naughty, shit-eating grin spread across his face.

Haley glanced at Saskia, who noticed nothing untoward in Simon's behavior. Saskia didn't like coffee drinks.

"No, thanks," Haley said. "Don't you have a project to get to or something?"

"I wanted a mocha for the road." He smirked. "You make them best." He was not generally a mocha man. Until this week, when he kept yanking her away from her work so he could get her alone in the break room.

"I'm busy, Simon."

"Come on, Haley," he whined like a fractious little boy. "I need your help." He glanced at Saskia's back as she turned away to answer a call, then he winked and crooked his finger.

She shouldn't. They were supposed to have one date, one time only. All this sexting and foreplay and mindfucking wasn't supposed to be a part of it. She liked it too much. It made her feel sexy and desired, beautiful and wanted.

She followed him into the break room as if she had no will of her own. That's exactly what she'd revealed to him in all those e-mails last Sunday night, that she needed a man to take control.

Simon was already tamping the coffee. Somehow all his muscles came into play, even his ass flexed. She couldn't count the number of times she'd sneaked a peek of his butt over the last week. He'd been in the office a lot more than usual. On purpose, she was sure.

"You're incorrigible," she muttered as she poured water into the small carafe.

"You ain't seen nothing yet, baby."

He closed in on her and Haley pointed to the refrigerator. "Milk, please."

"I love it when you order me around, sweetheart."

She couldn't help smiling. "Would you stop?"

He flirted nonstop as they got everything ready. When Simon turned on his charm, he could make a woman melt into a puddle at his feet.

The rich espresso brew reached the steam line on the carafe, and she opened the valve to froth the milk. Simon was right behind her, crowding her against the counter, touching her with his heat. She couldn't concentrate enough to steam the milk, something she'd done a thousand times.

"You were supposed to come into my office," Simon whispered at her ear.

"You are not supposed to send me dirty texts while we're at work," she answered sternly.

"I wouldn't have to if you'd come into my office and sucked my cock before Saskia arrived."

Haley laughed. Simon felt the rhythm of it vibrate against his chest, setting off shock waves through his body. She felt so damn good. He had no comparisons from his past; he'd found no one like her. He'd been hard since Monday. *Now, now, now,* his body screamed at him. *Take her, fuck her, make her yours.* He wasn't going to last much longer. Although he'd been having so much damn fun seducing her with text messages. Even if she didn't answer, his words had made her hot and wet. All he had to do was walk into a room and he could scent her on the air.

Sex first, love later. He would wear her down.

"Tonight." He rubbed his hips against her, letting her feel the rock of his cock. "I'll pick you up at eight."

Haley froze. Her body tensed where moments before she'd been pliable and, oh, so very fuckable. "Tonight? Why didn't you tell me sooner?"

"I was looking for the right person. I'm telling you as soon as I got word."

"Yes, but—"

He bent down to swipe his tongue along her earlobe. It shut her up.

"Tonight," he murmured again, his breath caressing her ear. "You wanted it, I got it for you. You don't really want to back out now."

The milk frothed, she shut off the steam valve and set the carafe on the counter.

He would not let her back out. This meant too much to him. The sexting was fun, sexy, the plans for tonight hot, exciting. Ultimately, this was all about getting her to see she needed him as much as he needed her. So he couldn't let her change her mind.

"This is probably your only chance to make your fantasy come true." He bracketed her with both arms against the counter, trapping her against him, seducing her with his body and her own desires. "You want it bad."

He heard and felt her swallow, smelled the musk of her arousal. He touched her hand, tracing his index finger over her skin. "You can't imagine how good this will feel. Two men doing anything and everything you've ever dreamed about. At their mercy. Being forced to let them make you come over and over."

Hell, he was seducing himself. "Say yes, Haley."

The phone rang in the outer office. Saskia called out in a lilting bellow, "Haley, it's Mr. Redmond from Primo Lumber."

"I'll be right there," she called.

"Tonight," he insisted. "I'll be at your house at eight."

She elbowed him. He backed off. By the time he left for the inspection he had out in Portola Valley, she still hadn't said yes. In his favor, she hadn't said no, either.

He texted as soon as the building inspector left. "There's a kitchen island I dream of putting you on so I can pull down your panties and make you come with my tongue."

She didn't answer.

"I need your come on my lips," he keyed as he waited at a red light.

She ignored him.

"You're so fucking hot in those tight jeans," he sexted over lunch, "and that tissue-paper-thin T-shirt that shows your nipples."

He imagined his messages set her pilot light burning.

At eight that night, when he pulled into her drive, the rush of relief turned him lightheaded.

She was waiting for him dressed in a tight black skirt and hot red top that screamed she was ready for action.

Simon would give her more than she'd ever dreamed of.

SIMON DROVE THE DODGE RAM WITH HIS USUAL CASUAL EXPERTISE. Haley had been too jittery to do the driving. Besides, the rugged manliness of the Ram appealed to her. He wore all black, jeans molded to the shape and thickness of his cock, black button-down workshirt, and his tan, steel-toed boots. He was hot, he was primal. Her body shuddered with the need to be taken by him. His sexting made her nuts. She hadn't gotten a thing done all day, and she'd left the office early. She'd soaked in the tub with a glass of wine to ease her tension. Along with the sexual excitement, there were also nerves rattling all over the place. She'd let her hands wander between her legs, rubbing lightly, riding the edge without falling off. That, too, eased the nerves while pulsing her excitement higher.

Simon took the winding curves of the mountain road easily. She turned in her seat, hooking one leg beneath her. "Where are we going?"

"A friend's house."

One goose bump rose in agitation. "Will your friend be there? Is that who's going to . . ." She searched for the right description. "The man who's going to help you entertain me?"

He laughed. She always felt Simon's deep, sexy laugh in the pit of her stomach.

Simon trailed a finger down her nose. "He is not going to be the one who spreads your legs and licks your sweet, delectable pussy until you flood his mouth with all your delicious come juice."

She blushed. He'd been saying things like that for days in his sexting, but it was different here face-to-face in the cab of his truck with the moon shining down through the trees. More intimate.

"My friend is letting me borrow his house because he has the necessary equipment."

A shiver traveled her spine. "Equipment?"

He reached out to stroke a knuckle over her cheek. "Don't worry. I won't make you use all of it." He winked in the dark. "Just certain things you asked for."

Damn. What had she asked for? All she remembered was wanting to be tied to the bed. In her frenzied e-mails, had she expressed an interest for—*gulp*—more?

Making a turn into a driveway, he grabbed a remote off the dashboard and opened the massive metal gate electronically. Driving through, he activated it again, enclosing them in the deep dark woods, only a row of ground-level garden lights and his high-beams pointing the way down the steep drive.

The house appeared around the next bend, a magnificent A-framed structure that seemed to cling to the side of the mountain.

Simon parked and shut off the engine, the lines of his face tense in the dimness of the cab. "You can change your mind."

She knew he didn't want her to. He'd intentionally seduced and teased her all week so she'd be too crazy to stop now. It touched her that he still offered.

"Once we're inside, you're mine."

The ownership in his tone sent a thrill straight to her belly. This was what she'd imagined in her fantasies. Total possession. She'd never dreamed it would be Simon.

That still terrified her. What about tomorrow? What about work on Monday?

"Last chance, Haley."

She glanced once more at the house, then back to him. "I'm not changing my mind."

His breath shot out as if he'd been holding it. Yanking on the door handle, he came round to her side and took her hand to help her down from the truck.

Unlocking the front door, he stepped aside, sweeping his hand out to allow her entry first. The back of the house was all windows opening to a magnificent view of the forest shimmering in moonlight. A huge loft overlooked the living room, a kitchen and dining area to the left.

Simon's big hand engulfed hers. "This way." Like an alley cat who could see in the dark, he led her down a short flight of stairs to a door. With one touch, a keypad lit up, and he punched in some numbers. The door lock clicked.

He hit another switch, lighting the staircase, and led her down. His big hand clasped around hers did funny things to her heart rate. The wall of windows from above continued down below with the same breathtaking view of the forest. A large four-poster bed dressed in a gold down comforter stood against mahogany paneling. Directly across, more wood paneling and a floor-to-ceiling mirror showcasing the bed. The back wall, built into the side of the hill, appeared to be made of irregular stone pieced together in a tight fit.

Her eyes seemed to widen involuntarily. Simon smiled. "Welcome to the dungeon, baby."

"Lord, Simon." She turned in a circle. Chains were sunk into the stone wall, manacles attached. There was more. A huge cross-like contraption, again with manacles. A machine like a horse's saddle with a great phallus in the middle. A sex machine. Bars were suspended horizontally from the ceiling, one in front of the mirror, another over the bed. Ankle and wrist restraints hung from the four posters of the bed.

"Do I need a safe word for all this?" She'd read enough on the Internet to pick up some of the terminology.

Simon chuckled, touched her cheek. "That's only for pain and gangbangs."

She shuddered.

"I have no intention of doing that stuff to you. If you really need to stop, all you have to do is tell me."

She stared at the metal bars hanging from the wood beams of the ceiling. Lined handcuffs dangled from the ends. The dungeon master would suspend his handcuffed victim from that horizontal bar.

"Don't be a pantywaist, baby. This is what you wanted." Simon moved in so close she dragged in his musky male scent instead of air. "You will love this," he murmured as if it were a command.

"Yes, Simon."

The smile that grew on his face was devil and angel all at once. He grabbed her, hauled her up his body, bunching her skirt, forcing her to latch on to his hips with her thighs to keep from falling.

He shoved her up against the stone wall. "You must always say *yes, Master.*"

Her breath fluttered in her throat. She felt so damn deliciously manhandled, wet and creamy as his cock nestled between her legs. "Are you really a BDSM dom?"

He nipped her neck, licked the bite, then rubbed his nose to hers. The small intimacies stole her breath.

"I've watched my friend perform. Tried it once." He shrugged. "Not for me." Grabbing her chin, he captured her in his hand. "I only do this for you."

For her. "I love the way you pick me up and toss me around. Like I'm some tiny little thing."

He nuzzled her hair. "You *are* a tiny little thing." He let her slide down his body. "Let's see what we're going to need for to-night's adventure."

Striding to a wide but shallow cabinet next to the mirror, he slid open the door to reveal an unnerving array of devices, the names of which she'd gathered from her Internet perusing. Dildos, short floggers, long whips, wrist and ankle restraints, ball gags, nipple clamps, ropes, brightly colored scarves, blindfolds, bars of varying lengths much the same as those that hung from the ceiling, plus instruments she was afraid to even ask the purpose. Her mind boggled.

Simon shot her that wicked angel smile again. "Oh baby, we are going to have so much fun."

She backed up a step, her heart clamoring, as he advanced on her. He stuck two fingers inside the waistband of her skirt and hauled her close.

"Now take off your clothes."

7

SHE WAS LIKE THE PROVERBIAL SQUIRREL IN THE MIDDLE OF THE road, twitching, not knowing which way to run.

Simon had dreamed about her naked body for twelve years. Now Haley was his. "Do you want to do it?" he said. Then he smiled. "Or do you want me to undress you?"

Her pupils dilated. Haley Ventura was the most gorgeous creature he'd ever seen in his entire life. Plump breasts a man could hold in his hands, full enough to take his cock in a slow, sweet titty fuck. Wide brown eyes, thick black lashes, long silky hair he could bury his face in and wrap around his hands to draw her close. Hips he could grab on to as he buried himself deep inside her. All the things he'd imagined were suddenly within his grasp, but only for this one night.

If he stripped her, he'd end up tearing her clothes. He backed off a step, eased his fingers from her waistband. "You do it."

She blinked, still the twitching squirrel. She needed some ordering around.

"Take your clothes off for me . . . now." He gave a split-second pause before that last all-important word. He then glanced down at her feet. "Leave the heels." Black suede fuck-me spikes.

Her gaze dropped, then she closed her lids.

"Look at me," he demanded.

Her eyes snapped back to his. As he watched, she tugged her tight T-shirt from her skirt, inching it up her delectable torso. Her breasts almost spilled from the lace cups of her bra.

His mouth watered. "Holy shit." She was more beautiful than he'd imagined.

She yanked the shirt over her head, her hair settling around her shoulders in a cloud, falling across her breasts. He pushed the soft strands back, reveling in the silky feel of hair and skin.

"Skirt next." He wanted her in bra and panties only.

Reaching behind for the back zipper, her breasts thrust forward for his view, her nipples beading against the lace bra. She shimmied deliciously, sliding the tight skirt over her hips.

"Nice," he whispered, a note of awe trimming his voice. She wore the tiniest thong of the sheerest black fabric. "Did you buy that for me?"

She nodded, her eyes wide.

"Excellent choice." He hated that he would eventually ruin the sensual lingerie, but he'd buy her a new set.

Grabbing a remote off the bedside table, he perused the controls. Okay, which one? He pointed at the suspension bar hung five feet back from the mirror, then pushed a button. The chain lowered from the ceiling. Ah, the correct one right out of the gate. His friend Damon was good to his submissives, and the restraints attached to the end of the suspension bar were lined with sheepskin.

In Haley's fantasy, she'd been tied to the bed, which was fine except for the fact she'd be either on her stomach or her back. The opposite side would be completely ignored. Unless he untied her and rolled her over.

The suspension bar was so much better. She'd have all the immobilization she required, with every inch of her available to be licked, kissed, nibbled, sucked, tasted, and fucked.

"Come here." He snapped his fingers and pointed straight down.

She jumped like a frightened rabbit. He wasn't sure how much of this she'd get off on. He'd never snapped his fingers at a woman in his life. That was something you did to a dog. Yet it was pretty damn fucking hot as, in bra and panties, she scurried to his side.

"Can you reach this?" He held up her arm, the tips of her fingers barely touching the metal. Her height required lowering the suspension bar a bit more. "Arms over your head," he ordered.

Her skin was warm to the touch, flushed a rosy pink, her pupils wide, eyes the color of rich 70-percent cocoa chocolate.

He thought of asking again if she was sure this was what she needed, but that would spoil the mood. He had to trust she would tell him when he pushed her too far, when enjoyment and excitement turned to fear and disgust. For now, her nostrils flared like a pedigreed filly as he cuffed one fine-boned wrist, then the other.

"Does this hurt?" He wanted no pain.

She shook her head.

He narrowed his eyes to slits. "Cat got your tongue?" He allowed a harsh tone to creep in.

"No. It feels fine."

"No, *what*?" he emphasized.

"No, *Master*." Her voice quivered.

The oddest, kinky thrill sizzled to the tip of his cock. If he wasn't careful, he'd get a wet spot on his jeans.

Using the remote, he raised the bar a couple of inches. He didn't want to yank her arms from their sockets, but he needed her to feel the slight tug of suspension, the pull of the restraints.

"Is this what you crave, slut?"

For the first time, a smile trembled on her lips, then she nodded. The game was on. And she liked it.

He stepped aside so they could both see her image in the mirror. Leaning close to her ear, he whispered, "Fucking hottttt . . ." letting his tongue hiss on the T.

He strode to the cabinet he'd opened earlier and grabbed a spreader bar. Standing in front of her once more, he nudged her feet apart, then hunkered down on the carpet to test the bar's length. Perfect. He buckled the ankle restraints lined with sheepskin. Eye level with the scrap of sheer thong over her mound, he blew warm breath on her hot pussy. She moaned, and her scent enveloped him.

Rising slowly, he dragged his fingers up her toned calves, over her firm thighs, squeezed her tight ass, pinched a beaded nipple, until he stood at his full height above her.

"I want nothing more than to climb behind you, sink my fingers into your hips, and impale you with my cock right in front of this fucking mirror."

With a sharp intake of breath, her lips parted, revealing the pink tip of her tongue.

"Later," he promised. They had a plan, a scenario. "Right now, I have a man waiting to do everything to you that I demand, giving you more pleasure than you can take."

His words set off a full-body shiver that rippled through her breasts. Putting his hand between her legs, he cupped her pussy. "*This* is mine," he said.

She gasped, then bit down on her lip as he stroked along the thong's crotch.

"I will allow the man I have chosen to pleasure you while I watch."

"Yes, Master." Her breath quickened.

He pinched one peak of her breast, hard, gauging her reaction, her delight. Her eyes damn near rolled back, and her head lolled on her shoulders before she straightened once again to meet his gaze. Oh yeah, she liked a small measure of pain with her pleasure.

"You will not come until I give you permission. Is that clear?"

"Yes, Master." Each time she said it, her voice grew stronger, more confident.

"When I say it's time, I will count to ten, and you will come right then." He tipped her chin with the tip of his finger. "Or you will not come at all. Understood?"

She nodded. "Yes, Master."

He was a quick study. He'd watched Damon work his magic. He knew the words Damon's submissives craved, and he fed Haley every line. Yet it was more than a recitation of acts he'd witnessed. She would come from another man's tongue, another man's fingers, but she would climax because Simon allowed her to and because he commanded it. It made him the key player.

Simon didn't believe that sex and love went hand in hand or that love precluded sharing. He'd had all his sex without being in love, and he could now allow someone else to pleasure the woman he loved. Because it was all about Haley's pleasure. Tonight, she would receive more than her wildest fantasies.

"I'm going to leave you now," he told her.

"What?" The pulse at her throat throbbed with anxiety.

A real dom would let her stew in her own thoughts and fears as punishment for not trusting him. That was part of the dom/slave relationship, no explanations, the sub simply accepted. That wasn't *their* relationship.

"I'm going to buzz our friend through the front gate."

"Do you know him?" she said, still with a bite of nerves.

"He's a courtesan through an agency I've utilized before," he explained. "I haven't met him, but I trust in the agency's recommendation. Isabel has chosen perfectly for me in the past."

"Who is Isabel?"

He recognized a thread of jealousy in the question. "She runs the agency."

"Is this guy, like, a hooker or something?" Her voice rose higher on the last word.

Simon cupped her throat. "He's a male courtesan trained to give you every pleasure that I instruct him to." He felt her nervous swallow against his palm. "Trust me, Haley."

Her eyes searched his face. "Yes, Master."

That was what he wanted to hear. And he left her alone down in the dungeon.

ALONE IN THE DUNGEON, HALEY STUDIED HERSELF IN THE MIRROR. Arms stretched over her head, the bar spreading her legs, high-heeled shoes sinking into the plush carpet. Yet it wasn't the bars or the cuffs that staggered her. It was her naked body. The heat in Simon's gaze had only worked its magic on her until he closed the dungeon door.

She exercised daily, considered herself in decent shape. She didn't hate the way she looked as some women did, but Simon should never have left her there to notice every bump and bulge. Artie's girlfriend had been model perfect—tall, blonde, svelte, and ten years younger than Haley. Now she was forty, but even ten years ago, Haley hadn't been flawless.

In contrast to Artie's nympho, Haley was . . . a fireplug.

She'd wanted to be tied to the bed and hadn't imagined that she'd be looking at herself. What was taking Simon so long?

Why did he hire a courtesan for this? *Hired* being the operative word. Now she was reduced to having to pay for a man.

She closed her eyes. This had been such a stupid idea. What was she thinking? She should have begged Simon to take her while he had her shoved up against the wall. He could have yanked her skirt to her waist, torn the tiny panties, and taken her. She'd been wet enough, wild enough, felt so good at that moment, no doubts, no queasy stomach. *That* was what she'd wanted. The feeling that he was the only man in the world among millions of women, and he chose *her*. Instead, she was alone, cold, and exposed.

Yet she must obey. She had to do whatever he wanted. She was tied, at his mercy. He could make her do anything, she'd have no choice. She must surrender to him.

That was exactly what she'd asked for.

The click of the door lock at the top of the stairs caught her ears. The shush of shoes on the steps accompanied by the thump of Simon's workboots.

She loved those boots, the pure masculinity of them, the rough-and-tumble maleness they exuded, the tan leather and steel toes. Add that to the way he'd picked her up as if she were light as a feather in his arms, she was wet all over again. Despite her fears, her nervousness, and her anxiety about her own body, she needed to surrender to Simon.

He entered the room and everything inside her tingled to life as if he had a live wire attached to the manacles. *Zing* to her nipples. *Zap* to her clit. She had enough maneuverability to grab the bar, clenching her fingers tightly around the metal, intensifying the sensations shooting through her body.

This was *Simon* she wanted so badly. Her husband's best friend. A man she'd known platonically for twelve years. Her best friend, too, for most of that time. Except that Artie had always been between them.

Artie wasn't here.

His gaze stroked her from head to foot, lingering on her breasts, the sheer thong. She forgot all her doubts. She wasn't thirty, tall, blonde, and perfect, but Simon didn't give a damn. He was hot for her the way she was for him.

She was aware of a man entering the room behind him, a vague shadow, but she had eyes only for Simon as he crossed the carpet silently, tall in his boots, big and beautiful in his black shirt and jeans.

He stopped directly in front of her, blocking her own image in the mirror. Electricity seemed to arc between their bodies.

He swept his hands over her without touching, the heat almost as potent as a real touch. "Sweet, gorgeous woman," he purred. "If I hadn't already promised you your fantasy"—his voice dropped, deep, guttural—"I'd fuck you now."

The words shivered through her. *God yes, please.*

He trailed a finger down the center of her chest, over one nipple, then down to her belly button. "We're going to make you come until you scream."

"Yes, Master," she murmured, loving the way his gray eyes smoked, hot and blazing.

The corner of his mouth quirked. "Christopher's going to worship your body first."

She could barely tear her gaze from Simon. She didn't need to see the other man, but Simon wanted her to look at the treat he'd bought her.

Medium height, scalp shaved smooth, he appeared close to fifty, but, oh my Lord, that was some physique. His gray T-shirt defined the sculpted muscles of his chest, the bulge of his thighs in tight jeans. The guy looked like a body builder. The bald head reminded her a bit of her late husband, but Artie had never taken care of himself like that. He'd never been meticulous about what he ate. He'd never worked out. While he hadn't been fat, Artie hadn't looked like Simon from all the years working out in the field with his crew.

He had never looked as good as this man—who did *not* resemble a Christopher. More like a Spike. Or Rocko.

"You like?" Simon whispered at her ear.

She bit her lip as she turned back to him. "He's all right." Her body, however, literally trembled in anticipation of her fantasy.

Simon gave one of his full-belly laughs that strummed a chord deep inside. "Maybe we should test that out."

He ate up the distance to the cabinet in two strides, grabbed something metal, and stopped in front of her once more to hold up his prize.

A thick, curved knife with a wrapped leather handle.

Her heart skidded to a halt.

Simon slipped the knife blade beneath the center of her bra. "I dreamed of tearing your clothes off," he murmured. "This is better." He flicked the blade through the thin lace. With two more twists of his wrist, he sliced through the straps, and the bra cascaded to the carpet, her breasts falling free.

Holding her gaze, he tossed Christopher the knife, and said, "Cut her out of her panties."

8

CHRISTOPHER CAUGHT THE KNIFE DEFTLY. "YES, MASTER. I'D LOVE to cut the fabric right from her body." The guy's voice, a deep, gravel pitch, was enough to make most ordinary women cream their panties.

Haley's jaw dropped. Simon grinned. Isabel's choice was right on the mark. The man was far from the stereotypical submissive. Simon had let himself be fooled by the name.

His fingers on Haley's throat, Simon circled her, coming to rest at her back, easing closer until his cock settled along the base of her spine. He wrapped his arm beneath her breasts, snugged her closer, and looked at their submissive over her shoulder.

"On your knees," Simon directed.

Christopher dropped immediately.

"Worship her body from that position."

"Yes, Master." Christopher slid the tip of the knife between her flesh and the thong riding her hip.

Snip.

He felt her intake of breath. Laying his cheek against hers, he watched as the short fluff of her pubic hair appeared. "Gorgeous," he whispered, his whole body aching to touch.

Christopher sliced through the other side of the thong and the material floated to the carpet. Simon gazed at Haley in the mirror, his pulse an irregular *ka-chunk* through his veins. "Look at you. Naked and open for us." Simon pointed to the reflection, indicating for Christopher to turn. "Have you ever beheld such beauty before?"

"No, Master. Your lady is the most beautiful creature I've ever seen."

"Mine," Simon said softly at her ear. She met his gaze in the mirror, blinked, then rolled her lips between her teeth as if she were trying to hide an emotion from him.

Simon tipped his head. "Do you have any idea how fucking gorgeous you are?"

Her lips parted. She swallowed. "I'm okay."

"Holy shit, baby, you're so much more than *okay*." He captured her chin, tipped her head to him, taking her mouth hard and fast, then slowed, drinking in her sweet taste. He circled her abdomen with both arms, hugged her up tight against him, letting her feel the ridge of his erection.

Had Artie's infidelity done this to her, demoralized her?

Well, he would fucking undo it. "Christopher's going to show you how desirable you are, how sensual." He nipped her earlobe. "Then it's my turn." Her body shivered against him. Christ, he wanted to feel her skin along his. The temptation to fuck her might be too great, but she needed the full impact of his body's reaction to her.

"Gotta get naked before Christopher starts," he warned her as he stepped away.

"Master, shall I get naked, too?"

Simon answered with a snap of his fingers. Christopher jumped to his feet and began tearing his clothes off, shirt and pants flying.

Simon undressed at a more leisurely pace, standing to Haley's side so she could see his unveiling in the mirror. He was man enough to appreciate the widening of her eyes and her gasp as his cock broke free, the shaft thick, his crown plum-colored with need, his balls full.

He let her caress his body with her gaze. "Do I pass muster, baby?"

"Simon, you're beautiful." Her voice soft, awed, it was enough to bring a hard man to his knees.

Metaphorically, that's right where Simon was. Luckily, though, he had a submissive willing to fulfill that role for now.

"On your knees before her, slave."

Christopher once again assumed the position, his dick bobbing. Simon took his place right behind her. Ah, God, the feel of her warm skin against his cock. For a moment, he couldn't speak, could only revel in the flesh-to-flesh sensation.

He found his voice. "See how hard he is for you, baby?"

A corner of her mouth lifted. "He's hard for *you*, Simon."

Simon tweaked her nipple, eliciting a squeal, then a moan of pleasure. "Christopher, are you gay or bisexual?"

"No, Master."

"Do you have any desire to suck my cock?"

"No, Master."

"You don't want me to fuck you?"

"No, Master. I love women. I'm not here to pleasure you, but to make your gorgeous lady feel better than she ever has in her life."

"See, baby, it's all for you." Simon bent at the knees, sliding his cock back up along the crease between Haley's cheeks as he rose. "So is this." He rotated his hips so there was no mistaking.

Simon felt so good against her body Haley couldn't help the shudder that coursed through her. The sight in the mirror, one man on his knees, the best man behind her, thick arms wrapped around her, a big hand splayed across her abdomen, it was enough to make her legs give way. If she hadn't been suspended from the ceiling with a bar spreading her wide.

"Are you ready for this, baby?"

She loved that he kept talking to her, hot words, endearments. *Baby.* She'd always wanted to be someone's baby. "I'm not sure, Simon." The words were for effect, maintaining the fantasy that she was being forced. Even without the manacles, though, she would have done anything he wanted.

"Don't be scared," he cajoled. He snapped his fingers lightly at her ear.

Ever obedient, Christopher ran his hands up her legs, slowly, lingering. At her thighs, his fingers curled inward and as he drew higher, he grazed the lips of her sex.

"I can smell your scent," Simon murmured.

"She's very wet, Master."

"Tell me how she tastes," Simon ordered.

She hissed in a breath as Christopher's tongue delved between her folds, licking, sucking, tasting. "Shit, she's sweet, Master."

"I knew she would be." Simon licked the shell of her ear.

She quivered, the sensation greater than the tongue between her legs.

"Pleasure her." Simon directed. Christopher complied.

Oh, she'd never felt anything like it. They were more than the sum of their parts, Simon fueling her with his breath in her hair, his whispers at her ear, his hard cock along her spine. He pinched both nipples hard, and she cried out, her hips bucking against Christopher's mouth.

It wasn't a climax, but a strong preshock. She couldn't close her legs, couldn't move except to writhe and wriggle like a fish on Simon's hook. Lord, how she loved being on that hook.

Her lids drifting down, she fell into Simon's voice.

"You're so fucking hot, your breasts pert." He flicked a nipple for emphasis. "I want to fuck them, squeeze them around my cock and fuck them." His fingers tickled down to her abdomen, tugged on her trimmed pubic hair. "You're so soft and pretty down there, too. Christopher, let me see more."

She opened her eyes as Christopher's mouth fell away, and he turned aside to reveal her reflection. Her pinkened clit burgeoned for the mirror. Her pussy lips were flushed and plump with desire, wet from Christopher's mouth. She looked wanton and desired. Simon tunneled into her folds, slicked his fingers with her juices— oh, his touch . . . rough, hot magic—and trailed the moisture all the way back up to her breasts, circling her nipples, turning them a deep rose red.

"Lick her some more," he demanded of Christopher.

The bald man's fingers entered her, searching for her G-spot as his tongue danced over her clit. She wasn't a G-spot girl, felt only the slightest response to his questing, but Simon, without even an erogenous touch, took her close to the edge with his voice.

Close, yet she couldn't fall over. Her legs trembled, her mind reeled.

"Do you need to come, baby?"

"Yes, please, God, please."

"Make her come, Christopher."

The courtesan's tongue and fingers made her wild, yet she needed Simon's permission, Simon's voice. "You have to count to ten," she burst out.

"One, two, three . . ." Simon counted slowly.

The ceiling chain jangled, her fingers clasped so tightly around the metal bar they hurt.

". . . five, six, seven . . ."

Her legs shook, buckled, her ankles swayed on the high heels, and she wanted so badly to plunge over the cliff. "Simon," she moaned, not knowing what she needed. More tongue? More fingers? Cock? Or Simon himself?

"Nine, ten, come."

She cried out, screamed, yet she seemed stuck on the precipice. Tears leaked from her eyes, but her body wouldn't perform. She'd asked for this, he'd provided, given her what she wanted, but it didn't seem to be what she needed anymore. He was going to be so pissed. "Please, Simon, I can't . . . don't be mad . . . please, Simon . . ."

Hands at her ankles and wrists. The chains fell away, freeing her. She felt lighter than air, carried on clouds to the bed. The mattress dipped, fingers trailed her abdomen, her thighs. She recognized Christopher's touch. Then Simon's body surrounded her. Laying in the vee of his legs, her back to his chest, head on his shoulder, she spoke with her lips against the skin of his neck. "I couldn't come standing up like that." His skin was so sweet, his scent so male and enticing.

"Poor baby." He kissed her temple. "Come like this." His finger tantalized her clit as Christopher petted her thighs, pushed her legs apart, and his tongue darted inside her.

Still, though she trembled, her body simply would not let go. It hadn't been the chains binding her or being forced to stand that held her back.

She threw her arm back, fisted her hand in Simon's hair. "You," she whispered.

"What, baby, what do you need?"

"I need you."

Christopher retreated from between her legs, and Simon gathered her close.

"You lick me, Simon. You make me come." The words hurt her throat, even the thoughts made her head ache, yet it was the only way she could come.

The only way she wanted to come.

Simon laid her flat across the big bed.

When he would have crawled down her body, Haley took his face in her hands. "Don't tie me up."

Simon felt something break loose around his heart. "I won't."

He'd never wanted to force her. He always wanted it to be her choice. Without physical restraints or mental reservations.

His body covering hers, he took what he'd been dying for, her lips. Her kiss was sweet, then she opened her mouth to him, and everything burst out of control. He sucked her tongue, delved deep. She tangled her fingers in his hair to the point of delicious pain. He could barely breathe, but more than air, he was starved for *her*. He rolled, bringing her atop him. His hand fell to her ass, while he cupped her head with the other, molding her mouth to his, her hair falling around them.

The words were there on the tip of his tongue, and if he hadn't been devouring her, they would have poured out. And terrified her. She wasn't ready for his emotions, but holy hell, she needed his kiss. She moaned, groaned, angled her head, backed off to take him the other way. She nipped his lips, sucked his tongue, laughed, came back for more. Fuck, this was making love with your mouth.

He needed what the courtesan had tasted.

His breath rasping in his throat, he held her off. "Let me make you come."

"Oh God, Simon." She writhed on top of him, wanting it badly, as badly as he needed to taste her climax.

He pulled her up to straddle him, her knees at his shoulders as he clasped her butt cheeks in his hand. "Lower the bar," he ordered the courtesan, pointing to the remote.

He licked Haley, one long swipe between her legs. "Holy Christ." She was so fucking sweet.

She glanced up at the whir of the bar's chain. "You said you wouldn't handcuff me."

"I won't, but I want you to hang on to the bar, to steady yourself while I lick you."

She grabbed it with first one hand, then the other, lifting herself over his face, and this time when he cupped her ass and brought her delectable pussy to his mouth, the position was perfect.

He impaled her with one finger, taking the nub of her clit in his mouth at the same time, sucking on her.

She arched. "Oh God, Simon."

"That's it," Christopher said, moving next to her, stroking her body, arms, breasts, abdomen, thighs. "Let him hear how good it feels."

She writhed above him. "Yes, yes, please, Simon, like that."

Her juices coated his mouth, eased the entry of another finger. He found the bump of her G-spot and worked it. She began to pant. "Simon, Simon. Oh God, oh God."

"Keep on talking to God, sweetheart," the courtesan urged, caressing her with words and gentle hands, adding to her pleasure, Simon was sure.

She flooded him with taste and scent and sound. His senses reeled. He worried her clit with his tongue, then sucked hard. Her voice, Haley's voice, saying his name the way he'd dreamed over and over in the middle of the night when he couldn't sleep.

She ground her body against his mouth, squeezed her thighs tightly to his temples, and her pussy contracted around his fingers, milked his hand as if it were his cock. She let loose, wailing his name. It was all he could do to hang on, pushing her further, higher.

Until finally, her fingers lost their grip on the suspension bar, and she fell on top of him. Gathering her close, he stroked her hair from her face, over her shoulders, wiped a tear of pure pleasure from beneath her eyes.

"That's my girl," he whispered, a meaningless endearment to hide the real things he wanted to say.

"Simon." She breathed warmth against his neck. "That was . . ." She seemed incapable of finishing. Holding him tightly, she bound him to her with her arms. "It's been so long. Make love to me, Simon."

She rarely cussed, the word *fuck* wasn't an everyday part of her vocabulary, and making love was just another euphemism. He was fifty years old, and countless women had said that to him. With them, it had been a sexual act, one he enjoyed immensely, but still just physical. Until Haley.

He kept his voice calm, his face impassive, hiding all his emotions so he didn't send her running. Only his words revealed everything he felt. "Yeah, baby, I need to make love to you."

If she let him, he would make love to her for the rest of his life.

9

HIS FACE CHANGED, HIS EYES SUDDENLY DARK GRAY, HIS LIPS UN-smiling. Oops. Simon had a phobia about the word *love*. Just as he had a phobia about commitment. Still, she'd said *making love* and he'd repeated it, and Haley would be damned if she'd take it back or ruin the moment.

Christopher rolled off the side of the bed, watching them in the mirror. Grabbing several packages of condoms from a bowl on the side table, he tossed them on the bed. "Please, Mistress, may I watch?"

Maybe he'd seen the night collapsing and sought to save it, she couldn't say for sure, but Haley laughed at his formality. "Simon's the master. I'm just another submissive."

The courtesan slowly shook his head. "No. You're not his submissive at all."

Christopher didn't comprehend enough to realize that Simon would never be dominated. He was considerate to her, accommodating her needs. "I've never been watched before." She'd never had one man stroke and caress her body as another man brought her to climax. The extra hands hadn't frightened her, simply enhanced the sensations Simon shot through her body. She was glad it was Simon, though, who'd made her come.

"I would be honored to observe such a glorious act," Christopher said with his most formal of tones.

Oh, he was good, and she found his decorum interesting. There was a ritual to the whole bondage relationship, right down to the language used. She rolled in Simon's arms. "What do you want?"

She couldn't read his expression. He'd gone . . . flat.

"Your choice, baby" was all he said.

Looking down at him, Haley was suddenly afraid to be alone with Simon. There was something about him, an intensity she couldn't fathom. If they were alone, she might very well give away too much of herself.

"Let Christopher stay." She rubbed the flat of her hand over Simon's chest, hairless, firm with hard muscles, his skin bronzed from the sun. She crawled down his body to the root of his manhood, wrapping his cock in her palm one finger at a time. "This cock is beautiful." She kissed the tip. He was big, thick, his pubic curls trimmed, his balls shaven smooth.

He gave her that intense yet indecipherable look, his eyes the dark gray of a storm cloud.

She felt like playing, needed it to somehow ease the tension riding his face. She spoke, holding his gaze. "Ask our master if he'd like me to suck his cock, Christopher."

Christopher was quick to comply. "Master, would you like Mistress to suck you?"

"Yes. I would like that."

Dammit, she still couldn't figure out what was in his head. She probably didn't want to know. "Ask Simon how he likes his cock sucked. Soft and slow? Hard and fast?"

"Master?" Christopher didn't bother repeating.

"Suck the head gently, then take me deep and slide all the way back up sucking hard, especially when you get to the crown."

"Wow, a man who knows exactly what he wants," she quipped.

She'd never enjoyed this with Artie, his taste was too salty. He liked to hold her head, make her take more than she could handle. She was never good enough for him.

Everything about Simon was different. Tonight was different, a night to experience new things.

He reached to the head of the bed, yanked a pillow down to stuff under his neck, then stacked his hands behind to rest on. "I like to watch, too."

Haley decided he was testing his control. Well, she would make him lose it, and he had just given her the recipe for success.

She enveloped the head with her lips, licking and sucking lightly, teasing the slit with her tongue as she gathered a drop of pre-come. He made a noise, but when she glanced up, his expression remained inscrutable. She slid down. He was thick and too large to take all the way. She allowed a scant more than was comfortable, testing herself, and he jerked in her mouth, his body tense as if he were trying not to force.

She sucked hard on the long glide up, cupped his smooth balls in her hand, squeezed lightly, then circled the crown of his cock. He slipped free, she grabbed him, took him, stroked him with two fingers right below the ridge of his cockhead.

His breath came harsh, and this time his body moved with her, the taste of pre-come filling her mouth, not too salty, almost sweet. He smelled of fresh soap and hot male musk, an erotic combination stealing through her head.

Weaving his fingers in her hair—"Oh fucking hell, baby, shit"—he pulled the mass of it away from her face so he could see. "That's too fucking good, yeah, shit, baby."

A flow of delicious, tantalizing words mixed with the thrust and grind of his body. Oh yes, she'd made him lose his control, and there was such power in it all. She sucked harder, deeper, better than she ever had in her life.

"Wait, wait, stop." He pulled gently on her hair. "Don't make me come, baby, I need to come inside you. Shit, please, don't make me come yet."

She gave him one last swipe of her tongue, and pulled away, straddling him on hands and knees.

He breathed hard, nostrils flared, pupils black and wide. "Pleased with yourself, aren't you."

She nodded. He'd had so many women, yet she'd made him beg. She wanted to ask how many women he pleaded for, but honestly, she didn't want to know.

"Mistress, that was magnificent."

She'd forgotten Christopher. He leaned against the bedpost, cock in hand. In her former self, she'd have been disgusted. Now, it made her want to give him a show.

Turning back to Simon, there was nothing flat about his expression now. His eyes smoked, his nipples were hard, lines of need etched his face, and his hands were clenched in fists as if he were trying not to grab her and haul her up against the door.

She placed a hand in the middle of Simon's chest, his heart beating wildly beneath her palm. "Christopher, ask your master how he wants me to fuck him." Simon loved the word. He would love that she used it for him.

He closed his eyes a long moment, dragging in a deep breath, his chest expanding, teeth gritted.

"Master, how would you like Mistress to make love to you?"

Geez, Christopher was laying it on thick, but Simon smiled, wrapping his big hands around her forearms. "I want your mistress to ride me so I can see her in the mirror."

Haley glanced over her shoulder. The position was fine for him, but she wouldn't be able to see unless she craned her neck. She nudged his thigh with her knee. "Move."

He scooted, lying horizontal to the mirror, his feet hanging over the edge of the bed. "Now we can both watch."

Christopher grabbed a condom that had gotten pushed beneath a fold of the comforter and tossed it. Simon caught it one-handed, tore it open, and donned it before she could count past ten.

He'd had a lot of practice.

She wouldn't think about that now.

"Take me, I'm yours," he said, offering up his cock to her.

She flipped off her high heels—she should have gotten rid of them long ago—and straddled him once again. His body heat traveled along her thigh, her calf. He was big. It had been over a year, but she was wet. Tipping her head back, she eased down on him as he guided himself inside her. Christopher was right beside them, caressing her flank as if she were a mare with her stallion.

"Oh Jesus," she whispered, stopping.

"Am I hurting you?" Simon's voice was hoarse.

"No." She drew in a deep breath, a smile growing on her lips, then she looked down. "You can't even begin to imagine how good that feels." He stretched her, filled her. So much more than just his cock, more than just her pussy. "Simon."

"I feel it, baby."

Two quick breaths, then she took him deeper. "How does it look?" she whispered.

He turned his head to the mirror. "So fucking hot." Sliding his hands from her butt up her back, his thumbs and fingers stretching along the outside of her breasts, he pulled her down. "Kiss me while you take me."

She'd never have thought Simon could be so . . . romantic. Because it was, his words, his reverent tone, the heat of his gaze. She'd pegged him for a wham-bam guy, but Simon knew how to treat his women.

She lay flush against his chest, her hair falling like a curtain over them. Christopher's hands fell away, the mattress shifted. Haley was alone with Simon in the drape of her hair. Leaning on her forearms, she kissed him, parted lips, a slight bit of tongue, not deep, yet soft and sensual, twisting one way, then the other, sucking his tongue, his mouth, his lips. Nipping, licking. All the while with his hands on her rear easing her down until he'd seated her fully on his cock.

"Oh, Simon." She buried her face against his neck, drew in his earthy scent. Goose bumps raced over her skin. Nothing had ever felt like this, the throb of his cock inside her, his heart beating against her breasts, the feel of thick hair in her fingers as she cupped the back of his head to hold him to her.

"It's good, baby," he murmured. "Now move. You're going to feel so much more when my cock is rubbing your G-spot."

He didn't understand. She couldn't explain. Sex had never been this good. Not ever. Where the feel of a man inside her was ecstasy, where his kiss, his scent, his taste were enough to make her heart skip beats.

Simon pushed her up slightly, brushed her hair out of the way, molded his palms to her cheeks. He wanted to say it, use the words *Make love to me.* Yet some part of him needed the minute protection of keeping them to himself. She could slaughter him. Christopher had seen it plainly, he was pussy-whipped. Ahh, what a euphemism for the way he felt. "Fuck me, baby. I need it so bad."

"Yes, Simon."

If she'd called him Master, he'd have shouted. He didn't want master and slave. Not even Master and Mistress. He wanted Simon and Haley.

She braced her hands by his shoulders and pushed back. He arched involuntarily, thrusting higher and deeper.

She sighed. "Simon."

He couldn't hear his name on her lips enough.

"Fuck me," he whispered, seduced, cajoled, begged.

Haley rode him, settling into her rhythm, faster, the bump of her G-spot cruising over his cock.

"That's it, baby, fucking perfect, shit, holy hell." He reached between them, adding his thumb to her clitoris, and she straightened, her hands rising to her hair, lifting it. She panted, moaned, made delicious sounds that rocked his cock. Her thighs tightened as she pushed herself to a faster pace.

He glanced in the mirror. "Jesus, you're fucking gorgeous. Beautiful. Perfect. Shit, oh man, God." Words spilled out of him, but none of them did justice to the picture she made. Like a goddess, a magnificent Valkyrie riding her stallion. Her body spasmed, and she cried out, her pussy contracting around him, turning him mindless. He grabbed her hips, hung on as she threw them both into Valhalla, Nirvana, the heavens.

He returned to his full senses with his cock still semi-erect and buried deep in her perfect pussy. Her hair had fallen all around them, cocooning them. The wild beat of his heart had calmed, but his ears continued ringing.

For the first time in his adult life, or rather since he'd had his first sexual experience at the age of fourteen, he didn't want to let a woman go. He'd spent the night a few times, but mostly he preferred to leave. He wasn't a cuddler.

Yet he could have cuddled Haley until morning light, then made love to her all over again with the sun falling across the sheets.

He wanted, but couldn't find the right words to ask. He needed, but couldn't beg. Twelve years. He'd watched her grow up, fall in love, get hurt, lose her confidence in herself.

Now a part of him wondered how he could have allowed Artie to do those things to her. He'd been aware of the affair, but he'd told himself it wasn't his business and let it go on. Haley was right. She'd been his friend, not just Artie's. She'd trusted him, he'd owed her the truth, yet he'd failed her.

"I'm sorry," he whispered, thinking her asleep.

"For what?" she murmured against his throat.

"For hurting you."

She pulled back a few scant inches. "You didn't hurt me, Simon. That was the most beautiful"—she stopped, swallowed—"fuck I've ever had."

Shit. He hated that word on her lips. Why couldn't she go back to *making love*? It ached that she didn't understand what he was trying to say.

He'd have explained if Christopher wasn't still sitting on the end of the bed. There were equal parts exhibitionist and voyeur in him. He got off on watching and being watched. Except now. Except with Haley in this moment, the first time he took her and she took him. The first time he truly gave himself to a woman.

"Time to go, baby."

He'd get her home. He'd explain there.

She rose to a seated position, stretched, groaned, twisted, moaned, and made his cock crazy inside her again. Then she met Christopher's gaze in the mirror. Her eyes widened, her skin flushed. The heat of the moment was definitely over.

"There's a bathroom over there, corner door." He pointed.

Damn if she didn't scurry off him, practically flying from the bed to grab her clothes and run for the restroom. It wasn't how he wanted it to end.

He removed the condom, disposed of it in the trash by the bed.

"Not exactly how you wanted it to turn out, was it." Christopher dropped the master/slave role, and it wasn't a question.

"It was fucking perfect." Simon rose, padded to his jeans, shirt, boots, and underwear. Haley's sliced underthings lay on top.

"No, sport, you're sorta screwed and not in a good way."

Simon pulled in a deep breath. He didn't get mad easily, go in for bar fights, or let off steam with his fists, but Christopher wasn't making it easy.

"Want some advice?"

He laughed. "No."

Christopher ignored him. "Tell her how you really feel. No games."

He scratched the side of his face in a seemingly easy gesture. "Time for you to go."

Christopher unfolded himself from the bed and donned his clothes. "I'd give a helluva lot to have what's at your fingertips."

The guy didn't know the history and Simon wasn't about to explain. "Thanks." He buttoned his shirt, tucked it in, then zipped his jeans. "You did a great job." He held a hand out indicating the stairs. "The gate will open automatically for you on the way out." He'd given the guy his cash when he arrived. Simon decided a price he was willing to pay, and took care of everything up front. If it didn't turn out as he'd expected, lesson learned, don't do it again at any price.

Christopher smiled, saluted, and backed up to the staircase. "Meditate on it, sport. You could have everything if you simply found your balls."

The guy was pushing it. Simon steeled himself not to react as Christopher disappeared up the stairs.

Maybe he did lack balls. He was afraid she'd never forgive him for not telling her about Artie and terrified to put himself on the line after what they'd shared on that bed.

Yeah. That qualified as lacking a pair of cajones.

10

HALEY FELT COMPLETELY NAKED WITHOUT HER BRA AND PANTIES. It was all so sexy while she was being stripped, not so much in the silence of Simon's truck, the big console separating them like a wall.

Christopher was gone by the time she came out of the bathroom. A good thing, since it was bad enough having to face Simon. Everything had been so darn hot up to that point. It didn't matter if Simon called it fucking, what he'd done was make love to her. She'd been drifting in that state of orgasmic satiation only to open her eyes to find Christopher staring at them. Even that wasn't bad, but it was what Christopher represented, the embodiment of Simon's way of life: kinky sex, exhibitionism, voyeurism. And lots of variety in his women.

He had such beautiful hands as he guided the truck around another mountain curve. Blunt masculine fingers, a thick palm, his hands practically spanned her waist. She'd always thought him handsome, but now she savored every detail. His silver hair was soft not coarse, his skin firm, muscles strong. Women constantly gave him a double-take. He noticed in return with an assessing eye. He didn't parade his ladies as if they were conquests. Most of what she believed about Simon and his women, Artie had told her, as he vicariously enjoyed Simon's exploits. The few times she'd met one of his dates, Simon appeared gracious and attentive. In the twelve years she'd known him, though, he'd never had a serious relationship. He was casual dating only. And casual sex. He used a sex agency, too, for heaven's sake. Courtesans. He hired women. One woman would never do for Simon.

She realized she was talking herself out of a relationship with him. Which meant she'd actually been considering it. Because the sex had been so phenomenal. Because she'd felt the same connection she'd had with him before Artie died. But Simon and a relationship? She was out of her mind. After Artie's infidelity—maybe there were more affairs she knew nothing about—she couldn't face the same thing from Simon. There was absolutely no chance for them. Not that he'd asked anyway.

Buried in her own thoughts, she didn't notice they were in her driveway until he shut off the engine.

"Thanks. It was great. You don't need to walk me to the door," she said as if they'd been on a date she couldn't get away from fast enough. She grabbed the door handle before he could come around, and she climbed out.

Simon's legs were longer and he moved faster, and he stood on the raised brick stoop before she made it up the last step.

"I never dump a lady off at night and simply drive away. I make sure she gets inside safely." He held out his hand. "Where's your key?"

His very statement reminded her of his vast experience with women. She clasped the house key to her chest. "Thanks. I can open my own door. Good night."

In the dim porch light, he was big, tall, overwhelming. With the proximity, his scent washed over her senses, heating her, the tactile feel of his body imprinted between her legs, the slight roughness of his body hair along her thighs.

"You don't want me to leave yet, Haley. There's so many things we haven't done."

She shivered. They'd kissed, he'd licked her, she'd sucked him, they'd fucked. What else was there? She wasn't stupid enough to ask aloud. "I'm tired, Simon. That was a quite a workout. Now I need my beauty sleep."

He caressed her cheek with his knuckles. "You're too beautiful for my sanity already."

See? He had all the right words to charm a woman out of her panties, though, in this case, charm wasn't necessary. She was naked under the skirt, her nipples clearly outlined beneath the thin shirt. His gaze dropped for a microsecond, noting the peaks coming to life.

She eased around him, managed to fit the key to the lock. Opening the door, she pivoted on her heel in the entryway, one hand on the jamb. He had a booted foot on the sill so she couldn't shut him out.

"Haley, don't end the night like this. We need to talk about it. So you're not all freaked out by tomorrow."

She was already freaked out at how much she loved what they'd done.

"Haley, let me in," he said softly, yet with a force of will that had her wanting to do anything he told her to.

She was weak. She stood on the threshold, wanting, needing. With one crook of his little finger, she'd buckle.

Simon didn't use his little finger. Hands on her rib cage, he lifted her, carried her inside, slammed the door with his foot. She had a choice, but she threw her arms around his neck anyway. Resistance was futile. Raising her legs, she crooked her knees at his hips and locked her ankles behind him.

"This is the last time," she murmured before he shoved her up against the wall and sealed her lips with a kiss.

Lord, the man could kiss. He devoured without being sloppy. He tasted and sucked and licked as if her mouth were a sweet treat. She moaned as he conquered her tongue. He ground his hot, hard cock between her legs, and she writhed. It hadn't been an hour since they'd left the mountain house, but he was ready. So big, he engulfed her, his whole body, touching her here, there, everywhere. She couldn't think. He made her not want to. She drowned in his minty taste, reveled in his earthy male scent, sipped and savored his mouth, his lips.

She had to pull back just to breathe, eyes closed, head against the wall. "Simon."

"Ride the wave with me, baby." He lifted her higher, cupped her breast, flicking her nipple, teasing, pinching, then he bent his head to suck right through her T-shirt.

She cupped his head, sifting her fingers through his hair, her body poised on the brink. Laying her head back, she rode the wave exactly the way he wanted her to, drifting in sensation, no thinking, no worrying.

His mouth on hers again, he slid his hands over her thighs and up her skirt as he braced her against the wall. Finding the warm, wet center of her, he played her in rhythm with his tongue between her lips. Her body shuddered. She gasped into his mouth. Lord, he had a way about him, knowing where to touch, for how long, how softly, how hard.

"Haley, Christ, baby, I need to be inside you." His breath was warm against her neck. "Let me inside." As he'd begged to enter her house, he begged to get inside her body.

"Yes."

He didn't even take her down off the wall. She wanted it like this. Elemental. The way she'd dreamed of him taking her since the moment he first lifted her in his arms against his office door. He kissed her again as she felt him reaching for his back pocket.

She held on with her arms and thighs as he ripped open the packet, leaned back, undid his belt and zipper.

The man definitely had practice.

Haley gulped back the thought. Not now. Later. But not now.

Rubber on, he eased the head of his cock past her opening, watching, a hand beneath her butt, balancing her on his strong, taut thighs. "You're so fucking pretty. The most gorgeous pussy I've ever seen in my life."

And he'd seen a lot.

Haley closed her eyes, shutting out the thought, opening her lids again when it was gone. "I love the way you talk while you have sex."

He laughed. "Sex is not a thing to be done quietly." He pushed home, and she cried out with the exquisite sensation. "See," he murmured, "so much better when you make noise."

She'd never been terribly vocal with Artie, and Simon was right, the louder she got, the more intense the feelings. She dug her fingernails into the firm muscles along the side of his neck as he rocked inside her. "Oh God, Simon."

"G-spot?"

"Yes, yes."

He was no wham-bam, taking his time, stoking her fire with words, touches, kisses, his voice. Lips on hers, he whispered, "Slow and easy over that special spot," as he rode deep, pulled out, tipped his pelvis to slide at just the right angle.

"Simon." She strained, arched, stretched.

"It's fucking good, isn't it." He put his head back, gave a long sigh, pumped short and sharp in her channel. "Shit, fuck. You're so perfect." He leaned in again, face to her throat, and thrust hard, growling, groaning. "I need this. I so fucking need this, baby. Tell me you need it, too."

Inside, she was molten liquid. "God, yes."

"Say it." His words heated her skin.

"I need you, Simon." Not just this, the sex, the way he made her body feel, but him, the emotions he evoked.

He rocked hard, faster. "Put your finger on your clit."

Clinging to his neck, she shoved her hand down between them, found her clit, swollen, sensitive, wet, and she rubbed. "Oh, oh." That was all she could manage, heat and sensation bursting inside, outside, as his cock rode her G-spot.

"Come for me, baby."

She was so damn close, almost there. The wall was hard against her back, knocking her spine, but she didn't care. She needed this from him, primal fucking like she was the only thing in the world that he wanted or needed. Ever.

His breath came harsh, and she reveled in it. Dirty words fell from his lips, and she loved them. Her body craved him, sucked him deeper. She came apart from the inside, clinging to him, crying his name, convulsing around the hardness of his cock, and the throb of his release inside her. She was sure he shouted her name and other things she couldn't understand, until orgasm shut out everything but the pulse of their bodies as they became one.

HOLY FUCKING HELL. SIMON CARRIED HER TO THE BEDROOM. SHE clung to him like a limpet, arms and legs wrapped around him, her head bobbing on his shoulder.

He'd never felt so replete. Or so complete. Yet he wanted her again, his cock surging to life inside her. Falling with her onto the bed, he rolled to the side so he wouldn't crush her. His pocket held more condoms that he'd grabbed off the bed in the dungeon, and he was damn well going to use every one. By the time she woke in the morning, she'd be his. He'd give her so much pleasure, more than she'd ever known. She'd said she needed him. He wouldn't let her get away.

"Let's get undressed, baby."

She mumbled, held him tighter.

"I want to make you come again."

She muttered, clung to him. He'd always been wary of clingy women, but this, the way she wouldn't let go . . . he craved it.

He needed to ditch the condom, toss the clothes, pull back the covers, and kiss every inch of her naked body. All night long. All weekend. All his life.

HALEY WOKE DELICIOUSLY SORE. HE'D MADE LOVE TO HER THREE more times in the night. She'd come so many times she'd lost count. She'd sucked him, licked him, kissed all of him until she could close her eyes and envisioned where each mole lay, each tiny scar, every sensitive spot that drove him crazy.

He was still sleeping, his head buried beneath a pillow to block out the morning sun. He'd slept next to her, his leg against hers, but he hadn't overheated her. Geez, the man didn't even snore. The sheet pushed aside, half his long, lean body lay exposed. Even his ass was gorgeous and squeezable. He was too perfect.

How many beds had he woken up in?

Knowing Simon, not many. He'd leave soon after he'd shown a woman a good time.

So why had he stayed with her? She wasn't stupid enough to believe "I need this" meant anything. He and Artie had been friends because they were both cut from the same cloth. They needed and wanted sex, it didn't matter who it was with and they'd take it wherever they could get it.

She sounded so damn bitter.

Pushing aside the covers, she climbed from the bed, her body achy in all the right places. Closing her eyes a moment, she thought about what he'd done to her. He'd truly turned her into his submissive, willing to take the crumbs he offered her.

Her breath hitched, her eyes prickled, and her temples ached. She was so very stupid. She'd always been attracted to him, but she'd known the kind of man he was. Artie made sure of that. She'd chosen Artie over him feeling they weren't the same. She'd been wrong, and here she was making the same mistake all over again.

Yanking her robe from the hook on the back of the bathroom door, she wrapped herself in its warmth and softness. She considered locking herself in the bathroom until he left, but she had a feeling he wouldn't go until they'd talked. He had an agenda. She didn't know what. Maybe it was just sex, but why had he chosen her now?

So she padded down the hallway to the kitchen. She needed a mocha in the worst way.

She was tamping and didn't hear him till he spoke. "I'll do that."

She jumped, spilling the coffee all over the counter. He'd pulled on his jeans and shirt, but left it unbuttoned to reveal a slice of his gorgeous torso. She couldn't deal with him when he looked so damn . . . suckable, and the words spilled out of her as easily as the coffee had strewn across the granite counter. "You need to leave now."

"Haley—"

She held up a hand, cutting him off without even looking at him. "Please, Simon. I have no idea what you want from me, I've seen your lifestyle, and despite what we did with Christopher, I am not capable of it."

"My lifestyle?" he said with an edge. She glanced at him to find his eyes a dark stormy gray.

She gulped and rushed in. "Women. Lots of them. I had enough of that with Artie." She pressed her lips together. "Live by the sword, die by the sword." The way Artie had died using Simon's bed to fuck another woman.

His nostrils flared. "I am not Artie." He tipped his head. "You don't get what this is all about, do you."

Oh, she got it. "Sex. But why did you have to pick me? We were going along fine without it."

"We weren't fine. You never forgave me for Artie. And you're fucking blind to the fact that I've been in love with you for twelve years."

She put her hand over her mouth. Stared at him, a jumble of emotions rioting through her. Then, God help her, she laughed.

11

SHE LAUGHED AT HIM. "YOU DON'T EVEN KNOW WHAT LOVE IS, Simon."

He wanted to be pissed. Here she stood in her perfect kitchen with sparkling counters and clean floor, oak cabinets and stainless refrigerator. He'd helped Artie do the work, hung the cabinets, added all the niceties she wanted such as roll-out shelves for her pots and pans, dual garbage containers for trash and recycle, corner cupboards with lazy Susans for the greatest utilization of space. He'd done it for her lovingly while Artie groused every step of the way. Yet she didn't think him capable of love. She'd taken the beautiful thing they'd done last night and turned it to shit in the morning light.

Admittedly, he'd never given her a reason to assume he had the capacity to love. He'd protected himself from his feelings for her by denying even to himself that he was capable of any strong emotion.

She held out her palms in a conciliatory gesture. "Don't get me wrong, Simon, I don't dislike you for it. That's who you are. You could never have just one woman. You're fine with that, but it's not for me."

She was still comparing him to Artie, and despite himself,

anger rose again. "I love sex, and I always will. But if I commit, I don't cheat." He slashed a hand through the air. "I'm not like Artie."

She turned back to the coffee as if she needed something to do. Or couldn't look him in the eye. "Maybe it's me then. I can't trust anymore. I won't go through every day worrying that I'm going to walk in to find you in bed with a woman. Or more than one woman."

He pinched the bridge of his nose, stuffing his anger down. "I can't deny that kinky sex and having multiple partners is a helluva lot of fun."

She laughed harshly, not an ounce of humor. "Right. Our first time was with another man and you had me cuffed and spread."

Goddammit. "You wanted that." He realized it was a puny excuse. He'd tricked her into answering his ad, then used her secret desires against her to get what he wanted.

She gave up all pretense of making her mocha and turned to him, leaning back against the granite counter he'd helped Artie install. "I don't know what I want anymore. You bowled me over."

He took advantage. "You're right. I found your weak spot." In addition to her G-spot. "I should have had the courage to tell you how I felt. So let me tell you." He wanted to step closer, touch her, even hold her while he whispered to her, but touching would be wrong, taking advantage again. "Sex won't be good anymore without you. I can never enjoy it with another woman. You've spoiled me for the rest of womankind."

She pursed her lips. Artie had complained bitterly about that *look*, yet Artie had always pushed her to it. "That's too trite, Simon."

Again, she was right. He'd never been good explaining his emotions. He'd never wanted to before. "I don't mean it tritely. I can have sex with any woman, but I can't make love unless it's you. Plain old sex with someone who doesn't matter isn't going to be good enough for me anymore."

Emotions flitted across her face. Doubt creased her brow, but there was also the tiniest glimmer of hope in her eyes. She wanted to believe. "A leopard doesn't change his spots."

"Maybe not." He turned, running his hands through his hair in frustration, then flattened his palms along the edge of the center island. "But I'm a man, with the ability to change." He'd done this to himself, sabotaged his own character in her eyes. "I should have fought Artie for you twelve years ago, but I wasn't ready for you then. I wouldn't have cheated on you, but I would have driven you mad pushing you to do all the kinky things I needed. That was a long time ago, and I'm a helluva lot older. I like women, but I need you. I don't want to face the rest of my life without you." He took a step toward her, braved reaching out a hand to cup the side of her face. "I surrender to you." He purposefully used the words he'd written in the ad to lure her. "I am your slave. It was never the other way around."

Haley let Simon touch her, but crossed her arms beneath her breasts. "I don't want a slave, Simon. I want a man. Someone to help me shoulder the burdens. It isn't just about sex. There's so much more." Artie had left her with a mountain of debt. All those credit cards she hadn't known about. He'd accused her of being a nag, but in the end, he'd proven she had good reason. She lowered her voice, spoke with feeling, all the yearning she'd felt in her marriage. "Sometimes I need to be taken care of."

Simon stroked a thumb beneath her eye as if to catch a tear that hadn't fallen. "That's what all those submissive ads were really about. The idea of someone making the decisions appealed to you."

She drew in a shuddery breath. "Yes." She stepped back. His

touch confused her, made her want to turn her face into his hand, kiss his palm, give in to whatever he wanted. "All the fantasizing about bondage and letting someone else take care of me was just that, a fantasy. The truth is I can't let a man have control. I can't even share the responsibility in case I let myself get fooled all over again." She couldn't trust. She *wouldn't* trust.

"Artie did a real number on you, didn't he?" His eyes were sad.

Maybe she'd done the number on herself. There was one thing she couldn't allow to go on, though. "I blamed you for not telling me he was cheating. I was wrong about that. You're not a liar or a cheat. I'm sorry for the things I accused you of. I can see what a bad position he put you in, smack in the middle between us. I realize you didn't want to hurt me."

He shook his head. "I didn't tell because—" He stopped, grimaced, then held her with a look. "Because I wanted you so badly that telling you seemed like dirty pool. I couldn't do it. I couldn't tell you, then let you cry on my shoulder, hoping that you'd turn to me for everything."

He was an honorable man. He always had been. He didn't fuck her then cheat on her or throw her aside. He let the supposedly better man have her. A man who then proceeded to screw her over, ruin her financially, cheat on her, and probably would have thrown her aside if he hadn't died. How much of what Artie had told her about Simon and his women was true? How many of the antics he related actually happened? She'd believed, yet time revealed Artie to be the liar, the cheat. Maybe Artie had lied about Simon, too, to get her to chose him.

She smiled, tears so close to the surface her lips trembled. "Our timing has sucked all along, hasn't it?"

Simon nodded.

"I can't let go of everything now. I can't get past it, Simon."

"Artie screwed you, and you won't trust anyone."

She swallowed, nodded. Because if she spoke, she would cry.

"So you want me to walk away."

She nodded again, sniffed, and forced her voice. "I'm sorry, Simon. It's not you. The problem is me."

He gazed at her a long moment, then his nostrils flared, his lips flattened. "That's bullshit, Haley. You're too scared to try."

"Of course I am."

"You accused me of not being able to change. You're not either."

"I can't, Simon." She couldn't risk getting hurt like she had with Artie.

"You *won't*."

If she told Simon about the debt, all the things besides the cheating, maybe he'd understand. She stared into his gaze that had turned hard and unyielding. No, he wouldn't understand. "You're right. I won't do it."

His jaw tensed. He turned and walked out of the kitchen, but was back in a matter of minutes, shirt buttoned and tucked, socks covering his bare feet, his boots dangling from one hand. Pulling out a kitchen chair, he sat, stuffing his feet in, lacing up.

When he was done, he braced his hands on his knees and rose. "You asked me to leave earlier, and I will for now." He moved quick as a predator, taking her chin in his big hand. "But I am not leaving you alone forever. You can look at me every day at work, and you can tell yourself that I'm like Artie, but one of these days it's going to dawn on you that I'm nothing like him. That you can trust me. That you love me." He bent and took her mouth in a hard yet sweet kiss. "We can be damn fucking good without Artie between us."

Then he walked out, leaving her heart in her throat, her pulse pounding in her ears.

He was right. She *did* love him, had for years, maybe from the first day she saw him, before all her fears and Artie got in the way.

But she was right, too. She might love him, but she could never let go long enough to trust him.

HALEY TOWELED OFF AS SHE STEPPED OUT OF THE SHOWER MONday morning. She'd half-expected Simon to stop by yesterday or at least call. Being contrary, she was disappointed he hadn't after that big emotional threat.

The tile floor warmed her feet. Artie and Simon had installed radiant heat when they remodeled the bathroom. She'd loved this house the moment she saw it, the old Eichler style from the fifties and sixties with a peaked roof, tall windows, high ceilings, open floor plan, and an atrium. The round pit fireplace took up the center of the living room. She'd adored that feature, too. The house, however, had all the original trappings, Formica countertops, even the old harvest gold appliances. Simon had helped with all the remodeling, one room at a time. She'd always made him those special dinners in payment. He had a fondness for her chicken scaloppini.

Her towel swooshed across the mirror, wiping away the steam. She was losing Simon all over again because after this there couldn't be even the pretense of friendship.

In an odd way, it was almost as if she'd had two husbands back then. All the nights the three of them had sat by the pit fireplace and laughed were gone forever. She mourned the loss. Artie told naughty-Simon stories. "Remember the time . . ." Simon would laugh, claiming Artie exaggerated everything.

In hindsight, Artie had been subtly undermining Simon's character with his embellished tales and other comments he made when Simon wasn't around, about how he'd screwed up this project or that client relationship. All the negative stuff about Simon had come from Artie. She'd never witnessed any of it herself.

She hadn't recognized all that when Artie died or even in the months right afterward, because she seemed to have lost so much at once. She used to have girlfriends, too, but she'd lost touch with them all over the last year. Working, worrying about the debts, struggling to come up with payment plans she could manage. There were so many things she had to let go of when Artie died.

Smoothing lotion over her legs and arms, she thought of Simon's hands on her. She would never feel that again. If she had sex, they would have to be casual one-week, one-month, or one-night stands. Anything else meant the same risk to her heart that she feared with Simon.

Stopping abruptly in the act of moisturizing her face, she stared in the mirror. She was attractive enough, even pretty, and she had a decent body despite the flaws that nagged at her. She could find sexual partners. Now. What would happen ten years in the future? Fifteen, twenty. What then? She would be alone, lacking Simon even as a friend. She'd never before thought of the years looming ahead without Artie. She'd been living each day, paying the bills, trying to keep her head above water and hold on to the house. Thank God the business had flourished or she didn't know what she'd have done. In all that time, she'd never once told Simon, never once asked him for help, or even thanked him.

What had she said to him on Saturday? That she wanted a man who could help shoulder her burdens. It was more than fidelity that Artie had made her lose faith in. She didn't trust a man to help out, bear his weight, in effect, to be a *man*. Artie was the one who'd lost clients and screwed up relationships, not Simon. She'd seen more than enough proof of that in the last year. Those first few months after Artie's death, she'd lived in panic, but the truth was, all she'd had to do was say, "Simon, I'm in trouble. Help me." He would have been there for her.

She'd struggled so hard to be independent. She'd done such a good job that now she was completely alone. If she didn't change, she would be alone for the rest of her life.

She'd accused Simon of being the leopard who couldn't change his spots. Maybe *she* was the leopard.

12

SATURDAY MORNING, HALEY HAD TORN OUT HIS HEART AND LEFT IT bleeding on her pristine kitchen floor. Goddamn Artie. A year later, and Simon was still paying for his best friend's sins.

Fuck. Fuck, fuck. What was the old saying? "Oh what a tangled web we weave when first we practice to deceive." He'd lied to himself as well as Haley. He should have told her Artie was cheating. He should have told her he loved her the day Artie died.

Simon hadn't stopped by her place or called all weekend. She needed time, he'd give it to her. Though he wasn't going to leave her alone forever. She needed him. He felt that in his gut. He would be so goddamn good for her. No more lies of omission, no more games. He would give her the real Simon Foster.

Monday morning, he had a few jobs to check on before he'd make it into the office. He had good crews, but there were always questions, things that came up needing his attention. Oftentimes he didn't make it into the office at all. From now on, though, he'd make it his priority, once a day, even if it was only for a few minutes. She had to see him often. He wouldn't let her forget him. Out of sight, out of mind. No way was he letting that happen.

He landed in the office at one-fifteen. Haley was still out for her walk. In the winter when the weather was cooler, she exercised over in the county park where there were good hiking trails. Rain or shine, Haley was out there. In the summer when it was hot, she rose early and walked before work. He knew her schedule, her routine, her likes and dislikes. Her favorite color was teal. She'd wanted soothing pink and gray tile in the bathroom that she could see when she sat in the Jacuzzi tub he and Artie had installed for her.

He knew everything. Except how to make Haley admit she was in love with him.

He was in the break room when she came in to grab a bottle of water from the fridge. Hair pulled back in a ponytail, she wore tight workout leggings and a sweatshirt. The clouds had rolled in late last night and cooled the day off. The good weather they'd been experiencing was over, the forecasters calling for rain by Wednesday, yet it had still been warm enough for a sheen of perspiration to gather on her face. She looked so damn lickable.

She stopped short when she saw him. In the outer office, the phone rang. Despite the drum of his heartbeat in his ears, he heard Saskia answer with her soft lilt. Haley glanced at the open doorway, her fists clenched. She widened her stance as if she were ready to do battle.

He held up his hands. "We don't need to fight."

"I wasn't going to." She drew in a long deep breath, let it ease out. "I wanted to tell you that I've missed having you as my friend since Artie's been gone. I've missed your jokes. The way you used to tug on my ponytail. How you always seemed to guess that something was bugging me."

All those things were true. He hadn't thought she'd noticed the absence of them.

"I want to be friends again, Simon."

He closed his eyes, the sentiment in her words filling him up, making him whole. If she wanted friendship, then in time . . .

He was a patient man. After all, he'd waited twelve years. Yet it was past time. Despite how much easier it would be, he couldn't let her go halfway on this. "Friendship is not going to be enough, Haley."

She tipped her head. "I didn't say friendship was all I wanted."

He'd always believed himself to be a strong man, yet his heart fluttered like a schoolboy's as he waited for her to go on.

"There are a lot of things I never told you about Artie, about our marriage, about the things I learned after he died. All of that has gone into making me wary of relationships and other men." She pursed her lips, then drew in another long breath as if she needed to find strength. "When I discovered he was cheating on me, I didn't have him to strike out at. So you had to take the brunt of all my disappointment and anger. I still believe you should have told me." Her eyes suddenly clouded. "There were so many things you didn't know, though. His infidelity was a drop in the bucket, Simon."

His heart bled for her.

"I wish to God I'd never pushed you away, because I needed you." Her voice trembled. "It would have been so much easier."

"I'm sorry, baby," he whispered. What Artie had done to her beyond the cheating, he'd ask later. More questions weren't what she needed. His comforting was. He took two steps toward her, but she shot out a hand.

"Don't touch me yet, please." She gulped. "I need to say this first or I'll never get it all out. I need to tell you everything that I figured out this weekend. You need to hear it."

He only needed to hear that she loved him, that she would be with him. But he waited.

"Back then, I wanted you both," she admitted. "There were so many things about you that made it hard. I couldn't compete with all those other women, and Artie, he was such a charmer." She swiped at a tear before it fell. "He was so easy. He wanted to marry me." She shrugged and spread her hands. "I couldn't let you go entirely so I made you my best friend. I put you in the difficult position between Artie and me. I tore you apart trying to figure out what the right thing to do was. The absolute truth is that if the circumstances were reversed, I probably wouldn't have told you your spouse was cheating."

He had to stop her right there. She was so willing to take the blame for everything. It was too damn wrong to let her do that. "Haley." He held up a hand.

"No." She got that militant look that had annoyed Artie. Yet for some reason it made Simon hot for her. "You will let me finish," she demanded. "I judged you based on the things Artie said and based on the things that *he* did. As if the fact you were friends and business partners made you the same. Look at me," she whispered, and he raised his gaze from her lips to her eyes. "I'm sorry I blamed you that he died in your bed and that he was cheating on me. Please forgive me, Simon."

Her words tore something inside him. He'd waited so long to hear them, yet he'd deserved her anger in the first place. He had been wrong, so very wrong. "A leopard can change his spots, Haley. I will never cheat on you. I will always be there when you need me. In whatever way you need me."

She closed the distance between them in one step and put her hand to his cheek. "You wouldn't cheat because you're a good man. With integrity. That's why I love you." Her body heat warmed him straight through to his heart. "I took a long time to figure it out. To stop painting you both with the same brush. I can change, too, Simon. I don't want to grow into a man hater because I couldn't let go of something that happened in the past." She laid her lips over his. "I want you. I need you. I love you."

If there was a heaven and a God who rewarded people for the

good things they did, then he must have done something so fucking good to deserve her.

"I want to give whatever is between us a chance," she whispered.

He dragged her up against him and hugged her so tightly she squeaked. "Love me forever, Haley."

"I will," she vowed. Spearing her hands through his hair, she pushed his head back to capture his gaze. "By the way, I'm not going to say *never* on all the kinky things, either?"

"Haley, I don't need all that stuff."

She kissed him gently, an erotic press of her lips to his. "*I* want to explore it with *you*. Baby steps. Starting with things like we did with Christopher. But I don't need to punish anyone with a dildo. Artie's gone, there's just us."

He couldn't believe she was giving him this gift. He didn't *need* all those other things, but there were so many sexual delights he could give her outside the privacy of their own bed. He could so get off on watching her enjoy taking a man with a dildo. Later, maybe. When she was ready. If. "Right now, I don't care about punishing Artie's facsimile or kinky sex. All I care about is that you're mine."

She cupped his jaw, traced her thumb along his bottom lip. "Yes, Simon, I'm yours."

He made a whoop and a holler, dancing around the break room with her in his arms, then he bent down and hauled her up in a fireman's carry, marching her through the door

Saskia's jaw dropped when she saw Haley over his shoulder. "Sas, hold all our calls. Haley and I will be in my office, and we don't want to be disturbed."

The vibration of Haley's laughter rumbled along the skin of his back. "Simon," she whispered harshly. "I'm all hot and sweaty."

He turned the corner into the hall. "Yeah. I'm going to lick it all off."

She bobbed on his back as he headed to his open door. "I cannot believe you did that in front of Saskia," she groused with laughter in her voice.

"I haven't made love to you in two days, and I cannot wait a second longer." He carried her in, slammed the door with his booted foot, let her down off his shoulder, and pushed her up against the wood, planting his body between her legs. Her face above him was flushed, her eyes bright, and the sweet hot scent of her arousal rose to his nose. She loved a little manhandling.

"You can call it fucking, Simon. It's fine. I adore fucking."

"I will fuck you so good, baby," he murmured, already shoving her sweatshirt up her torso. "For the rest of your life." One hand closed over her gorgeous plump breast, her nipple peaking against his palm. "I will love you with my last breath."

"The way I love you."

Then she made love to him with her lips, her hands, her body, and her heart.

ABOUT THE AUTHOR

Jasmine Haynes has been penning stories for as long as she's been able to write. With a bachelor's degree in accounting from Cal Poly San Luis Obispo, she has worked in the high-tech Silicon Valley for the last twenty years and hasn't met a boring accountant yet! Well, maybe a few. She and her husband live with Star, their mighty moose-hunting dog (if she weren't afraid of her own shadow), plus numerous wild cats (who have discovered that food out of a bowl is easier than slaying gophers and birds, though it would be great if they got rid of the gophers, but no such luck). Jasmine's pastimes, when not writing her heart out, are speed-walking through the Redwoods, hanging out with writer friends in coffee shops, and watching classic movies. Jasmine also writes as Jennifer Skully and J.B. Skully. She loves to hear from readers. Please e-mail her at skully@skullybuzz.com or visit www.jasminehaynes.com and www.jasminehaynes.blogspot.com.